JIMMIE DALE AND THE PHANTOM CLUE

FRANK L. PACKARD

BY FRANK L. PACKARD

JIMMIE DALE AND
THE PHANTOM CLUE

BY

FRANK L. PACKARD

AUTHOR OF "DOORS OF THE NIGHT," "PAWNED,"
"FROM NOW ON," "THE FURTHER ADVEN-
TURES OF JIMMIE DALE," ETC.

WILDSIDE PRESS

Published by
Wildside Press, LLC
P.O. Box 301
Holicong, PA 18928-0301 USA
www.wildsidepress.com

Wildside Press Edition: MMIII

JIMMIE DALE AND THE PHANTOM CLUE. I

CONTENTS

JIMMIE DALE AND THE
PHANTOM CLUE

JIMMIE DALE AND THE PHANTOM CLUE

THE TOCSIN

THE boat drifted on. In the distance a ferry churned its way across the river. From the farther shore the myriad lights of Brooklyn flung a soft glow into the sky, like a canopy between the city and the night.

And in the boat two figures merged as one in the darkness.

"Marie!" Jimmie Dale whispered. His arms tightened about her. "Marie!"

She made answer by a little pressure of her hand.

He looked behind him—in toward the nearer shore. Somewhere back there, somewhere amongst those irregular outlines that thrust out points of deeper darkness into the black, mirror-like surface of the water, was the old pier from beneath which they had escaped, and, above the pier, the shed where but a little while ago—or was it hours, or a lifetime ago?—Clarke, alias Wizard Marre, alias Hunchback Joe, had played his last card, and lost.

A grim smile touched Jimmie Dale's lips. Inside that shed the secret service men had found their quarry—dead. They were there now. In their hands lay the evidence that solved the murder of Jathan Lane; and in their hands, too, was the murderer himself—only Wizard Marre had taken the easier way, and was dead.

Jimmie Dale's smile softened. Inside that shed at the present moment there was commotion enough and light enough; but he could hear nothing, and he could see no light. The Tocsin here and himself were too far away. Too far away! Yes, that was it—at last! Too far away from the old life—forever. The road of fear lay behind them, and she was free, free to come out into the sunlight again. She had said so herself in that letter he had read at the club only a few hours ago. Free! Life lay before them now—and love. With the death of Wizard Marre there could now be an end of his, Jimmie Dale's, own rôles of the Gray Seal, and Larry the Bat, and Smarlinghue, and —no, not hers as the Tocsin, that could never change or terminate, for she would always be the Tocsin to him.

The Tocsin! Memory came surging upon him. That night in the long ago, before he had ever seen her, when he had known her only as the woman who addressed him as "Dear Philanthropic Crook" in those mysterious notes of hers that, supplying the data on which he had acted, the data for those "crimes," where no crime save that of rendering abortive the crimes of others had ever been, had made the name of the Gray Seal anathema to police and underworld alike; that night when, besides a note, he had also found a gold seal ring of hers, a dainty thing that bore a crest, a bell surmounted by a bishop's mitre, and underneath, in the scroll, a motto in French: *Sonnez le Tocsin!* It had seemed so apt! Ring the Tocsin! Sound the alarm! Always her notes had done that—calling the Gray Seal to arms that some one else might be the better or the happier for what she bade him do. The Tocsin! The word had seemed to visualise her then, and, knowing her by no other name, he had called her—the Tocsin.

She stirred a little in his arms.

"What time is it, Jimmie?" she asked.

He shook his head. Time! What did time matter now? To Marie LaSalle, who once had lived in hourly peril of her life as Silver Mag in the days of the old Crime Club, and later, yes even until to-night, had again been forced to live under cover of some rôle which she had never divulged to him and which he had never penetrated; and to him, Jimmie

Dale, in whose ears need never sound again that slogan of the underworld, "Death to the Gray Seal!" that reached to every nook and corner of the Bad Lands—to her and to him what did time count for now, save as a great, illimitable mine of happiness, a wealth beyond all telling that they were to spend *together!*

She spoke again:

"What time is it, Jimmie?"

And now he answered her.

"I don't know," he said happily. "It was just midnight when the shed back there was raided. Since then there hasn't been any such thing as time, Marie."

"Listen!" she said.

From somewhere across the water, faintly, a tower clock struck the hour.

"One o'clock!" she exclaimed, as though in dismay. "We must be getting ashore. I—I did not think it was so late. And please, Jimmie, I'd like to row the boat. I—I feel quite—quite cold."

He felt her shiver a little in his arms.

"Cold!" he echoed anxiously; and then, as he released her: "All right, if you really want to. It isn't very far. And I guess it's safe now. Pull in and skirt along the shore until we can find some good place to land."

She nodded as she picked up the oars, then turned the boat's head in toward the shore and began to row.

Jimmie Dale moved back into the stern of the boat and settled himself in his seat. He watched her, drinking in the lithe, graceful swing of her body, the rhythmic stroke of the heavy oars. He could not see her face for the night shadows hid it, but he could see the poise of her head and the contour of the full, perfect throat. And he clasped his hand behind his head, and a great happiness and a great peace fell upon him.

It seemed somehow as though the voyage of this little boat in which they had fled out here into the night for safety epitomised a voyage of great immensity that had begun in the very long ago, a voyage of interminable night through which his eyes had been straining and his soul had been yearning for a glimpse of the beacon light that should signal the approach to a wondrous Port of Dawn. And now the voyage was almost at an end. Marie there at the oars, and the peace and quiet around them, was the beacon light at last; and they could no more lose their way because the way was charted now to that Port of Dawn where there was no more any strife and peril and sordid crime, and where only love was.

He smiled at his fancy, and suddenly laughed out into the night.

"Keep in a little to the right, Marie," he called. "There's something that looks like a low wharf ahead that ought to do."

"Yes; I see it," she answered.

Jimmie Dale sat abruptly upright in his seat. Perhaps it was only the rasp and creak of the oars in the rowlocks, but it had sounded so *human*—like a short, quick, suppressed sob. He leaned forward.

"Was that you, Marie?" he asked quickly. "What is it?"

He could not see her face. Her voice came back to him steady and untroubled:

"Nothing, Jimmie."

Across the night, far up above them and in the distance, a great bridge stretched from shore to shore, its arc of sparkling lights like a tiara crowning the brow of the heavens. Faintly there came the roar of traffic, ever restless, ever sleepless. A trolley clanged its way unseen somewhere near the shore which the boat was now rapidly approaching; and here, where the lights showed but sparsely, many buildings, small and large, loomed out in queer, grotesque and fanciful shapes.

Jimmie Dale's dark eyes lighted. All this was as it always was and always had been—only it was *changed*. It held a promise now that it had never held before. He felt his pulse beat quicken.

The Port of Dawn!

"Here we are, Marie!" he cried.

The bow of the boat touched the edge of a low wharf—and then Jimmie Dale, like a man stunned, bewildered, his mind and brain in turmoil and riot, was standing up in the stern of the boat. Quick, like a flash, the Tocsin had lifted the oars from the rowlocks, flung them away in the water, and, springing to the string-piece of the wharf, had pushed the boat out again.

"Jimmie! Oh, Jimmie!" Her voice reached him in a low, broken sob. "There was no other way. It's in your pocket, Jimmie. I put it there when—when you were—were holding me."

"Marie!" he cried out wildly. "In God's name, what are you doing, Marie!" He flung himself upon his knees and began to paddle furiously with his hands. "Marie!" he cried again.

A shadow flitted swiftly along the wharf shorewards; it grew filmy and mingled with a thousand other shadows—and was lost.

She was gone! The Tocsin was gone—as she had gone so many times before. He paddled on with his hands, but the act was purely mechanical. Gone! A cold chill was at his heart; an agony of fear seized upon him. Gone—when life in all its fulness . . . Gone! Why? An abyss seemed to yawn before him.

After a time the boat bumped against the wharf. He sprang out and ran madly to the shore. He found himself groping like a blind man amongst buildings, in alleys, along dimly lighted streets. And then suddenly he stood still with the consciousness of stark futility upon him. Had he learned no lesson from the past? It was useless to search for her. He might have known that from the first! He *had* known it, only—only things had seemed so *changed* to-night.

Fear took its toll of him again. It brought the sweat beads out upon his forehead. *Fear for her.* Subconsciously he realised now that something, somewhere, had, after all, gone wrong to-night; that she was still in danger, a danger that she still meant he should not share: No other reason

save that brave, unselfish love of hers would have prompted
her to this.

"It's in your pocket, Jimmie." Her words came back to
him.

He searched quickly, and with a sharp little cry of pain
drew out a sealed envelope. Under a street lamp in a
deserted street, he tore it open. Words that he had never
thought to see again danced unsteadily before his eyes.

"Dear Philanthropic Crook—since you *must* be that again," he
read. "I do not know under what circumstances you will receive
this. I only know that before the night is over I shall be with
you, and we will be together—for a little while. And, Jimmie, I
am writing this instead of telling you what I must say, because I
am afraid of myself and our love, afraid that I would not be
strong enough to hold out against the plea of our hearts that
at all costs we should remain together, and against your arguments,
and perhaps against your physical restraint—for you *are* masterful,
Jimmie. I cannot bring you any more into the shadows in which
I know now I must live again. I must not, Jimmie; for it might
only too well mean your certain destruction, the certain revela-
tion to both the police and the underworld that the Gray Seal and
Larry the Bat and Smarlinghue are none other than Jimmie Dale,
the Riverside Drive millionaire and clubman. You see, I am
writing without reserve, putting upon paper what has never been
put upon paper before, because I know that in some way I shall
personally place this letter in your possession, and that no other
hands shall touch it and no other eyes shall see it save yours and
mine.

"I am writing this half an hour before midnight, while I am
waiting for midnight to come with its disclosure at the old junk-
shop on the East River that Hunchback Joe is Wizard Marre—and
Clarke. And only a day or so ago, Jimmie, I wrote you another
letter telling you that once Clarke was in the hands of the police
I would be safe for always. And Clarke *will* be caught to-night,
and you will believe that a new world stretches before us, and that
all our hopes and aspirations are to come true at last, and you will
be happier perhaps in that moment than you have ever been before.
Oh, Jimmie, it is so hard even to *write* this, for I love you so; but
it is because I do love you with all my heart and soul and life that
I will not, shall not, must not let a breath of suspicion exist that
there is anything between Marie LaSalle and Jimmie Dale. God
keep and guard you! I shall pray always and always for that.

And some day, some time perhaps—no, not perhaps, but surely, surely . . .

"Jimmie, I did not mean to write like this. Listen! You know, through the letter to which I referred above, why during all these past months I have 'disappeared.' You know that I was the *only* one who could identify Clarke as one of the leaders of the old Crime Club, and that it was a question of my life or his. You know that he went into hiding, and that there followed attempt after attempt upon my life. And then I 'left the city for an extended trip,' as my bankers informed you. And while you sought to find me, which, for the same reasons that still exist to-night, I could not let you do, I fought Clarke under cover with his own weapons. A few days ago I believed I had won; it seemed only a question of hours. I had placed Clarke in his true person as Marre, the shyster lawyer, and in his other alias as Hunchback Joe. And then suddenly, as though he had never existed, I lost him.

"You now know why. He and some of his band were at work under the bank making that opening into the president's private office that resulted this afternoon in the murder of Jathan Lane. I was too late to prevent that, but almost immediately afterwards I picked up Clarke's trail again. I found out that in some way, to cover their own tracks, to end all investigation, false evidence was somehow to be planted, and that to bear this out another murder was to be added to that of the bank president. Jimmie, what could I do? I could not stand passively aside, even when by so doing my own victory was assured. I had to go on. It was to save a man's life. There was a way to get the information necessary to forestall them, though it involved a risk that I would otherwise never have taken. In a measure I succeeded; I learned how the papers and money, and the blackjack with which the murder was committed, were to be placed in Klanner's, the bank janitor's, trunk in his boarding house, and that the man was to be lured into Baldy Jack's dance hall, where, in a riot staged for the occasion, their victim, apparently an innocent bystander, but with his reputation further blasted by being found in that unsavory resort, was to be shot. A dead man could refute no false evidence! I managed to get word to you, and, thank God, in time. But *I* was caught— and in my own character of Marie LaSalle. I was carried to one of Clarke's lairs, and left there a prisoner. They meant to finish me when the rest of the night's work was over.

"But I must hurry on, Jimmie. It is getting late.

"As I shall have been with you for a little while before you will have read this, you will know of course that I escaped. I have no time now to tell you how. The details do not matter. What matters is this: That while, before, Clarke was the only one who had any concern in putting me out of the way, and that for his own personal safety, that enmity is now transferred to an even more formidable enemy—those, and particularly one, who during the last year have been associated with Clarke. They will be actuated by two motives. First, revenge for the trap that will place Clarke in the hands of the police for the murder of Jathan Lane, and revenge for my interference in their attempt upon Klanner; and, second, the fear—a much more potent motive—that I know far more about them and who they are than I really do, the fear that I am in possession of all the knowledge needed to place them too behind the bars of the death house in Sing Sing. I do not know them, Jimmie—except one man, and that man I am not sure of at all. He is a bigger, brainier, far more crafty man than ever Clarke was, and far more powerful. There are times when I think I know him, and times when I am equally sure that I do not. I have come to call him the Phantom. If I am right, he has a score of aliases, a score of domiciles, and possesses the facility of appearing convincingly in each one of a bewildering number of different characters. I said that they had caught me in my own person. I do not need to tell you now, Jimmie, that if I were to go back to New York and resume my life as Marie LaSalle it would but be going to certain death.

"Just one thing more. I do not believe that the bank's papers, valuable as they were, that they took from Jathan Lane in his office, were the sole motive for his murder; indeed, I am not sure that they were the *real* motive. I do not know, of course. But I overheard snatches of something about a safe at Jathan Lane's house to-night at two o'clock, something that was to have its fulfilment later in a rendezvous at half-past three with an old acquaintance of yours, one Gentleman Laroque. I may be quite wrong; it may be that, even if I am right, my escape and Clarke's capture would effectually put a stop to anything further they might have schemed to do; but if there *is* anything in it, and if they go on, there will be others at Gentleman Laroque's who are not expected—the police. I will see to that. And so, perhaps, Jimmie, even to-night, after all, something may happen that will point the way to this Phantom and those with him—and to happiness for us.

"And now you must not be too anxious, Jimmie. In a measure I am safe. They have never penetrated the rôle which I have been playing, and I do not think they ever will. And you are going to help me, too, Jimmie, whenever—oh, Jimmie, those old days!—whenever I can 'sound the Tocsin' without allying you with me in the eyes of those upon whom Clarke's mantle has fallen."

Jimmie Dale raised haggard eyes. The signature seemed somehow blurred. "Marie . . . Marie . . . !"

THE GRAY SEAL

FOR a time Jimmie Dale stood motionless under the light, then he started automatically on along the street. He tore the letter into small fragments and the fragments into tiny shreds as he went along. The world seemed a void. No, not that! It was more as though fate jeered at him ironically. He was exactly, in respect of the Tocsin and in respect of the fulfilment of his hopes and plans, where he had been yesterday and a thousand yesterdays ago.

He walked on. The tiny shreds of paper, a few at a time, fluttered from his fingers and were lost. Mechanically he found himself boarding a street car. Thereafter he sat, his strong jaw clamped and hard, staring out through the window.

Who was the Phantom?

Twice, at long intervals, he changed cars. Finally, far uptown, he alighted, and, traversing several blocks, paused in front of a large corner house in a most select and exclusive neighbourhood. Ostensibly, had any one been observing his movements, he had paused in order that, under the street lamp, he might consult his watch. It was a quarter of two. A smile, half grim, half whimsical, as though he were suddenly aroused from some deep reverie to actual physical reality, flickered across his lips. The house on the corner was the residence of Jathan Lane, the bank president, who had been murdered that afternoon.

Jimmie Dale replaced his watch, and nonchalantly turned the corner; but the dark, steady eyes were alight now, sweeping the side street in every direction. His glance detected and held for a bare instant on the black mouth of a lane that showed at the rear of Jathan Lane's house. Jimmie Dale edged toward the inner side of the pavement, still walking nonchalantly. And then, gradually merging more and more with the shadow of the house itself, he came abreast of the lane—and the street was empty. A moment more, and lithe, active, silent as a cat in his movements, he had swung himself over a fence; still another moment, and lost utterly in the shadows of the porch, he was crouching at the basement door of the house.

It was Jimmie Dale, the Gray Seal again, in action now. From under his vest, from one of the multitudinous little upright pockets of that leather girdle where nestled an array of vicious blued-steel implements, a compact burglar's kit, he selected a pick-lock. From another pocket came a black silk mask. Jimmie Dale slipped the mask over his face, and leaned closer to the door. For perhaps five seconds the slim, sensitive fingers were at work, then the door opened noiselessly, and closed again, and was locked behind him.

He stood silent, motionless—listening. There was no sound. Apart from the staff, there should be no one in the house. The papers had overlooked few details in their account of the murder that afternoon. Mrs. Lane was away in Europe, and they had taken the body of Jathan Lane to the house of his married daughter. Under the mask there came again that grim flicker to Jimmie Dale's lips. There were only the servants then—since it was not yet *two o'clock!*

The round, white ray of a flashlight stabbed through the blackness, vanished, and blackness fell again.

"Stairs ahead and to the right," Jimmie Dale confided to himself. "Servants' quarters on top floor probably; only the cellar and storage here."

The flashlight played steadily, impudently now, pointing the way upstairs; and, as silent as the ray itself, Jimmie Dale followed. As he reached the head of the stairs he found a closed door before him. The light went out. He listened again; then, in the darkness, he opened the door and stepped through. Again he listened. Still there was no sound. The flashlight winked once inquisitively—then darkness again. He was standing at the rear of the hall. The basement stairs came up under what was evidently the main staircase.

And now a shadow flitted with incredible swiftness here and there; and doors opened, and some were closed again, and some were left open—and there was no sound. And presently Jimmie Dale stood again at the rear of the hall. He could command the open door that led to the basement stairs; and along the hall, where a slight rift in the blackness made by the plate glass panels was distinguishable, he could command the front doors.

He nodded in quiet satisfaction to himself. Jathan Lane's safe was in a sort of private den or office that opened off the rear of the library, and portières hung between the two rooms; each room had a door opening off the hall, and both doors stood open now. A clock struck somewhere in the house. His lips tightened. It was two o'clock.

Alert, tense, he listened—listened until the silence itself throbbed and beat at the ear drums, and palpitated, and made noises of its own.

There wasn't much chance. He knew that. After what had happened that night, unless under extraordinary conditions, Jathan Lane's safe should be the most inviolate piece of property to be found anywhere in New York. And even if any one came, the corollary of whatever held its premise in that safe was to be found at Gentleman Laroque's, and the Tocsin had said that the police would be warned in time. Yes, he understood. She had obviously made no effort to render anything abortive here at the source, for the very reason that she hoped it would but lead to the trap she would have prepared at Gentleman Laroque's. Her attitude had been quite logical, quite plausible. So why was *he* here?

Jimmie Dale's hands clenched at his sides. The answer was simple enough, and yet, too, in its very self seemed to hold a world of mockery and, yes, even futility. He was here to pick up the threads of yesterday and of those thousand yesterdays gone—anything—the grasping at any straw that might bring him into that arena where she was battling for her life, and from which, striving to shield him, she sought to bar him out.

He could not very well pick up those threads at Gentleman Laroque's, if indeed there were any threads *to* pick up, for the simple reason that the police would be there! And so he was *here*.

Gentleman Laroque! His brow furrowed. Yes, he remembered Gentleman Laroque—and Niccolo Sonnino—and a certain night that had so nearly cost young Clarie Archman his life. So Gentleman Laroque was in this new combine! Gentleman Laroque had played the rôle of safe-breaker that other night—but Gentleman Laroque had missed his calling, whether as a safe-breaker or as the gang leader that he was. He would have made an infinitely better confidence man, for he was educated, suave, and, when it suited him, polished to a degree; he possessed all the requisites, and, in abundance, the prime requisite of all—a cunning that was the cunning of a fox. Also he, Jimmie Dale, remembered something else about Gentleman Laroque; he remembered Gentleman Laroque's last words to the Gray Seal on that night in question, and now here in the darkness, waiting for he knew not what, with Laroque emerging so unexpectedly from the past, those words, hoarse in their rage and elemental fury, seemed to ring again with strange significance in his ears: "You win to-night, but we'll get you yet! Some day we'll get you, you cursed snitch, you——"

What was that?

The sound came neither from below through the open door of the basement staircase, nor yet from the front doors along the hall. The sound persisted. It was like the gnawing of a rat. And then Jimmie Dale placed its general location. It seemed to come from outside the house, and in direction from the little den or office at his right that contained the safe. He moved stealthily to the doorway, and, still in the hall, protected by the door jamb, peered into the darkness of the room. He could see nothing.

But now the sound was still more clearly defined, and he placed it exactly. Rather than a gnawing, it was a scratching

at the wall outside and below the window; and as it continued it seemed at times to grow almost human with impatience and irritability as it quickened its tempo.

And then suddenly Jimmie Dale turned his head. Imagination? No, there was another sound—and it, too, now
repeated itself, low, cautious, stealthy. Some one was
creeping down the third story stairs from the top of the
house.

For an instant Jimmie Dale stood without movement, then
a hard, quick smile compressed his lips. That scratching
sound outside the window, which still persisted, had not been
loud enough to *awaken* anybody. It was rather curious,
rather singular! His ears, acute, trained to the slightest
sound, caught the footfalls coming now along the upper hall,
still low, still cautious and stealthy—and Jimmie Dale slipped
across the threshold, and in an instant had passed into the
library and was crouched behind the portières that hung
between the two rooms.

A minute passed. A tread creaked softly on the main
staircase; then a form bulked in irregular outline in the doorway of the little den, paused for the fraction of a second,
came into the room, closed the door, and glided swiftly to the
window. The window was cautiously opened. There was
the soft *pad* of feet as a man crawled through and dropped
to the floor. A hoarse whisper vibrated through the room.

"Damn it, why didn't you keep me there all night?" a voice
demanded angrily. "You didn't go to *sleep,* did you, or
forget to leave the window of your room open so's you could
hear?"

Another voice answered. The words came in a choked,
broken way, as though with great effort:

"No; I—I didn't go to sleep. Not likely! I heard you
the minute you came, but—but I couldn't help it. I had a
—a bit of a turn. I came as soon as I could. I—I was sick."

A ray of a flashlight lanced through the blackness. It
played on the tall, gaunt figure of an old, gray-haired man
arrayed in a dressing gown, and on a face that was drawn
and pallor-like in colour.

Then darkness again.

Behind the portière, Jimmie Dale's face suddenly hardened. There were little gray "mutton-chop" side whiskers, that was the only change. He recognised the man in an instant. It was the "Minister," alias Patrick Denton, one of the cleverest "inside" crooks that had ever infested New York. The man, pronounced an incurable heart case, and even then supposed to be in a dying condition, had been pardoned two years ago while serving a sentence in Sing Sing. Since then he had dropped out of sight; and indeed, generally, was supposed to be dead.

There was a callous grunt from the man at the window. "Well, you look it!" said the man. "And that's no lie!" He laughed shortly. "And maybe it's a good thing. You could get away with the faithful-butler-mourning-for-his-dead-master stuff without batting an eyelid, if you had to."

There was no answer.

Jimmie Dale's hand slipped into his pocket and came out again with his automatic. So that was it! He began to understand. The Minister was back at his old inside game again—this time in the rôle of Jathan Lane's butler!

The man who had crawled in through the window spoke again—sharply now:

"Well, let's get busy! We've lost too much time, as it is. If a light's safe, shoot her on; we can work quicker that way."

"Yes," said the Minister. "It's—it's safe enough." He stifled a cough. "The rest are all asleep; and on account of what happened this afternoon, I had every shade in the house drawn. I——" He broke off with a quick gasp, as coincident with the faint click of an electric-light switch, a single, shaded incandescent on the desk in front of the safe went on. "You!" he exclaimed. "I—I thought it was to be Hunchback Joe."

The fold of the portière in Jimmie Dale's hand drew closer in against the edge of the wall projection until there was left but the veriest crack. A pucker came and nested in little wrinkles at the corners of his eyes. He was not so sure,

after all, that he had begun to understand. In view of the
Tocsin's letter, he did not understand at all. The man who
stood there in the room beside the Minister, the man with
the cool, contemptuous black eyes, the thin, cunning lips
parted in a grim smile, was Gentleman Laroque.

"So it was," said Laroque coolly. "You've got it straight.
Hunchback Joe was to come here for the sparklers, smear
the trail by bringing them back to me, and then I was going
to slip them to old Isaac Shiftel. But Hunchback Joe
couldn't come, and as it's a rather fussy job I didn't dare
trust any one else, so I came myself. I'll take them direct
from here to Shiftel's."

The pucker cleared from Jimmie Dale's eyes. Shiftel—
old Isaac Shiftel—the fence! The man was an outstanding
figure in the underworld! Yes, he *did* begin to understand.
But for once, for the first time since those days in the years
gone by when the Tocsin·had begun to sound those "calls to
arms," the Tocsin was astray. It was not her fault. It was
nothing that she could by any possibility have foreseen.
Only as matters now stood the police trap at Laroque's would
be abortive—it should have been at Isaac Shiftel's! Jimmie
Dale's lips pressed together. Well, he knew where Isaac
Shiftel lived, and instead of the police, it would perhaps
be——

Jimmie Dale's mental soliloquy ended abruptly. The Minister was walking with weak, unsteady steps across the room,
groping at the desk for support, and speaking as he went.

"There isn't anything the matter, is there?" he asked
anxiously. "I mean nothing's gone wrong with that other
thing to keep Hunchback Joe away? He's safe, isn't he?"

An oath fell softly from Gentleman Laroque's lips. He
still smiled; but the cool contempt had gone from his eyes,
and in its place was a smouldering passion.

"Wrong?" he echoed. "No; nothing's gone wrong, except
that the whole plant is blown, the papers pinched by the
police, and Hunchback Joe is dead."

"What's that, you say?" The old man swayed on his feet,
his face a ghastly white. "Dead! You said—dead? I——"

Jimmie Dale straightened up involuntarily. The old man was undeniably ill, desperately ill. He had reeled and would have fallen had not Laroque caught him and placed him in a chair.

"Brandy!" the old man gasped. "Over there—on—on that cabinet."

Laroque procured the stimulant. The Minister gulped it down eagerly. It seemed to revive him. He stared anxiously at Laroque.

"How—what—what happened?" he whispered hoarsely.

"The police were tipped off by some one you don't know, and by some one you do," said Laroque between his teeth. "The some one you know was—the Gray Seal."

"My God!" The white face was set with fear. "The police—and—Hunchback Joe dead! We—we can't go on with this—we'd——"

"We couldn't if Joe *weren't* either trapped or dead," Laroque broke in sharply. "Pull yourself together! We've no time to waste. Don't you understand? It's *safer* than ever it was! If Klanner, the bank janitor, had got his, and the fake evidence had been found the way we planted it, this little deal here to-night was all tucked away neat enough. But Klanner's skin was saved, by luck as we thought then, though we know better now, and that put everything up in the air as far as *this* was concerned—until the police copped Joe with the goods, and Joe snuffed out. That gave them the motive again for the murder this afternoon, and gave them the man who did it. The case is closed now tighter than we figured it could be sewed up even in the first place. Get me?"

The old man shook his head. He looked furtively around him.

"I'm afraid," he said huskily. "If the Gray Seal's in this, it—it ain't safe."

"But I tell you the Gray Seal isn't in this," snapped Laroque impatiently. "That's what I'm trying to get through your thick head! He and every one else will think the curtain rolled down on the *last* act when they got Hunchback Joe. It's safe enough! It's so safe there isn't anything to it,

if *your* end is safe. And you ought to know about that—
you've been a year getting the dope."

"I—I ain't afraid of that," said the old man. "There's no
one in the world knows how many he had. The family knew
he had a lot, of course, and knew it was his hobby, and that
he kept 'em here where he could look at 'em instead of in a
safety deposit vault—though I guess he figured no safety
deposit vault had anything on his—but they just knew he
had a lot, they didn't know how many."

A strange light came dawning suddenly in Jimmie Dale's
eyes. Had the Tocsin been right in this respect? Was this
the *real* motive for the murder—not the bank's papers?
Jathan Lane's hobby! It was no secret. Jathan Lane was a
fellow member of that most exclusive organization, the St.
James Club. Dimly there came back to memory a conversation one afternoon when four or five members, Jathan Lane
and himself amongst them, were gathered around one of the
smoking room tables, and——

"Sure!" said Gentleman Laroque brusquely. "Well, then,
what's the matter with you? There's no sign of any robbery; no sign of any entry into the house, not so much as
an unlocked door or a scratch on a window sill; and Jathan
Lane, the only man who could know that anything had been
taken—is dead. And his death"—Laroque grinned—"occurred in such a way as to make what's done here secure
from even suspicion. The bank game's a blind. This is what
we've been after, and now it's open and shut. And your
share is the biggest haul you ever made in your life."

The old man stared around him. Colour crept into his
cheeks and glowed in hectic spots. His eyes, deep in their
sockets, began to burn with a feverish light. He pulled himself up to his feet.

"Yes, yes!" he mumbled fiercely. "Rich—ha, ha!—rich!
It cannot fail; I am a fool"—he caught his breath, and
swayed again on his feet. "Come on! Come on! Hurry!"
he choked out.

Jimmie Dale watched them, his lips suddenly tight. They
had *passed by* the safe, and were coming directly toward

where he stood. Another yard and they would reach the portières. His automatic swung silently upward in his hand. And then the old man halted in front of an oil painting that hung from the wall a little less than shoulder high.

For an instant the man stood there breathing heavily, as though even the exertion of crossing the room had taxed him beyond his strength; and then with a quick movement he jerked at the edge of the frame, and the painting itself, as though it were the grooved cover of a box, slid to one side, exposing the wall, which was as bare and as innocent in appearance behind, or, rather, through the frame, as anywhere else in the room.

"Jathan Lane's safe deposit vault," coughed the Minister. He laughed. His cheeks were burning; his eyes were brighter. He leaned suddenly down toward the floor. "This knot in the wainscoting—see?"

Behind the empty frame, a door in the wall swung open—and the light from the room fell upon the nickel dial of a safe.

"That's the boy!" applauded Gentleman Laroque.

"Yes, yes!" whispered the old man. "I'll open it! Wait! A—a long time it took to get the combination, but—but I got it"—his fingers were working at the dial—"there—there it is!"

"Just a second!" said Laroque coolly, as the door of the little wall safe swung open. He glanced around him, then darted across the room to a small, square table on which stood a heavy bronze vase. "Here, this will do!" he said, and laying the vase on the floor, came back with the table. "Shoot the stuff out on this!"

It took a minute, perhaps two; and then upon the table there lay a number of jewellers' cases in both plush and leather, and a dozen or more little chamois bags. Laroque was rapidly opening and shutting the cases, and as he did so the contents of each in its turn, pendants, brooches, ornaments of many designs, all of them set with diamonds, seemed to leap thirstily at the light and hail it with eager scintillating flashes before the covers could be shut down upon them again.

"That all that's in there?" demanded Laroque.

"Yes," breathed the old man. "Yes"—he rubbed his hands rapaciously together—"all except the tray he uses to paw 'em over on."

"That's thoughtful of him!" grunted Gentleman Laroque. "Let's have it."

From the bottom of the safe the Minister pulled out and laid upon the table an oblong, plush-covered tray with raised edges.

"Now!" grunted Laroque again. "Open the bags, and dump the whities into the tray."

Jimmie Dale drew in his breath. It seemed as though little rivers of fire had begun to stream from the mouths of the bags. The men were working fast now; Laroque with almost cynical composure; the old man, wrought up, clumsy in his greed, his hands trembling, mumbling, crooning to himself.

Diamonds, unset stones, of all sizes, poured into the tray; they filled it, heaped it to its edges. An inch deep they lay. It was a fortune whose value Jimmie Dale did not dare attempt to compute—a pool of immortal beauty, restless with vitality, flashing, limpid, shifting, iridescent. Here the facet of a stone struck back at the light, fiery, passionate in its challenge; there another lay, soft in its radiance, glowing, pulsing, breathing, alive.

Laroque drew a cloth bag from his pocket and unfolded it. He ran his finger through the stones, separating them into two almost equal portions; the portion nearer him he began to put into his little sack.

"Slip the rest of them into the chamois bags again, and put 'em back in the safe," he directed tersely. "Divide 'em amongst the bags as equally as you can. And those gew-gaws in the cases, too, of course—put them back. We can't afford to monkey with anything but the unset stones; any one of those ornaments might happen to be just the one that somebody in the family would remember—and miss."

But now the Minister hesitated. The hectic colour had fled from his cheeks, only to enhance, it seemed, the fever fire in his eyes; the muscles of his face twitched; his hands, trembling before, shook now as with the ague.

"*All!*" he whispered fiercely, and touched his lips with the tip of his tongue. "Look at 'em! My God, look at 'em! We've got 'em all here! Take 'em! Take 'em! Let's take 'em all—all the unset stones anyhow! I'll make my get-away with you. Can't we take 'em all?"

Gentleman Laroque continued his work without looking up.

"*I've* never been in Sing Sing," he said, with a thin smile. "That's why I came here myself to-night. I couldn't trust you or anybody else, except Hunchback Joe, to stand up against the temptation of making the bum play that would land us there. All! That's what Sing Sing is full of! You poor fool, aren't you satisfied with a *sure* thing when the sure thing is a fortune? That's what the half we're taking is—a fortune. And nobody to know that any job has been pulled; and Shiftel with a free hand to dispose of the stones at market value! Would you rather pinch them all, make it next to impossible to sell them for anything like what they're worth, and on top of that dodge the police for the rest of your life? You'd have a rosy chance making your get-away—Mr. Jathan Lane's vanishing butler, alias the Minister, alias Patrick Denton, late of Sing Sing!" His voice hardened suddenly. "As I said, *I've* never been in Sing Sing. Hurry up, now! Put the rest of those stones and all the ornaments back in the safe."

The old man swept his hand across his eyes.

"Sure," he said thickly; "you're right, and I——" A spasm of pain contorted his features, and he clutched at his side and staggered; but as Laroque, with a sharp exclamation, reached out a steadying hand, the Minister shook his head. "I'm all right," he said—and began to return the diamonds Laroque had left on the tray to the little chamois bags.

A strange smile crossed Jimmie Dale's lips. Laroque was right—quite right. And from Laroque's standpoint—safe.

The scene of the two men at work there beyond the portière seemed suddenly to shift, and he, Jimmie Dale, was again one of that afternoon group gathered around the table in the smoking room of the St. James Club. Jathan Lane, one of the richest men in America, and his hobby! It had been pure pleasantry, the twitting to which they had subjected the multimillionaire. But the banker had answered seriously. "How many stones have I? What are they worth?" he had said in reply to a question. "I am sure I do not know myself, but I am equally sure there are no finer unset diamonds, in mass you understand, in America. I have been buying them, one, two, half a dozen at a time, for years. I love them; I take a pure delight in them; and I indulge myself without stint, since, after all, my hobby is by no means a bad one even in a business sense. At least, and what can hardly be said of most hobbies, the value is always there." "But your family?" the questioner had persisted. "I should think Mrs. Lane and your daughter would be raiding you all the time!" And then Jathan Lane had laughed. "Familiarity and contempt, you know," he had said. "A boy and his bag of marbles. They haven't looked at them for years."

Gentleman Laroque was speaking again.

"That's the idea!" he said more pleasantly. "They may be a little *disappointed,* perhaps even a little surprised that there aren't more, but that's where it ends so far as the family is concerned. No suspicion that everything isn't just as old man Lane left it; no suspicion that anything has been *taken.* And, speaking professionally, therein lies the difference between an artist and a hog!" He tucked the small cloth bag under his coat. The table was clear. "Close her up nice and tidy," he smiled, "and I'll beat it for Shiftel's."

The old man closed the wall safe, and slid the painting back in its grooved frame.

"Fine!" approved Gentleman Laroque. "I'll leave you to put the table back. Come on now, and lock the window behind me."

Jimmie Dale did not move; only his face set a little more grimly as he watched Gentleman Laroque climb through the window and disappear. It would be a pity to let Shiftel get out of this scot-free! His mind, alert, incisive, was sifting, weighing, formulating the details of a plan whose germ had taken root there, it seemed, almost from the moment he had begun to watch the men at work. Neither Gentleman Laroque nor the Minister would eventually escape, for they could be found anytime. . . . Shiftel was another member of the gang, an oily, craven little rat, and Shiftel in a corner with his own skin in danger was far more likely to *talk* than either of the other two . . . the Tocsin's letter and the Phantom . . . what Shiftel knew he could be made to tell . . . the *evidence* of this robbery here must be taken care of as soon as the Minister there had gone upstairs again to——

There came a low, dull thud; a broken cry:

"Brandy—I——"

With a sudden sweep of his arm Jimmie Dale brushed aside the portière and leaped forward—too late. The heavy bronze vase, fallen from nerveless fingers that had striven to lift it back on the table, was still rolling across the floor, as the old man, with arms outflung, pitched forward beside it, and lay still.

In an instant Jimmie Dale had reached the cabinet and procured the stimulant, and in another was kneeling beside the prostrate figure—and then, after a moment, in a strangely quiet and deliberate way Jimmie Dale laid the brandy aside.

It was very still in the house, still as the form stretched out there on the rug before him, still as the old, white, upturned face. The man was dead.

The grim, sharp lines that drooped the corners of Jimmie Dale's lips faded away, and something seemed to soften the hard, set immobility of his face as he rose finally to his feet. It was just a crook, just the Minister, alias Patrick Denton, just the end of a vicious, miserable career of crime—but it was also the end of a human life. And life even to this warped soul was as sweet, wasn't it, as to another?—more so perhaps for the very fact that death must have stood with beckoning finger for so long now at the other's elbow!

Jimmie Dale turned slowly away and walked across the room. Mechanically he slid the painting out along its grooves; mechanically he stooped and found the knot in the wainscoting. Perhaps it was as well, perhaps infinitely better this way, better that the end should come here than behind the steel bars and the gray stone walls where once it had so nearly come. They would not have pardoned the Minister *twice*.

The little door in the wall had swung open, the nickel dial of the safe glittered in the light—and suddenly Jimmie Dale's shoulders straightened, and for an instant his dark eyes studied the closed steel door. Then he leaned forward, his ear pressed against the face of the safe for the tumblers' fall, and the slim, sensitive fingers, the nerves throbbing at the tips, those magical masters of bolts and locks, were at work.

The minutes passed. There was no sound, save at times the faint, musical whir of the dial; then, abruptly, a deep breathed exclamation:

"All thumbs to-night!"

Again the minutes passed; again the dial moved, now with its musical whir, now slowly, with infinite care; and then a sound, so low as to be scarcely audible—the soft thud, muffled within the steel walls, of metal meeting metal, the bolts sliding in their sockets.

The door of the safe stood open.

Jimmie Dale swung around and stared about the room. He was provided with no little cloth sack such as Gentleman Laroque had had; true he had, instead, those little chamois bags, and his pockets might hold them all, but— With a quick stride he crossed the room to the desk, and picked up a black leather portfolio. It was quite large enough, and, used for carrying documents, its flap was fitted with a clasp. He opened it, dumped the papers it contained out on the desk, and returned to the wall safe.

Jimmie Dale was working with lightning speed now. The little chamois bags were tucked into the bottom of the portfolio; the small plush and leather jewellers' cases were opened in quick succession, their contents following the chamois bags, the cases themselves being tossed helter-skelter upon the floor.

The safe was empty.

Jimmie Dale closed the portfolio, and cast a sharp, critical glance around the room. He nodded grimly to himself. There was ample evidence now that there had been a robbery, quite ample—everybody knew that there had been *something* in the now empty safe—and it would not therefore be, as Gentleman Laroque expected, so blind a trail now that led to the source of the diamonds with which Isaac Shiftel was to be endowed! Also, for good measure in this respect, some of the ornaments, that were certainly the property of Mrs. Lane, and which Gentleman Laroque had been wise enough to leave alone, would not lack for a speedy identification! And, again, there was the yawning door of the wall safe, and the painting that still protruded so eloquently from its frame!

His eyes softened in their expression as they held now for an instant again on the form that lay upon the floor. Then he shook his head in quick decision. He needed time now before an alarm was sounded that might by any chance reach the ears of Gentleman Laroque, or, more particularly, one Isaac Shiftel!

Jimmie Dale consulted his watch. It was five minutes of three. The electric-light switch clicked under his fingers. The room was in darkness.

Then silence through the house.

And presently a figure crouched again in the shadows of the basement porch, and crossed the yard, and swung itself silently over the fence into the lane—and from here, slipping the black silk mask from his face, Jimmie Dale emerged on the street.

But now Jimmie Dale seemed to be no longer in haste. It was a long way from Jathan Lane's mansion to Mr. Isaac Shiftel's unsavory abode, which was now Jimmie

Dale's destination, and the subway would be the quicker, but, instead, Jimmie Dale hailed a belated taxi as it passed him. He was interested in reaching Isaac Shiftel's only *after* Gentleman Laroque had been there and gone. He gave the chauffeur an address on the Bowery that would bring him within a block of the tenement that Isaac Shiftel had chosen as his lair, and stepped into the taxi.

III

ONE ISAAC SHIFTEL

THE taxi rolled and swayed its way along. Jimmie Dale sat staring at the portfolio that bumped with the motion of the car upon his knees. In some thirty-odd minutes, at halfpast three to be exact, the police would be paying a visit to Laroque's quarters, and even if the man were not back there by then, the police were patient and would wait! They would get Laroque—but not the evidence. They might even let the man go again—temporarily. It would not matter. Laroque's freedom, if obtained at all, would be of very short duration. The evidence lacking at Gentleman Laroque's would be found within the hour and in abundant measure, together with Mr. Isaac Shiftel himself, at—Isaac Shiftel's!

But that was not all; nor, indeed, that which most vitally interested him. Despite the Tocsin's efforts to keep him out of those shadows, as she had termed it, that seemed to have closed down upon her blacker and more ominous even than before, the night's work had already brought him greater returns than he had ever dared to hope for or expect. He knew three of the pawns who moved at the criminal will of the unknown leader whom she had styled the Phantom. One of the three was dead, but there remained two; and of the two, one was Laroque, and the other was a miserable little rat-like creature, who, under *persuasion*, was not likely to prove over-secretive. And Shiftel's tongue, once made to wag, held promise of almost anything, even the "Open Sesame" to what was now his, Jimmie Dale's, ultimate goal—the Phantom.

Jimmie Dale's eyes travelled to the window, held there for a few minutes noting the taxi's progress, and then fixed introspectively again on the portfolio.

Shiftel! He knew Shiftel as only the *initiated* knew him, as only those knew him whose ears were attune to the whispered confidences of the underworld's exchanges in the dens and dives hidden away from the light of day, where he, Jimmie Dale, once as Larry the Bat, and now in the present day as Smarlinghue, the broken-down artist and hop-fighter, was welcomed as one of the élite of that inglorious realm. He had even seen Shiftel on one or two occasions—an unkempt, bearded, spectacled foreigner of uncertain age, a cringing little beast, hideously cunning, a master in his own peculiar line of deviltry. Shiftel ostensibly, for the benefit of the police should they ever prove inquisitive, made his living in his two-room, dirty, bachelor apartment, by working on garments which he brought from various sweat shops. If he were rarely at home and too lazy to work much, that was his misfortune, his loss, and his sole personal affair! But the underworld held him in quite other regard—as a "fence," a "shover of stolen goods," who was safe, and in cleverness without an equal. There were few crooks in the Bad Lands but were hungry for Isaac Shiftel's services, but Shiftel was not approachable to all; it was understood, and perforce had regretfully come to be accepted as a fact, that he dealt only with a small and select clientèle of his own choosing, whose personnel was more guessed at than known; and that to break into the charmed circle was a feat attempted by many but accomplished by few. And as far back as Jimmie Dale could remember, as far back as he could remember even Gentleman Laroque, Shiftel had lived in the same miserable rooms in the same miserable tenement.

The taxi rattled on. At intervals Jimmie Dale kept glancing out of the window. And then, as the taxi turned at last into the Bowery, he smiled suddenly, laid his handkerchief on the portfolio, and reached into one of the pockets of the leather girdle under his vest. Shiftel! He took out a thin metal case, like a cigarette case, and from the case, with a

pair of tiny tweezers that mocked at finger-prints, he lifted
out a diamond-shaped gray paper seal that was adhesive on
one side, and dropped it on the handkerchief. He returned
the metal case to its hiding place, folded the handkerchief
carefully, and replaced it in his pocket.

A moment later the taxi stopped. Jimmie Dale alighted,
paid and dismissed the chauffeur, and as he swung around
the corner, walking east from the Bowery, he looked at his
watch. It was twenty minutes past three. It became now
simply a question whether Laroque was still with Shiftel,
or had gone home.

The street, one of the most shabby of East Side streets,
was dark, poorly lighted, and free of pedestrians. Jimmie
Dale passed by a tenement whose shabbiness was quite in
keeping with its surroundings, passed by a narrow areaway
which separated the tenement from another which might
have been a duplicate of the first—and halted before the
entrance of the second tenement.

The outer door was unlocked. In a moment he was inside
the hallway, and in utter blackness now stood motionless,
listening. Then again the black silk mask was slipped over
his face, and again it was as though a shadow moved. Shiftel's apartment was the middle one on the ground floor facing
the other tenement across the areaway.

Jimmie Dale passed down the length of the hall, counting
the doors on his right by the sense of touch, and, returning,
crouched with his ear against the panel of the door he had
selected. From within, so faintly as to be indefinable in any
concrete way, there came the sound of movement. Still
Jimmie Dale listened, even while his fingers worked silently
at doorknob and lock. He nodded his head as he completed
his work. There had been no sound of voices. Gentleman
Laroque had evidently been and gone. Isaac Shiftel was
alone.

And then suddenly Jimmie Dale was on his feet, and in
a flash was in the room, the door closed and locked behind
him. Through the doorway of a connecting room ahead of
him he could see the unkempt, bearded figure of Shiftel as

the man, with a cry, sprang wildly to his feet from the chair in which he had been seated, clawing, even as he sprang, at the white, glittering array of diamonds strewn upon the table-top before him.

"Who's that? Who's there?" the man called out hoarsely.

Jimmie Dale's automatic covered the other as he moved swiftly forward to Shiftel's side.

"Quite an elaborate collection you've got here, Isaac," he said softly. "First water stones of course, or *you* wouldn't be handling them. And please don't wriggle, Isaac, until I—ah, thanks!" He had laid the portfolio down on the table, and his fingers passing deftly over Shiftel's clothing had whipped out a revolver from the other's pocket and trans-ferred it to his own.

But now Shiftel seemed to have got a sudden grip upon himself. He leaned forward, peering sharply from behind his spectacles at Jimmie Dale's masked face.

"No," he said with a snarl, "I don't know you, because I don't know *your* kind. But you evidently don't know Isaac Shiftel. Those stones, eh? That's it, is it? Well, you may get out of here with them, but afterwards—eh?—do you think Isaac Shiftel's arm is so short as that?"

Jimmie Dale made no answer. He retreated a step, and with his free hand began to unfasten the portfolio.

Shiftel shook his fist virulently now. The first shock once over, he was, through familiarity, apparently quite at his ease again in dealing with—a crook.

"How'd you get wise to this, eh?" he demanded fiercely. "How'd you——" His glance had travelled to the window that opened on the areaway. "Ah!" he exclaimed. "That's it, eh? The shade's down, but like a fool I left the window open. You had the luck to sneak into that areaway." He peered again into Jimmie Dale's face, and abruptly his tone and manner changed. He rubbed his hands together ingrati-atingly. "I said you didn't know Isaac Shiftel," he said smoothly; "but you do—everybody in your line of business knows Isaac Shiftel. I'll make a deal with you—a fair share

—eh? You don't want Isaac Shiftel as an enemy. I'll give you——"

"You're getting in ahead of me, Isaac," interrupted Jimmie Dale plaintively. He coughed slightly—and politely pressed his handkerchief to his moistened lips. "*I* meant to be the first to offer something." With a quick jerk of his revolver hand, he plucked a diamond necklace from the top of the portfolio, and tossed it upon the table. "That, for instance —Isaac."

The ornament seemed to fascinate Shiftel. As if drawn to it against his will, he leaned forward staring at it; and then, as though actuated by a sort of frightened incredulity, he reached out a hand toward it—but Jimmie Dale's hand that still held the handkerchief was the quicker. It fell and gripped like a vise upon the back of Shiftel's hand.

"Just a moment, Isaac," said Jimmie Dale coolly. "There is something else that I want you to have—as a little memento of the occasion."

There came a startled cry from Shiftel. Jimmie Dale had withdrawn his hand, and Shiftel was staring now, not at the diamond necklace, but at a diamond-shaped gray paper seal that was pasted on the back of his hand.

"I'll say it for you!" Jimmie Dale's smile was not inviting. "The Gray Seal! I apologise for the melodrama, but I think it will aid you, Isaac, to see things in a clearer light. You've got a little information that I want, and I imagine it will help to quicken your memory and loosen your tongue to know *who* wants it."

There was no answer. The man, his lips twitching, was still staring at the back of his hand.

With a sudden movement, Jimmie Dale emptied the contents of the portfolio upon the table. He brushed them into a heap with the diamonds already there.

"They belong together," said Jimmie Dale, in a curious monotone, "and I couldn't bear to see them left behind. They'll be *found* together too, Isaac, for I am afraid it will be impossible to make any one believe now that Jathan Lane's safe has never been disturbed." His voice hardened suddenly. "You're going up for this, Isaac. I make no bargain with you. The police are going to be tipped off over the phone, and they are going to find you here trussed up in that chair with the diamonds in front of you. But before the police get you, you are going to deal with me. I want to know who the man is you, and those with you, take your orders from. And before we are *through* you are going to tell me, Isaac—all you know."

Shiftel's tongue was circling his lips. He shook his head. He was cringing now, supplicating with his hands.

"I don't know anything," he protested wildly. "You're all wrong. You're all wrong about everything. I don't know anything about Jathan Lane. I don't know where the diamonds came from. I never ask questions in my business. They were brought in here for me to shove, and——"

"That's enough, Isaac!" snapped Jimmie Dale. "The game is up! Your friend, Patrick Denton, alias the Minister, is dead up there on the floor of Jathan Lane's private library, where he——"

"Dead!" Shiftel's hands had ceased their movements. The man stood rigid. Something stronger than himself seemed to have stripped him of further power to dissimulate. "Dead! You—you killed him?"

"Never mind about that!" Jimmie Dale bit off his words. "It's enough for you to know for the present that he is dead. You're not quite so innocent as you were—are you, Isaac? And as for the man who brought those stones here, a friend of mine has kindly arranged to have the police pay a little visit at Gentleman Laroque's at just about this time; to be precise"—he drew his watch from his pocket—"at——"

Jimmie Dale's words ended abruptly. He, too, was suddenly standing tense and rigid. A footstep, guarded, cautious, was coming along the areaway out there. It was coming nearer to the open window—the drawn shade did not *hide* the sound. Instinctively his eyes sought the dial of his watch.

It was halfpast three.

"At Laroque's!" Shiftel, his ears strained toward the

window, was whispering the words. "The police—at Laroque's!" And then he raised both fists in fury and shook
them above his head. "You snitch, you cursed snitch"—the
low, whispered words seemed but to accentuate the man's
sudden flood of passion—"we'll get you yet for this!"

For an instant Jimmie Dale's brain seemed to reel in turmoil and chaos. That voice was no longer Shiftel's. Those
words! Once he had heard those exact words before, and
—with a quick step forward, his hand reached out,
tearing beard and spectacles from the other's face.

"Gentleman Laroque!"

"Yes, you fool!" said Laroque, still whispering. "So
you've tripped at last, eh? You didn't know, and you've
brought the police *here*. Well, take the consequences! It's
you who's trapped!" He was backing slowly away from
both table and window toward the inner wall of the room.
"Perhaps *you'll* explain the possession of those stones! You
fool, you and that woman with you, you don't know what
you're up against, but——"

"Don't move!" ordered Jimmie Dale grimly.

"Just this far," smiled Laroque. "I hear them coming
along the hall inside now. Don't forget there's one of your
police on guard outside the window, and——"

The room was in instant darkness. The bare fraction of
a second passed, not more; there was a faint scraping sound
from the direction where Laroque had been standing—and
Jimmie Dale's flashlight, whipped from his pocket, was
sweeping around him.

The room was empty!

Jimmie Dale's face was set like chiselled marble. Empty!
Gone! The man was gone! But that was not all! Voices
were ringing that slogan of the old days in his ears again:
"Death to the Gray Seal!" He did not need to be told what
it meant to be caught by either police or underworld. He,
too, heard those guarded footsteps inside the tenement and
coming now along the hall. His mind, alert, virile, was working with lightning speed. The doorway was behind him, and
Laroque could not have gone that way—nor by the window

guarded by the police. There must be some secret exit from
the room. If so, given but a second, while he, Jimmie Dale,
was attempting an escape, Laroque could get back again
and secure the diamonds that lay upon the table. And he,
Jimmie Dale, was *responsible* for them now!

And now Jimmie Dale in action was swift as his racing
thoughts. Whether he could save himself or not, there was
at least a way to save the stones. With the flashlight
switched on, he propped it on the end of the table, its ray
streaming over the gems and playing in the opposite direction from the connecting door.

"If you can hear me, Laroque," he whispered, "I warn
you—don't try it! All you'll get off that table will be a bullet, whether I'm caught or not!"

It was utter blackness behind him. He backed swiftly,
silently through the connecting door, and across the outer
room to the door that led into the hall. His automatic held
a line on the table top. He crouched at the far side of the
door casing. They were here now. He heard a whispered
consultation outside, as his fingers, closing on the key, silently unlocked the door. Queer! His brain was racing
again. A queer sight! All blackness back here—and,
through the connecting doorway, a light, apparently coming
from nowhere, streamed over a shimmering, scintillating mass
of diamonds, and ended by imposing itself in a white, lumin-
ous circle on a dirty, greasy wall behind! His eyes never
left the table; his automatic never wavered in its line. Queer!
The Phantom! Gentleman Laroque—Isaac Shiftel! Could
it be? Was that a partial answer to the Tocsin's "score of
aliases and score of domiciles"? Was Gentleman Laroque
the Phantom? Yet how had she taken this for Laroque's
home if she hadn't known the two men were one? And she
hadn't known. She had said so. But—yes, it was not un-
explainable. It might easily have been—just as it had been
with him, Jimmie Dale, as Larry the Bat, or as Smarlinghue.
She might have seen Laroque come here some evening—
and Shiftel might have come out—while she thought Laroque

remained *at home*. It might easily be that she did not know Shiftel, and so——

"Bust it in!" The words came sharp, incisive, from the hall; then a quick exclamation: "Blamed if the door ain't unlocked! Come on!"

The door was flung violently open. A man swung forward into the room—and halted abruptly, staring toward the connecting doorway.

"For Heaven's sake, sergeant, look at that!" he burst out.

A man behind pushed eagerly forward. And Jimmie Dale, crouching low by the baseboard in the blackness, slipped through the doorway behind the other without a sound, and in a moment was outside the tenement and walking quietly along the street—in a direction that ignored the areaway.

Half an hour later Jimmie Dale mounted the steps of a palatial residence on Riverside Drive. He smiled softly as he stumbled and shuffled so noisily that before he had gained the topmost step the door was opened for him by the white-haired old butler, who had been butler to Jimmie Dale's father before him, and whose proudest boast was that he had dandled his Master Jim upon his knee. It would have been so easy to have slipped in, and passed the old man, and gone upstairs to bed—and broken the old man's heart to have been found out *asleep* at his self-appointed post.

"What!" said Jimmie Dale severely—and used identically the same words he had used on a hundred similar occasions: "Sitting up again for me, Jason? How many times am I to tell you that I won't have it? Jason, go to bed at once!"

"Yes, sir," said Jason. "Thank you, sir. Thank you, Master Jim, sir—I will."

IV

THREADS

TWO weeks had passed.
It was evening; and Jimmie Dale, as Smarlinghue now, the seedy, down-at-the-heels artist, better known as Smarly in the Bad Lands, and still better known again in the ultra-exclusive dens and dives, where the first citizens of New York's crimeland foregathered, as a dope fiend shattered beyond repair, a character shady enough from any angle to entitle him to homage even in that unhallowed circle of the élite, slouched along an East Side street—but the slouching gait was strangely and incredibly swift. He skulked in the night shadows of the buildings like some evil thing that sought darkness as kindred to itself. But at intervals, as he moved along with that strange illusive swiftness, the rays of a street lamp, as though in ironic mockery at his inability to evade them, brought out into sharp relief the disreputable figure whose coat was a size too small for him, and from the short sleeves of which protruded blatantly the frayed and soiled wristbands of his shirt, whose shoulders were stooped, and whose face, what could be seen of it under a battered felt hat, was hollow cheeked, and gaunt with a half starved look.

And now he entered a house that made the corner of a lane, a house that was as disreputable as himself, a dwelling of some old-time pretentions, but with the city's onward march a derelict now, metamorphosed into a mean and squalid tenement. He passed along the dark, musty hallway to the rear room on the ground floor, and, opening the door, stepped inside. He closed the door, locked it behind him, and for an instant stood still, his glance seeming to search into the very shadows themselves where they lay heaviest in the far corners of the room.

It was the Sanctuary that for a year now—or was it two? —had housed the character of Smarlinghue, as, in the days gone by, the old Sanctuary, before the fire had destroyed it, had housed the character of Larry the Bat. Through a top-light high up near the ceiling above the French window, which latter, a relic of past glory, opened on a level with the floor, the moonlight flickered in. It disclosed in nebulous outline a battered easel in one corner of the room, and near it, against the wall and strewn upon the floor, a number of canvases of different sizes. A cot bed, its covers in disorder, occupied the wall space opposite the door. For the rest, there were a filthy, threadbare rag of carpet upon the floor, a battered table, a rickety washstand, and two disabled chairs.

Satisfied that the moonlight was the sole intruder, Jimmie Dale nodded shortly to himself, and stepping abruptly forward examined the drawn roller shade on the French window, and particularly a rent therein that was fastened together with a pin. Again he nodded. Then a diminutive gas-jet, choked with air, hissed and spluttered under his match, and supplanting the moonlight, threw a sickly yellow glow about the room. He crossed then to the corner near the door, knelt down on the floor, and after an instant's work removed an ingeniously fitted section of the base-board. From the aperture he took out the carefully folded dinner suit which he had been wearing on the evening when he l.ad last left his residence on Riverside Drive.

He began to cast off the shabby, disreputable garments of Smarlinghue. He worked swiftly. With the clothes discarded, there came another change. The hollow cheeks, the thin, extended lips, the widened nostrils disappeared as little distorting pieces of wax were removed. Before a cracked mirror propped up on the rickety washstand, he washed away the stain that previously had given a jaundiced, unhealthy hue to his face and hands—and with minutest care took stock of the result in the mirror.

And then the light went out. The rest could be completed in the darkness. Smarlinghue was no longer at home.

It was like a shadow now flitting soundlessly here and there in the streak of moonlight. A minute, perhaps two, passed; and then the pin that held together the rent in the window shade was removed, and Jimmie Dale peered cautiously out into the narrow, squalid, moonlit courtyard beyond. Another instant, and the French window opened noiselessly on its carefully oiled hinges, and closed again. A figure, close hugged against the wall of the building, stole along the few intervening feet to the fence that divided the courtyard from the lane. Here, next to the wall, a loosened plank swung outward. The figure slipped through into the lane—and Jimmie Dale, immaculate and faultlessly attired, emerged upon the street from which, but a few minutes before, Smarlinghue, the dope fiend, had vanished.

He walked rapidly now, heading over toward the Bowery, and crossing that thoroughfare, innocuous now in the early evening hours, continued on deeper into the East Side. A half grim, half whimsical smile was on his lips. His objective was a little two-story, tumble-down house where an old widow by the name of Mrs. Kinsey still kept, as she had kept for more years than the East Side could remember, a small and woefully unpretentious confectionery store. It did not further the one interest he had in life now, this objective of his to-night; it would bring him no nearer to his goal, so far as he could see, though it held a logical and even intimate connection therewith. It was no "call to arms" from the Tocsin that he——

His pace slackened involuntarily, and there was a sudden droop to the broad shoulders that were usually so straight. The Tocsin! Where was she—while he, seeking to reach her, groped and groped in pitiful failure, a blind man, a child in strength, a fool in intellect! He clenched his hands. One of those black moments again! One more added to the thousand through which he had lived in the past two weeks. Was she still *alive?*

He choked back a cry of bitter agony, and quickened his

pace again; but though his shoulders were once more thrown back, a whiteness had been born into his face.

It was two weeks since she had left him that night in the little boat on the East River, two weeks since the night Gentleman Laroque, alias Isaac Shiftel, had so mysteriously disappeared from that tenement room, and she had begun again to battle alone for her existence, pitting her wits against that unknown super-fiend of the underworld whom she had styled the Phantom. And since that night Gentleman Laroque, both in that character and in the character of Isaac Shiftel, had vanished as effectually as though he had never existed; and there had been no word or sign from her, save a short note that he had found, as once before in the old days he had found one, hidden behind the movable section of the base-board in the Sanctuary—and that was now a week ago. He had destroyed it, torn it for safety's sake into the same minute fragments that he always tore her notes; but it still remained intact, for it had seared itself word for word indelibly upon his brain.

"Dear Philanthropic Crook," she had written. "Oh, why *will* you do it! You do not know your own danger. Apart from the police, there is only one man who could be interested in the secret of Shiftel's room. That's you, Jimmie. They know that. Keep away from the place. They expect you sooner or later. Oh, I beg of you to keep away! It is a trap. Mother Margot, the new tenant, is one of them. She is only there to throw dust in your eyes, and in the eyes of the police.

"As for myself, I am safe so far, Jimmie; but I do not know how much progress I have made. Sometimes I think I have already come far along the road—and sometimes I seem lost again. Yesterday I was sure of the Phantom's identity; to-day I am sure I was wrong; to-morrow I shall be sure again—but it will be of a totally different personality. You think, no doubt, that it is Shiftel, alias Laroque. Well, perhaps, it is; but unless you and I are both swept out of the road, neither in the one character nor the other will that man probably ever be heard of again. And so, oh, Jimmie, be careful—*and remember the trap*. Marie."

The last phrase was heavily underscored. The trap! It brought a grim twist to his lips. He had already been in and out of the trap—and, from what she had said in her note, at perhaps the only time when it had been safe so far as he was concerned, paradoxical though that seemed, for he had visited Shiftel's rooms again the night after the murder, and while the police had, so fortunately it now appeared, obligingly done unconscious picket duty for him without. The diamonds found in Shiftel's room had, thanks to the set pieces, been almost immediately identified; and these, coupled with their owner's murder, and the dead butler's identification as an ex-Sing Sing convict, had aroused a veritable furor in the papers. The police had wanted, and still wanted, Shiftel very badly indeed, and so plain-clothes-men for a week had unostentatiously watched the tenement day and night on the chance that Shiftel would return. But he, Jimmie Dale, had been even more interested in Shiftel's erstwhile domicile than had the police; therefore he had examined it, not entirely to his ultimate satisfaction, but certainly unknown to the headquarters men, whom, not being Shiftel, he had had little difficulty in eluding. The result had been—nothing.

Then, again unknown to the police, he had joined forces with them, and he, too, had watched the tenement. On the first of the month, a week after Shiftel's disappearance, the agent had re-rented the two miserable rooms to an old hag-like creature known as Mother Margot. He had been aware of that before the Tocsin's note had reached him. But prior to that again Mother Margot had passed muster with the police, who had thereupon withdrawn their forces, considering further surveillance of the premises unnecessary and their hopes from that quarter at an end. But Mother Margot had not passed muster with him, in spite of the fact that his own investigation of the woman had resulted in the discovery that she was, and had been for a year, a licensed pushcart vendor, a sort of travelling dry goods emporium, who hawked her wares in that ultra-foreign quarter on Thompson Street, just off West Broadway, where she with a hundred others of her ilk cluttered the narrow street until it was well nigh impassable. He knew what the police did not know. He knew that Shiftel's rooms held a secret that the man whom he, as well as the Tocsin, had now come to call the Phantom would strive his utmost to protect by one means or another. And so he had watched Mother Margot because logic would not down. The Tocsin's note had but confirmed his suspicions; and though her warning had not gone utterly unheeded, and he had thereafter evaded the "trap," he had kept even a still closer watch upon Mother Margot herself. For days at a stretch now he had lived as Smarlinghue—and that had brought him here to his errand to-night.

Jimmie Dale's face hardened suddenly. His errand! It was dirty, miserable, pitiful work that he had partially uncovered. Sooner or later, he had made sure that Mother Margot would bring him into touch with others of the same breed who owned allegiance to the Phantom. And she had at last, to-night—for it was neither probable nor tenable to imagine that, serving the Phantom, she was allied with any other band, or permitted a divided interest. An hour ago he had followed her to the Wistaria Café, one of the lowest type of dance halls in the Bad Lands, where she had joined two men; one named Little Sweeney, a smooth-tongued, oily little rat, fastidious in his dress, and whom he, Jimmie Dale, already knew in the same sense as he knew by sight and name a hundred other crooks of greater or less degree; the other, whom they had addressed not inaptly as Limpy Mack, a stoop-shouldered, bent-over figure in peaked cap, with unkempt gray hair and moustache, who walked with a distinct limp and by the aid of a cane whose tip was heavily rubber-capped like a crutch, he did not know at all. From the dance hall proper the three had adjourned to a private room in the rear; and anticipating their arrival there by the matter of a few seconds, he, Jimmie Dale, as Smarlinghue then, had adjourned to the alleyway without, and the window raised an imperceptible crack, the roller shade raised an equally imperceptible space above the sill, had afforded both sight and hearing—that is, within limitations, in so far as hearing went. He had seen Little Sweeney hand the man who limped a paper which the latter had carefully tucked away in his pocket; and then, as a waiter came in and left a tray of glasses, the three had got their heads together around a table.

Jimmie Dale's brows furrowed now as he hurried along. Again and again the blare of the jazz band had drowned out their low tones. In the ten minutes during which he had crouched there outside the window, he had caught no more than snatches of their conversation; but those snatches had been viciously significant. His mind mulled them over again now; a half completed sentence from one, an interjection from another. It had begun with Mother Margot.

"Mabbe dis Mrs. Kinsey person wid her tin-horn shop ain't got so much!" she had cackled. "Mabbe youse'll lose yer hundred!"

After that a jumble of words from one or other of the three:

". . . Forget it! . . . Never banked a cent in her life. . . . Up in the thousands, that's what; else where's the insurance alone that was a couple of thousand when the old man bumped off two years ago? . . . The Chief never pulls a bone. . . . The old girl's as deaf as a church congregation. . . . She'll lead us to it. . . . Cop the sale to-night. . . . Sure, about bedtime. . . . No night-hawk, though. . . . You watch downstairs, I'll watch up. . . ."

In actual detail he had learned little; but in general he had learned enough to know that old Mrs. Kinsey was supposed to possess a hidden store of savings, whose hiding place they in some way expected to trick her into disclosing. The thought of the police had come to him; that he might in some way with safety and without involving his own personality warn the police, instead of playing a lone hand in this himself. He smiled a little wanly. There was one very good reason why he should not communicate with the police. This Little Sweeney and the man who limped offered new fields for investigation, widened his range of action, and were, indeed, a reward for the days and nights that he had hung upon Mother Margot's trail. They might, or they might not, lead to something tangible; but certainly, for the moment,

he could not afford to see them in the toils of the police.
The alternative was stark enough. He could not stand by
inactive and see this miserable, sordid tragedy played out.

And so he had left the three in the back room of the Wistaria Café, and had hurried to the Sanctuary—and Smarlinghue had become Jimmie Dale. That was all. That was why
he was here now, why he was approaching that little store
on the corner ahead, which, early as the evening was, not
more than nine o'clock, had its modest show window already
darkened for the night—he had not dared risk "Smarlinghue"
here; Smarlinghue, whose position in the underworld, that
had literally come to mean life and death to him again, would
crumble to dust before the slightest breath of suspicion.

But his visit to the Sanctuary, imperative though it had
been, had nevertheless taken time. Against this, however,
was the fact that the Sanctuary was not hopelessly out of the
direct road between the dance hall and Mrs. Kinsey's little
shop; and, besides, he had hurried. He smiled a little grimly.
They might, or they might not, have arrived before him; but,
in any case, there would not have been time enough for them
to have reached here, played out their game, and made their
get-away. In that latter respect, at least, it was quite certain—the grim smile deepened—that he could not possibly
be too late.

He had halted now on the edge of the curb, the intersecting
side street between himself and the small, two-story frame
house, where Mrs. Kinsey both lived and transacted her daily
business. The house was in darkness, save for a lighted
window in a lower, rear room that opened on the cross street.
And for a moment he stood here, then suddenly he moved
forward again—but this time along and across the side street
itself until he stood directly beneath the lighted window. His
question had been answered. Even from across the street,
and muffled though it necessarily had been, his ear had caught
the sound of a voice raised to an abnormal degree from the
interior of the house; and now through the curtains of what
was a small, plainly-furnished sitting room, he caught a
glimpse of a faded little old white-haired woman, in a faded

little old black dress, whose wrinkled face was strained in earnest attention as she strove to hear through a huge ear-trumpet. Little Sweeney was standing in front of her, his lips to the mouth of the trumpet.

"I said you were never looking better, Mrs. Kinsey!" bawled Little Sweeney.

And then Jimmie Dale was gone.

A moment more, and he was standing nonchalantly at the door of the little shop. There was apparently no other entrance to the house, and if Mrs. Kinsey had admitted Little Sweeney as a caller, as appeared obvious, it must have been through the shop, and the door therefore, in spite of the shop itself being in darkness, should logically be unlocked. And being unlocked it would also have given entrance to one Limpy Mack and Mother Margot, who were both at the present moment undoubtedly hidden in the house.

"I'll watch upstairs, you watch down," repeated Jimmie Dale softly to himself.

It was possible, though scarcely probable in view of the fact that Mrs. Kinsey's deafness practically offered the freedom of the house, that he might run into that *downstairs* watcher skulking here just inside the shop itself. Well, in that case—he glanced sharply up and down the street that for the moment held no near-by pedestrians—the play would come to a very sudden and abrupt end!

His back was turned to the street now. From a pocket in that curious leather girdle around his waist and under his outer garments he took out a black silk mask and adjusted it over his face. And now the slim, sensitive fingers pressed down the door latch without a sound. His logic had not been at fault. The door was unlocked. It began to open. Still there was no sound. And then Jimmie Dale, his hand snuggled over his automatic in the side pocket of his dinner coat, stood inside the shop with the door closed behind him.

V

MOTHER MARGOT

NO challenge questioned Jimmie Dale's entry—there was only the strident voice of Little Sweeney from the rear room. The shop itself, as he had expected, was not the vantage point chosen by either of Little Sweeney's two confederates.

Jimmie Dale stole forward to the rear of the shop, where through an open door there showed a glimmer of light, which, though it seemed to be strangely obstructed, evidently came from some sort of passage that connected the living quarters of the house with the shop; and here, slipping in behind the single counter that the shop boasted, he listened. Little Sweeney was still bawling at the top of his voice.

"I've been thinking it over for the last few days," said Little Sweeney.

"Please speak a little louder." Mrs. Kinsey's voice came plaintively through the darkness.

"Damn it!" said Little Sweeney in low and fervent tones; and then in a veritable yell: "I said I'd been thinking it over! THINKING IT OVER! Our little talk, you know, of a few days ago, about buying out your confectionery business. I promised to come back and let you know what I was going to do about it."

"Yes," said Mrs. Kinsey.

"Well," shouted Little Sweeney, "I've decided to take a chance and buy it, and I've brought you a hundred dollars to bind the bargain."

"But I couldn't think of selling it for a hundred dollars," protested Mrs. Kinsey feebly.

"Not SELLING it, just to bind the bargain," screamed

Little Sweeney. "I'll give you the rest of the thousand when we sign the papers."

"Would you please speak a little louder," said Mrs. Kinsey anxiously. "Sometimes my hearing ain't quite so good as it used to be."

"I'll keep your secret!" gritted Little Sweeney in a hoarse whisper; then full-lunged again: "Here's a hundred-dollar bill. You don't even need to give me any receipt for it. I'll come across with the rest before the week's out. It's just to show that I'm in earnest, and to keep anybody else from buying the business."

"I don't think anybody else would buy it," said the old lady ingenuously.

"You've said a mouthful!" was Little Sweeney's *sotto voce* retort.

"But I'm so glad," said Mrs. Kinsey wistfully. "I'll be so glad, because I can't move around as spry as once I could. And I was afraid I'd—I wouldn't be able to go on with it much longer."

"That's all right, Mrs. Kinsey," bellowed Little Sweeney cordially. "I guess we're both satisfied with our bargain. Here's the money. And I guess I'll be moving along. I'll see you again in a day or so with the papers."

"Thank you very much indeed," said Mrs. Kinsey earnestly. "And I do so hope that you'll do well with it, and that you won't lose anything."

A chair scraped. Footsteps came from the back passageway, which, as Jimmie Dale crouched lower behind the counter, suddenly grew light. A moment more and Little Sweeney stepped into the shop, making for the front door; behind him followed Mrs. Kinsey, carrying in one hand a lamp, and clutched in the other her ear-trumpet and a hundred-dollar bill.

Jimmie Dale's lips set grimly. Back in the corridor that was now darkened again he thought he saw a shadow move; he distinctly caught the sound of a footstep. The downstairs watcher—and Mrs. Kinsey's hundred-dollar bill! It was quite clear now, the whole mean, sordid, contemptible business. The bait was cunning enough in a low, vicious way; amply cunning enough to succeed with a trusting, simple old woman already on the verge of her dotage. Where Mrs. Kinsey, who distrusted banks, had secreted her savings of years, she would secret a *hundred-dollar* bill.

Little Sweeney—in lieu, no doubt, of shouting on the street—bowed himself out politely.

"Good-night," said Mrs. Kinsey. "And thank you again."

She closed and locked the door, and came back through the shop, passing again into the rear hallway.

As the light receded, Jimmie Dale rose cautiously. Mrs. Kinsey's lamp, as she had passed, disclosed the fact that just beyond the rear door of the shop, the passageway made a jut at right angles. He nodded tersely to himself as he gained this with the trained step, so silent as to be almost uncanny, that had mocked at even the creaky boards of the old Sanctuary, and, in the shadows himself now, he peered along the hallway proper.

Steep, narrow stairs, to the left and a little way down the hall, led to the upper story. Mrs. Kinsey, still carrying her lamp, still clutching at her ear-trumpet and the hundred-dollar bill, was already near the top. The lower portion of the stairs and the hall itself, since her body shaded the lamp, were in almost complete darkness.

And then from somewhere above there came a sharp, whispered interrogation:

"Well?"

From along the lower hall, her figure shrouded in the blackness, a woman's voice answered:

"She's still got it. Watch her."

Mother Margot! Limpy Mack, then, was the upstairs watcher. There seemed something incongruous in this passage of words between the two, like a stage aside that was not supposed to be heard by the intervening figure of the old woman who was climbing the stairs; but it was not the incongruity in itself, it was the callous brutality, the vulture-like preying upon helpless infirmity, that hardened Jimmie Dale's face now in a sort of merciless intentness.

Mrs. Kinsey's light disappeared around the landing at the head of the stairs, and then, contemptuous of any exaggerated attempt at silence, another footstep sounded on the stair treads. Jimmie Dale could not see, it was pitch black in the lower hall now, but it was not necessary to *see* the obvious. Mother Margot was following Mrs. Kinsey upstairs.

And now there came the sound as of some one walking about in a room overhead for a moment or so, and then silence.

Jimmie Dale moved toward the stairs, and without a sound began to make his way upward. Halfway up he paused, and stood tight-pressed against the wall. He could just detect a glow of light filtering into the upper hallway, as though the door of a lighted room, almost directly above his head, stood open into the hall. Then a footstep and still another, starting from a position further back along the hall, moved toward the lighted doorway. Came then the sound as of a piece of furniture being moved on squeaky casters; and then a low-breathed, exultant oath in a man's voice, followed by a woman's vicious chuckle. He could almost discern the outlines of two figures there—Mother Margot and Limpy Mack.

"Pipe de lay!" chuckled Mother Margot. "Dere goes Little Sweeney's century buck. Look at her saltin' it!"

"Close your trap!" ordered Limpy Mack sharply. "Maybe she can't hear, but that's no reason for taking a chance of spilling the beans now we know where they are."

"Aw, forget it! Youse gives me a pain!" retorted Mother Margot acidly, but in a nevertheless more subdued tone. "Youse'd have to write her a letter to tell her youse was makin' a noise before she'd be wise to it, an' mabbe den she wouldn't believe youse!"

"Shut your face!" said Limpy Mack tersely.

The sound of what had seemed to Jimmie Dale like squeaky casters came again, then a footstep traversed the lighted room, a door—obviously one connecting with an adjoining room—opened and closed again, and the light was gone.

"Come on!" prompted Mother Margot's voice. "Dat's her bedroom she's gone into. It's all clear now. Wot're youse waitin' for?"

"I'm waiting till the old bird's tucked away in bed," Limpy Mack's voice answered out of the darkness. "I'm waiting till there isn't any chance of her moseying out for anything just as we're tapping the crib. I haven't noticed that there was anything the matter with her *eyes;* and she's not so *dumb* but that she might start something in the neighbourhood. I don't play the fool when I can play safe."

"Safe!" echoed Mother Margot sarcastically. "Wot's safer dan dis de way it is now? I wanter get home. Youse ought to go down to an antique dump an' buy yerself a suit of armour, an' walk around in dat. Youse'd look fine—an' youse'd always be safe. De pip, dat's wot I'm contractin' from youse!"

There was no answer.

Mother Margot grunted contemptuously, and relapsed into silence.

The minutes passed. There was utter silence now in the house, save for an occasional uneasy movement of one or other of the two watchers in the hall above Jimmie Dale's head.

Jimmie Dale stood in grim patience, close against the wall, still on the stairs, an integral part of the shadows around him. The time dragged interminably, the minutes seeming to expand into endless hours. And then suddenly Limpy Mack's voice broke the silence in a tense undertone:

"All right! Her light's out. Come on!"

There came then the sound of footsteps receding from the hall; and Jimmie Dale in an instant silently gained the head of the stairs, and lay there crouched, half on the landing and half on the topmost treads. From his position, slightly diagonal though it was from where he had placed the door, he had calculated he would be able to see clearly enough into the room that Mother Margot and her companion had obviously just entered. He nodded now in quick self-corroboration. Out of the darkness of the room, lancing it in a little white shaft of light, there came the ray of an electric torch, and two figures were outlined as they bent over a piece of furniture that stood against the far wall, and that looked like an old chest of drawers. But there was no squeak of casters now. Jimmie Dale smiled uninvitingly. They were becoming unduly cautious! The piece of furniture was being lifted, not rolled, until it stood out from the wall, the back of it exposed.

For a moment the two figures leaned over it, the flashlight playing on the back of the dresser; and then from its extreme edge, what looked like a very narrow drawer, its depth almost half of the dresser itself, was pulled out.

"S'help me!" Mother Margot's voice quivered in curious, sibilant excitement. "Say, de old skirt's rich!"

"*Was*," corrected Limpy Mack's voice curtly. "Keep your paws off! We'll make the split to-morrow. In the meantime I'll take care of it. See? Hold the flashlight."

"Sure!" sniffed Mother Margot. "Youse're de only honest one in de bunch. I know 'cause Little Sweeney told me!"

A man's hand dipped into the projecting drawer, disappeared nearly up to the elbow, and came out again with a fistful of banknotes which he stuffed into his pocket. Again the man plunged in his hand. Jimmie Dale rose to his feet, took a step forward—and halted abruptly, as Mother Margot's voice suddenly shrilled out tensely through the silence:

"My Gawd! Listen! Wot's dat? Over by de door!"

Jimmie Dale's jaws clamped together, as his automatic swung up into line. Strange! He could have sworn he had not made the slightest sound. He saw Limpy Mack step forward a pace and stand facing the doorway, listening intently. And then Jimmie Dale's face relaxed. Behind Limpy Mack's back Mother Margot's hand shot stealthily into the drawer, and a wad of bills disappeared stealthily inside her blouse. Once more she helped herself.

With a queer, grim droop to the corners of his mouth, Jimmie Dale retreated suddenly back along the hall, and a little beyond the head of the stairs. Mother Margot! The gods were good! There would be more in the night after all than the mere salvaging of old Mrs. Kinsey's savings. He had no intention now of interrupting the two at their work! Mother Margot had wrought a very drastic change in his plans!

"I don't hear anything!" Limpy Mack's voice growled after a moment. "What's the matter with you?"

"I guess I'm gettin' de creeps," Mother Margot's voice replied. "I t'ought I heard somethin' creak, but I guess it was de wind. Hurry up, Limpy! I wanter get out of dis. I'm gettin' de creeps, dat's wot's de matter wid me."

Perhaps another two minutes passed, and then Jimmie Dale, far back along the hall now, heard the footsteps of the two coming from the room. At the head of the stairs they paused, and Limpy Mack spoke gruffly:

"We don't want to take the chance of being seen leaving here together. You're safe enough, because if any one saw you, they'd think you were just a friend of the old dame. You wait here, give me five minutes, then beat it yourself. And you go straight home! You'll get what's coming to you to-morrow after the Chief's made the split. We don't meet again to-night unless something breaks, and in that case you know where to find me. Understand?"

Jimmie Dale smiled quietly in the darkness. He owed Limpy Mack thanks for that, at least—it would save him from following Mother Margot.

"Sure!" mocked Mother Margot. "Cookin' a pill in yer dump under Sen Yat's! Why don't youse come across wid de price of a bunk, an' give de Chink a chance once in a while?"

Limpy Mack, without answer, descended the stairs. From the lower hall, faintly, there came the soft *tap-tap* of his rubber-tipped cane. Presently the shop door opened and closed gently.

Jimmie Dale moved silently forward. He could just dis-

tinguish Mother Margot's figure as a dark blur at the head
of the stairs. She, too, now began to descend.

And then Jimmie Dale spoke.

"I'll keep you company downstairs, Mother Margot," he
said softly—and the flashlight in his hand, stabbing suddenly
through the darkness, played its ray upon her.

She whirled with a low, terrified cry, and put her hands
before her blinking eyes as though to ward off a blow.

"Who's dat? Who're youse?" she cried out.

"Go on, Mother Margot—downstairs," Jimmie Dale
prompted more brusquely.

She obeyed in a stumbling, uncertain way.

"My Gawd! My Gawd!" she mumbled wildly. "Who're
youse? A dick? I ain't done nothin'! I swear to Gawd,
I ain't! I swear——"

"Quite so!" interrupted Jimmie Dale coolly, as they
reached the lower hall. "But perhaps you will come across
just the same."

She stared at the hand which he had extended significantly
in the flashlight's glow, and from under a bedraggled hat
whose brim flapped over her straggling gray hair and fell
into her eyes, she blinked again; she drew the old threadbare
black shawl she wore closer around her shoulders, and
clutched at it where it met at her neck.

"I dunno wot youse mean," she croaked hoarsely. "Come
across wid wot?"

"With what Limpy Mack *didn't get.*" Jimmie Dale was
biting off his words now. "There *was* somebody at the door,
even if you didn't hear him. I can use that money myself
that you put inside your blouse. And I'm waiting—also I'm
in a hurry!"

"Youse ain't a dick, den!" She seemed relieved in the
sense that rage and fury now supplanted fear. She snarled
at him. "Why didn't youse touch Limpy? I only got a
dollar or two."

"I haven't forgotten Limpy," Jimmie Dale answered
evenly. His hand was still extended. "Quick!" he snapped
suddenly.

For an instant she hesitated, then snarling again, she felt inside her blouse and brought out a few crumpled banknotes.

Jimmie Dale thrust the money into his pocket—and extended his hand again.

"Dat's all!" she announced tartly. "Wot d'youse expect? I didn't have no chance!"

Jimmie Dale smiled thinly.

"Loosen the waistband of your blouse!" he ordered sharply.

She glared at him fiercely.

"I won't," she shrilled out. "Youse can go to blazes! I told youse dat was all. I won't!"

"Oh, yes; I think you will," returned Jimmie Dale grimly. "When I leave you I am going to call on your friend Limpy Mack, and if I explain the double cross you put over on him, I imagine——"

She changed front instantly. Fear seemed to have her in its grip again.

"Youse won't do dat!" She was whimpering suddenly. "My Gawd, youse won't do dat!"

"It depends," said Jimmie Dale.

"Den take it!" she mumbled in a frenzied way—and from the loosened blouse a small shower of banknotes fluttered to the floor.

Jimmie Dale stooped and gathered them up.

"That's better!" he observed coolly. "And now we'll go a little further, Mother Margot. I want quite a lot of information. First, this Limpy Mack's dump, as you called it on the stairs. Does he live there alone?"

"Oh, my Gawd!" She was wringing her hands together in terror. "Youse ain't still goin' dere, are youse? Youse ain't goin' to tell him, are youse? He'd pass de word along, an' if de Chief got wise dey'd bump me off for dis. I— dey'd clean me up before de mornin'!"

"So I imagined," said Jimmie Dale calmly. "That's why I refrained from any interference upstairs. You see, Mother Margot, I rather think we have become indispensable to each other."

"I dunno wot youse mean," she faltered.

"I mean this," said Jimmie Dale coldly, "that if you play straight with me, you are safe in so far as what you put over on your precious pals is concerned. Otherwise—" He shrugged his shoulders. "Is it quite plain?"

Mother Margot licked her lips feverishly.

"Dey'd cut me t'roat!" she whispered. "Dat's wot dey'd do. Wot do youse want? I—I ain't got no chance, have I?"

"We started with Limpy Mack, and we'll finish with him first," said Jimmie Dale tersely; "though you've just mentioned something much more important. Well, does he live alone?"

"Sure, he lives alone," Mother Margot answered. "He's got de basement——"

"Under Sen Yat's," completed Jimmie Dale smoothly. "All right! Now, the really important matter. This Chief you mentioned—who is he?"

Mother Margot shook her head.

"I dunno," she said.

"You don't know!" Jimmie Dale's voice hardened. "That won't do, Mother Margot! I wouldn't advise you to try another trick to-night."

"I ain't!" she protested wildly. "Honest to Gawd, I ain't! I dunno!" She was wringing her hands together again. "He ain't nobody, he's"—she glanced furtively around her, the act seemingly almost subconscious—"he's— he's just a voice."

Jimmie Dale studied her for a moment. The woman was evidently too frightened to be anything but truthful.

"Well, go on!" he prodded.

"Dat's all I knows about him," said Mother Margot fearfully. "Just a voice over de telephone dat youse're always wise to 'cause it's a kind of a queer, thick voice."

"Is that the way you get your orders, then?"

Mother Margot nodded assent.

"But there isn't any telephone in your room," said Jimmie Dale sharply. "I happen to know that you've just moved in where another pal of yours, Mr. Isaac Shiftel, used to live."

Mother Margot swallowed hard.   She drew back a little.
"How'd youse know?" she stammered.

"Never mind! How about that telephone?"

"It ain't done in de room," she said tremulously. "I didn't
know anythin' about to-night at all. Den dis afternoon w'en
I was wid my pushcart down on Thompson Street I'm called
into a store to de telephone, an'——"

"What store? Where is this telephone?" Jimmie Dale
interrupted tersely.

She hesitated.

"Aw, it's in a booth in de back room of Mezzo's second-
hand store, if youse've got to know," she blurted out.

"All right," said Jimmie Dale. "Go on!"

"Well, I was called to de telephone," she said, "an' told
to go to de Wistaria Café to-night an' meet Limpy Mack."

"And Little Sweeney," added Jimmie Dale quietly; then
abruptly: "Who else is in this gang?"

Again Mother Margot shook her head.

"I dunno dem all," she said. "I guess we don't all know
each other neither. I only know Limpy Mack an' Shiftel,
an' a man named Laroque; but I ain't seen neither of dem
last two for weeks, an' I dunno where dey've gone. Little
Sweeney was a new one on me to-night."

"H'm!" observed Jimmie Dale curtly. "Then who fixed it
for you to move into Shiftel's rooms?"

"The Voice," she replied readily. "I was told to go an'
hand de agent de rent in advance."

"Good!" said Jimmie Dale pleasantly. "We're getting
on, Mother Margot; and since you and I have become such
friends, I'm going to take the liberty of calling on you in a
day or so—unless perhaps you can tell me how, well, say, a
man like Shiftel can get in or out of those rooms without
bothering himself with either doors or windows?"

She drew still farther back, a startled look and a new
terror in her face.

"I know who youse are now," she gasped. "Little Sweeney an' Limpy was talkin' about youse. Youse are de Gray
Seal! My Gawd!" She wrung her hands. "Don't youse

come dere! I'm playin' straight wid youse. I don't know why, an' I don't know nothin' phoney about de rooms, but I knows dat's wot dey wants youse to do."

Again Jimmie Dale studied the dishevelled and distraught creature.

"Yes," he said quietly, "so I believe, and I believe you are playing straight. Well, we'll leave the rooms in abeyance for the time being. I shall always know where to find you—on Thompson Street. You may be called to the phone by *another* voice. Now, one thing more, Mother Margot—I don't want to keep Limpy Mack waiting! What was that paper Little Sweeney gave Limpy Mack in the back room of the Wistaria to-night?"

"Youse—youse know about dat, too?" She stared at him in terrified amazement.

"What was it?" repeated Jimmie Dale.

"Dey didn't let me see it," she said. "Some sort of dope about de gang, I guess, 'cause Little Sweeney was a new man. Little Sweeney just says, 'I got it pat,' he says, w'en he hands it over. I dunno wot was in it; dey didn't let me see it."

"Perhaps Limpy will be more considerate with me," observed Jimmie Dale dryly. He motioned along the hall, switched off the flashlight, and taking Mother Margot's arm, led her into the shop. "You go home now," he ordered.

She hesitated. His hand still on her arm, he felt her shiver.

"If youse—youse're goin' to Limpy Mack's," she quavered, "youse—youse won't split on me? Swear youse won't! Dey—dey'd kill me before de mornin'!"

"You needn't worry," said Jimmie Dale gruffly. "As long as you play straight with me, it's as much to my interest as yours to see that no harm comes to you. You're out of this. The only person I know is Limpy Mack, whom I saw come out of here alone—understand?—and I followed him because I thought perhaps he had made a little haul that—since you've saved me introducing myself—the Gray Seal could use himself."

"My Gawd!"   She was whimpering again.   "I—I'm afraid. Youse swear it?"

Jimmie Dale opened the door, and with a precautionary glance up and down the street, pushed her not ungently out into the night.

"I swear it," he said. "Good-night, Mother Margot."

VI

THE MAN WITH THE RUBBER-TIPPED CANE

THE black silk mask gone from his face, Jimmie Dale too stepped out of Mrs. Kinsey's little shop, and hurried away—but in an opposite direction to that taken by Mother Margot. And now he smiled as he went along. To-morrow, if he had luck, Mrs. Kinsey would get her money back, all of it, say by registered mail, and accompanied by a suggestion that she would be better advised to use a bank hereafter; a suggestion which fright at the discovery of her loss would probably have the salutary effect of causing her to act upon without loss of time!

He hurried on—and ten minutes later, deep in the Chinese quarter, in the neighbourhood of Chatham Square, in a narrow, crooked, evil-smelling, little street, in fact more an alleyway than a thoroughfare, he was strolling past the entrance of a shuttered tea store that bore the sign: SEN YAT. Again he smiled a little to himself—but now from a different cause. It was quite true that Sen Yat dealt in tea; but it was equally true that upstairs behind the shutters Sen Yat also specialised in another commodity of the East, and to those who had the price and were "safe" the sorry solace of the poppy was always at instant command.

An old and unkempt woman, mumbling to herself, shuffled by. A Chinaman, like a rat taking to its hole, disappeared down a basement entrance from the sidewalk a few yards away. Jimmie Dale turned suddenly. The street for the moment was clear. He retraced his steps to another basement entrance, the one below Sen Yat's, and out of the darkness of which, as he had previously passed by, a crack of light seeping from under the door sill had already informed him that Limpy Mack had returned home.

65

And then Jimmie Dale was gone from the street—and down the half dozen steps was crouching in the blackness below the sidewalk at Limpy Mack's door. Again the silk mask was slipped over his face; again his fingers sought a pocket in the little leather girdle—and the next instant were silently and deftly at work with a pick-lock.

Perhaps a minute passed. Then Jimmie Dale straightened up, swung the door open, and like a flash was inside the room with the door closed behind him.

A startled oath greeted his entrance. Limpy Mack, peaked cap drawn over his eyes, was seated at a table on which burned an oil lamp. His heavy, rubber-tipped cane also lay across the table. He snatched at this now in lieu of a sheaf of banknotes which he let fall from his hands, and which he had evidently been engaged in counting—and rose, half threateningly, half defensively, to his feet.

"Good evening!" said Jimmie Dale pleasantly. "I seem to be in luck to-night."

His automatic indicated the sheaf of notes, and then held on Limpy Mack. Jimmie Dale's glance swept swiftly, critically around the place. Its furnishings were few and of the crudest; a bed in one corner, near a second door that conveniently opened on the back yard no doubt; a washstand minus one leg, and therefore askew, that boasted a streaked and badly blistered mirror; the table and chair in front of the washstand; a dirty, unswept floor, bare of carpet—and that was all. The place reeked with filth.

"Nice quiet little resort you've got here," smiled Jimmie Dale. His eyes were apparently roving again about the cellar-like room, apparently everywhere save on Limpy Mack. "I'm sure you—*drop that!*"

A revolver, almost free from Limpy Mack's pocket, fell with a clatter to the floor. The man screamed out in rage.

"Why, Limpy, that's raw," said Jimmie Dale in a pained way. "I didn't think you'd fall for it. All I wanted was your gun." He advanced to the table, and kicked the weapon across the floor under the bed.

There was a sudden *swish* through the air, as, quick

without warning, Limpy Mack aimed a blow with his cane at Jimmie Dale's wrist and automatic. It missed. Again the man screamed out in fury.

Jimmie Dale's face set.

"Don't raise your voice again like that," he said in flat tones. "Sit down!" His automatic swung to the level of the other's eyes.

With a snarl, Limpy Mack subsided into the chair. He scowled at Jimmie Dale.

"Who are you, anyway, you damned thug?" he demanded thickly.

"I'll tell you," said Jimmie Dale. He was smiling whimsically now—not at Limpy Mack, but at the somewhat exacting demands of the situation in which he found himself. Mother Margot must in no way appear in this; and, besides that money on the table, there was the paper that Little Sweeney had given to Limpy Mack in Mother Margot's presence—a paper, in reference to the contents of which, he, Jimmie Dale, had acquired an intense curiosity. Ostensibly, therefore, he must appear—in order that no thought of Mother Margot might by any chance enter the other's mind—to be ignorant of even the existence of the paper, and yet, at the same time, get hold of it. "I'll tell you," said Jimmie Dale. "I was walking down a certain street to-night, and I saw you sneak out of a little confectionery store that looked as though it had all been closed up for the night, and I said to myself: 'That's funny, because Limpy Mack never plays for chicken feed.' And then I went and read the sign on the window, and I remembered that everybody said Mrs. Kinsey had a well-filled stocking hidden away somewhere. So I just took a chance, Limpy, thinking that maybe you'd found it, and I followed you. And as I said before, I seem to have played in luck."

"It's a lie!" growled Limpy Mack. "That ain't Mrs. Kinsey's, or anybody else's money. It's mine."

"I'm delighted to know it," murmured Jimmie Dale. "But even so, I still insist that I am in luck to-night. There must be quite a few thousand here." He began to thrust the bills into his pockets.

Limpy Mack sat crouched down in his chair, the posture seeming to accentuate almost to deformity his stooped shoulders.

"Damn you!" he shrieked out. He gnawed at his unkempt gray moustache, and flung another oath at Jimmie Dale.

Jimmie Dale swept the table clean. It was obviously all that Limpy Mack had stolen from Mrs. Kinsey, for he would obviously have had it *all* out to count it—but there was still a certain paper in Limpy Mack's pocket.

"I wonder—since you say it was yours—if you haven't got some more," suggested Jimmie Dale invitingly. "I'm afraid I'll have to trouble you to turn your pockets out, Limpy. Stand up!"

"I—I ain't got any more." The man seemed suddenly cowed. He crouched still lower in his chair.

"Stand up!" repeated Jimmie Dale sternly. "Now I'm quite sure you have!"

"No!" Limpy Mack was whining now. "I—I'll tell you the truth. I got it where you said. But that's all—all of it was on the table. Say, you believe me, don't you? I'd come across if I had any more, wouldn't I? I couldn't help myself."

The man was blatantly stalling now. The paper was—*no, it wasn't on account of the paper.* Behind Limpy Mack's back something showed in the blistered mirror—the head and shoulders of Little Sweeney protruding through the rear doorway, and in Little Sweeney's hand a levelled revolver. Limpy Mack's voice had drowned out any sound made by the opening of the door, if, indeed, there had been any sound at all.

Jimmie Dale's brain was working in lightning flashes now, but not a muscle of his face moved. His automatic dangling in his hand was useless. To swing it on the door with only a chance aim would be but the signal for Little Sweeney to fire.

"All right, Limpy," said Jimmie Dale, and leaned slightly toward the end of the table. "I'll take your word for it that——"

And then Jimmie Dale was in action. With a sweep of his hand he sent the lamp crashing from the table to the floor, and ducked instantly to one side.

There was a yell from Limpy Mack; and, in the sudden darkness as the lamp went out, from the doorway came the tongue-flame of Little Sweeney's revolver and the roar of the report. Then a rush of feet, the flash and roar of the revolver again, and the next instant Jimmie Dale was locked in a hand to hand struggle with Little Sweeney. Here and there they swayed, the breath of one, panting, hard, on the other's cheek; the table toppled to the floor, carrying the chair with it; their feet crunched on the splintered glass from the lamp and chimney—and then suddenly Jimmie Dale reeled from a terrific blow across the head.

"I got him!" screamed Limpy Mack's voice exultantly. "I got him, Sweeney! I beaned him with the loaded handle of my cane."

But though dazed, lurching, scarcely able to keep his feet, Jimmie Dale was still fighting like a wildcat. Twice since Little Sweeney had grappled with him, he had managed to strike the other with the butt of his automatic. He had only one chance now—to end it quickly—he was too nearly gone himself. He wrenched himself suddenly free, and swung again with all his strength. A gurgling voice—Little Sweeney's—answered the blow:

"Look out—Limpy—beat it—you know why—that paper —beat it—I——"

Again and again Jimmie Dale brushed his hand across his eyes. He fought desperately to clear his brain. His head was sick and dizzy. What was that sound, that strange, queer sound? *Tap, tap, tap!* Little Sweeney—that black outline on the floor was Little Sweeney—Little Sweeney wouldn't trouble any one for an hour or so—but that *tap, tap, tap*—it sounded from the direction of the rear door. And now it was gone, and there was silence—just silence.

But the silence, as nothing else had done, seemed now to penetrate Jimmie Dale's swimming head, and seemed to bring with it a sudden, swift significance.

Fool! He stumbled madly toward the rear door. Limpy Mack was gone—gone with the *tap, tap, tapping* of his cane. That paper! A clue to that super-crook perhaps, that the Tocsin called the Phantom, and Mother Margot called the Voice!

He was outside now. No, not too late! That was Limpy Mack there, wasn't it? That figure running, running! God, how his brain swam! His knees seemed weak under him, as though they were going to double up like the blades of a knife—but he was running too. His surroundings seemed mechanically, subconsciously, to be absorbed—just a back yard that ended in the black, irregular outline of the rear of what was evidently a three or four-story tenement.

On Jimmie Dale stumbled. He could not be more than ten or fifteen yards behind that figure ahead, which, to his whirling brain, seemed to take on the aspect of some grotesque jumping-jack, bobbing up and down in the darkness, until suddenly it disappeared through the back door of the tenement.

Jimmie Dale prodded himself into a spurt, reached the tenement door, found it open, and reeled inside. His faculties seemed miserably unreliable. Couldn't he *think* any more! He stood stock still, and again his hand swept fiercely across his eyes. The man couldn't have gone out of the front door, nor have gained the landing above, because he, Jimmie Dale, had been too close at the other's heels, and would have heard him, would be hearing him now. And there was not a sound—nothing but pitch, inky blackness. Therefore Limpy Mack must be somewhere here in the blackness.

That was better! At least his brain was striving to fight its way back to normal. But his eyes ached brutally. He bit his lips to keep back a groan of pain, and leaned against the wall for support. One of them, he or Limpy Mack, must sooner or later make a move. He forced a twisted

smile. If the blow from the loaded cane had not proved too·
much for him after all, it would not be he who made that
move!

And now, after a time, where he had heard no sound before, he became conscious of many sounds—the low indistinct sound of muffled things, the night sounds of a tenanted
building filtering vaguely out from behind closed doors only
to integrate themselves in a queer, throbbing way into the
very silence itself. How long had he been standing here?
Once he clutched frantically, but noiselessly, at the wall to
keep himself erect. Perhaps it would not be Limpy Mack
who moved first! His brain was swimming in that sick,
nauseating way again. Perhaps it would be——

A door began to open cautiously a few yards along the hall.
And then a man's head and shoulders, a man with a clean
shaven face and slouch hat showing quite distinctly in the
lighted doorway, was thrust out. The man peered around;
then from the threshold he whispered back into the room:

"It's a cinch he thought you beat it straight out through
the front door, and went out after you. I'll take a look, and
if he's still hanging around outside I'll spot him. You keep
under cover, Limpy. You're safe here anyway. I'll be back
in ten minutes. Savvy?"

The man, a broad-shouldered, well set-up fellow, stepped
out into the hall, and closed the door behind him. His footsteps echoed back as he walked rapidly toward the front of
the tenement; then the front door opened and closed again;
the footsteps rang faintly from the pavement without, died
away—and Jimmie Dale was standing before the door of the
room.

He had not heard the door being locked. He was sure of
that, in spite of the fact that his head was whirling like a
top. His fingers closed silently on the doorknob—and with
a swift movement, standing in the hall, his automatic thrown
forward, he flung the door wide open.

And then for a moment he stood there like a man stunned.
The room was empty. No, not empty! Dangling from the
gas-jet hung Limpy Mack's rubber-tipped cane; and stuck

upon the cane, flaunting itself in grim, ironical, mocking challenge—*was a diamond-shaped gray paper seal.*

A smile of understanding, bitter in its chagrin, flickered across Jimmie Dale's lips. He had stuck a gray seal on the back of Shiftel's hand that night two weeks ago. This one, he was sure, could have come from nowhere else; and, if that were so, then Shiftel, and Gentleman Laroque, and Limpy Mack, and Limpy Mack in still another guise, in the guise of the man who had just tricked him so neatly, were all one. And from that encounter in Shiftel's rooms, and one other encounter long before that at Niccolo Sonnino's place, Gentleman Laroque, alias Isaac Shiftel, in the character of Limpy Mack to-night, had known that he was dealing with the Gray Seal from the moment his room under Sen Yat's had been entered—could not help but have known it. And at the last here, the man, being then disarmed, had had no choice but to resort to his wits as the only means of escape. Yes, he, Jimmie Dale, quite understood!

He had sought, and found, and lost again—the Phantom.

VII

DAYS of searching! Days of futility! Days that had brought no reward! Since the night of Limpy Mack's disappearance there had been only failure. Nowhere had he been able to pick up again a thread or clue that would set him once more upon the Phantom's trail— until to-night. And to-night? Jimmie Dale shook his head. He was at sea, troubled—about to-night.

Threadbare, gaunt-cheeked, dissolute in appearance, his battered old felt hat pulled down over his eyes, he was slouching now, as Smarlinghue, with apparent aimlessness along the street. Past him, going to and fro, other figures shuffled by—for the most part Chinamen, their crossed hands tucked in the sleeves of their blouses. A slumming party from a "gape-wagon" disembarked its load of candidates for initiation into those most dark, drear, shivery and hidden things of Chinatown, whose storied mysteries in this more enlightened generation were now within the reach of all— for the insignificant sum of one dollar a ticket!

A twisted smile flickered across Jimmie Dale's lips. This jostling little crowd that was being herded into line now by the stentorian voiced barker would see many things, for the stage was always set. They would see most fearsome opium dens that reeked with the sickly sweetish smell of poppy, where no poppy was; they would see the worshippers at the Shrine of the Thousandth Ancestor; they would see the council chambers where the Tong wars were declared, and most ghastly murders hatched; they would see the Chinamen at their fan-tan; and—Jimmie Dale shrugged his shoulders—they would undeniably get their money's worth.

73

It was quite innocent, and everybody would be satisfied; but into Hip Foo's, for instance, where he was going now, from whose tortuous, bunk-lined, connecting sub-cellars there were two exits separated one from the other by almost a block, and again from the entrance by an entirely different street, their tickets would not take them. Hip Foo made no money from the gape-wagons!

The scene, though it was still before him, was gone from his consciousness as quickly as the train of thought that had obtruded itself upon him, and his mind was instantly back again now on the note that had been laid beside his plate by one of the attendants at the St. James Club, where he had been dining but little more than half an hour ago. The note had contained a single sentence—in the Tocsin's writing:

"Watch Mother Margot—at Hip Foo's to-night."

His lips closed tightly. Was there anything beneath the surface of that one sentence, anything more than its actual wording, anything of a *personal* nature? He had been turning it over and over in his mind from the moment he had received it, even while he had hurried to the Sanctuary and from a millionaire clubman had become the drug-wrecked Smarlinghue, even now again as he walked here along this none too well lighted and unsavory street in the heart of New York's Chinatown. The note was like none he had ever received from her before. Here there was no detailed plan laid out, no evident foreknowledge of what was afoot. It seemed almost a call for help where she herself was helpless, and so—it brought the blood pounding in quicker tempo through his veins—it might well be she had realised and was prepared at last to accept as inevitable the fact that, whether she would or no, he meant to force his way if it were humanly within his power into those shadows, as she termed them, with which the Phantom had surrounded her. Well, why not? She must know that he had already been in perhaps closer, more intimate touch than even herself with this master criminal of a score of aliases and a score of domiciles, first as Gentleman Laroque, then as Isaac Shiftel, and again as Limpy Mack. And besides there was her promise that—no! He shook his head a little bitterly. Why should he try to blind his own eyes? Her promise to call upon him for aid had contained the proviso that it would not identify him as an ally of hers in the Phantom's eyes.

It was a foolish hope fathered only by desire! A hope that out of this watching of Mother Margot to-night at Hip Foo's he and the woman that he loved would come together again, that he would see her, hear her voice, and after that —Yes, she knew that, too! She had said so in the letter she had slipped into the pocket of his coat when she had left him that night on the old East River wharf. She knew that once he found her again no legion of Phantoms, no pleading on her part, could keep him from her side until the end, whatever that end might be. He might shake his head if he chose, he might argue speciously with himself as his love prompted him to do, but in his heart he knew that her note to-night would not bring her and himself together unless—yes, that was it!—to-night saw the end of the Phantom's career.

The end! That brought still another angle into the Tocsin's message, an angle that was represented by this Mother Margot. His eyes grew grimly thoughtful as he walked along. How far was the old hag to be trusted? How much to be depended upon was the hold he had on her through having caught her in the act of purloining an extra share of the loot from one of her own confederates, who though she evidently did not know it herself, had been the Phantom in the guise of Limpy Mack that night at old Mrs. Kinsey's? His hands had been tied in a measure in respect of Mother Margot. True, since that night he had never lost track of her, but his means of communication had been restricted to the same means that the "Voice," as she called the Phantom, had employed—of calling her from her pushcart in Thompson Street to that telephone booth she had spoken of in Mezzo's second-hand store, and questioning her. This he had done each day, sometimes more than once; but the result had always been the same. Each time she had sworn that she had heard nothing further from the Voice. And yet to-night she was to be watched at Hip Foo's!

Was she playing fast and loose? He had not been in personal touch with her—that was where the weakness of his position lay. She knew him to be the Gray Seal, but she knew him only as a man with a mask on his face. He could not stand beside her pushcart on Thompson Street, and, wearing a mask, talk to her. He could not go to her as Smarlinghue and risk even the suspicion that Smarlinghue had any connection with the Gray Seal, let alone being the Gray Seal himself! A word from her, if that thought ever entered her mind, or anybody else's for that matter, and underworld and police would join hands in the one cause that could ever be common to both, and fight as only two packs of wolves might fight for the prey that only one could have.

It was not a pleasant thought!

He withdrew his hands suddenly from his ragged pockets, and, stooping down, picked up a crumpled newspaper from the gutter, as the flaring red type of a headline caught his eye. He glanced at it, and pitched it away again almost immediately. He had been interested to know if it were a special edition announcing some new development in the case of one Connie Pfeffer, alias the Mole. It did not. It was just re-hash.

He smiled wryly. The Gray Seal, "that depraved and degenerate glutton who feasted and lived like some ghoul upon his foul notoriety, and who, with inhuman boastfulness, left his diamond-shaped gray seal upon the scene of every one of his fiendish crimes," the usual stand-by of the sensational headliners, had of late been relegated to obscurity by the newspapers. It was a relief! For the time being the crime that held the public attention was that in which this Connie Pfeffer was involved, but this was more, as a matter of fact, because of the opportunity it afforded for a jeer at the police rather than on account of the actual crime itself.

For two days the journals had been full of the Levenson Bank robbery, a private bank in the Wall Street district, where a customer, having just drawn out ten thousand dollars in twenty five-hundred-dollar bills, had been held up almost in front of the teller's wicket at the point of a revolver and relieved of his cash. Connie Pfeffer, alias the Mole, who had answered to the description of the robber, had been apprehended within an hour of the crime by the police, released again for lack of evidence against him—and then had promptly disappeared. New evidence establishing the fact that Connie Pfeffer was the man who had entered the bank had almost immediately come to light, but Connie Pfeffer was no longer to be found, and the police——

Jimmie Dale swung sharply around. Some one was plucking at his sleeve—a tattered and stoop-shouldered old man, who had a tray slung around his neck upon which was displayed a pitiful array of cheap collar buttons.

"Hello, Smarly!" The man spoke low, out of the corner of his mouth. "Say, Smarly, I wanter ask youse somethin'."

For an instant Jimmie Dale surveyed the other. It was Pedler Joe, and Pedler Joe lived just around the corner from the Sanctuary and was therefore in the category of an old acquaintance and neighbour; but his, Jimmie Dale's, business to-night was at Hip Foo's, and he had no time to waste.

"Hello, Joe!" he returned a little ungraciously. "Didn't know you went in for night work. There's a gape-bus back there, and the bunch have gone into Charlie Wong's lay-out. If you stick around when they come you may get away with something."

"I ain't out for business—not dat kind," the man whispered —and still holding Jimmie Dale's coat sleeve, edged out to the curb and halted. "I'm lookin' for some one. Everybody says youse're on de level, Smarly. Youse bats around a lot in places dey won't let me into, so hand it to me straight. Have youse seen Connie anywhere, youse knows who I mean, de Mole?"

Jimmie Dale stared. It was rather curious, rather much of

a coincidence! He had been thinking of Connie Pfeffer, alias the Mole, at the moment Pedler Joe had accosted him. And coincidences in the Bad Lands were not always—coincidences!

It was Smarlinghue of the underworld, not Jimmie Dale the millionaire clubman, who .spoke.

"What's the lay?" His tones pointed the inquiry with almost exaggerated suspicion.

"Aw, it's straight!" the old man answered. "I'm askin' youse just dat. Have youse seen him, or heard anythin' about him?"

Jimmie Dale still parried the question.

"Sounds like you'd shoved your stake in with the bulls," he scowled. "Did they give you a badge to pin inside your vest? What have you got to do with Connie?"

The old man's face was haggard; he evidently had not shaved for several days, and the short white bristles seemed to accentuate a general woe-begone aspect and feebleness that age and the thin, stooped shoulders already proclaimed loudly enough.

"I got a lot to do wid him," the old man said hoarsely. "He's like my own kid, dat's wot he is. I ain't done much for him mabbe, but I done wot I could to keep him straight, an'——"

"You!" Jimmie Dale laughed outright. Pedler Joe's life history was written on the police blotters! The man had served at least a half dozen sentences in prison. True, Pedler Joe in his declining years—he must be verging on the seventies now—had, outwardly at least, reformed to the extent of earning his living as a legalised mendicant, as witness the collar buttons. But as a guardian and sponsor for young morals— Jimmie Dale, as Smarlinghue, grinned viciously. "Say, it's no wonder he pulled that bank job! He comes by it honestly! Say, what's the——"

Jimmie Dale's grin had died away. Something was wrong here; there was something deeper than appeared on the surface, something that he did not understand. The tears had come suddenly into the faded old eyes, and were trickling now down the wrinkled cheeks.

"Forget it, Joe!" Jimmie Dale laid his hand in quick sympathy on the other's shoulder. "I didn't mean to hand you nothing. Spill the story, Joe—only hurry, 'cause I got a date."

"I picked him outer de gutter w'en he could hardly walk," said Pedler Joe. "An' w'en I wasn't doin' spaces up de river, I kept my eye on him. Sounds like hell from an old lag, don't it? But it's true, Smarly, so help me Gawd, it's true! I wasn't runnin' straight myself, but wot chance I got I tried to show de kid my line wasn't any good. Only I was away a lot, an' I let him down, so it ain't all his fault. Dere wasn't no one to keep him from goin' wild w'en I was doin' time—see? He ain't lived wid me for years, but dat didn't keep him from comin' frequent to see me, I'll say dat for him. An' den dis bank job happened. If youse read de papers youse know he was pinched in my place dat afternoon. He blew in to get a little stake from me, an'——"

"From you!" Jimmie Dale interrupted. "I didn't know you had loose change to——"

"Some days," said the old man simply, "I pick up more'n youse'd t'ink. But dat ain't nothin' to do wid it. Dere was always a few dollars for Connie w'en he was on his uppers. Well, youse know dey didn't have anythin' on him to hold him for de job, an' dey let him go."

"And he beat it, and he ain't been seen since," commented Jimmie Dale judicially in his rôle of Smarlinghue. "And now some one else comes along and swears too it was him at the bank. It's open and shut now that he pulled the job all right, and ducked with the cash. That's why they're laughing at the police. You're wasting your time looking for him. He's gone."

"Yes," said Pedler Joe; "he's gone—dat's wot's de matter." He glanced furtively about him. "But he ain't gone de way youse t'ink. I don't say now he didn't pull de job, though I didn't t'ink so until last night; an' I was handin' de police straight goods w'en dey was puttin' me through down at de Chief's de afternoon dey put de nippers on Connie at my place. He's gone—but he ain't gone de way youse t'ink. Dere's somethin' else bein' pulled besides dat. Take a look at dis!"

Jimmie Dale leaned forward. Pedler Joe had loosened his collar. The man's neck and throat were a mass of ugly bruises, discolored, swollen, finger-printed in angry, purplish blotches.

"Good God!" muttered Jimmie Dale. "How'd you get that?"

"It was last night"—Pedler Joe again glanced furtively around him, as he rearranged his collar—"dey nearly bumped me off before dey was satisfied dat I didn't know any more'n wot I'd told de police. Dey wanted to know where de cash was, de ten t'ousand bucks dat Connie stole. Dat's wot dey did to *me*, an' dat's why I'm askin' youse if youse have seen or heard anythin' of Connie."

Jimmie Dale's lips had tightened.

"You think," he said slowly, "they had tried the same game with Connie, and that's why he's—*disappeared?* You mean you've doped it out that they hadn't been able to make him talk up to last night, and that they tried you then on a chance?"

The old man nodded.

"Sure, dey got him," he said miserably. "Dey got him cold. Dat's wot makes me t'ink now dat Connie pulled de job all right, 'cause dey're wise to him."

"Yes," said Jimmie Dale; "but who was it that laid you out?"

"I ain't dead sure," said Pedler Joe. "I woke up last night in bed wid a pair of hands around my t'roat, chokin' me. It was pretty dark in the room. Dere was two of 'em, an' I wasn't sure, an' I ain't sure now, but I thought one of 'em, the little fellow, was Bunty Myers, who used to travel wid Gentleman Laroque's gang."

Gentleman Laroque! *The Phantom!* Jimmie Dale was fumbling aimlessly with the brim of his battered old felt hat. Mother Margot, Hip Foo's, the Phantom—and Connie

Pfeffer, alias the Mole! Was this what was at the bottom of the Tocsin's note? Intuitively he was instantly sure of it. It dovetailed perfectly. The Phantom was not likely to be playing *two* games to-night, therefore——

Pedler Joe was whispering hoarsely again:

"Youse're on de level, Smarly, an' on de inside everywhere. I—I thought mabbe youse'd help me. An' if youse heard anythin' or saw anythin' youse'd tip me off."

Jimmie Dale held out his hand.

"Sure, I will, Joe!" he said. He leaned closer to the other. "You keep your map closed about having spoken to me—see? I know Bunty Myers. I'll do my best for you."

"T'anks, Smarly," said the old man gratefully. "I knew youse would."

"Sure!" said Jimmie Dale again. "Well, that goes—and so-long, Joe."

He turned and slouched on again down the street. His face was impassive, but his hands in his pockets were clenched now. So the Phantom's hand was in this, too, was it? And the old broken figure with the tray of collar buttons slung around his neck was one of the victims! It brought the hot anger surging upon him. There was something that struck deep to the root of his sympathy, something pathetic in the queer, strange loyalty, the curious love that old Pedler Joe, himself a thief by profession in the days gone by, held for the gutter snipe that he had tried—and failed—to bring up in the paths of virtue! The Phantom! Well, perhaps, to-night, if at Hip Foo's there was——

Jimmie Dale turned the corner, and halted suddenly in a dazed, stunned way. As at the door of Charlie Wong's back there on the other street, a wagon was drawn up here at the curb in front of Hip Foo's, and a little crowd was disembarking from the wagon and was being marshalled into line, but it was not a gape-wagon that stood at Hip Foo's front door; it was a wagon of quite a very different sort—a police van. And then in an instant, his wits at work again after the first shock of surprise, Jimmie Dale slouched back out of

sight around the corner again.   Here he broke into a run.
A raid! Hip Foo's was being raided.

Jimmie Dale ran on at top speed.   His chances were just
even—that was all.   There were *two* exits a block apart.   He
could not watch both at once.   Which one would Mother
Margot use?   The police would not get her, nor any of those
with her.   The police would gather in a few Chinese attendants who would be as phlegmatic and informative as so
many cows; the police would collect a little opium-smoking
paraphernalia, and Hip Foo would be fined—but that would
be all.   Before the first blue-coat crossed the threshold of
the entrance, the exodus through the sub-cellars would have
begun.

And now Jimmie Dale drew into the shadows at the mouth
of a dark and narrow lane.   It was the toss of a coin.   This
one or the other!   Yes—here they came now, like rats running from a sinking ship.   He crouched against the wall unnoticed, or if noticed accepted as one of their own ilk, and
watched them.   Man after man, woman after woman, passed
out into the street.   The procession dwindled to a few belated stragglers—and ceased.   He waited a minute longer.
There was no one else.

Tight-lipped then, Jimmie Dale turned away.   Mother
Margot had not been amongst them.   He had lost the toss,
that was all.   She had gone out the other way.

He walked rapidly now.   There was only one thing left
to do, one way left open to him.   It would not be very difficult to find Mother Margot—at her home—in those rooms
from which, on that first night, the Phantom had so mysteriously disappeared.   He had even promised her a visit!

He smiled a little grimly.   His promise so far had been
unfulfilled.   Not because the Tocsin had warned him that
the place was a trap, and even Mother Margot, evidently
terror-stricken that night at Mrs. Kinsey's, had done likewise; but because, prior to that warning and prior to
Mother Margot's occupancy of the rooms, he had already
searched the premises and found nothing; and because, until
now, it had not seemed that there was anything to be gained

by a move which might result in warning the Phantom that he, Jimmie Dale, had been in communication with Mother Margot.

But to-night there was no choice but to go there—unless perhaps she had gone back to her pushcart in Thompson Street. He would try that first, and if she were there call her to the phone as he always did, and arrange a meeting somewhere under conditions such that she would discover no more of his actual identity than that of the man in the mask whom she already knew as the Gray Seal.

He was hurrying now. Time, as measured in minutes, might or might not be precious. He did not know. What had taken place at Hip Foo's, whether for instance the rendezvous that Mother Margot had presumably had there had been prematurely interrupted by the raid, or what were the details of the scheme the Phantom was hatching, he did not know. But in any case, one thing was vital, not only to himself but to the Tocsin, vital to all he hoped for—that the *character* of Smarlinghue should not be endangered. And this, not only because it was in itself the key that opened for him the innermost portals of the underworld, that again and again had alone stood between him and recognition as the Gray Seal, but because to-night he must meet Mother Margot, not as Smarlinghue, but in the only character that she would recognise, and, yes—the grim smile came again—*obey*. And so, first of all, must come the Sanctuary; after that—his shoulders under the ragged coat lifted in a queer, almost fatalistic little shrug—who knew!

VIII

JIMMIE DALE PAYS A VISIT

IT was Smarlinghue, the drug-wrecked artist, who, ten minutes later, by the street entrance, inviting even the nods of recognition from some of the loungers round about, entered the dingy tenement and scuffled along the musty, dark, unlighted hallway to the squalid rear room on the ground floor—the Sanctuary; it was Jimmie Dale, in dinner jacket, the millionaire clubman, who stealthily gained the street again by way of the old French window, the refuse-strewn courtyard, the board in the high fence that swung aside at a touch, and finally the lane.

Another ten minutes, and he was sauntering nonchalantly along a narrow crowded street, whose curbs were lined with pushcarts, whose sidewalks were thronged with shawled women and coatless, swarthy men, whose gutters were the playground for almost naked children. Thompson Street was in the heart of New York, just off West Broadway, not far from the homes of the old-time aristocracy of Washington Square, but it was also in a foreign land!

But Mother Margot with her pushcart was not here to-night. He had hardly expected she would be. His face was set as he made his way back now to the Bowery, and from there headed still deeper into the East Side. There was nothing for it now but Mother Margot's rooms.

A few blocks farther brought him within sight of the tenement that was his destination, and his pace slowed as he passed the narrow alleyway over which the police had kept abortive guard on the night they had pounded at Isaac Shiftel's door inside. There was a light in the window, the same window through which he and the Phantom, alias Isaac

Shiftel, or perhaps better on that occasion, alias Gentleman Laroque, had first had warning that the police were without. Mother Margot, then, had presumably returned home.

He was opposite the tenement door now. He halted abruptly, ostensibly to watch the efforts of a man across the road who was attempting to start an old car that was backfiring viciously, in reality to allow some near-by pedestrians to pass by and then suddenly Jimmie Dale had disappeared from the street, and in another instant, in the dark, murky hall, was standing before Mother Margot's door.

From one of the pockets in the leather girdle beneath his outer garments, that harboured too its little blued-steel burglar's kit, he took out his black silk mask and slipped it over his face. His lips tightened a little, as his right hand closed over the automatic in the side pocket of his dinner jacket. Who knew! There was a light in there, it was true; but he was not necessarily *sure* that it was Mother Margot—or that Mother Margot was alone.

He knocked upon the door. There was no answer. He knocked again. This time there came the sound of a shuffling footstep crossing the floor within, and then the door was cautiously opened, and Mother Margot, holding a candle above her head, peered out into the hallway.

"My Gawd—youse!" she whispered hoarsely. "Wot're youse doin' here?"

Jimmie Dale smiled beneath his mask.

"Have you forgotten, Mother Margot?" he said softly. "I promised you a visit, you know."

He stepped forward, but she blocked his way at the threshold.

"Go away! Go away from here!" she breathed wildly.

"I don't see why I should—just yet," said Jimmie Dale quietly. "And wouldn't it be better if we had our interview *inside* instead of out here? It wouldn't be quite so public."

"No!" she said frantically. She kept glancing behind her, over her shoulder in a terrified way. "Aw, go away! For the love of Gawd, go away before we'se gets caught!"

"Who's in there, then?" demanded Jimmie Dale sharply.

"No one!" she answered. "Dere ain't no one dere—at least I don't know whether dere is or not."

Jimmie Dale stared at the old hag for a moment speculatively.

"You don't know!" He injected a caustic note into his voice. "What do you mean by that?"

"Didn't I tell youse de other night!" She was still whispering hoarsely. "Didn't I tell youse wot dey said—dat dey was figurin' on youse comin' here sometime. Dat's wot I means. I ain't never seen no one in here but me, but sometimes I'm scared. Sometimes I'm sure some one is watchin' me—an'—an' I can't *see* no one. Don't youse see I'm playin' straight wid youse. If I wasn't, I'd let youse in, an'—aw, my Gawd, get away from here! If I'm caught tippin' youse off dey'd put a knife into me, dat's wot dey'd do!"

"We'll be less likely to be seen or caught without that light, then," said Jimmie Dale coolly. He leaned forward suddenly, caught her arm, and blew the candle out. "Now, don't move!" He was past her in an instant, and with quick, silent tread, his step as noiseless as though he possessed the padded paws of a cat, he made the circuit of the two rooms. And then he was back again beside her at the threshold. The rooms, so far as any outward and visible evidence of human presence was concerned, were empty. Nevertheless, he drew Mother Margot out into the dark hallway now, and closed the door silently behind them.

"Wot is it?" she faltered. "Wot is it youse wants?"

"A little information—perhaps a little more than information," said Jimmie Dale evenly. "You said something a minute ago about playing straight with me. I'm not so sure about you, Mother Margot. That's why I'm here. I telephoned you this morning, and you swore you had not heard from the Voice since that night at Mrs. Kinsey's."

"It was de truth," she said quickly.

"I'm so glad you always tell the truth," he said tersely, "because then, of course, you'll tell me now all about Hip Foo's to-night."

She drew in her breath sharply.

"My Gawd!" she stammered. "Youse—youse knows about dat?"

"Go on, Mother Margot!" Jimmie Dale prompted curtly.

"Dere—dere ain't nothin' to tell." She was obviously groping for inspiration. "De bulls raided de place almost as soon as I got dere, an' I beat it on de jump for home."

"Don't lie!" snapped Jimmie Dale sternly. "There is a good deal to tell! Shall I help your memory?" He was quite sure of his ground. Pedler Joe's story made the Phantom's and Bunty Myers' connection with the night's work a practical certainty. "Don't you think Bunty Myers, and Connie Pfeffer's ten thousand is worth telling about— Mother Margot?"

The shot went home. The old hag shrank back against the wall. He heard her mumbling incoherently.

"I'm waiting!" said Jimmie Dale coldly.

"I—I can't!" she burst out. "I—I daresn't!"

"I think you can," Jimmie Dale answered sharply. "And I am sure that it will be much the *safer* thing for you to do. As a last resort, for instance, if you forced my hand, the police might be very much interested to learn that Mother Margot knew something about the Levenson Bank robbery, and——"

"I—I'll tell youse!" she broke in. "My Gawd, wot can I do? Wot else can I do? I—I'll come across. W'en youse telephoned me to-day I hadn't heard nothin'. It was only about six o'clock dat de Voice told me to take de message over to Hip Foo's, an' be dere by half past eight. See? Dere wasn't no way I could tell youse, was dere? I ain't de only one dat don't know where de Gray Seal lives, am I?"

"No," said Jimmie Dale evenly; "and we'll dispense with any discussion as to what you would have done if you had known. Go on!"

"It was to meet Bunty Myers an' another of Gentleman Laroque's gang named Muller." Mother Margot's whisper was scarcely audible. "An'—an' it was about Connie Pfeffer, all right. I was to tell 'em dat Connie had seen de error of his ways an' opened up, an' dat de coin was in de house wid de broken stairs, an' shoved in under one of dem."

She paused, and in the semi-darkness Jimmie Dale could see her jerking her head in a queer birdlike way furtively about her.

"What's its other name?" demanded Jimmie Dale shortly.

She looked at him puzzled.

"De other name of wot?"

"The house with the broken stairs." Jimmie Dale's tones were uncompromising.

"Why, it's Pedler Joe's, of course!" she answered. "Youse knows where dat is. Everybody does."

Pedler Joe! For a moment Jimmie Dale stared at her. Was Pedler Joe, too, playing a game? The figure of the old man, full of misery from what seemed genuine distress and fear, rose before him. But against this was Pedler Joe's record. Was this the way he had brought up his young protégé—to play in with him hand and glove? And yet those bruises on the man's neck and throat—*they* were genuine enough.

Again Jimmie Dale lunged in the dark, and won.

"Pedler Joe had nothing to do with it!" he snapped. "Don't try any holding out on me, Mother Margot!"

"I ain't holdin' out nothin' on youse," she protested. "I didn't say Pedler Joe was in it. Connie beat it for Joe's after pullin' de robbery at de bank dat day, so's to work up an alibi—see? But de bulls pinched him quicker'n he figured. He hears dem comin' while he's dere—see?—an' w'en Pedler Joe ain't lookin' he shoves de envelope wid de cash in under one of de broken stairs, an' w'en de bulls bust in dey don't find nothin', an' dey ain't got nothin' on Connie, an' after puttin' him through for a few hours down at headquarters dey has to let him go."

Jimmie Dale nodded.

"Exactly!" he said tersely. "And the reason he didn't go back for the money was because he never got a chance. Your gang got him, and started in to apply less humane but evidently more effective measures to make him talk than the police did."

Mother Margot drew in her breath.

"I guess youse knows de whole lay. My Gawd, youse ain't human, are youse?"

"There's Hip Foo's," suggested Jimmie Dale grimly.

"Yes," she mumbled. "But dere ain't nothin' much to dat now youse knows de rest. I had just give 'em de message w'en de bulls started de raid, an' we beat it. Dey're to go down dere after Pedler Joe gets to sleep, an' pinch de dough—dat's all."

"Not quite!" said Jimmie Dale. "There's Connie Pfeffer. Did they go the limit with him? Is he dead?"

Mother Margot shook her head.

"No, he ain't—not quite. He'll be all right after a while, but I guess he just come through wid de dope in time. Him an' one of Laroque's men, dat's supposed to be a man-nurse in charge of an invalid—see?—is on deir way west for somewhere now. Dat gets Connie outer here so's he don't get a chance to butt in an' spill anythin' to Pedler Joe or some other pal dat'd help him out, an' besides it's a kind of a stake dey're givin' him so's de bulls won't bother him no more."

Again Jimmie Dale was silent for a moment. It was clear-cut, wasn't it, the work that was ahead now? There was no choice, was there? There was only one thing to do. He could not go to a telephone, say, and tip the police off to the hiding place of the money; for the fact that it would be found in Pedler Joe's would convict Pedler Joe as an accomplice. The man, innocent though he was, would not have a chance. His known intimacy with the Mole, and the fact that Connie Pfeffer had been found there shortly after the robbery, both of which reasons had already resulted in a grilling for the old man from the authorities, and above all Pedler Joe's own record would——

"All right!" said Jimmie Dale abruptly. "Let's go!"

"Go!" Mother Margot crouched back against the wall. "Go where?"

"To Pedler Joe's," said Jimmie Dale curtly.

"Me!" She flung out her arms wildly. "Me—go dere! Aw, my Gawd, not dat! If dey caught me dey'd—dey'd croak me. I don't dare! My Gawd, I don't dare! Dey'd kill me. I've told youse all I knows. Youse ain't got no use for me dere."

"Oh, yes, I think I have," said Jimmie Dale coolly. "I'd feel a little more comfortable if I knew where Mother Margot was and what she was doing during the next half hour."

"But—but youse can trust me," she faltered.

"Possibly!" admitted Jimmie Dale evenly. "But not to the extent of staking my life on it. It would be rather awkward for me if you communicated with the Voice, say, while I was——"

"No, no; I swear I won't!" she whispered frantically. "Aw, for Gawd's sake, don't make me do dat! If dey sees me, if dey catches me dey'll know I snitched, an' dey'll twist me t'roat or put a knife into me."

It was quite true. If caught under any such circumstances Mother Margot's life would not be worth a moment's purchase. But then Mother Margot would not be caught. Bunty Myers and whoever was to accompany him were not to go there until late to-night, not until they would expect Pedler Joe to be in bed and asleep; and at the present moment Pedler Joe was out roaming miserably about the streets in his hopeless search. The place would be empty. There would be no risk for Mother Margot—and he, Jimmie Dale, was certainly by no means sure enough of her to leave her free to communicate with her confederates and trap him like a rat if she chose to do so.

"They won't catch you." His tones were peremptory now. "You go ahead. I'll follow—where I can keep my eye on you. I can't very well walk through the streets with a mask on my face, and I would a little rather prefer, Mother Margot, that all you saw was—a mask. And, besides, it might be just as well for your sake that you should not be seen in company with any one. You say you know Pedler Joe's place. Well, so do I. When you turn into the wagon drive I'll join you. Now then!"

Again she shrank back.

"No, no!" she pleaded. "I—I'm scared. Youse don't know wot youse're doin'. Youse're goin' to get me killed, dat's wot it means."

"I don't want to make any noise that might be heard back there in your room by the unseen watcher that you appear to be so much afraid of," he said coldly; "but you are either going with me, or it is going to be a showdown right here, Mother Margot. You understand?" He caught her by the arm, and pushed her toward the front door. "Now go!"

She moved forward along the hall. He could see her wringing her hands.

"My Gawd!" she whispered; and again: "My Gawd!"

IX

THE HOUSE WITH THE BROKEN STAIRS

MOTHER MARGOT passed out through the door. Jimmie Dale, a few paces behind, removed his mask as he stepped out to the sidewalk. He crossed instantly to the other side of the road, and, keeping pace with her, followed her as she shuffled down the street.

He was smiling grimly now. The Phantom apparently was becoming cautious—in a personal sense. As Gentleman Laroque, as Isaac Shiftel, as Limpy Mack, the man had but narrowly escaped; to-night, it seemed fairly obvious, he was playing a safer game by delegating the actual work to the members of his old gang over whom he evidently still preserved his authority. Jimmie Dale's smile gave place to tight, set lips. It was a compliment in a way, and a very genuine compliment, to him, Jimmie Dale; but if there was no Phantom to-night, no chance at the man in that personal way, then, equally, there would be no Tocsin to-night either at the end of the quest!

He went on down the street, following the shawled figure of the old hag. Why dwell on that? What good would it do? What would it bring him? Some night, some time, it would be the last night and the last time, and there would be—the end. Meanwhile to-night, at least, he could checkmate the Phantom's game.

His thoughts swept back to the immediate present. Something struck him for the moment as incongruous, out of keeping, a little illogical, in view of the open brutality they had dealt out to Pedler Joe last night when they had not hesitated to break into the old man's house, that to-night the Phantom had switched his tactics to those of almost exaggerated stealth. And then he shook his head. No—it was far from illogical. He saw it now. He owed the Phantom a compliment in return. Mentally he paid it. The man had a sort of super cunning and cleverness cradled in his devil's brain! Pedler Joe knew nothing; Pedler Joe would continue to know nothing. Connie Pfeffer's lips were sealed unless to confess his own guilt. And so the disappearance of the money would remain a mystery—that was all!

The shawled figure on the opposite side shuffled on. It was not far now to Pedler Joe's. He followed her across the Bowery, down a side street again, past the Sanctuary, and around the next corner. Here he closed the gap between them, crossing to her side of the street—and as she disappeared into the blackness of a sort of arched driveway, he joined her.

He slipped the mask over his face again, and took her arm.

"Come on!" he whispered.

The driveway was a wretched, dirty place, once used no doubt for a delivery wagon when the store in front had been in its prime; now it was Pedler Joe's entrance to his domain, which, in turn, had once been an out-house of some kind, perhaps even the stable, or wagon shed, a miserable little wooden shack, neglected now and in hopeless disrepair.

Jimmie Dale, still holding Mother Margot's arm, emerged from the driveway, crossed the small yard beyond, and halted at the door of the hovel.

It was dark here; nothing showed but the looming shadows of the surrounding buildings. Mother Margot was whimpering again:

"Pedler Joe! Pedler Joe'll see me, an' den——"

"Pedler Joe is out," said Jimmie Dale crisply. "There's no one inside. You won't get into any trouble, Mother Margot, unless you make it yourself. I'll see to that!"

The door was locked. From the leather girdle Jimmie Dale selected a pick-lock. A moment, two, passed. The slim, sensitive fingers of Jimmie Dale, that mocked at even the intricate locks and bolts devised by modern ingenuity, were working quickly, almost contemptuously now, at Pedler Joe's cheap, flimsy fastening. The door swung open. Jimmie Dale motioned Mother Margot to enter, and, following, closed and locked the door again behind them.

For an instant he stood motionless, then his flashlight swept the interior, lancing the blackness with its round, white ray. The place was one of utter, poverty-stricken desolation. There was but a single room, with no furniture in it save an old table and chair; the floor sagged and had rotted away in places; even a window was lacking, for where one once had been, it was now, in lieu of broken panes no doubt, nailed up with boards.

And now the flashlight focussed and held on a flight of stairs obliquely across from the door and on the far side of the room. Mother Margot had called the place "the house with the broken stairs," and it was well named! Half a dozen of the treads at least were broken away and were little more now than so many gaping holes; and for the rest, the whole staircase leaned drunkenly to one side as though scarcely able any longer to sustain its own weight, let alone the added burden of any one desirous of reaching the floor above.

"Whereabouts in the stairs is it?" Jimmie Dale demanded abruptly.

Mother Margot was crouched close against the door in a frightened attitude. She shook her head.

"I dunno," she answered. "I wish to Gawd I did, so's we could get outer here quick. It's in one of dem holes in de stairs. Connie said he didn't remember which one 'cause he had to act on de jump. He heard de bulls comin', an' Pedler Joe was upstairs, an' he said he hadn't time to figure anythin' except to get de cash outer sight."

"All right!" said Jimmie Dale quietly. "It doesn't much matter. We'll begin at the beginning."

He moved across the room, and with his flashlight began his search under the broken stair treads. But it was not until the fourth attempt that his hand, in under a tread up to the elbow, encountered a sealed envelope. He drew it out quickly, and tore the end open. Yes, here it was! He took out the money and counted it rapidly—twenty five-hundred-dollar banknotes. It was all here—ten thousand dollars. He thrust the money into his pocket, and laid the empty envelope on the stair beside him.

"It's all right, Mother Margot!" he called softly. "We'll go in a minute."

From another pocket in the leather girdle he drew out now the thin metallic case that contained its store of diamond-shaped, gray-paper seals, and with the tiny tweezers—that there might be no tell-tale finger prints—lifted out one of the seals and moistened the adhesive side with his lips. There was Pedler Joe to be considered. Pedler Joe must not be held accountable by the Phantom, any more than by the police. He picked up the empty envelope and pressed the gray seal firmly down upon it. When Bunty Myers and his fellow thugs arrived and found the money gone, Pedler Joe would naturally be the first one they would think of, and their former suspicions that the old man knew more than he pretended would be aroused again with disastrous results for Pedler Joe. But the gray seal here on the envelope would square Pedler Joe and settle all doubts on that score. The Phantom, for instance, was fully——

Mother Margot's whisper cut tensely, suddenly through the room:

"Dey're comin'! Dey're comin'! Aw, for Gawd's sake, dey're comin', an' dere ain't no way to get out!"

In an instant Jimmie Dale was across the room beside her. He caught her wrist fiercely.

"I told youse so!" She was crooning in a queer, low way. "Dey'll kill me for dis!"

"Keep quiet!" breathed Jimmie Dale.

Cool, possessed, motionless, he stood there. Mother Margot was right. He could hear the footsteps of three or four men close to the door outside. There was no way out. They were trapped, and Mother Margot——

The door rattled as it was tried. A voice in a low callous laugh reached him through the panels:

"It's a good thing youse piped old Pedler down de line,

Bunty; it's saved us wastin' de night hangin' round waitin' for him to hit de hay!"

And then another voice, impatiently:

"Aw, get de door open! Wot's de use playin' wid de lock? Bust it in, an' strike a light! Youse don't have to be careful of de noise when Pedler ain't dere."

Mother Margot! There was a chance. Just one. Not for both of them perhaps, but for Mother Margot. He owed it to her. He had brought her here—to her death—if the chance failed.

He leaned toward her, his lips close against her ear.

"Flatten back here against the wall. The door opens away from you. Don't move till they make a rush, then slip through the door behind them, and get to the street. I'll guarantee at least that no one will *follow* you, and with a little luck you won't be seen at all."

"But youse"—a strange note had come suddenly into her voice—"but youse—youse mean dat——"

"Never mind what I mean," said Jimmie Dale between set teeth. "Do as I tell you, or *neither* of us'll get out!"

The door lock yielded with a little snap—but Jimmie Dale was no longer there. Silent as a shadow in his movements, he was already halfway up the stairs.

He halted here. He was still holding the envelope with its gray seal, but instead of his flashlight his automatic now was in his other hand.

And then for the first time Jimmie Dale made a sound—at the moment that the door swung open. It was as though, suddenly alarmed, he had tripped and fallen upon the rickety stairs. There was a chorus of startled oaths, a rush of feet across the floor in his direction, the white gleam of a flashlight thrown upon him, the chorused shouts again—and he turned, dropping the envelope from his hand, and as it fluttered downward to the floor, he dashed madly up the stairs.

Came the crash and roar of a revolver shot, the spurt of flame, the ugly *spat* of a bullet as it embedded itself in the woodwork somewhere above his head, another, and still another—but Jimmie Dale did not fire in return. There was

Mother Margot. They had not noticed her and she should be gone by now, but he could not see. He dared not take the chance of any of them running back for cover in the direction of the door. Just a few seconds more, and then— he flung himself over the topmost stair—yes, it was safe now surely to check their rush if he could. He fired—his shot directed high over their heads. Snarls and curses answered him. The flashlights, more than one of them now, made almost daylight of the place. And suddenly a new shout went up. Some one had picked up the envelope!

"The Gray Seal!"

A hail of lead came up the staircase—and a concerted rush of dark, swarming figures. He could not tell how many— three or four—but it seemed as though there were a dozen.

The window! There must be a window here. He remembered that Pedler Joe had spoken of a window. Yes, there it was just across from the stairhead. He hurled himself toward it, flung it open, and swung out over the sill. It could not be very high. In any case it was the only chance. A flashlight's ray caught him now from the head of the stairs, and was accompanied almost simultaneously by an oath and the tongue flame of a revolver.

He let go his hold and dropped. Something, a heap of rubbish, an uneven surface, threw him violently upon his face as he landed, but in an instant he was on his feet again. There was no way out of the place except across the yard and through the archway, and he raced in that direction. He heard a shout signalling his whereabouts from the window. It was echoed by shouts from within.

If he could but gain the street before they poured out of the shack in pursuit! No—here they came now! Over his shoulder he caught a glimpse of shadowy forms behind him.

He had a start of ten yards, perhaps fifteen at the outside. He swerved out into the street. Strange the commotion back there had not aroused the neighbourhood! But it would not take long to do so now if the chase remained in the open!

"The Gray Seal! Get him! Stop him!"

The shouts, the pound of feet rang from behind him. But now a queer, half choked, panting laugh came grimly from Jimmie Dale as a dark shawled figure peered suddenly out from a doorway and drew back again as he dashed by. Mother Margot! Well, at least, he had kept his promise to Mother Margot.

And now windows began to open; people to emerge from the houses. The pound of feet, the shouts seemed to grow even nearer. Jimmie Dale was straining every muscle now, running like a deer. Another few minutes of this in the open and it would be the end. Thank God, the Sanctuary was just around the corner! If he had ever needed it in his life, he needed it now. They might see him enter the tenement; but by the time they had been able to search the place even cursorily the Gray Seal would have vanished, and only Smarlinghue of the underworld, the drug-wrecked peer of that inglorious realm to which they themselves belonged, would be found.

He turned the corner, ran on the few yards up the block to the Sanctuary, and as he flung himself inside the tenement door he saw them swing into the street behind him, and heard them like a pack of bloodhounds give tongue again at sight of their quarry. But in a second now he was along the dark hallway and inside the Sanctuary itself, the door locked behind him.

And now he worked with lightning speed. He could have run on out through the French window, and by the lane perhaps might have had a fair chance of getting away—but almost as important as his life was the vital necessity of protecting the character of Smarlinghue from suspicion, and the Gray Seal making straight for Smarlinghue's room and disappearing thereby, marked an intimacy in time of stress with Smarlinghue's habitation too significant to go unchallenged. He tore off his evening clothes, wrenched open the movable section of the baseboard, brought out the seedy, tattered garments of Smarlinghue, and put them on.

He needed no light—only a few more precious seconds. They were stumbling around outside in the hall now; and now he could hear them break into one of the other rooms. Just a few more seconds—that was all he needed. There were still the little pieces of wax that distorted lips and nostrils, that gave a peculiar set to cheeks and ears; still the facial solution to give the gaunt, pallor-like effect that Smarlinghue— Cold beads of sweat stood out suddenly on Jimmie Dale's forehead. His mask as he pulled it off was sticky; his hand as he put it to his face came away *wet*. No, there was no need for light. He knew! It was blood. His face had been bruised and cut when he had fallen from the window. No make-up, no clothes, no "Smarlinghue" would explain that!

They were coming to his door now, weren't they? His wits—if he had ever possessed any! A chance for his life—and Smarlinghue's! The wax went into the nostrils, under the lips, behind the ears, inside the cheeks—there was no need for pallor on blood-stained skin—and the mask was over his face again.

A footstep was almost at the door.

And then, not Jimmie Dale, but Smarlinghue spoke.

"Help! Help!" he cried in a strange, gurgling, strangled voice. "Help! Let me alone! Help!"

He loosened the catch on the inside of the French window, but without opening the window itself; then, seizing a chair, he hurled it over his head in the direction of the easels and canvases that stood against the far wall. There was an answering crash. He scuffled with his feet, as he flung the evening clothes he had just taken off—saving out only his hat, which he put on—into the hiding place, and put back the movable section of the baseboard again. Another instant, and he had sent the table in the centre of the room hurtling to the floor, and had sprung—silently now—to the door.

They were pounding upon it, flinging themselves against it in an effort to break it in. In the darkness of the hall they would not be able to distinguish clothes. If they followed him, then, with luck, he might still save both himself and Smarlinghue; if they didn't, then—well, it was the end.

He turned the key with a sudden twist of his fingers, and swept the door open. Dark forms loomed before him. He struck right and left with all his body weight behind his blows, cleaving a passage for himself as he plunged forward.

A volley of furious oaths greeted the unexpected attack. Hands snatched at him. He broke from their clutches as they tried to grasp him, and sped down the hall. Yes, they were following! Thank God, they were following!

It was only a step from the street door to the lane, and in barely the fraction of a second he had gained the latter, leaving his hat behind him on the sidewalk as though it had been swept from his head in his flight; in another second he was through the board in the fence that swung aside at a touch of his hand, and was creeping along the rear of the tenement to the French window of the Sanctuary. An instant here he listened as he slipped the mask from his face, then the French window opened and closed silently again—and Smarlinghue, with battered, blood-stained face lay prone and motionless upon the floor amidst the débris and ruin of his squalid room.

A minute passed—two. Fellow tenants began to gather at the doorway, and finally to crowd into the room. The poverty-stricken gas-jet hissed as some one lighted it, and threw a pale, yellow, inadequate light over the surroundings. Jimmie Dale felt some one grasp him by the shoulders and lift him to a sitting posture. He rubbed his hand across his eyes, and stared dazedly around him. Then suddenly he seemed to rouse himself. He shook his fist wildly.

"Get the police!" he croaked hoarsely, as he recognised as Bunty Myers a man who was elbowing his way forward. "Get the police! I want the police! Some one bust in here and said if I made a peep he'd lay me out. I—I was scared for a minute, mabbe two, and then I—I started something."

"Sure! You look it!" snapped Bunty Myers. He swung fiercely on the little crowd and brushed them back to the doorway. "Get outer here!" he snarled. "Dis ain't yer hunt!" He turned again to Jimmie Dale. "Blast youse, Smarly!" he swore. "I ain't blamin' youse, but if youse'd kept quiet we'd have had him cornered cold. He's got away now down the lane." He lowered his voice. "Wot I come back for was to find out if youse'd got a better look at him dan some of de boys wid me on account of his mask, an' if youse'd know him again if youse saw him?"

Jimmie Dale shook his head.

"No, I didn't get no look at him," he said viciously. "But I'll have the police on him, and——"

"De police!" Bunty Myers' laugh was forced, unmirthful. "De police'll be a long time findin' dat bird, youse can take it from me! Say, youse give me de pip, Smarly! Dat was de Gray Seal!"

Jimmie Dale's jaw dropped. He stared helplessly.

"My God!" gasped Jimmie Dale. "The Gray Seal! Him!"

And he was still staring in a dazed and helpless way about him as Bunty Myers swung hurriedly from the room again, presumably to join his companions in their search along the lane.

X

THE street lights showed mistily, like vague, filmy patches in the darkness. It was raining in torrents, pitilessly. The water dripped from the brim of Smarlinghue's old felt hat, and beating into his face soaked the bandage around his cheek, threatening to displace it. He smiled grimly in reminiscence, as he raised his hand and tightened the dressing a little in its place.

It was four nights ago now since his accident when he had made his escape from Pedler Joe's window, and subsequently had saved himself by playing the dual rôle in the imaginary fight he had staged between Smarlinghue and the Gray Seal in the Sanctuary; and since then the character of Smarlinghue had virtually been a little Old Man of the Sea that had clung with almost sinister tenacity to him, and that he had not been able to shake off and discard as before at will. It was strange! A queer trick of fate, perhaps; and not an over-kindly one, for it had tied his hands, and for the moment had left him seriously crippled in his efforts to pick up the clues, already found and lost so many times, that must eventually, if there were ever to be life and freedom for the Tocsin, happiness for himself and the woman that he loved, lead to—the Phantom.

Jimmie Dale's face grew hard, anxious, perturbed. Things had not gone well in those four days. Smarlinghue, if such a thing were possible when his life itself had been the stake, had played his part too well that night in the Sanctuary! Already one of the acknowledged aristocracy of the underworld, he had been suddenly elevated to the status of little less than demi-god. Smarlinghue had been in actual, physi-

cal combat with the Gray Seal! Smarlinghue had become
the idol of a morbid awe and curiosity! It was subsiding
now, but while it lasted it had made the "disappearance" of
Smarlinghue, even for a few hours, far too dangerous a
move to consider; he had been too much the attraction, too
much on exhibition, as it were. But even if this had not been
so, there was still another and perhaps even stronger reason
that had temporarily chained him to the rôle of the drug-
wrecked artist and to the environment of the Sanctuary.
The underworld had eyes and ears, and so too had the
police; while, still more to be feared as one who seemed to
reach out with cunning versatility into so many different
spheres, as one who, of all others, would have his suspicions
the most quickly aroused, there was the Phantom. Jimmie
Dale, if he had returned to his ordinary life, would have had
to do so with a bandaged face curiously like Smarlinghue's!
It invited far too much! And so he had telephoned to
Jason, that peer of butlers, that he had been called out of
town for a few days; and whatever personal fears the old
man might have entertained for the safety of his young
master, whom, as he was wont to say, he had dandled on
his knee as a child, Jason could be trusted to account, both
ingeniously and to the entire satisfaction of any one interested, for the temporary absence of Jimmie Dale from his
usual haunts.

In a personal sense, therefore, there had been no serious
cause for anxiety; but in those four days it seemed, somehow, as though a wall, impenetrable, thick, had been reared
across his path, halting him, and shutting out from both sight
and hearing those things that concerned him far more than
the consideration of his own security. There had been no
word from the Tocsin, no note, no sign, no straw of evidence
out of the whispered confidences in the hidden places of the
underworld that he could grasp at as indicative of even her
continued existence. The old question gnawed at his heart.
Was she still alive to-night? What move had the Phantom
made in those four days, and if any, had the man with his
hell-born cunning been at last successful?

The days had been as a blank. Even Mother Margot had been denied him, for no mask could have hidden the bandages from her eyes. But yet, after all, he had not been idle. He had done what he could. The wave of notoriety that for the moment had swept him to a pinnacle high above his fellows of the underworld had seemed to present the only opportunity for activity left open to him, and he had seized upon it to cultivate the very men who were unconsciously responsible for the ruse to which he had been forced to resort that night in the Sanctuary to save his life, the men who had hammered at his door, voicing for the moment the one rallying cry that alone could unite the myriad, vicious interests of gangland in one common bond, "Death to the Gray Seal!" And in a measure he had been successful, though, as far as results had gone, he might, it seemed, have saved himself the effort. Bunty Myers, Muller and the rest—Gentleman Laroque's, alias the Phantom's, gang—had admitted him, rather pleased to bask in his reflected glory, to their hang-out in the upstairs rear room of Wally Kerrigan's ill-favoured "club," which was half restaurant, half gambling den, and the resort of the worst in the Bad Lands, but he had learned nothing. They had loafed and smoked and played cards and drunk an amazing quantity of liquor, but that was all. There had always been Bunty Myers and Muller, and at times as many as three or four more, but had he, Jimmie Dale, not known that back of it all Gentleman Laroque, unseen, held these men in allegiance, he never would have discovered it there!

He had learned nothing; but though to-night, for perhaps the first time, he could have dispensed with the bandages to the extent of at least being able to use the black silk mask without the risk of Mother Margot suspecting the tell-tale hurt that lay beneath, he was on his way now to Kerrigan's again as the first part of his night's work. Afterwards— He shrugged his shoulders. Afterwards he would see! Certainly there was always a chance at Kerrigan's. He felt that he had already worked himself into an intimacy that was not far from breeding confidences. Their apparent inaction was also not without its measure of satisfaction, and this in itself alone was worth knowing. It might very well, and probably did, augur that the Phantom too was for the moment inactive, that there was a momentary stagnation, as it were, in that master crook's field of endeavour, and——

Jimmie Dale stopped short. He was opposite the swinging doors of a saloon, run by one Gypsy Dan, from which there emanated a stentorian-lunged voice high-pitched in song, accompanied by the thumping of many fists evidently upon the bar, and the stamping of many feet obviously upon the floor. Subconsciously, he was now aware, he had heard the row half a block away. It was not by any means a select and exclusive neighbourhood; it was one more of squalor than anything else and accustomed to disturbances more strenuous and decidedly more vicious than this, but it was at least within the purlieus of the city and supposedly under the domination of law and order. And now from the opposite corner ahead he caught the ray of a street lamp glinting on the rubber-cloaked shoulders of an officer, as the man crossed the street and headed for the saloon.

Jimmie Dale, as Smarlinghue, smiled thinly. Whoever they were in there, they were friends of Smarlinghue, the riff-raff, the rank and file of the citizenry of that sordid fatherland of the underworld in which he held so high a station! The character of Gypsy Dan's saloon guaranteed that. He turned quickly, pushed the swinging doors open, and stepped to the side of the ragged, unkempt figure at the bar who was yelling at the top of his voice.

"Forget it!" said Smarlinghue roughly. "There's a harness bull on the move out there."

The man, too immersed in his vocal efforts and the liquor he had imbibed, paid no attention; but the barkeeper was alert in an instant.

"T'anks, Smarly!" he grunted. He leaned across the bar and clapped his hand over the singer's mouth, effectually shutting off the flow of song. "Close yer face!" he ordered peremptorily. "Dat'll be Riley out dere, an' he's all to de good if youse'll give him half a chance. D'ye hear? Dat goes for de whole of youse!"

The half dozen loungers around the bar subsided. Comparative silence reigned for a moment, then a slow, measured step sounded outside, a night-stick rattled softly on the swinging doors, as though both in warning and in acknowledgment that the amenities had been observed, and the step died away.

"T'anks, Smarly!" said the barkeeper again, as he once more leaned back against the far side of the bar.

The erstwhile singer blinked.

"Have a drink," he invited cordially; and digging into his pocket, he produced a fistful of bills which he waved with a lordly, inebriated air about him.

Jimmie Dale stared. A moniker in the Bad Lands was always apt and incisive, and it had been particularly so in this instance. He knew the ragged, down-at-the-heels vagrant, as everybody else in the East Side knew the man. *Beggar* Pete! The man was known at times to do odd jobs perhaps if pushed to extremity for food and particularly for drink, but otherwise he lived a miserable, poverty-stricken existence—not criminal, perhaps, just a drifter, lost to all sense of responsibility and self-respect.

"Hello!" said Jimmie Dale, half seriously, half facetiously. "Who stuck you in his will, Pete?"

Some one at the bar guffawed.

"A nice old geezer wid gold spectacles dat Pete croaked wid a black-jack," said the man. "Dere wasn't no one else to inherit wot was in de stiff's pocket!"

Beggar Pete swung suddenly upon the speaker.

"Dat's a damn lie!" he shouted furiously. "Youse t'inks youse're funny, don't youse? Well, mabbe youse won't laugh so loud wid a bust face—see?"

Jimmie Dale edged in between the two men. Beggar Pete was huge-framed and, in spite of dissipation, muscular, and his face, working with rage, was indicative of a row that would bring more than Riley rapping softly in admonition with his night-stick on the swinging doors.

"Sure, I'll have a drink," said Jimmie Dale, diplomatically. He nodded to the barkeeper. "Suds for mine!" Then to Beggar Pete: "Here's how, Pete!"

Beggar Pete's scowl gradually subsided.

"Youse're all right, Smarly!" he said. He grew suddenly confidential. "Say, it came my way all right, an' 'twasn't more'n half an hour ago, neither. I'll tell youse. I was walkin' along an' broke for fair, an' an old gent goes brushin' by in a hurry in de rain. De Mouser t'inks he's funny, but de old geezer did have gold spectacles 'cause just after he gets by me he stops an' reaches into his pocket for a box of matches, an' I sees his face under de umbrella as he lights his cigar. Den he goes on again, an' as he puts de box of matches back in his pocket I sees somet'ing drop out on de sidewalk. I slips along an' grabs it up." Beggar Pete licked his lips, and scowled again at the little crowd. "It's his purse, dat's wot it is, an' a fat one. I ain't no saint, an' jest den I t'ought me luck was out, 'cause I t'ought he looked 'round an' saw me pickin' it up, so I runs after him an' hands it back. Say, he slips me wot I t'ought was one buck, an' wot I guess he t'ought was only one too, but w'en I gets into Kelly's place dat was near dere an' had a snifter it took all de money in de cash register to make change—see? Fifty, dat's wot it was—a fifty-dollar bill."

"Well, den," suggested one of the crowd to whom the story had evidently been retailed before, "set 'em up again, Pete—youse must be dry talkin' about it."

Jimmie Dale, included in the invitation which Beggar Pete promptly accorded, shook his head and left the place.

He smiled a little curiously to himself as he went on again through the rain. It was an incident, that was all; an incident that could have no bearing on him in a personal way, that could carry with it no significance so far as he was concerned, save that it was one of the many little cross-sections of life, queer, bizarre, a scratch under the surface of things, here in the Bad Lands. Yet, naturally enough, it remained uppermost in his thoughts for a few moments as he walked along.

He knew Beggar Pete, and he was not at all convinced by Beggar Pete's story. Benevolent, gold-spectacled gentlemen were not in the habit of handing out fifty-dollar bills—even on a dark and rainy night! There would always be a street lamp within a few paces under whose light the award could be made without any mistake on the donor's part. A five-dollar bill for the service Beggar Pete had rendered—yes; a fifty-dollar bill—no. He found himself growing more and more skeptical. Indeed, he was not sure, for instance, that the gibe the lounger at the bar had flung at Beggar Pete had not more nearly hit the truth, to the extent at least that Beggar Pete had come by the money by methods that would not stand any very close scrutiny.

Jimmie Dale shrugged his shoulders. One thing at least seemed certain. Beggar Pete would sooner or later come to grief, and perhaps the sooner the better. There were too many Beggar Petes who had drifted on the reefs to become broken hulks, worthless to themselves and a menace to others!

He drew his coat collar closer around his throat. What a beastly night! Head down against the storm, he ploughed along. Thank Heaven, he was not far from Kerrigan's now—just around the next corner. For all it's evil-smelling, reeking atmosphere, where about the only air there was stole in like a sneak thief through the broken window pane that was covered with cardboard, there would be even *physical* comfort to-night in the company of Bunty Myers and his fellow gangsters in that upstairs back room! There would even be a sort of compensation in the fact that he was under cover and in shelter should the real object of his visit, as it probably would, prove as futile to-night as it had in the past. His face hardened suddenly. What was the matter with him? Was he growing childish, his thoughts feeble-minded and astray? Shelter! A bit of a rain storm! Where was the Tocsin to-night? Where was she? What was *sheltering* her from a storm, not of pattering rain drops, but from one where every moment her life itself stood in peril, where her——

He raised his head. Along the street, through the murk, he noticed a shadowy form, the only other pedestrian in sight. It was too far off in the storm to distinguish even whether it was a woman, or a man wearing what might be a long raincoat, but strangely enough, unaccountably enough, yet nevertheless existent in h's mind was the consciousness of something familiar about the figure. And then, almost the next moment, his impression was verified in a measure that brought every faculty, alert and tense now, into instant action. The figure was turning the corner, passing under the street lamp. It was Mother Margot!

He did not quicken his pace. He was Smarlinghue! His lips tightened grimly. Mother Margot owed the man she knew as the Gray Seal her life, but how far her gratitude extended he did not know—perhaps not at all in view of the fact that her life would not have been in jeopardy if the Gray Seal had not literally forced her into the situation that had so nearly proved fatal to her that night at Pedler Joe's! In any case, it would be trusting her very far, too far, farther than he would ever dream of doing, if he risked the consequences of handing himself over utterly to her mercy in allowing even a suspicion to arise in her mind that the Gray Seal and Smarlinghue were one! A word of that, a hint, and Smarlinghue, the idol now of the underworld, would know instead a hatred and a vengeance that would not only bring exposure and disgrace to the name of Jimmie Dale, not only play into the Phantom's hands and leave the Tocsin to stand alone, as prompted by that brave, unselfish love of hers she sought to do, but would cost him his life as well. And so, as Smarlinghue, though that was Mother Margot there, he could make no move to intercept her.

But in a moment more he reached the corner. Mother Margot had disappeared. He nodded his head. She had gone in through Wally Kerrigan's side entrance, her objective beyond question of doubt that upstairs room at the back.

Jimmie Dale moved swiftly now. At last, then, there was something afoot again. Mother Margot was the mouthpiece of the "Voice," as she called the Phantom. For a moment he experienced a sense of chagrin that he should have lost those few minutes in Gypsy Dan's saloon, for otherwise he would have been upstairs with Bunty Myers and the rest on Mother Margot's arrival, and Smarlinghue would have been introduced to Mother Margot, and— He shook his head again. No! He had lost nothing. His intimacy had not *quite* reached the point where they would talk before him. They would more likely have kicked him out. It was much better as it was; better that Smarlinghue should not have been in evidence at all if the aftermath of this visit of Mother Margot meant anything that would bring him into any game that might be played to-night.

And now he smiled with grim whimsicality as his thought of *shelter* came back to him. Instead of the back room upstairs, if he was to have any part in the proceedings whatever, he was much more likely to be a silent and unobtrusive occupant of the fire escape outside the window, than which he could imagine no place less sheltered or more uncomfortable in New York that night!

The door of Wally Kerrigan's side entrance closed silently behind Jimmie Dale. It was utterly dark here. The clientele that favored Kerrigan with its patronage, in so far as this portion of his premises was concerned, made no demand for any such extravagance as light! A footstep sounded from above, a woman's footstep; it died away, and a door closed. Mother Margot had run true to form!

Jimmie Dale moved forward as a shadow moves, and began to mount the narrow stairway with which he was already so well acquainted. There was no sound. It was the silence learned in the days of the old Sanctuary on the creaky, rickety stairs there, where an untrained step would have sounded the alarm from top to bottom of the tenement.

He gained the landing. There were three or four rooms here, he knew, but save for a tiny thread of light that seeped out under the threshold of the rear room, which was the rendezvous of Laroque's gang, everything was in darkness. It was early yet, which might be one reason, and the stormy

night another, why the other rooms were as yet evidently
unoccupied.

And now he was crouching against the door itself, his ear
pressed against the panel. It was a possibility, that was
all—a possible alternative to the uninviting fire escape.
Again he shook his head, then turned swiftly to the window
almost at his elbow that gave on the rear of the little hall.
He had caught the sound of movement through the panels,
even the sound of voices, but the words had been hopelessly
indistinguishable.

Cautiously he opened the window, slipped out on the fire
escape, and, against the possibility of any of the occupants
of the room stepping out into the hall to notice an opened
window, he closed it again behind him. Another moment,
and, flat on his face, he had crept along the iron platform
until he lay beneath the window of the rear room. He would
be able to hear now. He had taken no chances on that
score. Open or closed, the window above him with its
square of cardboard tacked over the broken pane could hardly
be improved upon for his purpose. And now, keeping a
little back from the wall, he raised himself up and peered in.
Mother Margot was talking excitedly, gesticulating with
her hands, while gathered around her at the table were
Muller, Bunty Myers, and two men he had met there before, who, leaving aside a score of aliases, were known as
the Kitten and Spud MacGuire.

A pretty quartette! Jimmie Dale's lips thinned, as, the
sense of sight gratified, he shifted his position, placing his
ear as close to the edge of the window casing as he dared
without exposing himself to the risk of being seen. Yes,
he could hear now, but—a dismayed frown furrowed his
forehead—Mother Margot appeared already to have imparted whatever information had brought her there.

". . . Youse understand, don't youse?" she was saying.
"'Cause if youse have got it straight, I'm goin' to beat it
outer dis, an' get home an' get dry."

"It kinder took de wind outer us, dat's all!" Bunty Myers'

voice responded in a puzzled growl. "I t'ought de whole works was blown up an' we was done!"

"I told youse once," snapped Mother Margot. "It's de panel in de wall."

"Sure!" said Bunty Myers. "We ain't deef, an' we got dat, all right—de middle one at de back of de room. But, den, wot's de use of waitin'?" He broke into a coarse, un-pleasant laugh. "I guess old Miser Scroff ain't at home to queer anythin'!"

"De use of waitin'," returned Mother Margot tartly, "is 'cause de Chief says so, an' 'cause some of youse pulled a bum play dat he's got to make good, an' I wouldn't like to be de one dat done it 'cause de Chief is seein' red. Anyway, don't youse make no mistakes again. Youse ain't to make a move until as near ten as'll give youse time to get away wid it, but youse're to be through by den, 'cause at ten de bulls get tipped off."

"All right," agreed Bunty Myers. And then abruptly, as Mother Margot evidently started to leave the room: "Say, wait a minute, mother! Mabbe youse have got de answer to somethin' we'se can't figure out. Wot's de big idea be-hind de Chief's keepin' under cover? We ain't seen him for weeks—nothin' but telephones an' messages. Where is he?"

"Why don't youse ask him?" suggested Mother Margot acidly.

"Ask him!" echoed Bunty Myers helplessly. "How de hell can I, w'en I don't know where——" ,

"Dat's de answer!" Mother Margot's interruption was a cackling laugh. "Youse knows all I knows. Do youse t'ink me an' de Chief goes to a picture show every evenin', an' den spends de rest of de night together eatin' hot frankfurters an' stewed ice cream? Say, youse give me a pain! Good-night!"

The door in the hall closed.

For an instant Jimmie Dale stood motionless, then he turned, and, in lieu of an exit via the hall window, began to make his way down the fire escape. And now what? Go to Mother Margot as the Gray Seal and force a detailed ex-

planation from her as he had the other night? He shook his
head. It wasn't necessary to-night, was it? He had learned
enough, hadn't he?

His mind was working swiftly, in a precise, virile way,
as he descended the wet, dripping iron treads. The middle
panel at the back of old Miser Scroff's room—and old Miser
Scroff was not at home. That was clear enough. And there
was no question but that Miser Scroff had money hidden
away somewhere. It was only a wonder that it had not been
taken from him before. The old man was almost senile. It
was common property on the East Side that he had been
caught fondling and crooning over packages of banknotes
in his room on more than one occasion. For more years than
any one could remember the man, already old, had just kept
on growing older in a solitary life in his sordid surroundings.
He was supposed to have a small income from some source,
but however small it might have been it was certain he saved
on it for he never spent a cent save to keep absolute famine
from his door. Undoubtedly he had money. Robbery, therefore, as the motive, was equally clear. And at ten o'clock,
for some reason, the police were to be notified of the crime
by the actual perpetrators themselves. Ten o'clock. It could
not be much after nine yet. There should be at least half an
hour then before Bunty Myers need be considered as a
factor. Meanwhile the Phantom was at work in an effort
to rectify some misplay made by his underlings. Was it at
Miser Scroff's that the Phantom in person would be employed prior to the arrival of Bunty Myers and his confederates? Was it luck like that? Luck at last! If so,
then——

Jimmie Dale dropped from the bottom of the fire escape
to the ground. And then, in the shelter of the lane where
the fire escape had landed him, he broke instantly into a run.

"Not as Smarlinghue," confided Jimmie Dale grimly to
himself as he ran. "I can't risk Smarlinghue—it's got to be
the other way in spite of a patched face."

XI

THE PANELLED WALL

JIMMIE DALE, a long coat, sodden with rain, covering his evening clothes, crept up the narrow tenement stairs, crept along a bare and dirty hallway, and halted before a closed door. Softly, cautiously, he tried the door. It was locked. His fingers reached in under his outer garments, and then shot swiftly to the door again. There was a moment of utter silence, then a faint *snip,* and the door began to open guardedly, the fraction of an inch at a time. Another instant and Jimmie Dale stood inside the room.

The door closed behind him. A minute he listened, then the round, white ray from his flashlight lanced through the blackness, swept its surroundings in a swift, comprehensive circle—and a low, startled exclamation, involuntary, before it could be checked, came from Jimmie Dale's lips. This was old Miser Scroff's squalid, hovel-like abode, niggardly alike in its furnishings and its cleanliness, since even cleanliness cost money—but—but—it was strange! He did not understand! He had not been very long on his trip to the Sanctuary and back. It had not taken him long. Certainly it could not even yet be half-past nine. And yet it seemed as though, in spite of that, he was already too late.

The flashlight circled again, but more slowly this time, as though puzzled and nonplussed itself. The small room was in dire confusion. The bedding from the cheap cot was flung here and there on the floor; the drawers of an old desk had been pulled out and their contents strewn about, and the desk itself had been hacked to pieces as though on the chance that it might have possessed a hidden receptacle; while even the ragged strip of oilcloth, that was the sole floor covering, had been ripped up and flung into a corner. Where a hiding place might have existed before, there existed now nothing but a pitiful state of wreckage!

Jimmie Dale's mind seemed to echo the confusion. It did not seem possible that Bunty Myers and his companions could already have been here. And besides—the flashlight's ray shot suddenly to the rear of the room—what had all this to do with the panelled wall?

An ironic smile tinged his lips now. Yes, it might by a stretch of imagination be called panelled, but it was simply an extra height of boarding that ran up to meet the plaster all around the room some three or four feet from the flooring. He stepped quickly across the room, and knelt, as nearly as he could judge his position by the flashlight, in front of the middle boards. He nodded grimly. These were at least intact if nothing else in the room was! From a pocket in the leather girdle around his waist he drew out now a small, but incredibly strong and powerful "jimmy." It would have been a useless waste of time to seek for any secret spring that, while it probably existed, was also certainly well and cleverly hidden.

He was working rapidly now, the point of the "jimmy" prying tentatively into, and up and down, the joints of the boards. A low-breathed exclamation of satisfaction came almost instantly from his lips. The "jimmy" had slipped through one of the cracks into an open space behind. It was here, then, the hiding place of old Miser Scroff's hoard that Bunty Myers——

Jimmie Dale stood suddenly erect, tense, every muscle rigid, listening. A footstep, low and stealthy though it was, had caught his ear from the hall outside. It was not another lodger, it was too cautious for that, too guarded; and for the same reason it could not be Miser Scroff. It was not Bunty Myers and his confederates, because there was only *one* footstep. The Phantom, then! The Phantom had required time for something somewhere. And he, Jimmie Dale, had dared to hope that it might be here. Luck! If he was in luck at last, he would play it to the full. He was crossing the room swiftly, without a sound. There would be a settlement this time from which there would be no escape! It was almost at the door now, that footstep; but he, too, was at the door—on the inside, crouched against the wall.

A grim smile twisted his lips as he stood there, his automatic flung forward, his flashlight ready in his left hand. Here was a good place for that settlement, here in old Miser Scroff's room, here on the scene of one of the Phantom's hell-hatched crimes—there could be no better place for that *final* reckoning!

The doorknob turned, the door began to open slowly. A form, shadowy, a little blacker than the surrounding blackness, bulked in the opening, then stole across the threshold, and the door closed.

And then Jimmie Dale spoke in a cold, merciless whisper, as the stream of his flashlight cut through the black, and his automatic lifted to a level with the line of light:

"Put up your——"

The sentence died on his lips. It seemed to Jimmie Dale that the room was whirling around him, that he was robbed of all power of movement, that his brain had lost the faculty of reason. The light was boring into a pair of brown eyes, startled, it was true, but brave, calm, self-reliant brown eyes that looked out from a wondrously glorious face, the only face in all the world. And then his pulses leaped, and the blood in a furious tide went whipping through his veins. The Tocsin! The Tocsin! Was he mad? Could it be true? The Tocsin!

"Marie!" he cried out hoarsely.

"Jimmie! Is it you? I could not see with the light in my eyes. Oh, Jimmie!" Her voice faltered. Relief was there, but relief was not the note he caught; it was love, yearning, the woman's soul that was in her tones.

The flashlight, the automatic, were thrust into his pockets. She was in his arms. He held her close. Years had gone since he had held her there before! He had fought for this, risked all and everything for this, hoped for it when hope itself seemed dead, and now she was here, close to him, clinging to him—and it was not just for the moment, not just a stolen, pitiful instant out of all eternity, but for always, for all time. He had her now. She would never go again. There was no power on earth would keep him from her side now!

Half laughing, half crying, she struggled to free herself a little.

"Jimmie," she breathed, "don't you know that you are terribly *strong,* dear?"

He released her a little, grudgingly, but still he held her close. His lips found hers, her eyes, her hair—the dark silken strands that, playing truant from under her hat, swept his face.

Her hand had crept up and found his mask, slipped under it, and was resting gently against the strips of plaster on his cheek.

"I—I know of course about the night when—when you got this," she said brokenly. "All the underworld has been talking about Smarlinghue. They very nearly caught you, Jimmie. Oh, Jimmie, why will you do it? I have begged you so, done all I could to keep you out of this. And now to-night again! What are you doing here? What brought you here?"

His arms tightened about her again.

"To find you," he said.

She drew away in amazement, her hands on his shoulders now, holding him at arms'-length.

"To find me!" she echoed helplessly. "But how could you have expected to find me here? You did not know. I sent you no note, no word, for after I heard about that night at Pedler Joe's and what happened later in the Sanctuary, I ʌade up my mind not to——"

He laid his hand softly across her lips.

"I have ʌot been anywhere, done anything, since that night on the East River, Marie," he said quietly, "except with the one end in view of finding you. And had I not found you again now I should still have kept on in the same way. I'm quite sure you know every move that Smarlinghue has made, and you therefore ought to know that I have already gone too far, that I've already been too close to the Phantom more than once to have let anything you did keep me out of this, Marie. The fewer the notes, the more I should have worried, and the harder I should have worked. But that's all at an end now, thank God! There'll be no more separation. We'll work together from now on until we've found the Phantom."

For a moment she did not answer, then she turned her head away.

"No, Jimmie!" she said firmly. "I cannot! I will not! Nothing has been changed since that night on the East River. I cannot prevent you from doing as you have been doing, but there is a great difference between your actions as the Gray Seal and as one who is known to be working hand in glove with Marie LaSalle. It—it would make it almost impossible for me to go on, for I—I could not do anything then without the fear of putting your life in danger. Oh, Jimmie, you do not know, you do not understand, and—and I cannot tell you!" She turned quickly toward him again. "Go, Jimmie, please—at once. There is something that I must do here."

Jimmie Dale reached out for the door.

"We'll go together, Marie—now," he said calmly. heard Mother Margot talking about Scroff's panel here. "I was on the fire escape outside Kerrigan's place. That's what you mean, isn't it? But *you* are what *I* came for, so we'll go, for there is nothing else that counts here now against the risk of you being caught by Bunty Myers and his crowd, to say nothing of old Miser Scroff himself turning up any minute to——"

"Miser Scroff is dead," she interrupted dully.

"Dead!" he repeated in a startled way.

"Murdered," she said. And then her voice broke again. "Oh, Jimmie, I have failed miserably to-night. I—I have cost a man his life, I am afraid. The least I can do now is to keep them from getting the money—it's in an old leather bag behind the panel—but that I must do. You—you must let me work this out, Jimmie. I have no choice. If you force me out of here, or if you insist on staying to help me, then in an hour, two hours, somehow, Jimmie, I warn you frankly that I will get away from you again."

"I don't think you will—not this time, Marie!" said Jimmie Dale grimly. "I've got you now, and I'm going to keep you no matter what happens."

She smiled at him wanly.

"Very well, Jimmie, if you think so," she said quietly. "Only remember what I have said. Meanwhile there is the panel. *I* can't go until I have got the money."

She started across the room, only to stumble over the broken desk. And then Jimmie Dale's flashlight was in play again, and he followed her.

"Murdered, you said!" He spoke quickly. "Why? I don't understand. And I don't understand what has happened here. The place has been turned inside out."

"The panel, Jimmie!" she answered. "It's near the middle. Get it open! I'll tell you while you work."

"I had already found it before you came in," said Jimmie Dale coolly. He was kneeling by the wall, the "jimmy" in his hand again. "Go on, Marie!"

A joint in the wood gave with a low, rending, creaking sound. She stood at his shoulder, whispering swiftly:

"Some of the gang under the Phantom's orders inveigled Miser Scroff down somewhere in the neighbourhood of that old junk yard near Kelly's saloon, with the intention of keeping him out of the way for an hour or two while the rest of them came here and searched for his money. But Scroff was an old man, and the blow he was hit by the black-jack killed him; and the search here resulted in nothing."

The "jimmy" pried away a narrow board from top to bottom. Jimmie Dale reached in his hand. Yes, there was something in here, a bag of some kind.

"How do you know all this?" he demanded. "And if you know it, where was the Phantom all this time?"

"Under cover," she answered. "I told you long ago that he was a man with a score of domiciles and a score of aliases.

Lately he has been driven from one to another—and robbed of some of them by the Gray Seal."

"I thought so!" said Jimmie Dale swiftly. "Well, you've lost your case, now, Marie. It would appear, then, that the Gray Seal has been of service, so why should you attempt to keep him at a distance?"

Her hand found and touched his shoulder.

"It's no good, Jimmie," she said softly. "Shall we call it a woman's inconsistency? I cannot give you any other answer."

Another board came loose. Jimmie Dale frowned. What was the matter? He was not working with his usual deftness and silence. It seemed as though the creaking of the board could be heard throughout the building.

"You said you had failed miserably to-night, and that you were afraid you had cost a man his life," he said. "You mean Miser Scroff?"

"No," she said heavily. "I did not know anything about to-night until after Miser Scroff was killed. That brought the Phantom into it in a personal way. There had been no murder intended, and failure to find anything here would otherwise have ended the matter; but in old Miser Scroff's pocket they found, besides some stock certificates made out in his name, a dirty old piece of paper with a tracing of his room upon it, and a position on the rear wall marked with an arrow, so they knew then where the money was. But this was after the first search had been made and the room torn to pieces as you see it, and though they knew then where the money was, there was a *murder* that had to be covered up."

Jimmie Dale drew out a worn yellow leather bag from the aperture. He opened it, and uttered a sharp exclamation. It was crammed full of loose banknotes.

"How do you know all this?" he asked for the second time, as he shut the bag.

The Tocsin shook her head.

"It is useless to ask me, Jimmie," she said steadily. "If I told you, I might as well enter into the partnership with you that you are so insistent upon—it would amount to the same thing. I cannot tell you. I can only tell you that I know the Phantom means to plant the crime on some outsider's shoulders, some one he has picked out as *suitable,* a seedy character who—it's horrible, Jimmie!—will not have a chance for his life. The securities with Scroff's name on them are to be placed under the innocent victim's mattress; then, with the panel rifled here, the police are to be tipped off about the murder, and where to find the 'murderer' and the evidence. I did my best; I did all I could, but—but I lost the trail, and so I came here to save at least the money, and as a sort of last hope that somehow I might pick up the clue again. The only thing I am sure of is that the Phantom was playing the part of an old gentleman with gold spectacles to-night, and——"

Jimmie Dale had taken the Tocsin's arm, and, carrying the bag, had started back for the door; but now he halted suddenly as though rooted to the spot, and stared at her.

"An old gentleman with gold spectacles!" he ejaculated sharply.

She caught at his sleeve.

"Jimmie!" she whispered tensely. "You—you know something about it! You—you've seen him! You know who it is they mean to railroad to his death for this?"

The room, his surroundings, even the Tocsin, had fled from Jimmie Dale's consciousness for the moment; instead, there came again the scene in Gypsy Dan's saloon, when Beggar Pete had told his story, which he, Jimmie Dale, had but so short a time ago dismissed almost summarily from his mind as having no personal significance for him. Beggar Pete and the gentleman with the gold spectacles! Beggar Pete and his sudden affluence! He had not believed Beggar Pete then, but he believed him now. There was no shadow of doubt but that Beggar Pete was the Phantom's intended cat's-paw, and that the snare was the low, viciously-cunning handiwork of the Phantom. Beggar Pete's story, once those securities were found beneath his mattress, would, out of its own improbability, only *assure* the man's conviction. Nobody knew how much or how little cash Miser Scroff had had! So this was what the Phantom wanted that extra time for—to plant those securities. God, if he could *catch* the Phantom at Beggar Pete's! No! There was the Tocsin here—he had her now—he would never leave her again. And besides it was too late now. He knew where Beggar Pete lived because of late it had been almost a source of gossip on the East Side, for the simple reason that, for perhaps the first time in his life, Beggar Pete now had a *permanent* address—the cellar of a somewhat questionable lodging house run by a yegg named Harry the Dip—and this in return for the more than questionable agreement on Beggar Pete's part to make himself generally useful when called upon to do so! It was a long way to Beggar Pete's—almost across the whole of the East Side. The Phantom would have completed his work by now, or at least long before he, Jimmie Dale, could reach Beggar Pete's lodging, and that would——

"You *know!* Oh, thank God!" she cried tremulously. "And I—I was so afraid!"

"It is Beggar Pete," he answered mechanically.

"Then quick, Jimmie!" she pleaded. "There is not an instant to lose. You must get those securities before the police do!"

He did not move.

She shook frantically at his sleeve.

"You see that, don't you, Jimmie?" she cried again. "Oh, there's not an instant, not a second to spare—and besides, the rest of them will be here any minute."

He looked at her.

"And you?" he said.

"I'll take the bag of money and see that it reaches the authorities," she replied quickly. "You can't be hampered with that. It will be all you can do to win the race against the police."

"No!" he said fiercely. "Let you get away out of my life again? Not for a dozen Beggar Petes!"

A strange smile, wistful, drooped her lips; and suddenly

her eyes were wet; and as suddenly she reached up and drew his face to hers and kissed him.

"You are too big a man for that, Jimmie," she whispered. "And there is no other way, and—and, besides, you know what I have told you. You are too big a man for that, Jimmie, and that—that is why I love you."

He held her close.

"It's no use!" he said hoarsely. "There's been more planted on him than you know anything about; enough so that the robbery here would almost cast suspicion on Beggar Pete without the securities being found at all. He has been spending more money in the saloons to-night than he ever had in all his life before; and he is accounting for its possession in a manner that no one would believe."

"But there's a way out of that," she answered quickly. "A way that the Gray Seal has taken before. Take it again now, Jimmie—because it's a man's way, *my* man's way."

He knew what she meant, but he did not answer. She was gathered in his arms. He could not let her go. He had given his all to find her—he could not let her go.

"Jimmie," she said, steadying her voice with an effort, "every second that we stand here may mean that it has cost a man his life."

With a low cry that seemed wrenched from him in agony, Jimmie Dale's hands dropped to his sides. Through the darkness, that was now a strange mist before his eyes, he saw her pick up the leather bag. And then her whisper came to him:

"Thank God for you, Jimmie! I'll stand guard at the door until you're through."

He found himself at the rear of the room again, working with frantic speed in front of the broken panelling. He knew what she meant; it must be his mind, of course, that was functioning, governing him, and yet his actions seemed purely mechanical. From the leather girdle he drew out the thin metallic case; and from the case, with the tiny tweezers, he lifted out a diamond-shaped, gray-paper seal. If he succeeded in getting the securities before the police did, and if

the police found here on the scene of the robbery the insignia of the Gray Seal that they knew so well, then Beggar
Pete, a worthless, broken hulk, would go free, and——

Her whisper, from the door now, reached him again:
"Quick, Jimmie! They're coming now. I hear them
downstairs. Quick, Jimmie, and—and—good-bye!"

It took an instant, no more, to moisten the adhesive side
of the paper seal, and stick it into place on the edge of the
broken panelling; and then Jimmy Dale was across the room,
and, the door closed behind him, was standing in the blackness of the hallway.

She was gone! His face was set and rigid. Perhaps she
was still somewhere here in the hall; but he could not see,
and he did not dare call out. The stealthy tread of two or
three men was distinctly audible coming up the stairs. He
drew farther back along the hall and crouched there in the
darkness. Low whisperings reached him; indistinct forms
clustered around the door of Miser Scroff's room—and then
the door opened and closed again, and the hall was empty.
Empty! Where was she? Still here—still within touch
perhaps? A bitter smile curved his lips. He was beaten—
beaten by a worthless, broken hulk that had drifted on the
reefs—a human wreck!

He was crouched outside the door again, and now silently,
quickly, with the little steel pick-lock, he locked the men inside. If she were still in the hall here, she too would have
her chance, enough time to get away before they discovered
that gray seal in there and came pouring out of the room
again!

And then he went down the stairs, and in another instant,
the mask removed from his face, was outside the tenement,
and racing madly through the night. And as he went he
looked about him. He had hoped for a passing taxi or a
vehicle of some sort, but there was only the torrential rain.
And so he could but run. Time! It would take him all of
twenty minutes, and it must be later than twenty minutes of
ten now, and—he paused for a second under a street lamp
to consult his watch—yes, it was a quarter to ten. At ten

the Phantom would notify the police—in some anonymous way, of course. But there was still a little leeway. Perhaps ten minutes. The time it would take the police to get to Beggar Pete's *after* ten o'clock.

He ran on and on. Still no taxis, no vehicles—only deserted streets. It seemed as though he had run for hours. He did not stop to look at his watch again. He heard a clock from somewhere boom out the hour.

Was he in time? He glanced up and down the street now, as he halted finally before a small, tumble-down, shabby dwelling house. He did not know. At least there was no one in sight.

Harry the Dip's door was never locked! His lodgers kept hours too uncertain and varied! Jimmie Dale smiled grimly, as slipping suddenly into the shadows of the doorway, he stepped silently inside the place. Another item, this choice of lodging, even if it were the choice of necessity, that would not help Beggar Pete's reputation in a jury's eyes!

The cellar entrance! Where was it? It was dark in here —but not silent. From upstairs he could hear talking and the sound of movement. And then his ear caught another sound—the sound of loud, heavy, stertorous breathing that seemed to come from a direction ahead of him. He risked his flashlight. He was in a short and narrow hall. And now he advanced cautiously. Yes, here it was; and here, too, was the explanation of those laboured, stertorous sounds. Under the stairs at the back of the hall, a door stood half open.

The flashlight's ray played down a flight of bare, ladderlike steps—and coincidentally Jimmie Dale's face set in hard, bitter lines. At the bottom of the steps, a little to one side, in a filthy cellar, sprawled on a torn and filthy mattress from which wisps of mildewed straw protruded blatantly, Beggar Pete lay in a drunken stupor. The man had already been pretty well along at Gypsy Dan's, and in the hour since then it was obvious that he had lost no time!

Jimmie Dale's hand clenched. The sight seemed to fan a latent fury, a merciless passion into flame. It was for this, to save *this,* a vagrant, a bum, a drunken sot, a beast, that he had lost all that was most dear to him in life to-night; it was for this that he had done what he had never thought to do under any circumstances, under any pressure, while life remained to him—lose the Tocsin again if once he ever found her! It seemed to plumb the depths of irony; it seemed as though he could *wish* for nothing better than that this besotted beast should experience exactly what the Phantom had prepared for him!

And yet, mechanically, Jimmie Dale went down the cellar stairs. He stooped over the man. There was no danger of *disturbing* Beggar Pete! He pulled the man aside, and over-turned the mattress. A little bundle of stock certificates, held together by a rubber band, lay there. He picked them up. They were made out in the name of Heinrich Scroff.

For an instant he stood staring from the certificates in his hand to the sprawled form upon the floor—and slowly, gradually, the hard, embittered look on Jimmie Dale's face softened. Was he so sure after all that he had paid too much? In his hand he held the death warrant of an *innocent* man, a fellow creature, sunken, low, it was true, but a human being with hopes and fears like his own perhaps, though one, unlike himself, who had had only the rougher road to travel, where plenty was unknown and life's sunshine meagre.

He stooped again, and replaced the mattress, and laid Beggar Pete upon it. He was smiling now softly, as sometimes a woman smiles when her lips mirror her heart. And somehow he was glad.

And then Jimmie Dale turned away and went out into the storm again. To-morrow the city would awake to find that the Gray Seal had committed another crime!

— XII —

THE air was heavy with drifting layers of smoke, as it always was in this back, upstairs room of Wally Kerrigan's "club," that was the hang-out of Gentleman Laroque's, alias the Phantom's, gang. Four men sat at the table playing stud, and Jimmie Dale, as Smarlinghue, seated a little apart, watched them now as he fumbled with the dirty, frayed sleeves and wristbands of his coat and shirt, and, fumbling then in his pocket, drew out a hypodermic syringe, its nickel-plating worn and brassy, its general appearance as disreputable as himself.

How many nights had he come to this room, as he had come to-night, playing a game, that was not a game of cards, with Bunty Myers here, and the Kitten, and Muller, and Spud MacGuire! How many nights? He had almost lost track of time. The wound in his cheek had healed. He had even resumed, in so far as an occasional appearance at the St. James Club, and here and there a social function went, his normal life as Jimmie Dale. He must have been coming here for many nights!

Through half closed, apparently drug-drowsed eyes, he watched the players at the table. Yes, it must have been for many nights. It was over a week since—his fingers tightened involuntarily in a fierce, spasmodic grip upon the hypodermic—since that night when he had held the Tocsin once again in his arms in old Miser Scroff's room, and had lost her again. Since then he had continued to cultivate these men. They were only pawns, they moved only at the will of that unseen yet ever present spirit of evil, the Phantom; but to be one of them opened the Avenue of a Thousand Chances that might lead to the Phantom himself. He had had no other clue to follow.

But so far nothing had come of it. They did not distrust him—who in the underworld would distrust Smarlinghue, who had the entrée everywhere!—but they had made no advances toward offering him full membership in that unhallowed fraternity to which he knew they belonged. At times he had believed they had been on the verge of doing so, and that applied especially to Bunty Myers, who was the Phantom's apparent chief of staff; but there had been nothing definite, nothing concrete, nothing tangible.

And yet, even in a negative sense, the nights he had spent here of late had not been futile. He was in possession of the fact that there had been *inactivity*. And that meant that the Phantom, whatever might be germinating in that master mind of crime, had for the time being been quiescent; and, as a corollary to that, the almost certain deduction that no further blow had been struck at the Tocsin—that she was still safe. And this had been borne out by Mother Margot, who, so far, had always been the Phantom's mouthpiece. As the Gray Seal, and through the hold that, as the Gray Seal, he had upon her, he had continued to call her daily from her pushcart to the telephone and question her. But she had still protested vehemently each time that she had had no further word of any move, and he was satisfied that she was telling the truth for the simple reason that he did not believe she would dare do anything else. But, even so, unknown to her, he had still maintained, in so far as he could, a personal surveillance over her movements, and there had been nothing to disprove her statements. She still tended her pushcart in Thompson Street; she still lived in those rooms from which the Phantom, in the dual guise of Shiftel, the fence, and Gentleman Laroque, who once had openly led this very gang here, had so mysteriously disappeared.

Smarlinghue's face was vapid, but into the dark eyes behind the drooping eyelids there came a troubled gleam. Those rooms where the Voice, as Mother Margot called the Phantom, had installed the old hag! What was the secret that they held? He was certain that Mother Margot did not know. And twice again, of late, in Mother Margot's absence, and despite the Tocsin's warning that they were a trap for himself, he had explored them, searched them—and found nothing.

And now the men around the table, the room itself, his immediate surroundings, existed only in a subconscious way in Jimmie Dale's mind. That was the negative side of the week just past. There was equally the positive side.

Shiftel had returned to the underworld.

Not openly. Not to his old quarters. At first the rumour had flown from mouth to mouth through the underground exchanges of the Bad Lands that Shiftel was back; that he had been seen a dozen times in the hidden places, the lairs, the hang-outs, the breeding dens of vice; that crooks of his old, exclusive clientele had talked with him, done business with him. And at first, he, Jimmie Dale, had not believed it; and then he had seen the man himself. He was sure of it. Shiftel! Isaac Shiftel, alias Gentleman Laroque, alias Limpy Mack, alias the Gentleman with the Gold Spectacles—the Phantom! The man that the Tocsin had so truly said possessed a score of domiciles and, yes—entities—there was no better word, for in each of his disguises the man seemed to have established himself as a known and breathing entity in the life and surroundings of the particular character which for the moment he might have assumed. As witness Shiftel, the fence, known far and wide in the underworld; as witness Gentleman Laroque, long the leader of this band here, long the most notorious gangster in the Bad Lands.

He had seen Shiftel three nights ago in the Green Dragon, a dance hall of unsavoury repute. And Shiftel, the man who was the cause of his, Jimmie Dale's, return to the life of Smarlinghue and the squalor of the Sanctuary, the man who sought the Tocsin's life, the one man that he, Jimmie Dale, would gladly have sacrificed his all to bring to a final reckoning and account, had escaped him that night in the Green Dragon.

He shook his head, mumbling to himself, almost mechani-

cally continuing to play his part in the presence of these
underlings around the table even while his mind was far
away. It was not his fault that Shiftel, once seen, had got
away. He could not in any fairness hold himself to blame.
He had caught but a glimpse of the man far across the hall,
as in the swirl of the bunny-hug the dancers on the polished
centre of the floor had opened for a moment and closed
again. When he had reached the other end of the room
Shiftel had disappeared. That was all.

It was strange! What was the game? What was the
meaning of this reappearance? The man was running a
tremendous risk, and the motive must certainly be commen-
surate with the danger. What was that motive? Shiftel
was wanted, and wanted badly, by the police for his connection with the diamonds stolen from Jathan Lane, the
murdered banker. There was no such person, of course, as
Shiftel—it was the Phantom. Shiftel was only one of the
Phantom's disguises to be put on or off at will. But it was
the known character of Shiftel that the police sought. Why
had the man shown himself in that character, lived it again?
He need only have discarded it utterly, never returned to it,
and as far as "Shiftel" was concerned he could have laughed
at the police until the day he died.

What was it? What was at the back of that crafty brain
whose evil genius had prompted this move? No little thing!
Had the Tocsin's note that he, Jimmie Dale, had found
amongst the mail Jason had handed him when he had appeared at home for his lunch yesterday, any bearing on the
Phantom's motive? He did not think so; rather, out of the
ruck of explanations that had suggested themselves, and
which were for the most part hopelessly untenable, there had
finally come one that he was almost ready to accept.

Smarlinghue's lips twisted in a grin—apparently one inspired by Spud MacGuire as the man scooped a pot on a
barefaced bluff. Well, why not? Even if it was a back-
handed compliment to himself! The Phantom was shy of
funds. Time after time of late he, Jimmie Dale, as the
Gray Seal, had forestalled the other, and snatched away the

fruits of the man's criminal schemes. Where, in the past few weeks, the Phantom had counted upon thousands, many of them, and had even spent lavishly to pave the way to the expected profits, he had received instead not a single penny. The Phantom, therefore, unless he possessed the reserve wealth of a Crœsus, was certainly shy of funds. Yes, that was it. It *must* be it. And as almost irrefutable evidence of this was the fact that the Phantom, as Shiftel, was said to be in communication again with some of those who composed that carefully selected circle of crooks who had been tried and successful business associates in the past; and that was why, too, it was as *Shiftel,* and not as Limpy Mack, not as Gentleman Laroque, or any one of his other aliases, that the Phantom had ventured, cautionsly it was true, but nevertheless had ventured out into the underworld again.

The Tocsin's note! It came uppermost into his mind now. It was the first sign of existence she had given since that night at old Miser Scroff's.

His lips were still twisted in a smile, but there was something cold, forbidding, far removed from smiles, that seemed suddenly now to weigh upon his spirits. She had written; but it had only been to accentuate, as it were, her decision, what she had *said* that night when he had been so sure of taking his place again beside her. Alone! That was it— alone! It was her love, of course, her great unselfish love, that prompted her to try to keep him out of the "shadows," out of *her* dangers. The note reiterated it; he knew it word for word:

"Dear Philanthropic Crook:—I see that you are incorrigible. If I thought that it would do any good I would implore you again— oh, Jimmie, I *do* implore you to leave all this to me, and to go back at once to your own life. I am half mad with fear for you. There is something, some trap being laid, and I cannot find out what it is. I only know that the Phantom has become suspicious that behind the Gray Seal's repeated blows there is more than a mere desire to reap where the Phantom has sown. I only know that the Phantom is convinced that he himself is the Gray Seal's one and only object; and, in turn, the Phantom means to move heaven and earth now to get the Gray Seal—first. Oh, I know you won't do as

I ask you! I know you too well. I know that, if anything, this hint of danger will perhaps even urge you on. But I *had* to write. I had to warn you because I am afraid, and because I know that in some way, with all his hideous cunning behind it, the Phantom is laying a trap for you that——"

Bunty Myers swung around in his chair, and made a grimace at the hypodermic syringe with whose needle Jimmie Dale was now pricking the skin of his forearm.

"Say, can dat, Smarly!" he complained. "Youse give me nerves. Youse've been monkeyin' wid dat squirt gun for de last half hour. If it won't work, for Gawd's sake go down to de Chink's, or somewhere else, and hit a pipe."

The door opened.

Mechanically Jimmie Dale restored the hypodermic to his pocket. He was staring at the doorway. It was not the sudden appearance of that hag-like, black-shawled figure that set his brains at work in swift, lightning flashes, and brought every faculty he possessed into play to preserve the indifference, even apathy, that became the supposedly drug-dulled Smarlinghue, for Mother Margot, he knew, was a frequent visitor here. It was not Mother Margot who caused his pulse to stir now; it was the man who had stepped into the room behind her—Little Sweeney.

It seemed somehow to dovetail and fit most curiously into his thoughts of Shiftel of a few moments gone. His hand, inside his pocket, as it released the hypodermic closed instead upon his automatic. He kept staring at the door—behind Little Sweeney. Was there still *some one* else? The last time these two had been together there had been another with them. That night at Mrs. Kinsey's, when they had tried to rob the old deaf woman of her savings! There had been another with them then—Limpy Mack. But Limpy Mack was also Shiftel, also Gentleman Laroque; in a word, the Phantom. Was Shiftel, or the Phantom in whatever guise he chose to assume, there behind these two to-night? Little Sweeney had not been heard of or seen since that night. This was Little Sweeney's first appearance, and——

The door closed.

Little Sweeney, with a nod that embraced everybody, leaned nonchalantly back against the door and lighted a cigarette. Mother Margot stared around the room, and then her eyes fixed on Jimmie Dale. He saw her glance swiftly then, interrogatively, at Bunty Myers.

Bunty Myers waved his hand.

"Smarly, meet Mother Margot," he said off-handedly. "Mabbe youse knows Little Sweeney."

Meet Mother Margot! There was something exquisitely ironical in this, wasn't there? If Mother Margot but knew how many times and under what circumstances they had met before!

Mother Margot loosened her shawl, and slumped down in a chair.

"Everybody knows Smarlinghue," she grunted.

"Sure," said Little Sweeney from the door.

"Glad to meet you both," said Smarlinghue cordially.

There was silence for a moment. Mother Margot folded her hands patiently in her lap. The silence, prolonged, grew embarrassed. Bunty Myers broke it.

"Beat it!" he suggested uncompromisingly to Jimmie Dale.

Jimmie Dale, as Smarlinghue, vacant eyed as he looked around the room, rose from his chair. It was a little awkward—a little awkward to carry it off as though it were quite a matter of course. He grinned around the circle.

"See you all again," said Smarlinghue pleasantly.

Little Sweeney opened the door.

"Damned thick in here, this smoke," said Little Sweeney, as Smarlinghue shuffled through. "I'll leave it open till the room clears out a bit. 'Night, Smarly!"

"Good-night!" said Jimmie Dale still pleasantly; but out in the hall, and as he turned and went down the stairs, his lips tightened into a straight line.

Little Sweeney was no fool! The fire escape, just within reach, just outside the window of the room where the broken pane mended with cardboard had once before supplied him, Jimmie Dale, with a vantage point from which he could both see and hear all that went on within, was barred to him now by the open door; also the open door, with Little Sweeney standing there, offered no alternative to a prompt and unhesitating exit via the stairs from even the building itself!

Jimmie Dale's lips drew still tighter together as he went on down the stairs. In spite of Smarlinghue's high station in the underworld, he had been treated with scant ceremony! But it was not the hurt of pride in that, as one of the élite of gangland, the honour and deference that was his due had been withheld from him, that brought the grim, set expression to his face now; it was the consciousness of defeat where he had foreseen victory. He had counted too much on the intimacy that he had first cultivated and then believed he had established with Bunty Myers and his fellow gangsters. He had believed and hoped that he was not far from being upon the verge of initiation into their unholy fold, of being invited, in plain words, to become one of them.

He shrugged his shoulders as he stepped out on the street. Well, he had lost on that score for the time being, at least. He was wrong, that was all. But he had burned no bridges behind him. To-morrow night Smarlinghue could still go back there, and be welcome. And as for to-night—well, he was not yet through with to-night! There was something undoubtedly afoot again. What was it? He crossed to the other side of the street, and just opposite the side door of Wally Kerrigan's "club," where he could watch that door unseen, he slipped, unnoticed, into the shadows of a high flight of dwelling house steps.

What was it? He could not, as Smarlinghue, accost Mother Margot when she came out; and by the time he had gone to the Sanctuary and become the man in the evening clothes that she knew as the Gray Seal, she would as likely as not have left Kerrigan's and have disappeared. Queer! Somehow, he was not interested in *what* was afoot to-night in so far as its specific nature was an essential feature. He was more interested in this sudden appearance of Little Sweeney in conjunction with the fact that Shiftel, too, had broken cover. It was the Phantom that interested him—and Shiftel was the Phantom. Was there any connection between this return of both Little Sweeney and Isaac Shiftel to activity? He meant to see! The two had been very closely allied that night at Mrs. Kinsey's, and particularly later on that same night in Limpy Mack's hang-out under Sen Yat's "tea shop."

And so, somehow—he smiled grimly—he was more concerned with Little Sweeney than with Mother Margot tonight. Little Sweeney *might* lead him to Shiftel; Mother Margot he had already tried too often to have any hopeful expectations raised on that score. To reach the Phantom, in the guise of Shiftel, or any other, was the one thing in life that he sought; to meet the man once again face to face was why he was here now, why night after night, and day after day, he still risked his life playing this precarious rôle of Smarlinghue in the underworld. Even a *chance* was worth while. It was rather curious that Little Sweeney and Shiftel, both of whom had dropped completely out of sight for so long a time, should both now have made their appearance again! And so, at the present moment, he was exceedingly interested in Little Sweeney!

Jimmie Dale crouched there in the shadows. Pedestrians passed up and down. Perhaps a quarter of an hour went by. Then the side door of Kerrigan's opened, and a shawled figure stepped out and scurried away. Mother Margot! And then presently the door opened again, and Little Sweeney and Bunty Myers came out together.

Jimmie Dale slipped out on the street, and, on the opposite side, followed the two men as they went down the block. At the corner they separated, and Jimmie Dale took up Little Sweeney's trail.

Block after block the man traversed. Jimmie Dale, hugging the shadows of the buildings, kept a position as nearly opposite the man across the street as he dared, wary always of a corner around which the man might turn, and, with too great a distance separating them, disappear into some place— should that be his objective—before he, Jimmie Dale, could round the corner and pick up the trail again.

Little Sweeney walked fast, obviously unconscious of pursuit, and obviously with some set and fixed destination in view. The chase headed down toward the water front. The quarter now was one of small stores and dwellings, dark for the most part, save for the saloons. Jimmie Dale's face set grimly. It was not an over-inviting neighbourhood.

And then suddenly Little Sweeney swung around a corner.

Jimmie Dale quickened his step, and reached the corner himself in time to see the other, after skirting a fence that enclosed either a vacant lot or a store yard of some sort, turn abruptly at the end of the fence and disappear. In an instant, Jimmie Dale, silent in his movements, though he was running now, crossed the street, and in turn was skirting the fence. There was a lane beyond, of course—that was it! Little Sweeney had not entered any house; he had just turned around the far corner of the fence, and— Jimmie Dale stood suddenly stock still. Out from the corner of the fence, flooding the sidewalk, came streaming a powerful ray of light.

And then Little Sweeney's voice, rasping:

"Of course, it's me! Shut off them damned lights!"

The light disappeared as quickly as it had come. Footsteps crunched faintly in the lane, receding. Jimmie Dale edged quickly forward to the corner of the fence, and peered cautiously around it.

It was quite clear now; there was nothing mysterious about the light that had flung its beams across the sidewalk; it was even commonplace. From a rickety-looking metal garage, which was perhaps twenty-five yards back from the street and in which there stood an automobile, some one had sent the headlights playing along the lane.

For a moment Jimmie Dale stood there watching. There was a single incandescent light burning in the garage which illuminated the place dimly, and, aside from Little Sweeney who was just stepping inside, he could make out the forms of two men standing beside the car. He dared not enter the lane, of course. It would be the act of a fool! A chance sound, those headlights switched upon him, and——

The slouching, bent, almost decrepit figure of Smarlinghue

drew back; and the next instant, after a swift glance around him to make sure that he was unobserved, with a spring, lithe and agile as a cat, he swung himself over the fence from the sidewalk, and dropped without a sound to the yard on the other side. He began to move noiselessly along the section of the fence which flanked the lane. It ran straight to the edge of the garage, he had observed from the street, and— yes, it ended there! He was in luck! He was crouched now against the wall of the garage itself, which obviously, though it was too dark to see, served to complete the enclosure, in lieu of fence, at this corner of the yard.

He could hear them talking now as plainly as though he were inside, for he was separated from them only by the thin metal sheeting of the garage; and, furthermore, just above his head, shoulder high, where a faint light seeped out, the window was open.

"This is a sweet, juicy place for a meeting!" Little Sweeney's voice grumbled.

"Wot's de matter wid it?" another voice demanded, with a hint of truculency. "It's as good as anywhere else, I guess, an' a blamed sight better'n most. I told youse I had to make a trip first with some swag for a friend of mine."

"Oh, all right, Goldie!" said Little Sweeney placatingly. "All right! I know you did. Forget it!"

Jimmie Dale raised himself cautiously, and, back at an angle from the window sash that precluded the possibility of being seen, looked inside. His lips tightened suddenly. The other two were no strangers, either to any one in the underworld or to the police. Goldie Kline and the Weasel! Goldie Kline was one of the cleverest box-workers in the business; the Weasel, a shrivelled little runt, was without a peer as a second-story man.

It was the Weasel now who spoke.

"Me," he said, "I tell youse straight I wouldn't touch dem stones on a bet if any one but old Shiftel was goin' to fence 'em, 'cause dere ain't no one else could get away wid 'em. De Melville-Dane emerald necklace! Swipe me! Dere ain't a stone in de bunch dat ain't known all over de lot, an' it'll take *some* shovin', even by Shiftel, to cash in on 'em. De lady wid de name parted in de middle'll be——"

"Close your face!" said Little Sweeney politely. "You've seen Shiftel, haven't you, and he's settled that to your satisfaction? All you fellows have to do is get the stones tonight, and leave the rest to him."

"Sure!" said the Weasel blithely. "I ain't kickin'! I'm only sayin' dat I wouldn't go in on de deal wid nobody else but Shiftel. Well, spill de rest of it! We're to slip him de stones as soon as we pinches 'em. Dat's understood. An' youse have come down here to tell us where he's layin' low to-night, an' where we're goin' to find him; so let's have it."

Jimmie Dale leaned forward a little in strained attention. Shiftel! The one man he would risk, that he *had* risked, limb and life and liberty to reach! He had made no mistake in following Little Sweeney!

And then a blank look, that changed swiftly to one of bitter dismay, settled on Jimmie Dale's face. The roar of the engine starting up had suddenly drowned out all other sound. No—it was subsiding a little now. He caught Goldie Kline's voice:

"Aw, we can talk in de car. I gotta get dat job I was tellin' youse about done before ten o'clock. ·Dat's de only t'ing dere's any hurry about. De necklace job don't come off till de early mornin' when de dame's gone bye-bye. Jump in, Sweeney; we'll drop youse anywhere youse like."

They were gone—the car, Little Sweeney, the Weasel, Goldie Kline! Jimmie Dale stood there alone in the blackness of the yard. He could not follow them. They were gone. It had seemed that success at last had been actually within his grasp. It numbed him now somehow that it had been so swiftly and unexpectedly snatched away. He had little or no chance of finding Little Sweeney again to-night; he *might,* with luck, pick up the trail of Goldie Kline or the Weasel somewhere in the underworld, but— He had turned away from the garage, making his way back toward the street, and now he halted abruptly, staring into the darkness. Had he lost his wits? What was this that his subconscious mind had kept whispering over and over to him as the key-note of everything from the moment the name had been mentioned? Melville-Dane! Melville-Dane! That was in his *own* world, wasn't it? They were his own friends. Strange! Curious! Yes, he remembered now. Soon after he had ventured home again following his "absence" from the city, due to that night at Pedler Joe's, he had found an invitation to some affair, a reception, if he were not mis-taken, at the Melville-Danes' for to-night. He had sent his regrets, it was true; but he was on too intimate a footing with them to have that make any difference.

And now Jimmie Dale moved on again, reached the fence, and gained the sidewalk on the other side. He was also well acquainted with that emerald necklace—a priceless thing that seldom left the shelter of its safe deposit vault. Mrs. Melville-Dane was evidently wearing it to-night at the recep-tion!

He started on along the street. A word of warning, then, to the Melville-Danes—or the police? He shook his head. By the time Goldie Kline and the Weasel attempted the proposed robbery in the Melville-Dane home, they would be in possession of something far more valuable to him, Jimmie Dale, than all the emeralds in existence—*they would know where Shiftel could be found to-night.*

"And I think," said Jimmie Dale softly to himself, as he quickened his pace, "I think, Smarlinghue, that we'll leave you at the Sanctuary for the rest of the night!"

XIII

THE LESSER BREED

FROM somewhere in the darkness there came a faint musical purr as of metal whirring swiftly upon metal. It stopped; began again; and stopped again. Then utter silence reigned; then there came a low, deep-breathed exclamation, and simultaneously the ray of a flashlight cut through the black, flooded the interior of a small safe, and reflected back upon a masked figure in evening dress.

"One of the X—38 type," murmured Jimmie Dale to himself; "and, as per catalogue, especially adapted for private residences. Tough little nuts to crack! I haven't seen one since the old days at the plant when dad used to turn them out by the gross!"

He reached inside the safe, lifted out a morocco-leather jewel case, and opened it. For an instant he held it under the light, staring at a magnificent emerald necklace of flawless, matched stones. The Weasel had been quite right! Stones such as these must have been garnered and selected from the markets of more than one continent. They would be, through the usual underworld channels, extremely hard to "fence"; for a small and ordinary emerald was not of any great value, and to "cut" one of these and so disguise it, would instantly rob it of the great part of its worth. It was certainly a job for Shiftel! It quite accounted for Shiftel's reappearance!

Jimmie Dale laid the jewel case, still open, on the top of the safe, and from the leather girdle hidden beneath his vest drew out the thin metal box that was stocked with its little gray, adhesive, diamond-shaped seals. He moistened one of these, lifting it with the tweezers, and stuck it on the inside of the jewel case; then he replaced the metal box in his girdle, and slipped the morocco-leather jewel case into his pocket.

And now the light bored into the safe again. There was nothing else there of value from a thief's standpoint. It contained what were evidently some of Mr. Melville-Dane's private papers; it had only been a temporary refuge for the emerald necklace, in lieu of the safe deposit vault from which it had been removed to grace the evening's reception. Satisfied on this point, Jimmie Dale closed and locked the safe again.

He drew back now across the room, and, smiling curiously, arranged two low-backed chairs side by side before the library table. Then his flashlight played for a moment on the wall, locating precisely the electric-light switch just beside a little alcove that was hung with heavy portières; and then the room was in darkness, and Jimmie Dale sat stretched at ease in a lounging chair in the alcove behind the hangings.

His lips twitched grimly now. It was quite a transition from Smarlinghue and the back room of Wally Kerrigan's "club!" It was somewhat different, too, in another way. At Wally Kerrigan's, night after night, he had waited and watched for something, anything, that would open the road to the goal he had set himself—the Phantom; to-night he waited and watched here, quite sure in his own mind as to the exact nature of what would happen, and with no misgivings any longer but that his goal was in sight! In an hour, two hours, at any rate some time before dawn, he would have run Shiftel, alias the Phantom, to earth. It was the end in sight at last; life, happiness, for the Tocsin and himself.

It was very dark, very still in the library of the Melville-Dane mansion here. Again the twisted smile crossed his lips. Here too was quite a transition from the brilliant assembly of but an hour before when he had been one of the guests at a social function that had been, from a society point of view, one of the events of the season. His smile became a little whimsical. Mrs. Melville-Dane had been superb in that emerald necklace. He had paid her almost marked attention throughout the entire evening! Not once had she been out of his sight, even up to the time when she had taken off the necklace and had handed it to her husband to be placed in the safe here in the library. It had been quite simple. He had bidden his host and hostess good-night— and in the confusion of the departing guests, instead of departing himself, had secreted himself in the house.

He shrugged his shoulders. His attentions had been quite wholly unnecessary perhaps. He had not expected the Weasel and Goldie Kline to make any attempt upon the necklace until, say—*now*. It was highly improbable that they would have attempted to stage anything with the house full of people; and yet, if the Phantom's brain was behind the scheme, such an attempt had always remained a possibility. And since he, Jimmie Dale, for his own ends, to pick up the final clue that would bring him face to face with the Phantom, had elected to give no warning either to the Melville-Danes or to the police, then, of necessity, the moral responsibility for the safety of the necklace was his alone— and so he had taken no chances.

The minutes, the quarter hours dragged by. A clock struck through the silence with a clashing, resonant sound. That would be half past two. It was time now surely for the Weasel and Goldie Kline, for they had already allowed ample leeway for the household to retire and settle down for the night.

He stared into the dark. His brain seemed strangely, abnormally active to-night. It was due, wasn't it, to a sort of exhilaration, an uplift, that was upon him? The promise of the end! The Tocsin might be quite right, and probably was, in her belief that the Phantom was planning a trap for him, Jimmie Dale, for the Gray Seal. But her fears now were groundless. It was a plot that, however cunning, however clever it might be, would never come to maturity. It would not be the Phantom now who struck the *first* blow. After to-night she need never fear the Phantom again.

A faint sound, the sound of a cautious, guarded footstep, caught his ear. He stood up silently, his automatic in his hand. The door at the far end of the library creaked slightly; and then, through the parting of the hangings in front of him, Jimmie Dale saw the white gleam of an electric torch flash around the room.

Low whisperings reached him now. He parted the hangings another half inch. The flashlight was playing on the safe; two dark forms were moving quickly toward it; and now one of the two knelt before the safe and began to manipulate the dial, while the other held the light over the kneeling man's shoulder.

Jimmie Dale stepped noiselessly from behind the portières. His hand reached upward, there was a faint *click* as his fingers closed on the electric-light switch, and the room was ablaze with light. A smothered oath came from the kneeling man as he sprang to his feet; the other, startled, dropped his electric torch to the floor. And then silence, an absence of all movement, save that, in obedience to an eloquent gesture from the muzzle of Jimmie Dale's automatic into which they stared, the two men slowly raised their hands above their heads.

"Hello, Goldie! Hello, Weasel!" said Jimmie Dale softly from behind his mask. "I was almost beginning to think you weren't coming." He waved his hand toward the two chairs by the table. "I've been waiting for you, you see. Sit down, won't you?"

The Weasel, licking at his lips, his shrivelled little face working, swore under his breath.

"Who—who are youse?" he demanded shakily.

"We'll talk about that presently, Weasel," Jimmie Dale answered coolly. "In the meantime"—his voice hardened suddenly, rasping, cold—"go over there and sit down!"

Truculently, hesitatingly, their hands still above their heads, the two men moved forward and sat down in the chairs.

"Now"—Jimmie Dale was biting off his words, as he stepped swiftly behind them—"one at a time. You first,

Goldie. Put your hands around the back of the chair, palms together." And then as the man obeyed, Jimmy Dale thrust his left hand into the tail pocket of his evening coat, produced a small coil of stout cord, and shook it out to its full length. It had two loops near the centre in the form of slip knots. He slipped one of the loops over Goldie Kline's wrists, and tightened it. "Now you, Weasel!"

The other loop closed upon the Weasel's wrists. A moment more, and the respective ends of the cord were lashed to the respective chairs, and Jimmie Dale stepped around to the other side of the table to face the two men.

He smiled at them for a moment speculatively.

Goldie Kline burst suddenly into a torrent of blasphemy.

Jimmie Dale's smile became plaintive.

"That's rather foolish of you, Goldie," he said. "You are making quite a little noise, and from your standpoint I should say that was the one thing to avoid."

The Weasel squirmed in his chair.

"Who are youse?" he demanded hoarsely again. "Wot's de lay? Youse're no dick wid dat mask on yer map."

"You are quite right," said Jimmie Dale calmly. "As a matter of fact, I am afraid I am in the same category as yourselves to-night. Shall we say—fellow thieves? The only difference being that I have got what I came for, and you haven't."

The Weasel's rat-like little eyes narrowed. He leaned forward.

"Wot do youse mean?" he snarled.

Jimmie Dale took the morocco-leather jewel case from his pocket, opened it, and laid it down on the table in front of the two men.

"This!" he said tersely.

The men bent forward, staring. It was a minute before either spoke. Goldie Kline raised his eyes and cast a furtive, fear-startled glance at Jimmie Dale. The Weasel licked his lips again.

"My Gawd!" whispered the Weasel thickly. "It's de Gray Seal!"

Jimmie Dale made no answer.

It was Goldie Kline who spoke now. The man seemed to have pulled himself together, and in his tones was a sort of blustering bravado.

"So youse're de Gray Seal, are youse? Well, den, I don't get youse! Youse've beat us to it an' pinched de goods, damn youse! I can see dat! But wot's de big idea in hangin' around after youse've got de swag, an' stickin' up de Weasel an' me?"

Jimmie Dale closed the jewel case, and returned it to his pocket.

"That's a fair question, Goldie," he said pleasantly; "and I'll answer it. It's no cinch to shove that necklace. There's only one man who would have much chance—and that's old Isaac Shiftel." He smiled at them engagingly. "I'm sure you'll agree with me, because—the source of my information is really of no consequence at the moment—I happen to know that it was mainly, if not wholly, because Shiftel agreed to dispose of the stones that you figured the job of getting them would pay. Well, I am in exactly the same position." Jimmie Dale's smile broadened a little. "Without Shiftel the stones wouldn't pay me. I think this answers your question. I have the necklace, and you haven't; but you know where Shiftel, who seems to be extremely difficult of late to locate, can be found to-night, and I don't. And so I waited for you, because I was sure you would be kind enough to give me his address."

Goldie Kline's jaw had dropped. He shut it now with a snap.

"Well, by Gawd!" he burst out furiously. "Can youse beat dat! Say, youse've got yer nerve! Youse grabs de stuff from under our noses, an' den youse has de gall to ask us to wise youse up so's youse can get rid of it! Say, we'll see youse in hell first, won't we, Weasel?"

"Youse have said somethin', Goldie!" agreed the Weasel earnestly. "We sure will!"

"I'm so sorry," said Jimmie Dale patiently. "I really

thought you would help me out. In fact, I actually counted on it."

"Youse don't say!" The Weasel was quite at his ease now, sneering broadly.

And then Jimmie Dale leaned suddenly across the table. All trace of facetiousness was gone from both voice and manner now. He drew his watch from his pocket.

"Listen, you two—and listen *hard!*" he said evenly. "I'm going to give you two minutes to come across. It might be compounding a felony to let you get away from here, but you didn't steal anything—though that's not your fault— and I'm thinking of the long terms you would get, even for 'breaking and entering,' with your records behind you. Am I making myself clear? A little noise down here will bring the family and servants about your ears in short order—while I go out the way you came in. If they find you here, even trussed up as you are, I imagine you will find it rather difficult to explain to the police how you came to visit Mr. Melville-Dane at half past two o'clock in the morning. On the other hand, an earnest half-hour's work—the time I should like to feel I was guaranteed against any interference on your part—will free you from that cord, and once free you can walk out of here. I still hope I am making myself clear." He glanced at his watch. "One minute has already gone. Where were you to meet Shiftel?"

A whitish tinge had crept into Goldie Kline's face.

"Damn youse!" he whispered fervently.

The Weasel squirmed again in his chair. He looked at Goldie Kline.

"I ain't for goin' up for nothin'!" There was a sudden nerveless whine in his voice. "He's got de goods anyhow. We ain't goin' to *lose* nothin' by tellin'. Wot—wot d'youse say, Goldie?"

Goldie Kline gnawed at his lips.

"All right," he muttered after a moment. "Spill it. I guess dere ain't nothing else to do."

"Just a minute," said Jimmie Dale coolly. He replaced his watch in his pocket. "It would be unfortunate if there were a *mistake* in the address. I am sure your memories are good enough to recall certain instances in the underworld that will reassure on the point that the Gray Seal always pays his *debts*. I mention this simply in passing. And now— where is Shiftel waiting for you?"

It was the Weasel who answered.

"He's in de room off de back yard, down at Morley's dope joint," he said sullenly.

"Thank you!" said Jimmie Dale grimly. "I know where that is." He moved away from the table and toward the door. Here he paused for a moment. The two men were already tugging and struggling with their bonds. "I forgot to say," he said quietly, "that there is nothing of any value left in the safe! Good-night!"

And then Jimmie Dale was gone.

XIV

FIVE minutes later, Jimmie Dale climbed into the light runabout that, prior to the reception, he had unobtrusively parked in an alleyway a block from the Melville-Dane residence. He replaced his silk hat with a peaked cap which he drew out from under the seat—and the car shot forward into the street.

He drove fast now. He had no thought of speed laws. Shiftel—the Phantom—the end in sight! He had no thought for anything but that; he asked for nothing more than just this, which was at last to be granted him, of playing out the final hand with this inhuman fiend to whom murder was a trade, and crime of the basest sort a pastime. There was room now for only one of them—the Phantom or himself— in this world. The debt that lay between them was too abysmal to be plumbed or spanned in any other way.

And yet the man should have his chance; a chance to fight for his life. He was not entitled to it; he, the Phantom, under the same conditions would have struck as quickly and murderously as he could. In fact, if the Tocsin was right, as no doubt she was, the Phantom even now was preparing a trap which, to-morrow, the next day, or the day after, was intended to be sprung in the hope of snaring him, Jimmie Dale, the Gray Seal; and that trap once sprung successfully he, Jimmie Dale, would go out with no more chance for life than the flame of a candle flung to the storm! But there would be no to-morrow, or the next day, or the day after, for the Phantom and his trap; to-night, now, within the next few minutes, there would be no longer need for the Phantom to cudgel his brain for tricks and devices to lure the Gray Seal into his web!

The streets were deserted. A strange, queer silence seemed to reign over the city. Somehow it seemed sinister, premonitive—aptly so. Still Jimmie Dale drove fast. And then finally, far over on the East Side, deep in a neighbourhood as vicious and abandoned as New York had to offer, he parked his car again in a lane, sprang out, and started at a brisk walk along the block.

There was a grim, set look on his face now, as his hand, slipping into his pocket for his automatic, encountered the morocco-leather jewel case. Shiftel was waiting for the necklace! Well, Shiftel should have it—for a moment. But, at that, its safety was nowhere nearly so greatly imperilled as if it had been left as a temptation for Goldie Kline and the Weasel! To-morrow, in some way, it would be back in the Melville-Danes' possession again.

Jimmie Dale swerved sharply into a cross street, and from there into an alleyway. His pace slackened, became guarded, cautious. He knew Morley's opium den by more than hearsay. As Smarlinghue, he had been a supposed client more than once. Yes, here it was—the back of it, anyway, over this fence here, and across the yard. Well, it was the back of it he sought, wasn't it? That was what the Weasel had said—the room off the back yard.

He drew himself up to the top of the fence, dropped silently to the other side, and suddenly his pulse beat fast. Across the yard was an open, lighted window, almost on a level with the ground. Unbridled now, almost overwhelming, that sense of exhilaration was upon him again. The end of the chase! What did it not mean—for the Tocsin—for himself!

Jimmie Dale moved forward quietly, noiselessly—ten yards —another ten. He was not far from the window now, not more than another five yards. And now he could see inside. Shiftel! And now he knew another emotion—something cold, merciless, primitive in its naked thirst for retribution. The Weasel had made no "mistake!" Shiftel was there! He could see the bent form in its greasy black coat; he could see the bearded face of the old "fence" bending over a table, as he had seen it once before on a night when he had thought he had run the man to earth in the rooms old Mother Margot lived in now.

A yard more! Yes, the window was not more than a couple of feet above the ground. His automatic was in his hand now, his face masked again. Another yard—and then Jimmie Dale whirled sharply around, his face drawn suddenly in hard, tense lines. Out of the darkness, out of the nowhere, came a voice, ugly in its menace, a voice he recognised—Bunty Myers':

"There he is! Get him! The Gray Seal!"

Out of the darkness, out of the nowhere, a circle of flying shadows seemed to arise and converge upon him.

The trap!

Like lightning his brain worked; like lightning he moved now. The trap! In a flash, out of a strange bewilderment, he grasped the fact that somehow the trap of which the Tocsin had so earnestly warned him, the trap that he had so self-confidently thought he would nip in the making, was even now being sprung upon him; that his own confident plan of reaching Shiftel was in fact the very trap that had been laid for him.

The trap! And the jaws of it were that open window! And there was no other way to turn. Those on-rushing shadows, that were snarling, cursing men now, were almost upon him, blocking his retreat.

Retreat! He had no mind to retreat. It would be the end without a doubt to-night now; he had at least been right in that. But it would not be his end alone. Inside there, in through the jaws of the trap—was Shiftel!

The brain works fast. In the winking of an eye Jimmie Dale had leaped forward, and had sprung for the window sill. It was intuition perhaps that prompted him. The figure at the table, at a slight angle away from the direct line of the window, had risen, revolver levelled. Jimmie Dale plunged forward, as a man plunges in a long, low dive, over the sill and to the floor. And as he plunged, like a machine gun in action behind him, came the roar and flash of what seemed a myriad revolver shots.

It happened quick—quicker almost than the brain could grasp. The bearded, greasy old figure, intent evidently upon his victim alone, had overstepped the zone of safety, stepped a little forward into the line of the window; and now, with a wild cry, with suddenly upflung arms, as the hail of lead swept in, had pitched face forward to the floor.

And something in Jimmie Dale's soul, amidst the turmoil that was raging physically about him, gave quiet, fervent thanks. Not for a man's death—but that the burden and guilt, if it should be termed guilt to destroy such a one as this, one that, to save the life of the woman he loved, he *must* have destroyed if he could before his own end came, had been lifted from his shoulders. Shiftel was dead!

Jimmie Dale had wriggled around on the floor. He was facing the window now, firing in turn with his automatic. The low sill afforded a measure of protection. He fired from the floor over it. Shouts, yells, curses answered him; but the rush was checked, though the shots still poured in from without.

And now pandemonium seemed loosed! He glanced around him quickly. The door of the room was locked. That was obvious because they were pounding upon it now, trying to burst it in; and it had been locked, quite obviously and quite logically, in preparation for his entry into the trap, and against the possibility of any escape through what was the only means of exit he could see—except the window with its hail of bullets!

It was the end! He slipped a fresh clip of cartridges into his automatic. But now he fired with more restraint. True, it was the end, but he must be careful of his ammunition now; he would need it even more when that door gave!

It was an even break. Himself for Shiftel! It was worth it; it had been worth it—for her sake. Shiftel, the Phantom, was——

Was he mad? Had this scene from the pit of the inferno, that bursting door, these shots that hummed with hell's venom above his head, this smoke-filled, acrid-stinking room, turned his brain? Shiftel! That was not Shiftel there! Nor Gentleman Laroque! He was staring now for the first time at the still, motionless figure on the floor. The beard on the upturned face hung awry. He reached for it, and snatched it off. A thousand noises, a thousand sounds pounded at his eardrums and made mockery of the crashing blows upon the door, the vicious *spat* of bullets, the hideous yowling of those human wolves who had the Gray Seal trapped at last. This man on the floor here dead was not Shiftel, nor the Phantom in the guise of Shiftel, nor the Phantom in any other guise. *It was Little Sweeney!*

The door was yielding now. And somehow—he did not understand why or how for his brain seemed stunned—the noise and the shouts without seemed to increase in intensity. He wriggled back a little way across the room where he could best command both window and door. He had still one clip of cartridges left. He had only one hope now—that he could use them to the last one. In another minute the door would give, and——

"Jimmie!"

Yes, he was mad! Reason at the last had fled from him. That was her voice, the Tocsin's voice. As those shadows outside the window had suddenly closed in upon him out of the nowhere, so this voice, the voice he loved, came suddenly to him now out of the nowhere.

"Jimmie!"

His eyes strained over in the direction of the desk. He could see nothing. There was nothing there, unless—yes, yes, the floor seemed to have risen up a few inches above the surrounding level. A trap door!

"You!" he cried.

"Yes! Quick! Quick, Jimmie, quick!" her voice answered from below.

He flung himself forward, and wrenched the trap door wide open. It was pitch black below; he could see nothing.

"Drop, Jimmie; it's only a few feet," she called up to him.

"Bolt the trap door behind you. And, oh, hurry, Jimmie, hurry!"

He swung himself through the opening, and dropped; then reached upward behind him and closed the trap door. His fingers searched for the bolt, found it, and shot it home. He could not stand upright; he had to stoop, the opening was so low. And it was so dark he could not see his hand before his face.

"Where are you?" he cried out. "Marie, thank God for you! Marie, where are you?"

"Here," her voice replied. "Follow me; come this way."

"I can't see you—I can't see anything," he said; then quickly: "Wait! I've got a flashlight."

"No!" Her voice came back instantly. "You mustn't show a light here under any circumstances. Keep your head down, and feel your way. You can touch the walls on each side of you."

"All right!" he answered.

He could hear her moving ahead of him. Half bent over, he followed. Soft earth was under foot. It was a low, narrow tunnel of some sort, that was evident. An underground passage, of course. Morley's drug-den was well equipped!

His brain was in chaos. Shiftel, Bunty Myers, the emerald necklace, Little Sweeney! And the Tocsin here!

"Marie, I don't understand!" he burst out.

"It was the trap I warned you about," she answered back.

"Yes; I know that now," he said. "But Shiftel! That wasn't Shiftel up there. It was Little Sweeney."

"He was the cat's-paw," she said.

He stumbled on. Where did this passage lead to? Was there no end to it?

"Hold on a minute, Marie! Stop!" he pleaded suddenly. "You——"

"There is no time; there is not an instant to lose," she broke in swiftly "I—I—but never mind that. I can tell you in a few words what you do not understand as we go on. Are you listening, Jimmie?"

Listening! Listening to *her,* to her voice!

"Yes," he said; "since you will not wait."

"Well, then," she said rapidly, "the Phantom was not fool enough to close his eyes to what looked as though there were a leak somewhere on the inside. The Gray Seal had put in an appearance with too great *regularity.* He thought, too, at last, as I wrote you, that you were after him in a personal way. Therefore he meant to strike first. And so for to-night's work he sent out his orders and his plans through the *usual* channels. Is that clear?"

"Yes," said Jimmie Dale, as he groped his way along.

"If, then, there was a leak," she went on, "the plan for the night's work would reach the Gray Seal also as usual. But though the Phantom inclined strongly to the belief that *he* was the one you were after, and that the spoils of the various affairs in which you had intervened were a secondary matter, he was still not absolutely sure of it—and therefore, whether he was right or wrong, and while he hoped to get you by offering what you would believe to be himself as a bait, it was not his intention to take any chances with that emerald necklace to-night, and—" She broke off suddenly. "I don't see how you found that out!"

Jimmie Dale brought up abruptly against a sharp turning in the tunnel. He bit his lips in chagrin. In the utter darkness, in spite of the cramped posture he was forced to assume, he had tried to catch up with her, reach her.

"I followed Little Sweeney from Kerrigan's," he said. "He met Goldie Kline and the Weasel, and I overheard enough to know what was going on before I lost Little Sweeney again. They got away in an automobile."

"I see." Her voice floated back. "Well, that part of the plan was *not* passed out through the usual channels. All that was given out to the gang was that Shiftel would be here at Morley's to-night to receive some swag; but it was not until the last minute, not until an hour ago that the gang themselves were ordered to be on hand to get you if you came. After that they were kept *together* so that a leak *then,* when a leak would no longer be a lure but a warning, was impossible. If you were only after spoils, you would know nothing about the necklace, and so would not get it; but if you were after *him* you would come here, and he would get *you!* Do you still understand, Jimmie?"

"Yes," he answered; "all but Little Sweeney's part."

"It was risky business playing the part of Shiftel—something might go wrong," she said bitterly. "And the Phantom takes no risks—when he can let some one else assume them! That is why he had some one play the part of Shiftel. Little Sweeney received his orders through Limpy Mack with whom, as you know, he had worked before, not knowing that Limpy Mack and Shiftel and the unknown 'Chief' were one; and Little Sweeney of course thought it was a clever way to induce two crooks to steal the jewels, for Little Sweeney was made to believe that Shiftel had left the country for good. Limpy Mack supplied the disguise, which was actually of course the one worn by himself when he masqueraded as Shiftel."

"Good God!" gasped Jimmie Dale. "I see now!"

"Yes!" she said. "There is not much more. Little Sweeney was chosen because he had been away during your later appearances, and was therefore free from suspicion that any leak had come through him; and Goldie Kline and the Weasel were chosen for the same reason—they were wholly *outsiders*. That's all—except my share. *I* had sent you no word, no note. I didn't think you could possibly know anything about to-night; and so I didn't expect you would come here, and in that respect I thought the Phantom would fail. But I knew that Shiftel was to be here at this hour—for I believed then that it was actually Shiftel himself—and so I notified the police. If they got Shiftel, then that was the end of our troubles. They—they are there now. They came just as I reached the trap door—but"—her voice seemed to dull a little—"they haven't got the Phantom."

Jimmie Dale made no answer. His lips were tight and grimly set. The Phantom was still alive, still at liberty, still free to carry on his fiendish machinations! But—Jimmie Dale's face relaxed a little the next instant—it was not all utter failure and defeat. *She* was here! The Tocsin was here with him. And he, Jimmie Dale, was alive, where but a few minutes before he had seen no chance of life. They were together—Marie and himself. In a moment more now the tunnel must end, and she——

Her voice, suddenly low and guarded, reached him.

"Wait!" she whispered. "Stay where you are. I'll see if the way is clear."

He stood still.

A minute passed, and then she called again:

"It's all right. Come on!"

His hands still groped out before him as he moved forward again, and, groping, discovered that the tunnel here took an abrupt right-angled bend. And then as he turned the corner, and a cool, fresh current of air fanned his face, he found himself on a flight of steps, and he could straighten up and there was head room as he mounted them.

And then he was standing outside a doorway on a dark and deserted street. He could hear the sound of shouts, of revolver shots, but the sounds came faintly from the distance. They were safe now, quite safe, the Tocsin and himself. He looked quickly, eagerly around him. He called her softly.

But there was no answer—and of the Tocsin there was no sign.

XV

BEHIND THE DOORS OF THE UNDERWORLD

J IMMIE DALE turned softly, without sound, upon the bunk, easing his position. Around him were whisperings, murmurings, the stir of humans in troubled sleep, a hundred conglomerate, sinister sounds; and everywhere the sickly sweetish smell of opium.

His face was haggard, worn, drawn, in sharp, pinched lines, and there was a dull, weary look about the eyes that no "make-up" could have supplied, as a smile, grim, unbidden, settled now upon his lips. Was this reality? Perhaps it was all a dream—a dream such as the poppy brought to these dregs and lees of the underworld who stole in here, where no daylight had ever shone, to burn their suicidal incense to the God of Gray Things!

Reality! Could even his existence in itself be reality? Was it any more reality than he, as Smarlinghue, as one known far and wide throughout the underworld as a hopelessly confirmed dope fiend, represented reality? He was not Smarlinghue. There was no such person as Smarlinghue. And yet in that very character which he had created, unkempt and ragged, he lay here now in one of Hip Foo's "private" rooms, hidden deep down in the chain of sub-cellars that housed perhaps the most infamous opium joint in all New York! He was not a dope fiend. Neither taste nor drop of the drug had he ever known. And yet he had burned a thousand "pills," he had toyed with a hypodermic syringe a thousand times, and before him even now lay the pipe that the Chinese attendant had brought him but a few moments since! Was it then reality, or but a dream, ceaseless, unending, whose vividness was so acute that it aped reality? Was it a dream that somewhere, always elusive, always just beyond his reach, always just evading him, a *phantom,* evil as no other human being was evil, cunning as only one from the fiend's pit itself was cunning, diced with him out of the shadows for his life—and hers, the Tocsin's?

Jimmie Dale's eyes closed. He was conscious of great fatigue; not physical—mental. Days of striving, days of utter failure, of futility, nights of unceasing, sleepless effort lay behind him. Reality! The question answered itself. He had but to listen for an instant through these thin, flimsy partitions to know that it was not only reality, but a reality stripped of all glamour, ugly in its nakedness and its menace. It was only his brain voicing its plea for rest, giving warning that it was nearing the breaking point and that the lash could be applied too often to the slave, that had prompted the groping question.

He listened now for a moment almost involuntarily. Here was one of those underground exchanges where the secrets of the underworld passed from mouth to mouth; where the gossip of the Bad Lands circulated; where crimes were born; where he had even heard his own death, the death of the Gray Seal, decreed a score of times.

Whispers reached him. Two yeggs of the lesser breed, whose names he did not know, were in there. Their conversation was snatchy, desultory, due presumably to the fact that the opium was beginning to get in its work. There was a reference to an uptown "job" of a week ago; a dance hall fracas that had ended in a murder; the approval of the sentence passed upon one English Steve by the fellow members of his gang, and the speculation as to how many of the gang English Steve would succeed in "bumping off" before in turn English Steve finally received his own quietus.

Again Jimmie Dale turned noiselessly on his bunk. He was not interested. Ten minutes before he had made a tour of the sub-cellar here; and then, playing his part as Smarlinghue, he had flung himself down on this bunk and given his order. Neither Bunty Myers nor any other of the Phantom's underlings were in evidence. He had not actually expected to find them already here, he did not even expect them later on; but in half an hour, or an hour, luck might change, and they *might* come. He had simply made Hip Foo's his first stopping place night after night of late because it had once been the rendezvous of the men he wanted, because it was here that some of them had met on the night the place had been raided, and because, since the night that the Phantom had laid the trap for him at Morley's, Bunty Myers and the Kitten and Spud MacGuire and Muller no longer met in the back, upstairs room of Wally Kerrigan's "club." Perhaps they would again in the future—some of them—perhaps not!

Jimmie Dale's lips tightened. It had gone very badly with the Phantom's plans that night. Apart from Little Sweeney, Spud MacGuire and Muller, in the subsequent fight with the police, had both been killed. Also, it had apparently forced Bunty Myers and the Kitten into hiding. Certainly, since that night, he, Jimmie Dale, had not been able to pick up the slightest trace of either of them.

He swept his hand heavily across his eyes. He was not so sure that he could wholly glory in the outcome of that night. If the Phantom had received a blow, he, Jimmie Dale, had perhaps received one that was even more disastrous. The Phantom was still at large, still free to pursue his heinous activities, but with the abandonment of Wally Kerrigan's back room, even if only temporarily, by Bunty Myers and the rest of his associates who hung on the Phantom's orders, he, Jimmie Dale, had lost touch with everything and every one connected with the Phantom—except Mother Margot!

Mother Margot! His lips twisted in a weary smile. She had been of little service to him! So far as any information he had been able to obtain from her was concerned, she might as well have been non-existent. Not that she had attempted to mislead or lie to him; he was satisfied on that score because, being the sole connecting link with the Phantom that was left to him, he had naturally watched her more carefully than ever before. As the man in the black silk mask, the man she knew as the Gray Seal, he had held her closely to account; but he was convinced that of the Phantom's plans and movements since that night at Morley's, she was as ignorant as he was himself. Where before she had been the mouthpiece of the "Voice," as she called the Phantom, her office now had apparently become a sinecure. It was as though the Phantom, failing in the supreme effort he had made to find the "leak" among his trusted subordinates, and afraid perhaps to place further trust anywhere, had withdrawn himself completely from every one of those that formerly he had moved as pawns upon his miserable chess-board of crime.

But that did not mean the Tocsin's safety. The Phantom, as she had so well named him, master of impersonation, the Phantom alias Gentleman Laroque, alias Shiftel, alias Limpy Mack, alias heaven alone knew what else, the Phantom with his score of domiciles, if he meant now to play a lone hand, was a far more dangerous antagonist than ever before; one far harder to come at, more elusive, more safely and deeply entrenched behind——

Jimmie Dale's hand reached swiftly out for the opium pipe that lay on the stand beside the bunk. A footstep, one accompanied by a low, soft swish, was coming along the boarded corridor outside. It was probably one of the Chinese attendants, and the swish was the usual swish of the slippered feet; but if there was any one den or dive in the Bad Lands more than another where it meant literally life and death to preserve the character of Smarlinghue from all suspicion, it was here in Hip Foo's where a whisper was alone sufficient to bring down upon him, darting from its every corner and crevice, the drug crazed rat-horde of the underworld that infested the place.

The step came nearer. Jimmie Dale, the pipe apparently at his lips, lay back again upon the bunk. If the Phantom were playing a lone hand now, if he had sloughed off, as dangerous and unfit, the tools he had formerly employed, then he, Jimmie Dale, since the Tocsin was obviously steadfast in her determination to afford him no opportunity of picking up any further clue, was facing a blank wall. If, however, the veil that had shrouded the movements of the Phantom and all those who had been connected with him since that night at Morley's was simply the natural caution inspired by what had so nearly been complete disaster, then certainly, sooner or later, he, Jimmie Dale, would pick up the trail again of those, such as were left of them, who once had congregated at Wally Kerrigan's. That was why he was here in Hip Foo's to-night—on the chance that, either through their appearance in person, or through the mumbled gossip which was the freer in dens like this where the incense burned to the God of Poppy loosened men's and women's tongues, he might find the lost threads again.

He asked no more than that—only to go on to the end while there was yet time. And he was afraid to-night, afraid with a great fear. How did he even know that it was not already too late? How did he know that in her battle of wits with the Phantom which she insisted in waging alone, unaided, with her life at stake, the Tocsin, brave, resourceful, clever though she was, had not already——

Through half-closed eyes Jimmie Dale watched the curtain that hung across the doorway. Yes, undoubtedly, the footstep was no longer in evidence, and undoubtedly the curtain was being drawn stealthily aside. He made no movement. The opening widened, widened still further—and suddenly the blood went whipping through Jimmie Dale's veins in a mad, elated tide, and weariness was gone.

Reward! The light was dim, low, flickering, but he could see well enough. It was not one of the Chinese attendants. It was the shawled head of an old hag that was peering in there. Mother Margot!

Still Jimmie Dale gave no sign that he was aware of the other's presence. It was a reward at last for the days and nights that were gone! Once before she had come here to meet Bunty Myers, once before this had been the rendezvous—what else would she be here for to-night? He had evidently been right then in hoping more from Hip Foo's than from any other place. And it did not mean that she had lied to him as the Gray Seal either. It might very well be, and probably was, that, since last he had communicated with her, the Phantom had suddenly broken silence and through her was issuing his orders again.

She stood there on the threshold now, peering toward the bunk, shading her eyes with her hand as though, even in the dim light, it helped her the better to distinguish objects. And for a moment she hesitated, then she came slowly through the doorway and let the curtain fall behind her.

"Dat's youse, ain't it, Smarly?" she whispered.

Jimmie Dale sat up on the bunk, and blinked at her. There was something of grim, sardonic humour in the situation. They had been formally "introduced" that night at Wally Kerrigan's, and she knew Smarlinghue—as *Smarlinghue*. But between Smarlinghue and the man she knew, yes, and *obeyed,* as the Gray Seal, there was a gulf that she had never crossed. The trumps were very much in his hands!

Jimmie Dale blinked again, rubbed his eyes, and stared at her.

"Oh, hello!" he said, a little ungraciously. "It's Mother Margot, eh?"

She nodded without speaking.

"Well?" It was Smarlinghue who spoke. "What's the idea? I ain't standing any free rides to dreamland—the price has gone up."

Mother Margot shook her head.

"Nobody's askin' youse to," she replied a little tartly. "I ain't never been on dat kind of stuff, t'ank Gawd! I'm lookin' for some one, dat's wot I'm here for."

Jimmie Dale permitted a slightly malicious grin to flicker across his lips.

"You didn't seem to fall in love with me the night I got shown out at Wally's," he observed, "so I guess it ain't me. Try next door!"

She came a little closer, and lowered her voice.

"No, it ain't for youse," she said; "but mabbe youse'll do, if youse ain't too stewed on coke."

Jimmie Dale did not answer for a moment. Was the entrée into the Phantom's circle here at last, an entrée in the sense that, if only in a minor way, he was to be offered the opportunity of participating in the activities of Gentleman Laroque's, alias the Phantom's, gang? She was looking for some one. Who? She was, he knew, the one through whom the Phantom, always invisible himself, issued all his orders. Who, then, would she be searching for to-night save the very men that he himself would willingly pay any price to find— Bunty Myers for one, the Kitten for another!

"I ain't been here long enough, without being butted in on, to get stewed," said Jimmie Dale caustically.

She came still closer, peering at him through her spectacles, drawing her shawl with quick nervous little clutches tighter around her shoulders and throat. And then suddenly her whole manner changed; she seemed frightened, almost in despair.

"Yes, youse're all right, I can see dat now," she burst out in a hoarse, shaken whisper. "Dat was de only thing I was scared of w'en I sees youse in here—dat youse'd be stewed. Listen, Smarly, I got to get some help. An' I want youse to help me. Dere ain't no one on de whole East Side could do it de way youse could, if youse only will."

Jimmie Dale lounged back on the bunk. Mother Margot would at least not find him *eager*.

"Thanks for the bouquet!" he grinned. "The last time all you handed me was a frozen mitt."

"Aw, forget it!" she whispered passionately. "For Gawd's sake forget dat, Smarly. I ain't handin' youse no jolly. Everybody knows Smarlinghue; an' everybody knows dere ain't a dump in de Bad Lands dat he ain't wise to, an' where he don't get de glad hand. An'—an' everybody knows dey can trust Smarlinghue. *I'm* trustin' youse now. Say, give me yer word youse'll keep yer trap closed about me whether youse sits in de game or not, an' I'll come across."

"Sure!" said Jimmie Dale. "That don't cost nothing. I've never seen you to-night, if that suits you. Go ahead! Spill it!"

Mother Margot glanced furtively around her. She listened for a moment to the voices, grown thicker now and almost inaudible, coming through the partition, then she leaned close to Jimmie Dale. Her lips scarcely moved.

"I'll get mine if I'm heard, or youse snitches on me," she breathed in a frightened, jerky way. "But I got to do it. I got to do it. I've been lookin' for hours, ever since early in de afternoon, an' it ain't no good. I've looked everywhere, an' I can't find him, an'—an' I didn't darst get too nosey wid questions. Youse understand, Smarly? It's English Steve. I got to get a message to English Steve, an' if I don't he goes out. My Gawd, Smarly, youse gets dat, don't youse? He goes out."

Jimmie Dale stared at her. He experienced a sudden loss of the elation, the uplift, that he had known but a moment before in such full measure. English Steve! All the underworld knew about English Steve! It was no secret. Even those two hop-fighters in the next room, who ranked little higher than stalls and steerers in the citizenry of the Bad Lands, knew all about English Steve and his gang troubles. He, Jimmie Dale, knew all about it. As Larry the Bat he had even been personally acquainted with English Steve in the olden days. Therefore he also knew—which was the one thing that concerned him now—that English Steve had nothing to do with Bunty Myers. And it was of Bunty Myers, as the first step toward picking up again the Phantom's trail, that he had expected Mother Margot to unburden herself.

His eyes shifted to the ragged sleeve of his coat, to the dirty, frayed, protruding wristband of his shirt. He had hoped for too much evidently. Perhaps he should have known better, but that did not lessen the disappointment. True, he had called this woman from her pushcart on Thompson Street only that morning, and had talked to her as the Gray Seal over the telephone, and he had been thoroughly satisfied then that she was as ignorant as he was of either Bunty Myers' or the Phantom's movements; but until a moment ago, in view of her appearance here, he had thought that in the meantime the Phantom had communicated with her. Well, he had been wrong, it seemed, and to-night was to be only another night of hollow results added to the nights that had gone before. He had lost track of how many! It didn't matter. He had hoped for too much, that was all.

She clutched at his sleeve frantically, in pitiful pleading.

"Youse ain't afraid, are youse, Smarly?" she quavered. "Youse don't have to get in between. All I'm askin' youse is to help me find him, an' if youse finds him first to slip him a message. Youse don't have to do nothin' else."

"What's the message?" inquired Jimmie Dale, a little gruffly.

"Just tell him to duck his nut out of New York to-night, dat's all. Just tell him dat."

Jimmie Dale as Smarlinghue shook his head critically.

"He ain't that kind," he said. "I suppose you're talking about him and his gang, but everybody that ain't deaf knows he swore he'd get every last one of the outfit he used to work with before they got him, if they tried any funny business. What's the use of handing him any steer like that?"

"Never youse mind about dat," said Mother Margot quickly. "He'll go if youse tells him it was me sent de word. He ain't for runnin' into a trap, is he? Nobody but a fool 'ud do dat."

Jimmie Dale appeared to ponder the matter.

"What's the trap?" he demanded after a moment.

"I don't know," she answered miserably.

"Well then," prodded Jimmie Dale, "if you don't know that, how do you know it's to-night they're laying for him, and where do you come in? He ain't a long lost son you've discovered, is he?"

She wrung her hands suddenly.

"Oh, my Gawd, Smarly," she whispered wildly, "we're losin' time, an'—an' I'm afraid. Mabbe it's too late even now. Dere ain't no use askin' me questions dat I can't answer. I don't know how, an' I don't know where, but I knows English Steve gets his to-night if he ain't tipped off in time. For Gawd's sake don't ask me nothin' more. I owe it to English Steve to wise him up. I got to do it if I can, an' I'm askin' youse to help me. Youse will, won't youse,

Smarly? Aw, for Gawd's sake, say youse will! Youse won't be sorry. I—I'll make it up to youse. Mother Margot don't never forget."

Jimmie Dale swung his leg slowly over the edge of the bunk. Well, why not? Mother Margot's advent had brought him anything but what he had hoped for, but he was certainly no worse off than he had been before her arrival. English Steve and his gang affairs were too well known, too public, to warrant any suspicion that there was any ulterior object in Mother Margot's actions. He had not the slightest doubt but that the gang had laid their plans for the removal of English Steve to-night. It was quite on the cards. In some way Mother Margot had got an inkling of this. She probably owed English Steve a debt of some kind, due, as probably, to some crooked work in the past in which they had been engaged together. That, too, was quite on the cards. Well, why not? He had no particular interest in English Steve, but certainly he had no desire to stand by and allow a murder, even the murder of a crook, to be committed if he could prevent it. And then, too, there was another angle to the affair. Mother Margot as a *friend* of Smarlinghue might well mean far more than Mother Margot constrained by fear to be the unwilling ally of the Gray Seal. And, besides, from now until dawn his own search would be continued through the underworld anyhow; and where he looked for Bunty Myers or the Kitten, he would, as naturally as though that were his sole quest, look for English Steve.

"All right," said Jimmie Dale abruptly, as he stood up. "I'll help you if I can. I guess I know a few dumps you don't, but you keep on going yourself. We'll cover more ground that way, and get on quicker. And it wouldn't do either of us any good to be seen hunting together, neither. Beat it!"

Mother Margot caught his hand impulsively.

"I knew youse would, Smarly! I knew youse would!" she whispered in a choked voice. "Gawd bless youse, Smarly, youse're——"

It was Smarlinghue who grinned a little sheepishly, and Smarlinghue who spoke.

"Aw, forget it!" he said. "I thought you said we was losing time." He brushed past her toward the doorway. "I'll go out by the lane, you go out the other way. See?"

"Yes," she answered; "but——"

"So long!" said Smarlinghue, alias Jimmie Dale—and vanished through the doorway.

XVI

ENGLISH STEVE

IT was growing late, near midnight. Through the murk of an uninviting, almost ominous-looking basement entrance, whose light, such as it was, seeped upward to the sidewalk, Jimmie Dale emerged, and stood for a moment staring up and down the dirty, shabby street.

A grim smile was playing on his lips. Behind him, down those few dark, rickety steps up which he had just come, and thence through an ill-lighted little cobbler's shop, where a cobbler, who was a cobbler in but little more than name, held an inner door against the invasion of undesirables and the law, was a thug's den than which New York knew no worse. Debauchery and crime, unbridled and unlicensed, held sway there. None entered save the initiated—or those the initiated lured there to fleece and work their will upon. Likewise, it was a refuge from the law, and, as a refuge, was without its peer. Mickey the Cobbler might not be a very good cobbler or a past master of his art, but he was a cheery sort and always paid his bills, and never overcharged the poverty-stricken neighbourhood that innocently believed it supported him with its patronage! So why should it not be safe? Mickey the Cobbler stood high in the estimation of the community, and therefore brought no suspicion upon himself from the police.

Jimmie Dale shrugged his shoulders. What did it matter? There were dozens of places like that—and he had been in and out of dozens of them since he had left Mother Margot at Hip Foo's a few hours ago. What did it matter the degree of pest hole from which he had just come? In so far as he was concerned it had yielded him nothing, and in that respect it was like all the rest. His search to-night had been doubly fruitless because he had had a double errand. He had found no trace of Bunty Myers on his own account, or of English Steve on Mother Margot's.

Again he shrugged his shoulders. He had about given the latter up. As a matter of fact, it had only been secondary in any case. And yet he had kept faith with Mother Margot. He had visited English Steve's lodging house, and he had visited the known haunts of the gang that now held English Steve's life forfeit—and all this before even he had widened his search to embrace the secret pest holes of Crimeland such as the one he had just left. And he had been rewarded only by failure everywhere.

He could go on, of course, and he would go on until dawn broke, prompted by the prime urge to find Bunty Myers; but now, for the moment, the weariness of it all seemed to be creeping back upon him again, and this time not without its physical as well as its mental demands for at least a measure of consideration. His eyes roved down the street. At the corner, drawn up to the curb, there was a lunch wagon. He was tired and hungry. A queer, whimsical little smile touched his lips. What could be better? A lunch wagon and Smarlinghue, unkempt, ragged, dissolute in appearance, went well and in perfect harmony one with the other!

Jimmie Dale turned abruptly, and walked to the corner. Here he climbed the three wooden, abbreviated steps that permitted entrance to the antiquated vehicle, and sidled up to the counter.

The lunch wagon for the moment was without customers. The proprietor, rousing himself from a doze, laid a mug of hot coffee and a sandwich on the counter at Jimmie Dale's mumbled request, slid a pot of mustard in the general direction of the sandwich, and subsided again into semi-unconsciousness upon some amazingly existent resting place in the crowded space behind the counter.

Jimmie Dale stared around him, and, as he ate, a sort of ironic facetiousness settled upon him. A picture of the St. James Club, with its polished silver and its snowy napery, rose before his mind's eye. Here he was Smarlinghue; there he was Jimmie Dale, the millionaire. He was almost beginning to wonder which of the two was his real, actual entity. Jimmie Dale; Smarlinghue—the Gray Seal! If it were ever known! His eyes fastened on the ungraceful proprietor, whose white coat was long overdue at the washtub, and whose white cook's hat was limp and grease spotted. It seemed a far cry to the white-haired, immaculate, perfectly trained Jason, his own butler, who, too, sometimes served him with coffee and sandwiches!

His mind mulled on. He kept staring about him. It was strange! The place somehow seemed familiar. Well, why shouldn't it? He had been in a lunch wagon before. Not this one probably, but there wasn't much difference in the genus lunch wagon, was there? No, that wasn't it! It seemed rather to be striving to revive a memory that somehow had to do with——

Yes, he had it now! English Steve! But that was years ago—back in the days when he, Jimmie Dale, was Larry the Bat in the underworld instead of the Smarlinghue of to-day. It was in a lunch wagon just like this. English Steve had been there, and two or three others of like ilk. They had adjourned to English Steve's room for a game of cards, and he, Jimmie Dale, as Larry the Bat, had accepted the invitation to join them. Well, what of it? That wasn't where English Steve lived now. English Steve had gone up in his profession since he had lived in what was little better than a shed behind old Michael's ship-chandler's shop. And he, Jimmie Dale, had already been to English Steve's more pretentious, if still seedy, quarters of to-day.

Strange, the stirring of that memory! What was it trying to suggest? That English Steve still— It was absurd, of course! That was years ago. It was the last place in all New York that any one would look for English Steve to-day. The last place that any one would——

Jimmie Dale's fingers fumbled in his pockets, and extracted a coin. He laid it on the counter, mumbled again at the proprietor—this time, a good-night—and shuffled his way out to the street.

The *last* place! The phrase battered at his mind now. If that were so, it was the *one* place to look! And why was it so absurd? There was more than one man in New York who maintained two establishments, and on a far more extensive scale, without publishing the fact broadcast! English Steve was a crook of no mean order, and such an arrangement might well have stood him in good stead more than once in respect of the police, and, for that matter, with his erstwhile associates—as it perhaps was serving him now at this minute. With his increasing prominence, his rise in the sordid realm of crime, English Steve had publicly moved into a more "exclusive" neighbourhood among the élite of Crimeland; but it might well be that he had continued to pay rent for his former lodging—without any one being the wiser for it save old Michael, his landlord, whose shop was stocked with merchandise which consisted mainly of ships' stores and fittings purloined by the wharf rats along the river front! Birds of a feather!

It was worth putting to the test, at least. Certainly it was a tangible, definite objective—something he had not had before all night. He hurried now, twisting and turning through alleyways and narrow, darkened streets, until finally he had worked his way into a neighbourhood down near the East River shore.

The buildings were fewer here, more scattered; there was a generous sprinkling of vacant lots; few lights, and no pedestrians. He halted at last in front of a low, squat, dingy building, with large double doors and a grimy, unwashed show window, through which latter, from the rays of a distant street lamp, was just discernible a display of miscellaneous second-hand ships' fittings—a heap of tarpaulin, ropes, blocks, tackles and other articles of like nature. This was old Michael's. If the man had another name, he, Jimmie Dale, did not know what it was. There was only one old Michael on the East Side, and that was enough.

The place was in darkness. It stood detached, unprotected

by either fence or enclosure, and Jimmie Dale now made his way rapidly around to the rear. Here a sort of extension, in the shape of an exaggerated lean-to, projected out from the back of the building. It was here that in the days gone by, a miserable, barely weather-proof hole, English Steve had made his home. And here, too, as in front, the place was in utter darkness.

Jimmie Dale stepped to the door, and knocked softly upon it. There was no answer. He knocked louder, insistently. There was still no response. And then he smiled a little ironically at himself. He had come quite a long way—and quite probably on a fool's errand. Certainly English Steve did not appear either to be at home or in hiding here!

He stood at the door for a moment frowning. He had begun to doubt very much now that English Steve had ever cast eyes on the place again from the day he had taken up his quarters nearer the Bowery; but mere doubt did not in any way disprove the theory that, somehow, back there in the lunch wagon, had suddenly taken possession of him. English Steve might very well be absent at this precise moment—and might very well at the same time still be old Michael's tenant.

Jimmie Dale's jaws snapped suddenly together. He had come quite far enough to make it worth while to find out that much anyhow! He tried the door. It was locked, of course.

From one of the upright pockets in the leather girdle beneath his threadbare vest, Jimmie Dale drew out a little blued-steel pick-lock, and from another a diminutive, though none the less powerful, flashlight. For a moment the trained fingers worked swiftly at the lock, then the door swung open, and Jimmie Dale stepped inside.

He closed the door quietly behind him, and for an instant stood still, listening; then the white ray of the flashlight lanced suddenly through the blackness, darting here and there over walls and floor.

A smile crept grimly to Jimmie Dale's lips. English Steve for the moment might not be at home; but he, Jimmie Dale, or his intuition, or what had seemed perhaps a far-fetched deduction from a memory of years gone by, or whatever else one might call it, had after all not been at fault. English Steve still lived here—when it suited English Steve to do so! The room was in no way changed since the night he had played cards here with English Steve. Even the man's clothes were strewn about, here across a chair, there even on the floor. An empty beer bottle, and beside it a slab of cheese and a portion of a loaf of bread, stood upon the table. But it was not these proofs of occupancy that caused Jimmie Dale's smile to tighten now. *They* might belong to anybody. The flashlight was holding steadily on a large, half-page photograph, cut from a Sunday supplement, that was tacked on the wall. He remembered it very well because English Steve while still sober that night had pointed it out with pride, and thereafter when not so sober had pointed it out another dozen times. It was a treasured possession of English Steve, and whatever else English Steve might have left behind him had he vacated the place for good, he most certainly would not have left that. It did not amount to much; it was utterly valueless; but to English Steve it had been, and still was obviously, a source of intense, if somewhat childish, gratification. It was a photograph intended to demonstrate the extent of a record crowd at a race course somewhere, and in the foreground, perhaps the most prominent figure of all, the photographer by chance had snapped the heavy black-moustached, rather rakish-looking figure of English Steve.

Jimmie Dale leaned back against the table in the centre of the room. Well, that was settled, and for such satisfaction as the establishment of his theory afforded him his trip had had its reward. But what was he to do now? Wait here for English Steve's return? English Steve might return in an hour, or in two days from now—or *never,* if Mother Margot was right, and English Steve fell into whatever trap was set for him to-night! On the other hand, to resume a blind search through the underworld again seemed to offer no greater likelihood of finding the man than was presented by the possibility of English Steve returning here. Indeed, if the man were keeping under cover, as seemed more than probable, since, after hours of search, he, Jimmie Dale, had been able to find not a single trace of the other, then the chance that right here was where English Steve might be met with sooner than anywhere else was not without its logical argument. And yet——

The flashlight was still circling inquisitively about the room. Jimmie Dale's eyes followed the ray abstractedly. It passed across the open doorway of an inner room. There had been a cot in there, he remembered—English Steve's bedroom.

Mechanically he moved forward in that direction from the table; and then suddenly, with a low, sharp cry, as the flashlight shot forward into the inner room, he halted, hardfaced, staring ahead of him across the threshold. He had been right in his theory, doubly right, for the search ended here; and Mother Margot had been right, and her fears had been only too well justified! Sprawled across the floor, his head in a dark, crimson pool, lay the body of English Steve.

For the fraction of a second, no more, Jimmie Dale remained motionless, and then he was across the threshold and on his knees beside the other. Yes, the man was dead. Jimmie Dale turned a little then, and the flashlight circled swiftly in all directions about him. There was no weapon— only the bullet hole in English Steve's right temple. The end of the search, the warning that Mother Margot had tried to give, had come too late. English Steve had been murdered.

So the gang had had their way, had they? It was dirty, miserable work, crook though English Steve might be! Jimmie Dale's jaws were clamped now, as he leaned forward again and drew a paper, already protruding as though it had half dropped out when the man had fallen, from the inside pocket of English Steve's coat. It was a folded sheet of foolscap size. He opened it out, his flashlight playing upon it. In the folds was a small newspaper clipping; while the paper itself was covered with a rough design, or plan, as of some interior.

He stared in a perplexed way at the clipping for a moment. It had been cut from the middle of a paragraph, and contained only one complete sentence; but from the sentence itself, and the fragments of context that preceded and followed, it was obviously the report of some jewellery auction. He read it once—and again:

unusually good value. The pendant was finally knocked down to Mr. Max Linesthal after spirited bidding for four thousand, three hundred and eighty-five dollars. A cluster ring set with the

From the clipping Jimmie Dale looked again at the roughly drawn sketch, then his eyes reverted to the still form on the floor. A minute, two, passed as he stood there. Something seemed to tighten in Jimmie Dale's throat.

"Poor devil!" he whispered—and thrust the clipping and paper abruptly into his own pocket.

He turned away then, and began a rapid search of the two rooms.

Still another ten minutes passed, and then Jimmie Dale stepped out into the night again, locked the door behind him, and, hurrying now, headed back into the East Side.

XVII

JIMMIE DALE'S face was drawn in sharp, set lines, as he went swiftly along. In a sense the brutal, sordid affair was clear enough. The clipping spoke for itself; there had been an auction sale of jewellery, and Max Linesthal had bought in a pendant worth roughly four thousand dollars. The drawing was probably a sketch of old man Linesthal's place. Jimmie Dale nodded his head sharply. Everybody knew Linesthal. Max Linesthal was a prominent, if somewhat eccentric figure on the East Side, who lived alone in a combined office and dwelling that consisted of the ground floor of a small, two-story house on a cross street within a block of the Bowery. The old man, sometimes on his own account, sometimes acting for private interests on commission, or even for the bigger jewellers who for very justifiable business reasons did not wish to appear at the auctions, was a large and well-known buyer of second-hand jewellery of the better sort.

This was quite plain, and the inference from it seemed equally so. English Steve had seen the account of the auction, knew that a valuable pendant was in Linesthal's possession, and had in some way managed to obtain the information that had enabled him to make a rough, working sketch of the old jeweller's flat. Following out the inference to its logical conclusion, therefore, English Steve either had already robbed Max Linesthal of the pendant, or had proposed to do so before the night was out.

A puzzled light for an instant crept into Jimmie Dale's dark eyes. What was the *date* of the clipping? It might be a week old; the auction might have been held days ago! He shook his head impatiently, as though irritated at his own momentary stupidity. It was nothing of the sort; or, if it was, then what he had found in English Steve's pocket meant nothing at all. No robbery of any such nature as that could be committed without its being known everywhere in the underworld at least within a short time after the police were on the scene. Therefore, unless the robbery had been committed yesterday, or the day before, or a week ago, which it most certainly had not, since nothing was known of it in the underworld, the clipping, to have any present significance, must almost certainly have been cut from a paper of very recent date, for English Steve would realise that there was no guarantee, rather the opposite in fact, that Max Linesthal would keep the pendant in his possession for any length of time before he disposed of it again.

The whole thing narrowed down then to two suppositions: English Steve had not yet carried out his plans when he was shot down, presumably, by the gang; or he had already committed the robbery just previous to his murder and the pendant was then, at that time, either in his immediate possession or hidden somewhere, probably in his rooms. But he, Jimmie Dale, had searched and had found nothing. It might still be there, still craftily hidden, of course; but if not, and the robbery *had* been committed, then the alternative seemed blatantly obvious. The gang, sworn to English Steve's destruction, had found the pendant in their victim's possession, and taken it—that was all.

Jimmie Dale went on, traversing block after block. And now a queer, whimsical smile brought a softer expression to his face. Those papers were damning evidence, and he had appropriated them without right or reason! He shrugged his shoulders. Perhaps! It had been impulse. He admitted that; but it was not an impulse that he regretted, or would undo now if he could. If it had been only an *intended* robbery, one that had not known fruition, there was sorrow and shame enough for some one—perhaps a mother; perhaps an old father; certainly some one who loved even English Steve—without needlessly adding to a measure already so miserably full. There would be time enough for those papers to come into the hands of the police if they were needed to point the way to a more thorough search of English Steve's rooms than he, Jimmie Dale, had made; or failing that, to English Steve's erstwhile gang and present murderers in whose possession the pendant then must be.

The softer expression vanished, and there came again a troubled look into Jimmie Dale's face. There was still another angle to the affair, one he did not like. If the robbery *had* been committed, it must have taken place, say, quite a little while before midnight in order to have allowed English Steve time enough for its actual accomplishment, the time to get back from Max Linesthal's to old Michael's, and, on top of that, the time to account for what had then occurred in his own rooms. That, then, would be long before he, Jimmie Dale, had started out from the lunch wagon, and had anything come to the ears of the police up to that time, it would as certainly have been known in the resorts. And there had been not even a whisper of it. Why then had not Max Linesthal sent out an alarm, or, rather—*what had happened to Max Linesthal?* Jimmie Dale shook his head again. No; that was putting it in its worst phase. English Steve would not have hesitated at anything in the nature of violence perhaps, if, for instance, he had been caught in the act; but it was far more likely that his work would have been done so secretly and successfully that it had not even now been discovered. And yet, at a fairly early hour of night, before possibly the old jeweller had even gone to bed, to break in, blow a safe, and——

Jimmie Dale shrugged his shoulders. The answer lay at Max Linesthal's. He was going there now—he smiled grimly to himself—via the lane and the back door, secretively, like a thief himself. It would hardly do for Smarlinghue to present himself at the front door, and, if Max Linesthal responded to the summons, inquire if a robbery had been perpetrated! It would be even worse, if a robbery and perhaps violence to Max Linesthal had taken place, should Smarlinghue have been seen in or near the house. And that was the vital question. He could not morally side-step it. The old jeweller lived alone. Had Max Linesthal come to any harm?

Jimmie Dale's pace slowed now suddenly to one of almost hesitancy. He was very near the place now; it was just around the corner. Perhaps it would be safer if, even by the back door, instead of Smarlinghue, it was Jimmie Dale who went! But it was quite a little distance from here to the Sanctuary where through one door Smarlinghue could enter, and through the French window on the squalid court-yard, and thence to the lane, Jimmie Dale could emerge. No! It would take too much time to go to the Sanctuary; and, besides, it could serve no real purpose. He did not propose to be seen—or heard. If nothing had happened in Max Linesthal's place yet, nothing would happen now since English Steve was dead, and he, Jimmie Dale, would leave as unostentatiously as he entered; if, on the other hand, the break had been made, he would leave with equal unos-tentatiousness and the police in some way, anonymously, could be notified. Even as Smarlinghue then, well known as Smarlinghue was in that neighbourhood, he was quite safe.

He slipped suddenly into the mouth of a lane that opened beside him. The slouching gait was gone now. He was running swiftly, silently, in the darkness. There was no question of locating Max Linesthal's back yard. His years of Larry the Bat in the old Sanctuary, of Smarl-inghue in the new, where his life had literally depended upon it, had taught him every inch of the network of lanes and alleyways in this section of the East Side.

And now, with a lithe spring Jimmie Dale was over a fence, and in another instant, running across the yard, was crouched before a door that opened almost on a level with the ground. There was no light anywhere. He could hear no sound—save the distant rumble of the elevated from the direction of the Bowery. And then the slim, sensitive fingers of Jimmie Dale, no less deft or agile for the grime and uncared-for appearance that was theirs as an integral part of Smarlinghue, were at work again with the little pick-lock.

The door opened, closed—without a sound. Jimmie Dale stood inside. It was as though a shadow of but a moment ago outside in the darkness and silence had moved—and vanished.

But it was not dark here in the narrow hallway. A little ahead, a faint light showed through from a partially open doorway. Nor was it silent. Voices reached him, though the words themselves were not distinguishable.

Jimmie Dale stood for an instant motionless. What did it mean? A mare's nest? A late visitor? Something equally commonplace? The sketch in his pocket reproduced itself in a mental picture before his eyes. The four rooms from front to rear each had a door opening into the one next to it, and each had a door opening on this narrow passage here. The room ahead from which the light came was the second one from the front, the room that showed the safe marked on the plan. There had been no light showing as he had come along the lane, of course, because the rooms were on the opposite side of the house, and there were apparently no windows in the hallway here.

What did it mean? If nothing had happened, nothing would happen since English Steve was dead. His mind insisted on reiterating that statement. What was it, then? An ordinary, perhaps business, visitor; or the aftermath of the robbery in the shape of the presence of the police?

He stole forward cautiously, without sound, hugging the wall. The voices grew more distinct. And then, back against the wall, himself unseen, protected both by the angle at which he stood and the angle of the partially opened door, he stood staring into the lighted room.

Reality! Strange how that thought had obsessed him all night. Well, at least, this wasn't reality—or else his reason was in collapse, his sanity a gibing mockery. The room was evidently used by Max Linesthal as a bedroom, even though he kept his safe there, for the bed was there too, and Max Linesthal in his nightclothes sat lashed, a prisoner in a chair. He could understand that; but after that he was either mad or it was all a myth. A man was kneeling at the safe. He knew the man; he knew him quite well. He had even been with him that evening, had even left him not more than half an hour ago—only he had left the man lying dead upon the floor of a miserable shack with a bullet hole through his right temple, and it was the dead man who was kneeling there now at the safe. The man at the safe was English Steve.

Brain and vision now both seemed blurred. Jimmie Dale hung there. He was trying to fight his way out of some mental morass, wasn't he? The man was dead, and he was lying in a pool of blood miles away, and yet he was here, moving, yes, and speaking, just as though he were alive.

"Come on, now! Come across!" the man snapped at the bound figure in the chair. "You know what'll happen if you don't! You know me, don't you? You've seen me often enough around these parts."

"Yes, I—I know you." Max Linesthal was an old man; and it was perhaps only the cords that held him from collapsing in his chair, for his face was deathlike in its fear. "You—you're English Steve."

"Bull's-eye!" snapped the man at the safe again. "Well, that ought to be enough to teach you what's good for your health. You get just one minute. Take your choice. If I have to blow the safe, I might as well set you up against it for the pad! Get me? Now then, what's the combination? Quick!" He reached out and gave a sudden, vicious wrench at the leg of the chair.

"I—I'll tell you," the old man cried out hoarsely. "Wait! I—I'll tell you. It's twenty-eight and a half left, nineteen——"

Jimmie Dale was not listening. Was he *really* mad? Yes, perhaps; but whether the man was dead or not, he was robbing the safe. And he, Jimmie Dale, could do nothing! He was Smarlinghue. To interfere with any crook's work was to bring the enmity of the underworld down upon the offender. It was the law of the underworld. It would destroy Smarlinghue. Better that Linesthal should lose his jewels—a thousand times better. Smarlinghue was the one chance he, Jimmie Dale, had to find the Phantom, the one chance he had to stand between the woman that he loved and the death that threatened her. With the doors of the underworld once closed against Smarlinghue, there was no——

Slowly, as though the act were almost subconscious, his hand crept now toward his pocket, crept into it, snuggled around the butt of his automatic, and, snuggling, tightened suddenly in a fierce, convulsive grip. The safe was open now, and the man kneeling there had his back to Linesthal in the chair, his side face to the door. He was ransacking the interior of the safe. Books and papers were being flung on the floor. A diamond pendant glistened in the light. It was laid on the table beside the safe. There were other jewels. They began to make a glittering little heap. But it was curious, strangely curious that the heavy black moustache should suddenly have seemed to sag down at one side; strange that the man should be taking the time now to pause in his work to twirl at it like some sophisticated dandy! No—it was off! And now the man was carefully readjusting it.

Through Jimmie Dale's veins, as though some floodgates were suddenly rent asunder, his blood was racing now in a wild, mad, surging tide. Laroque! It was Gentleman Laroque, alias *the Phantom!* The master of impersonation! Yes, he understood now! There was no madness in his brain. He understood! It was hellish in its cunning—a devil's alibi. The Phantom, if he were not entirely playing a lone hand through lack of trust in his erstwhile tools and pawns, was at least playing the major rôle. A safe rôle! *His alibi was a dead man!*

Swift as lightning flashes Jimmie Dale's mind worked now. Yes, he understood. It was the Phantom, not the gang, who had murdered English Steve. It was the Phantom, not English Steve, who had taken that clipping from the paper, made that sketch, and placed them in the dead man's pocket. Max Linesthal would be robbed, and would swear that it was English Steve—the Phantom had but a moment gone taken care to make doubly sure of that point—then English Steve would be found murdered; the police would attribute the murder without an instant's hesitation to the gang who had boasted everywhere that they would take English Steve's life; and to the gang, too, having failed to find the jewels elsewhere, would be attributed, even as he, Jimmie Dale, had thought might be the case, the possession of the proceeds of the robbery from Max Linesthal's safe. That was why the robbery was being pulled here now in so open and bare-faced a manner, intentionally so, as part of the plan, an integral, vital part of the plan—to establish the alibi that English Steve could never now refute!

The room seemed to swim before Jimmie Dale's eyes— *red*. Smarlinghue! What did it matter now if Smarlinghue were seen, if Smarlinghue lived or died, so that this inhuman fiend found his end too at the same time! That was what Smarlinghue existed for—the final reckoning—the end. And it was here now. There was the man he had sought through days and nights of ceaseless, torturing effort. The Phantom! Primal, elemental, his soul itself seemed stripped of all else but a blind, savage——

What was that? The doorbell, wasn't it? The doorbell in two quick, short rings! Jimmie Dale, about to step forward into the other room, his automatic already flung forward, instinctively held motionless for an instant—and in that instant he saw the Phantom leap to his feet, and whirl to the electric-light switch just beside the safe. There was a *click*. The house was in utter blackness.

But Jimmie Dale was in action now. A signal, of course, those two rings! Why? From whom? But it didn't matter now. Nothing mattered save to come to grips with the Phantom in there. It was pitch black, but he knew what the other's next move would be as well as though the room were still alight.

With a bound, Jimmie Dale was through the doorway and into the room. The table—those jewels! They were what the Phantom had come here for—and signal or no signal, be its meaning what it might, the Phantom would not leave without them if he could help it.

Jimmie Dale brought up against the table with a crash. His hand swept swiftly across its top, and as he brushed the jewels to the floor, to safety, a hand, groping it seemed, touched his—and was instantly drawn away before he could grasp it.

A snarl came out of the darkness on the other side of the table. A cry of terror rang out from the old man lashed in the chair. And then a blinding flash, the roar of a revolver shot, as the Phantom fired—and missed.

And Jimmie Dale laughed now, laughed with the tongue flame of the shot still hot upon his cheek, and, hurling the table out of the way, he flung himself forward again. He could not see. He could only spring straight for the spot where the shot had come from. He could not fire in return—he might hit the old man in the chair.

His fingers closed, gripped at a sleeve, tightened, and his other hand, with clubbed automatic, swung upward in a fierce, short-arm jab. And his soul cried out in joy as he felt the blow go home.

There was a sharp cry of pain; then a sudden, furious wrench that tore the sleeve from Jimmie Dale's grasp—and then the sound, deadened now, almost lost in Max Linesthal's terrified cries, of a step racing across the floor.

Jimmie Dale's jaws clamped hard together. To use his flashlight was to offer himself as a target that would not be missed a second time. But the man was making for the door, of course. Jimmie Dale leaped back in the darkness across the room—too late! The door slammed. He heard it locked. He heard the footsteps racing down the little hallway toward the back entrance.

But if there was no time to unlock this one, there was still another door—the connecting door from this room into the next, and from there into the hall. His flashlight now! It gleamed as he wrenched it from his pocket and ran to the connecting door. Was this, too, locked! Strange, those scattered jewels on the floor; that uncouth creature in a nightgown lashed in a chair and screaming in fright! He wrenched again at the door. No, it was not locked; but it was badly warped, and it stuck. His shoulder, all his body weight, went against it. It gave now, almost bursting from its hinges.

Jimmie Dale lunged through. It had cost him time; time enough, he was afraid, to allow the Phantom to get away across the yard, and—— Yes! He had gained the rear door himself now. No one was in sight. But it was dark, damnably dark, and— What was that noise? It seemed to be a commotion of some sort going on in the street out in front of the house. The neighbours must have heard the old jeweller's screams. He was still screaming. Well, it didn't matter what it was! There was still a chance. The Phantom could not yet be very far away, and he must have gone by the lane.

Jimmie Dale was running now. In an instant he had crossed the yard; and then, as he poised to swing himself over the fence, he drew suddenly back instead, and crouched down in the shadows. Some one was climbing over the fence *from* the lane not ten yards away from where he stood. A voice, muffled, gruff, reached him:

"Look out for that damned nail, sergeant!"

The police! A form, silhouetted against the night, showed on the top of the fence for a moment, then dropped to the ground. It was followed by another. Jimmie Dale crouched closer in against the fence in the shadows. He gnawed his lip now in bitter chagrin. He was not afraid of being discovered, it was far too dark for that; but he knew that with this further delay any hope of finding the Phantom again was definitely at an end.

The two men were joined by a third. They crossed the yard, and disappeared inside the house.

Cautiously now, Jimmie Dale moved farther on along the side of the fence away from the house. With the Phantom gone, it became purely a question of self-preservation now. Smarlinghue found here by the police and subjected to a search, held perhaps until the make-up, worn off in a police cell, disclosed Jimmie Dale, was but little more pleasant to contemplate than was the present realisation of the Phantom's escape!

Well, it should be safe enough here. He was at the far end of the yard now; and silently, quickly, he swung himself over the fence into the lane. He broke into a run, swerved into an alleyway that crossed the lane some fifty yards farther on, and, following this, finally emerged on a cross street a block away from the old jeweller's house.

There was a certain strange, abnormally cold composure upon him now; a sort of philosophical acceptance of the fact that the Phantom had got away. But his mind was probing, sifting, searching for the answer that would explain the direct cause of the Phantom's escape, leaving him, Jimmie Dale, victor only to the extent of having saved for the old jeweller the contents of his safe. Who was it who had given that signal, which, so evidently now, had been a warning that the police were at hand? And how did it happen that the police had known anything about what was going on in Max Linesthal's? It wasn't the shot or Max Linesthal's screams—there hadn't been any disturbance up to the time the doorbell had rung!

Jimmie Dale, shuffling along, as Smarlinghue always shuffled, went up the block, turned the corner of the street on which Max Linesthal's house stood—and as though suddenly attracted by the little crowd that had gathered in front of the old jeweller's, made his way forward in that direction. He reached the fringe of the crowd as a man in the uniform of a police lieutenant, jumping from a car, pushed his way unceremoniously through the rather tough-looking aggregation on the sidewalk, and halted before a policeman who stood on duty at the door. Jimmie Dale's eyes narrowed for an instant. That was Klinger, a lieutenant in the precinct. It might be worth while!

Jimmie Dale, as Smarlinghue, was apparently actuated now by no other motive than an ill-mannered, morbid curiosity that prompted him to secure the best vantage point that he could, for, as he wormed and elbowed his way nearer the lieutenant, his mouth was agape, breathless with interest, in a sort of senile way.

He caught the lieutenant's quick flung question to the officer at the door:

"Did you get him, Lynch?"

"No, sir," the man answered.

"You didn't! How's that? That woman, whoever she was, handed us a fake tip over the phone, then?"

Smarlinghue's ragged form edged still closer to the two officers, as though his curiosity were now beyond the bounds of restraint, as though he were not only utterly oblivious to, but quite innocent of the impropriety of standing there with blear, blinking eyes and gaping mouth, greedily drinking in a conversation by no means intended for his ears. The woman, whoever she was! It was the Tocsin, then, who had sent the warning to the police. It couldn't have been any one else.

"No, sir," the man addressed as Lynch answered. "It was straight enough, only there was an outside worker on the job, I guess. Anyway, just as we got to the corner over there and started to cross the street, a man ran up to Linesthal's door here, and then beat it like blazes down the street, and got away."

"Did you get a look at him? Know who he was?"

"We aren't sure," Lynch replied. "But O'Grady said he thought it looked like the Kitten."

The Kitten! Jimmie Dale was fumbling with his battered hat. The crowd, as it jostled, had suddenly pushed him none too gently against the police lieutenant's elbow.

Lieutenant Klinger swung sharply around.

"Send this damned mob about their business!" he snapped at the policeman. "And maybe it wouldn't be a bad idea to run in one or two of them while you're at it. Some of 'em look as though they were due for it!" He stared suddenly into Jimmie Dale's face. "You, eh, Smarlinghue? Hop-fighting, I suppose! What the hell are you doing around here?"

"Me?" Smarlinghue circled his lips with his tongue. "I—I ain't doing nothing," he mumbled—and shrinking back through the crowd, and casting furtive glances over his shoulder in the direction of the police lieutenant while the crowd laughed, Smarlinghue scurried hurriedly down the street.

XVIII

THE VOICE

IT was like the glow of a firefly. It flitted here and there, lancing its tiny stabs of light indefatigably through the darkness. From somewhere without, in the distance, muffled, there came faintly the rumbling of wheels, the clatter of a horse's hoofs on the pavement. There was no other sound.

Jimmie Dale rose from his hands and knees, and, with the diminutive flashlight switched off now, stood staring around him in the darkness. Under the black silk mask his forehead furrowed. This was one of Mother Margot's rooms—the room from which the Phantom had so mysteriously disappeared on that first night. He had searched here before—more than once—in an effort to discover the secret of the Phantom's disappearance. But he had never found anything. To-night, because he had never been satisfied with his previous efforts, and because he had now been afforded a better opportunity of searching the place than ever before, he had returned to it again. He had been at it for two hours now. And still he had found nothing.

Both Mother Margot and the Tocsin had warned him to beware of the place—that it was a trap. Both had warned him that the Phantom asked nothing better than to lure him here. He shook his head. That might well have been true of a month ago, when, in the guise of Isaac Shiftel, alias Gentleman Laroque, the Phantom's unaccountable disappearance from this room before his, Jimmie Dale's, eyes, might naturally have been relied upon to bring him back without loss of time in the hope of getting at the bottom of the mystery. But not to-day. It was too long ago now.

If, as a trap, it had not proved effective almost immediately after it was baited, the Phantom, from the standpoint of pure logic, must long since have given over any hope of it ever proving effective as a trap at all.

Jimmie Dale smiled grimly. He had, in spite of warnings, invaded the place almost immediately after that night—and he had not been able to find even a trap, let alone the secret of the Phantom's disappearance! Nor was Mother Margot in the secret. He was convinced of that. True, she had been installed here by the Phantom when the latter had been forced to vacate the premises after the police raid, and she had obviously been installed here for the purpose of keeping any stranger from renting the rooms, and therefore, by her occupancy, of safeguarding that secret for the Phantom, but of its nature he was sure she was ignorant. He doubted, indeed, if the Phantom trusted any one to that extent!

But, in any case, Mother Margot was away to-night. And so to-night's conditions offered him the opportunity for a search that, prolong it as he chose, was almost guaranteed against any interruption, or, as he felt confident now, any risk of the place proving a trap. Mother Margot was away. He did not know where she was. It did not matter. Presumably there was devil's work afoot again to-night, and she was engaged in her share of it. He only knew that for the first time since she had succeeded the Phantom as the tenant of these rooms, she had absented herself from her usual haunts. As Smarlinghue, who at her request had haunted the dens and dives of the underworld for one English Steve last night, he had been free, without risk of bringing any suspicion upon the character of "Smarlinghue," to seek her out openly at her pushcart—which covered her real activities —on Thompson Street that morning. But she had not been there. She had, however, in view of what had transpired the previous night, obviously expected him, for he had found a message waiting for him with an old Italian who had his cart next to hers.

"You Smarly?" the old Italian had said. "Margot go away one, two day—come back."

Through the darkness Jimmie Dale stared around him, his brows still knitted. The best opportunity he had ever had of searching these rooms had been his to-night, and he had seized it, but was there any use in continuing the search? He had the rest of the night before him, for that matter, if he chose to devote it to that purpose—but was it worth while? He had covered every inch of the floor, every inch of the walls up to a reasonable height, and his search had gone utterly unrewarded. He had been minute, painstaking, exact, thorough to a degree, and he had found nothing. Was there any use in going all over it again?

He half turned away toward the door, but halted again. There was a secret here—even if he had never been able to find it. There was a clue here—even if so far it had proved but a phantom clue. That fact would not down. He hesitated an instant, and then, with a shrug of his shoulders, moved softly halfway across the room. Well, once more, then!

He began to reconstruct again the scene of that first night— here in this room, the inner one of the two that Mother Margot now occupied. It was exactly here he had stood when Isaac Shiftel, stripped of his disguise, had suddenly turned off the light and in the ensuing darkness had vanished, as that trite saying had it, into thin air. The man could not have gone by the door, because there was only one door, and he, Jimmie Dale, had been blocking the doorway; nor could the man have gone by the single window, because at that time the police had been on guard in the alleyway outside. Through the wall or the floor then? Yes. But how? Where? Neither wall nor floor showed any——

Out of the darkness, without warning, there came suddenly a low, ugly laugh.

"The Gray Seal!" said a voice.

In an instant, strained and tense, his automatic whipped from his pocket and outflung before him, Jimmie Dale drew back against the wall. A trap after all! The trap he had so logically proven to have outlived its usefulness! He strained his eyes through the blackness. Nothing! He could see nothing. Nor was there any further sound. A minute passed. Was it a minute—or some vast, immeasurable æon of time? He stood rigid, motionless—waiting.

"Where?" said a voice abruptly.

Jimmie Dale turned his head; his automatic swung swiftly. The voice seemed to have come almost from his elbow. Then his jaws locked hard together. No; it was not from there! They were playing with him, were they? A cat-and-mouse game! Well then, he——

A voice spoke again:

"Worth anywhere from thirty to fifty thousand. Easy money."

Jimmie Dale pushed back his hat, and above his mask flirted away a bead of sweat from his forehead. He understood now. There wasn't any one in the room save himself. It wasn't a trap. It was only uncanny. He was simply listening to snatches of a conversation that came from the nowhere, out of the darkness.

He leaned forward a little, striving to the utmost to *place* the direction of the sounds. The voices, he realised now, while quite distinct, had been curiously heavy and uneven. He nodded sharply to himself. A pipe, a hollow space, almost anything might act as a conductor for the sound waves, and bring them here from no little distance at that!

Once more a voice broke through the stillness:

"Easy money, yes; but old Twisty Munn's no fool, and neither is Kid Gregg. The stuff will be pinched by now, but we've plenty of time left—enough to see that there are no mistakes made."

Again there came the low, ugly laugh.

"There won't be any! One o'clock at Twisty's——"

The voice ended as abruptly as though, if speaking over a telephone, the wire had been suddenly cut. There seemed to Jimmie Dale no other way to describe it. He stared around him in a queer, helpless way. Now the voices had seemed to come from here, now from there. His lips twisted in grim self-mockery. The longer he had listened the more confusing it had become. The voices simply came from *everywhere* in the room.

Had they ended now?

The tiny glow of the flashlight played for an instant on the crystal of his watch. It was fourteen minutes past twelve.

Noiselessly now Jimmie Dale moved across the room to a chair. The sort of finality with which that last sentence had been broken off held out little hope, he felt intuitively, of his hearing anything more. But there was a chance. He sat down quietly. Strange! Where had the voices come from? From below, above—where? He did not know. He knew only that *one* of those voices must be the Phantom's. It did not require proof. It was axiomatic. He could not locate the direction from which the voices had come, but the opening through which the Phantom had once vanished from this room was obviously the medium through which the voices entered. How cleverly deduced! He snapped at himself mentally. The only trouble was that after prolonged and laborious search he had not been able to locate that opening either!

His fingers played softly in a curiously caressing way over his automatic. It hadn't been any trap. The allusion to the Gray Seal that had so startled him had been only a snatch of the conversation which had at first, through some cause or other that he was unable to define, reached him only in broken fragments. Or perhaps, after all, it was a trap—the other way around. A trap for the trapper! If he could not locate the voices here, it might not possibly be so difficult to do so at, say, one Twisty Munn's—at one o'clock!

He sat there in the darkness listening, his mind at work. One of the voices had been the Phantom's, that was beyond question or doubt; but which one of the two it was he did not know. He could, he was certain, have recognised Gentleman Laroque's, alias the Phantom's, voice anywhere under ordinary circumstances, but here, due unquestionably to the mysterious way in which the sound waves had been transmitted, all sense of inflexion had been lost. Nor did the conversation itself, as he went over it again in his mind, help to differentiate in that respect one speaker from the other. Either one of the two, from what had been said, might have been the Phantom.

Twisty Munn's at one o'clock! He smiled grimly. One of the two voices at least, possibly both of them, would be at Twisty Munn's at one o'clock. Well, if nothing further eventuated here, he, too, would be at Twisty Munn's at that hour. His search, the hours he had spent here, had perhaps not been so fruitless after all! It was an even chance at least that, in spite of the continued silence in this room now, he would hear *the* voice again to-night. And if he did——

His face hardened suddenly. Last night he had held the Phantom at his mercy, last night he could have shot to kill before the man had even been aware of his presence; and last night, because he had failed to realise that it was a Thing blood-flecked with murder, a Thing that preyed upon every decency in life, and not a human being, the Phantom had escaped. Last night this had happened. *There would be no second time.* There was another life at stake—hers— the Tocsin's. Last night he had jeopardised that life because he had not fought the Phantom with the Phantom's own weapons, but all that was now at an end.

And as he sat there listening, and there was still no further sound, he found himself strangely, abnormally calm, strangely callous even, as though this decision were but commonplace and one of everyday occurrence. He asked now only for one more meeting with the Phantom. Where, or how, it did not matter. Just once more!

The minutes passed. The tiny flashlight winked again through the darkness and lighted up the dial of Jimmie Dale's watch.

It was twenty-five minutes of one.

Jimmie Dale stood up. There was evidently nothing more to be heard here, or if there was, and he waited any longer, then the chance of hearing anything at Twisty Munn's must go by the board—and as a choice between the two he very much inclined toward Twisty Munn's now. He moved softly through the connecting doorway, and traversed the adjoining room that opened on the hall. Here, the door opened and closed silently behind him, and Jimmie Dale, lost in the darkness of the unlighted hallway, reached the rear door of the tenement, and stepped out into a small back yard. A moment more, and he was over the fence, and, slipping his mask from his face, was running noiselessly along a lane.

Two blocks away he emerged upon a dingy, ill-lighted and uninviting street. He smiled a little whimsically, as he pulled his soft felt hat somewhat rakishly to one side and well down over his eyes, and, hunching the perfectly fitting dinner coat at one of the shoulders, turned up the collar around his neck. True, the costume was hardly *de rigueur* in the East Side, but he was Jimmie Dale, not Smarlinghue, to-night. He shrugged his shoulders. Well, did it matter? He was not on his way to attend any *public* function, and as for the streets there were always the shadows of the buildings to hug a little closer, always a loose, slouching gait to assume.

Twisty Munn! Kid Gregg! What was the game these two were playing to-night? He shook his head impatiently. That did not matter either. It mattered only that the Phantom was concerned in their movements. It was common knowledge in the underworld that Twisty Munn was a "buyer" for a certain class of apparently honest establishments, where, if the alibi were good enough, stolen goods, disguised of course, were offered over the counters to the public at prices well in excess of what could be obtained through the underground channels employed by the regular "fences." It was profitable for all concerned, even taking into account the commission charged by the crafty Twisty Munn, who lived apparently—for the benefit of the police— in a condition approaching almost abject poverty in a squalid, ill-furnished room at the top of a seedy and somewhat questionable tenement over in the direction of the East River. Kid Gregg, less known save by the inner circle of the underworld, which latter had already marked him for preferment, was a young and budding crook, still outside the ken of the police, who showed exceeding promise in the profession he had chosen. In a word, neither of them had ever had any dealings or were in any way connected with Gentleman Laroque's, alias the Phantom's gang.

Jimmie Dale's dark eyes narrowed grimly as he went along. The conclusion was somewhat obvious. The Phantom was by no means averse to plucking the plums ripened by some one else, and it was fairly evident that in some way or another he had got wind of one that had been ripened by Twisty Munn and Kid Gregg. It looked very much therefore as though the night were likely to develop into a three-cornered game, counting in himself, Jimmie Dale, with the added possibility that the trumps perhaps might be in the hand that neither Twisty Munn nor Kid Gregg in the first place, nor the Phantom in the second, suspected!

Jimmie Dale covered block after block at a swinging stride. His mind reverted to Mother Margot's rooms. It was strange where those voices had come from! He could not tear the building down to find out. He had already known there was a secret exit from that room. The voices in that respect had not proved anything further. His mind mulled on. A search of the rooms adjacent to Mother Margot's offered no prospect of help in the solution of the problem. If the room itself, where he *knew* the secret exit to be, was so apparently search proof, what better chance would any other room offer? Or why, as a matter of fact, should the secret exit even lead into any other room? Well, the cellar then, for the Phantom could not have gone up through the roof! There was no cellar! The ground floor was a sort of basement in itself! Those voices——

Cycles! He was beginning all over again. He shook his head in self-exasperation, and with a mental effort dismissed these thoughts from his mind. He had almost reached his destination, and the immediate present demanded his full attention.

Under a street lamp he looked at his watch. Twelve minutes to one. He nodded. He was well on time. Just ahead of him was the three-story tenement where Twisty Munn made his home.

XIX

JACKALS

THE street was deserted. The tenement itself was dark. Not a light showed from any window. But Twisty Munn lived in an upstairs room at the rear, therefore the fact that no light could be seen from the street had no bearing whatever on Twisty Munn.

Jimmie Dale stepped suddenly into the doorway. The door itself, the entrance common to heaven alone knew how many who hived in wretchedness and squalor within, and to whom a latchkey would have been not far removed from mockery, was unlocked as he had expected. He moved noiselessly into the hall. The place was close and dank to the nostrils; also it reeked with the odour of garlic. It was dark, too; but through the murk he could just make out the stairs ahead of him and to the left.

There was a curious tightening of Jimmie Dale's lips as he moved forward and tested the tread of the first stair cautiously. Yes, he knew the breed! Old and in disrepair, the stairs would certainly shriek their protest to high heaven if any liberty were taken with them. But it was Jimmie Dale of the old days, Jimmie Dale of the days of Larry the Bat and the rickety stairs of the old Sanctuary, worse even than these stairs were, where his life had literally depended upon his silence a score of times, as he went upward now.

He gained the first landing. There were doors around him here, and, because they were flimsy doors and flimsy partitions, from behind them the night sounds reached him—the restless movement of a sleeper, the sick, querulous cry of a child, a stertorous snore.

Twelve minutes of one! Ten now, wasn't it?

There were three flights. At the third landing Jimmie Dale paused for an instant to adjust the black silk mask over his face again, then stole forward, feeling out with his hand along the wall, toward a thin, irregular thread of light that seeped out from under the ill-fitting threshold of a door at the rear end of the hall. Twisty Munn, at least, was evidently keeping the rendezvous!

Faintly, no more than a murmur, voices reached Jimmie Dale from the other side of the door now as he stood before it. And now a pick-lock in his hand was silently at work. Perhaps half a minute passed. Then, by the barest fraction of an inch at a time, the doorknob turned without sound under the slim, trained, sensitive fingers, and the door opened by a crack. The murmur from within became distinct, disintegrated itself into words and sentences.

". . . Sure, de goods is all right, but wot about de rest of it? De guys I have to slip dese over to ain't takin' chances, not if youse handed 'em de stuff for nothin' an' paid 'em for takin' it."

The door opened another crack. Twisty Munn and Kid Gregg! Yes, that was what the voice in Mother Margot's room had said. Jimmie Dale could just see the two. They were at a table in the upper corner of the room. His eyes narrowed. There was what looked like a small fortune in the shape of jewellery on the table between them. Twisty Munn! The stoop-shouldered, almost hunch-backed form of the shabby old man was bent forward over the table, while his thin, hooked fingers clawed at the jewels, picking up one after the other to hold it close to short-sighted, squinting eyes. And opposite him Kid Gregg, young, in an over-loud checked suit, a peaked cap pulled so low over his forehead as almost to hide the small, roving black eyes, scowled in evident impatience.

"Aw, it's sewed up—tight!" the latter snapped. "Ain't I told youse dat?"

"Sure, youse told me dat," agreed the old man sharply. "Two days ago youse told me youse had it all fixed for to-night, an' dat everythin' was safe, an' dat youse'd bring me

de sparklers. Well, dat's all right, youse've brought 'em,
an' *dey're* all right; but I ain't heard yet how safe dey are,
an' dat's wot puts de deal across wid de crowd I works for.
See?"

A cigarette dangled from Kid Gregg's upper lip. With
the tip of his tongue he deftly transferred it to the corner of
his mouth.

"Well, den, listen!" he grinned complacently. "Some job,
Twisty; an' all me own—see? I used to know a guy dat
worked for old Froomes up on de Avenue, an' he was forever shootin' off his face about de sparklers de family wore.
Well, a month ago I gets a job dere myself—taken on regular. Get me? Polishin' de hardwood floors, an' keepin' de
windows of de mansion washed. Ah, say, it was soft! I
hadn't been dere a week before I knew where de combination of de safe was kept in a drawer in de library right along-
side de safe itself—so's Mrs. Froomes wouldn't have to walk
far to get it!"

Kid Gregg chuckled, and sucking at his cigarette only to
find it out, began to search through his pockets for a match.

Jimmie Dale stared. Froomes! It was Martin K.
Froomes, of course, the retired broker. He knew Froomes
very well indeed, and on several "stag" occasions had been
in Froomes' house; and Froomes knew him—as Jimmie Dale,
a fellow member of the St. James Club. So that was where
that haul of jewellery on the table there had come from!
What was it the voice in Mother Margot's room had said?
—"anywhere from thirty to fifty thousand." He could well
believe it. Froomes was an exceedingly wealthy man, and,
besides a wife, had two daughters who moved constantly in
society.

"Go on!" prompted Twisty Munn impatiently.

"Watch me!" boasted Kid Gregg. "I could have made de
pinch anytime, but den I'd have had to make me get-away,
an' duck outer little old New York. I wasn't for dat—not
some! I've still got me job polishin' de floors, an' to-morrow
mornin' I'll be polishin' 'em de same as though nothin' had
happened. See? Some day de bulls may write up me auto-

beeography an' keep me photograph handy to look at w'en dey wants to see somethin' handsome—but not if I sees 'em first! Nix on dat stuff! So far I'm a nice, quiet, hard-working young man. Get me? Well, dere ain't no hurry, an' I sits tight, keepin' me lamps open lookin' for goats. An' I don't have to wait long, neither. One day I was out on a window sill washin' de window, an' I hears de boss in de next room handin' out a Sunday school spiel like he was talkin' to a naughty son. 'From a business standpoint,' says de old man, 'dis has nearly lost youse yer job here, an' no man ever made anythin' out of himself on that basis. An' from a moral standpoint,' he says, 'it's simply de road dat leads from bad to worse.'"

Jimmie Dale, an ominous droop at the corners of his mouth, dared another half inch of door space, as Kid Gregg paused for a moment to drag on his cigarette. Was there a wall switch for that single, dangling incandescent that lighted the room? Yes, there it was—just inside the door. He could almost have reached in and touched it from where he stood.

"Well, dat's all I heard," went on Kid Gregg; "but, take it from me, I watches to see who comes outer dat room. Say, can youse beat it! It's a little red-headed dude named Culver, dat's a typewriter, or secretary, or somethin' like dat to de boss. After dat, dere's nothin' to it. Culver's de bird I'm after, an' I gets his number for fair. Some high-roller wid his dinkey shirts an' his imitation diamond shirt studs! He don't live dere wid de boss, y'understand, but he dresses up every night like he owned a bank, an' hits de high spots on de first speed. Youse knows de kind, don't youse?"

Twisty Munn was twining the long, bony fingers of his hands in and out of the heap of brooches, pins, rings and pendants in front of him, seemingly fascinated by the fiery little gleams of light that he made to flash from their count-less facets.

"Up de river," observed Twisty Munn, "dere's a whole cageful of dem birds dat dress up *all* de time—only dey don't sport de shirt studs any more. I get youse! Wot did youse do wid *Mister* Culver?"

Kid Gregg indulged in a fresh cigarette. There was a smirk of unabashed conceit upon his face, as he blew a smoke ring in the air.

"Him? He's down at Hoy Loo's."

Twisty Munn leaned suddenly across the table.

"Wot's dat?" he demanded tensely. "Hoy Loo's?"

"Youse said it!" nodded Kig Gregg complacently. "He's gone bye-bye down at Hoy Loo's wid a nice little pipe of coke laid out beside de bunk."

Twisty Munn squinted blear eyes at the other.

"I don't get youse!" he grunted after a moment. "Dat don't stick nothin' on him. I don't get youse!"

Kid Gregg smiled pityingly.

"Dat's why youse won't never be nothin' more dan youse are to-day, Twisty," he murmured; "just runnin' around an' doin' de dirty work. It's de bean dat counts."

"Youse close yer face!" snapped Twisty Munn. "Go on, an' spill de rest of it."

"All right," grinned Kid Gregg. "I fixed it up for to-night, after I'd tipped off another guy I knows to make up wid Culver about a week ago. Me pal plays de game. Savvy? He chums up wid Culver, an' promises to show Culver some of de *real* goods around town. Youse gets it now, don't youse? To-night de two of dem goes to Hoy Loo's, an' dey starts in wid a drink, an' Culver gets a pill slipped into his, an' den he's laid out peaceful on a bunk just as though he'd got stewed on too many pipes. Soft, eh? He'll be dere to-morrow mornin'. He don't know who me pal is because somehow me pal ain't got a good memory even for his own name; an' besides, bein' dolled up for de occasion wid a little waxed moustache an' a cute little beard, youse'd have taken him for a French Count—which he ain't. Well, de bulls get Mister Culver dere in de mornin'—an' Hoy Loo gets a piece of de money youse're goin' to hand out 'cause he's got to stand for a police fine."

Kid Gregg paused and grinned at Twisty Munn, as the

latter puckered the leathery skin of his forehead into wrinkles.

"Never mind about de bean stuff dis time," said Twisty Munn gruffly. "I ain't wise yet, but I'll say it begins to listen good. How'd youse hang it onto him?"

"De easiest thing youse know," said the Kid cheerfully. "A letter—dat's wot. Dere's a letter in de mail now dat de police gets in de mornin', just about de same time dat de family on de Avenue wakes up an' t'rows a fit w'en dey finds de safe open an' de sparklers gone. De letter just says dat mabbe de police'd like to know dat a guy blew into Hoy Foo's to-night, an' got stewed to de eyes hittin' de pipe, an' got frisked of a bagful of rings an' jewels an' stuff by some yeggs dat was floatin' around dere. An' it's signed: 'A Friend.' I guess dat's all to de mustard, ain't it? Dat takes care of de missin' goods! De bulls slip over dere, an' dey finds it's me red-headed friend Culver, de typewriter expert for Mr. Froomes dat owns de safe dat's been cracked."

Twisty Munn blinked.

"Dat's all right," he said judicially; "but it don't actually prove he pulled de job. If he was frisked, which he wasn't, den——"

"Sure, he was frisked!" said Kid Gregg with a vicious grin. "All dis happened before I went up to de nabob's house an hour ago. Dat was midnight, y'understand, an' de Froomes bunch was all in bed. I wasn't takin' no chances. He was frisked, all right!" The Kid with studied effect blew another smoke ring in the air. "I frisked him— of one of dose near-diamond shirt studs of his dat youse can buy from de hawkers at three for a nickel!"

Enlightenment was dawning on Twisty Munn's wily countenance.

"Say dat again!" he whispered hoarsely.

"Sure!" said Kid Gregg. "Dat's wot! D'youse know of anythin' dat's easier to lose widout youse bein' wise to it dan a shirt stud dat falls out w'en youse're pawin' over de stuff in a safe youse've cracked? Dat's where it is now—on

de floor up dere in de Froomes' library under some papers
dat was yanked out of de safe."

For a moment Twisty Munn stared at his companion, then
his long, bony hand shot out across the table.

"Youse'll go a long way, Kid! Shake!" he cackled ad-
miringly. "Take it from me, youse will—a long way!"

"Youse bet yer life—an' nothin' but dust behind me!"
agreed Kid Gregg boastfully. "Youse said somethin',
Twisty!"

"'S'help me!" gulped Twisty Munn. His fingers clawed
the jewels on the table again. "As sweet a haul as ever I've
seen, an' open an' shut—open an' shut!" He pushed the
heap suddenly toward Kid Gregg. "Put 'em back in dat little
sack," he gloated. "I'll take 'em, Kid—dere's big money in
dis all round."

Under his mask a dull red had suffused Jimmie Dale's
cheeks; subconsciously almost his hand had crept into his
pocket, and his fingers had closed around the stock of his
automatic. It was brutal work; miserable, inhuman work.
A shirt stud, three for a nickel—and five, ten, fifteen years,
the best of a man's life, behind the drear walls and the steel
bars of Sing Sing. Was it possible that men like these two
lived, festering God's green earth! His automatic came
from his pocket. They were stuffing the jewels into a small
canvas bag now. Well, the game wasn't finished yet; there
was still another hand to play! The little sack would prove
a convenient receptacle. It ought not to take but a moment
more before *all* the jewels were inside, and——

Jimmie Dale drew suddenly back from the doorway. Had
he *forgotten?* In the natural sweep of anger, in the hot-
blooded fury that the scene in there had brought him, had he
forgotten—those voices in Mother Margot's rooms! What
was that now? A creak upon the stairs? Yes, he was sure
of it! Another! One o'clock! It must be after one o'clock.
Some one was coming!

Every faculty alert, he crouched back now—farther back,
away from the door, where he was lost in the darkness of the
hall. Yes, there was some one almost at the head of the

stairs now, coming stealthily, almost without sound—only once in a while a faint, protesting squeak from a stair tread that would not be audible inside Twisty Munn's room. Those jewels, Twisty Munn, Kid Gregg were the lesser issue now. It was the Phantom who had brought him here, the hope that the Phantom would come himself in person.

Tense, silent, Jimmie Dale crouched there. The Phantom! If it were the Phantom in any one of the characters that he, Jimmie Dale, could recognise, there would be no failure this time such as there had been last night! Whoever passed from the hall into that room would stand out, if only for an instant, clearly defined in the lighted doorway—and an instant would be enough!

A second passed—still another. A dark form bulked at the head of the stairs. It was joined by another. Two of them, then! And now there was no sound—yet the two dark forms there moved. They came on down the hall like queer, wavering, intangible shapes that seemed almost like brain hallucinations in the darkness.

Outflung before him, Jimmie Dale's automatic held a bead on the doorway. They had stopped there now, stopped in that thin crack of light that seeped out through the inch of open door that he himself had left. And the face of one came into the light. Bunty Myers! It was not the Phantom; it was Bunty Myers, the Phantom's unholy chief-of-staff! But *both* of the men could not be the Phantom. The other! Who was the other?

A whisper came. A revolver barrel glinted in the light-thread. Jimmie Dale strained forward. The other! Just a glimpse of the man's face! There could be no disguise that would blind his eyes to Gentleman Laroque, the *real* man, any longer; no disguise however clever that could——

The door crashed inward, a wave of light flooded out into the hall, and the two forms at the door leaped forward into the room. But, for the single instant Jimmie Dale had asked, the light had shone on the second man's face—and upon Jimmie Dale there surged a sense of bitter disappointment that seemed to engulf him, seemed to hold him

momentarily stunned. Neither was the second man the
Phantom; it was only the Kitten, one of the gang that used
to rendezvous in the back upstairs room of Wally Kerrigan's "club." The Kitten who only last night had— Well,
he might have known! It was the Phantom's way. It was
the Phantom and Bunty Myers he had heard talking—he
knew that now—but the Phantom had left the actual work,
as he had done a score of times before, to his tools and
pawns.

His mind seemed strangely numbed. He stared into the
room. Two men had just leaped through that lighted doorway. It was like some scene flashing upon a cinema screen,
wasn't it? Shirt studs, three for a nickel—and the best of a
man's life behind the bars of Sing Sing! He shook himself
free as from some clogging mental weight. Yes, that was
what it meant, whether Bunty Myers or Kid Gregg came off
the victor—and there wasn't any other issue now because
the Phantom wasn't here.

He crept forward to the door. Old Twisty Munn was
cringing in a corner, twining his claw-like fingers in and out
of each other, licking at his lips, his face gray with fear.
On the table stood the little canvas bag, tied now with a
string at the top—and behind the table, Kid Gregg, a cigarette
still dangling from his upper lip, had risen from his chair,
and was staring with a queer, inane smile into the muzzle of
Bunty Myers' revolver a yard or so away.

"Put up your hands!" snarled Bunty Myers.

"Sure!" smiled Kid Gregg; and—the revolver in his hand
previously hidden by the edge of the table—whipped up the
weapon and fired.

It was answered by almost simultaneous reports as Bunty
Myers and the Kitten fired together; it was answered by a
scream of terror from Twisty Munn—and then the crash
of the overturned table as Kid Gregg spun half around like
a spent top and pitched against it.

But Jimmie Dale, too, was in action now. From the edge
of the door jamb his hand shot forward, closed upon the

electric-light switch, and the room was in darkness. And the next instant he had flung himself forward across the room. The little canvas bag! He had marked the exact spot on the floor where it had fallen from the table. Queer, this scuffling of feet around him; savage oaths; snarls of confusion; doors opening somewhere below in the tenement; the creak of stairs, and— Yes, here it was! His hand closed upon the bag and thrust it into his pocket. He turned and sprang for the doorway again. Something blocked his way, struck at him viciously, clutched at his clothing. He struck back with a short-arm jab, tore himself free, and lunged forward again.

A revolver flash lanced through the blackness behind him —another. Twisty Munn still screamed in terror. And a bedlam seemed loosed now throughout the tenement. But Jimmie Dale had gained the door.

He slammed it shut behind him, and, springing for the stairs, took them three and four at a jump. A man holding a candle, peering upward from the landing below, blocked his way for an instant—and went down before Jimmie Dale's rush.

Two more flights to go! Doors opened. Frightened faces were thrust out. There came the cries of children—and then from above the pound of feet, racing as madly as his own down the upper stairs.

Jimmie Dale laughed strangely to himself. That would be Bunty Myers and the Kitten, but they mattered nothing now. There had been murder above, Kid Gregg was dead, and their one concern would be to hunt cover without loss of time, because if they were known to Twisty Munn they were in desperate case indeed!

He was not concerned with any pursuit from Bunty Myers or the Kitten. It was a question only of what margin he himself had before the uproar here would have brought the police upon the scene. It was the shouts and yells that pursued him from the awakened and terrified occupants of the tenement wherein lay his real source of danger.

A minute! That was all he asked. The margin of a
minute! He risked a leap of almost half the length of the
lower stairs, stumbled at the bottom, recovered himself,
jumped for the front door, wrenched it open and dashed out.
The street was still empty. Thank God! He ran like a
deer for the corner, gained it, doubled at the next one, and
then dropped into an nonchalant walk.

XX

H E was safe now. He laughed shortly, without mirth.
Safe! Yes, for the moment—but the night wasn't
ended yet. He laboured under no delusions on that
score. The rendezvous at Twisty's, instead of the hoped-
for meeting with the Phantom, had left him with the heri-
tage of a little canvas bag whose physical contents became
but a handful of miserable, worthless baubles compared with
the potentialities it held for a long-term penitentiary sentence for an innocent man. Nothing that had transpired at
Twisty Munn's had changed by one iota the vile, low, cunning trap that Kid Gregg had laid for his victim—and had
now paid for with his own life. The police would receive
the letter; the police would find that shirt stud at the scene
of the robbery, find this young fool Culver at Hoy Loo's,
and find in Culver's shirt that a stud was missing from
amongst its fellows.

Jimmie Dale's face darkened now, as he turned at the next
street and headed over in the direction of the Bowery.
Young fool! Yes, that was it! Why should he take any
further risk? He did not know Culver. He knew nothing
about Culver except that he had a red head, and was evidently somewhat of a bounder who probably very richly
deserved what— No; he knew more than that. He knew
that Culver was *innocent*.

And then a smile came to Jimmie Dale's lips, a half whimsical, half troubled smile. Yes, of course! It was inevitable!
He knew that. He had known it all along. Why else had
he taken the risk of snatching up that little bag in Twisty
Munn's room? Well, then?

Hoy Loo's? He shook his head. He would find nothing there but a limp, red-headed boy, drugged into unconsciousness. He could do nothing with Culver; for, even if he managed to get Culver out of and away from the dope joint, there still remained the one outstanding, damning piece of evidence in the shape of that shirt stud in the library of the Froomes' home. Neither would Culver's removal from Hoy Loo's offset the letter that the police would receive simply because they did not find the boy there, for they would find that Culver *had* been there, had spent most of the night there. Equally, there were no means of intercepting that letter.

There was only one alternative. Jimmie Dale shrugged his shoulders, and again the whimsical smile broke across his lips. It was perhaps a fortunate thing for Culver that he, Jimmie Dale, was not red-headed too!

He hurried on now, breaking at times almost into a run. There was only one way, and—yes—he saw that way clearly enough now. It remained merely a question of whether by any chance the robbery at the Froomes' mansion would be discovered before he could act. It was not likely, since Kid Gregg had said the household had all retired by midnight; but it nevertheless left the matter of time an unknown factor whose latent possibilities were by no means to be ignored. Well, he would lose no time!

Near the Bowery, in an all-night café, he entered the telephone booth. He gave the number of his residence on Riverside Drive, and as he waited for the connection into his dark eyes, strangely, there crept a softer light. Old Jason would answer the phone. Faithful old Jason, butler to the father, more than butler to the son! Despite injunctions, despite the nights, many and many of them, when he, Jimmie Dale, did not return at all, Jason would even now probably be maintaining his self-appointed vigil in the arm-chair in the vestibule waiting for his Master Jim—and almost certainly asleep! Jason was an old man, and nature was stronger than the flesh. Well, it was Jason's way, a rather splendid way, a way of great devotion. Strange? No—not strange!

It was just Jason. Jason knew perhaps too little or too much; enough, in any case, so that the old man lived in constant anxiety anent the safety of his Master Jim, and——

"Yes! Hello! That you, Jason?" said Jimmie Dale quickly.

"Yes, sir—Master Jim, sir," the old man answered.

"Listen, Jason!" said Jimmie Dale. "Rouse up Benson, and send him down here with the light car as fast as he can make it. Tell him the Palace—he knows where that is."

"Yes, sir; at once," Jason replied; and then, a curious hesitancy, a curious yearning, in his voice: "Is there any—anything else, Master Jim, sir?"

"Yes!" said Jimmie Dale sharply. "You've been sitting up again, Jason!" Jimmie Dale's smile belied the severity of his tone. How many times had he used exactly the same words to Jason—and with probably the same effect! "Go to bed, Jason! Good-night!"

"Yes, sir, Master Jim," said Jason. "Good-night, sir."

Jimmie Dale hung up the receiver and went out into the street again, making for the Bowery now, and walking in an uptown direction. It would save time to meet Benson by part of the way. By the time he walked to the Palace Saloon, Benson should have about reached there too.

He began a mental calculation as he went along. Say, twenty-five minutes for Benson to get downtown, then another twenty for himself, Jimmie Dale, to reach his objective on Fifth Avenue, still another twenty for the work there was to do, and, yes, that was pretty close figuring, though it gave Benson, who was far safer away from the car and would have to walk, a leeway of twenty minutes. Allow an extra ten minutes, then, as a factor of safety. That made seventy-five minutes—an hour and a quarter. He looked at his watch. It was exactly half-past one. That would bring it, then, to a quarter to three.

He nodded. A quarter to three! He could depend on Benson literally to the extent of his life, and indeed had done so on more than one occasion; Benson as a chauffeur was almost on the same plane with Jason as a butler. As he had remarked many times before, there was perhaps no man in New York who was served as he was—and it was not a service of money. Rare thing? Yes! But it was true. It *did* exist in the world. Thank God for it!

Jimmie Dale walked briskly. He reached the corner in front of the Palace Saloon that he had given his chauffeur as a rendezvous. Benson had not yet arrived. Consulting his watch, Jimmie Dale waited a minute, and then taking out a little notebook began to write rapidly under the rays of the street lamp. This, too, would save time—or, at least, preserve the schedule. It would save the two or three minutes necessary to give Benson verbal instructions, though he could, of course, take Benson along with him in the car since their roads would lie in the same direction for part of the way, but he had definitely decided against that. If anything went amiss, it would be infinitely better for Benson that there should be no possibility of the two of them having been seen *together* in the car. He owed that to Benson. It was quite another matter that Benson, obeying orders, should have turned the car over to his employer here where he had been instructed to do so.

He tore the leaf from his notebook and folded it carefully. There was one minute left for Benson to make the rendezvous on the timetable set for— Yes, here he was now!

A car drew up at the curb. Benson's clean-cut, strong, young face showed in the light as he touched his cap.

"Good work, Benson!" said Jimmie Dale approvingly. "What time is it?"

Benson leaned forward to consult the car's clock.

"By your *watch*, Benson," said Jimmie Dale. He held his own in his hand.

Benson looked at his wrist watch.

"Five minutes of two, sir," he said.

"Right!" said Jimmie Dale. He motioned Benson from the car. "I'll take the car, Benson." And then, as he swung into the driver's seat, he leaned out and handed Benson the folded note. "Follow these instructions to the letter, Benson," he said quietly. "And *destroy* that note. Good-night."

The car turned and headed uptown. Jimmie Dale drove fast. The streets were deserted. The minutes passed—ten, fifteen, eighteen. He kept glancing at the time—and nodded as he finally parked his car on a side street within half a block of one of the most exclusive residential sections of Fifth Avenue. He had taken nineteen minutes from the Palace Saloon.

The black silk mask covered his face again, as he stole forward now and slipped into an areaway that ran in the rear of the corner house on the Avenue. The rest would be slower work. This was Martin K. Froomes' residence.

It was moonlight; light enough to see. There was a high fence here that flanked both sides of what was evidently a garage. Jimmie Dale swung himself over the fence, and alighted in a small, cement-floored courtyard. He was across this in an instant, and in another was lost in the shadows of a basement entrance.

Again the little steel pick-lock was at work. The door opened and closed—silently. Jimmie Dale stood inside. For a moment he listened; and then, the diminutive flashlight in service again, darting its tiny gleams before him, Jimmie Dale moved forward once more, and, locating the stairs, began to climb them—and a moment later found himself standing in the main hall of the house.

So far, all was well! The library now—no, first, the telephone! He must make sure that his memory had served him right on that score. He had been here once or twice before —under quite different auspices!—as a guest. The flashlight's ray played down the hall. Yes, it was all right! It was there on a little stand in an alcove near the foot of the central staircase. He could hardly have forgotten that rather unique door, shaped in a half circle, which at will could transform the alcove into a booth!

Jimmie Dale turned now. He was not quite so sure of the library, but the impression was strong that it was here at the rear. He tried a door on his right. The dining room. He stepped back then into the hall, and opened a door on the opposite side. The flashlight circled the interior, went out—

and Jimmie Dale closed the door softly behind him.

His lips, beneath the mask, tightened now, as the flash-light, playing again through the darkness, focused on an open safe near the window at the rear of the room, and upon what had evidently been a very large proportion of the contents of the safe which were now strewn about on the floor in front of it. He stepped forward quickly, and kneeling on the floor began to search carefully beneath the litter of documents, papers and books. A minute, two, three, went by—and then Jimmie Dale stood up again. Between his fingers he held a cheap and tawdry shirt stud.

He stood looking at it for a moment, balancing it now in his hand. And a softer light crept into his eyes, and a strange smile tempered the grimness of his tightened lips. No, it wasn't worth much, just a rhinestone—just ten years in the penitentiary, that was all!

And then Jimmie Dale shrugged his shoulders. The margin of time was narrowing. He slipped the shirt stud into his pocket, and sent the flashlight's ray playing inquisitively around the room. There was still the letter that the police would receive in the morning, and which must be made to disprove even itself, be made to stand out so glaringly as a plant to saddle a crime on an innocent man's shoulders that none could mistake it for what it was. And there was only one way to accomplish that!

His eyes followed the ray of the flashlight. Yes, that single bracket light over there would do when the time came. He could not afford to be too generous! And now the window. He walked over to it and raised the drawn shade. It looked out on the courtyard. Silently, cautiously, he opened the window wide. Ten feet to the ground. Well, it might be worse!

At a quarter to three! He returned to the centre of the room, and consulted his watch. He had not needed all of that extra ten minutes. He was four minutes to the good.

He stood there in the darkness. It was very silent in the house, and yet it was strange what queer noises even silence possessed if one listened for them. They began very low, and grew louder, but always in a palpitating sort of way, and finally beat with almost thunderous clamour at the ear drums.

The flashlight was on the dial of the watch again. Seventeen minutes to three. Benson would be at work now. It would take a minute or two, of course. He smiled with grim whimsicality. It always did! He had allowed for that.

The flashlight held on the dial of the watch—and suddenly went out.

A quarter to three.

Faintly, from the front of the house, the telephone rang —and Jimmie Dale was in action. The side light went on, filling the room with a soft mellow glow. He stepped silently to the closed door, and with his ear to the panel listened. The telephone rang again—and still gain. And then, barely audible on the thickly carpeted stairs, he caught the sound of a footstep descending.

And presently Jimmie Dale's lips twisted again in a grim smile. He could not hear, he did not have the receiver at his ear, but it was Benson speaking from a slot booth in the Grand Central station where, though they might eventually trace the call, they would never trace Benson. It was Benson speaking, but the words were his, Jimmie Dale's:

"I don't want to appear in this, so never mind who I am. I couldn't find a phone any nearer, so it's about ten minutes ago that I saw a man climb over your back fence and steal into your house. I guess if you've got such a thing as a safe there, you'll know where to find him; and if you're quiet enough about it you ought to get him yet."

That was what Benson was saying! It was quite all right. The call *would* be traced—but it would "hold water." The Grand Central was just about within a ten-minute range of the Froomes' residence.

Jimmie Dale's ear was still pressed against the door panel. The footstep was mounting the stairs now—but evidently with extreme caution, for Jimmie Dale could scarcely catch a sound. It was probably the butler. Reinforcements! He would return with Mr. Froomes, perhaps, and an added footman or two!

A minute—two! The cautious tread was coming *down* the stairs again.

Jimmie Dale retreated across the room to the open door of the safe. He crouched there, tense, his muscles rigid. In his hand now he held the little canvas sack of jewels, the string at the top untied. They were almost at the door there. And now——

The door burst open.

With a well simulated startled cry of alarm, Jimmie Dale jumped to the window side of the safe—and as he jumped he allowed his arm apparently to hit sharply against the top of the safe door and knock the canvas bag from his grasp, strewing the floor with a sparkling heap of gems. He was darting for the window now. A voice roared out to him to halt. Froomes! Froomes himself in dressing gown, and behind Froomes two other men. And for a bare instant Jimmie Dale faced them, then he vaulted for the window sill. They had seen him, hadn't they—quite plainly—seen that he wasn't Culver!

"Stop! Stop, or I'll fire!" Froomes yelled out.

But Jimmie Dale was astride the window sill now, and— a vivid flash like a fork of lightning seemed to leap toward him to sting and blister and bring him agony, and the room seemed to swirl and be full of deafening, racketing reports. He dropped to the ground outside, staggered, steadied himself, leaped across the courtyard, and swung the fence, as a fusilade of shots followed him from the window.

He was racing along the areaway now. Another instant, and he had flung himself into his car. It shot forward with a bound. He whipped off his mask, as he bent over the wheel. He was gnawing at his lips now until the blood came.

The car swung the corner and tore uptown. But it wouldn't steer properly. It swayed from side to side. No, it wasn't the car, it was himself. Something in his side tortured him, and something hot, sticky hot, was running down his leg. His head swam. Nausea strove to set its grip upon him. He fought it off. He had been hit, of course, but it wasn't far to go—not far to go—not far to go—and—queer sing-song brain—what—what was the matter? Everything was all right, wasn't it? They had seen the man who had tried to rob the safe and had left the jewels on the floor, hadn't they; and they knew it wasn't Culver because—it was extremely funny, wasn't it?—because Culver had a red head.

Giddiness, nausea, hot and cold flashes! Jimmie Dale fought frantically for his senses. He drove clinging to the wheel. It wasn't far. There wasn't any pursuit; they'd never find him—if—if he could hold out just a little longer.

A sort of mental fog settled upon him that blotted out time and distance; and action was purely mechanical—and then he found himself staggering up the steps of his home on Riverside Drive. And at the top of the steps the door opened. He brushed his hand across his eyes. That was Jason, wasn't it? Jason had been sitting up again!

"Go to bed, Jason!" said Jimmie Dale severely.

The old man's face was ashen.

"My God, Master Jim, sir, what's the matter?" he cried out wildly.

Jimmie Dale lunged through the doorway.

"Nothing," said Jimmie Dale. "I—I was just looking for a shirt stud. You know the kind, Jason, three for a nickel, and——"

Jimmie Dale pitched forward unconscious to the floor.

— XXI —

THE CALL OF THE NIGHT

A NIGHT light on the stand beside the bed glowed dimly, throwing curious little shadowy patterns on walls and ceilings. Jimmie Dale turned restlessly in the bed. His hand stole beneath his pajamas and mechanically, in a sort of tentative way, felt over his tightly bandaged side. There was a nervous disquiet upon him, growing with the minutes, obsessing him. He reached out to the bed table for his watch. Half past nine.

For a moment he lay still, tracing with his eyes the shadows' fanciful shapes on the ceiling; and then suddenly he flung the covers from him, got out of bed, snatched up a dressing gown, and crossed the room to an easy chair by the window. He sat down and stared out into the night.

Rest! Quiet! He could no longer rest, because his mind would no longer remain quiet but ground on and on like the turning of a mill wheel that never ceased. The first night— when he had been wounded and the loss of blood had weakened him—yes. But not now! Thank God, he had regained consciousness in time that night to prevent Jason telephoning for a doctor! With the papers full of the burglar in evening clothes who was believed to have been hit by a shot as he had leaped through the library window of the Froomes' mansion on Fifth Avenue, it would have been perhaps a little awkward for Jimmie Dale to explain a bullet wound in his side even to a trusted physician! It had been only a flesh wound. Jason and Benson between them had done famously with him here at home. It was healing now. That was three nights ago. It was still sore and stiff—he gritted his teeth as a twinge of pain caught him suddenly— but it was healing nicely.

217

He had not stayed in bed any more than he could help after the first day—when he could elude Jason's watchfulness. He had been afraid of that, more afraid of doing that than of the wound itself. One got weak staying in bed. One's legs needed exercise—and there had been the combined lengths of the dressing room and bedroom for surreptitious constitutionals!

Well, he had been well repaid for the wound; not merely in the sense that young Culver was probably walking the streets to-night a free man, but in the sense that there had come into his hands another clue, another instrument through which his chances of running the Phantom to earth became at once now definite, tangible and concrete. Bunty Myers, the rat-faced underling, the chief tool of the Phantom! It was Bunty Myers who had been talking to the Phantom that night when he, Jimmie Dale, had heard those voices which had seemed to come out of the nowhere in Mother Margot's room. Therefore Bunty Myers knew *where* that conversation had taken place; and therefore, whether the man himself realised the full significance of it or not, Bunty Myers held the secret of the phantom clue to the lair where his master hatched his devil's work.

Jimmie Dale nodded to himself. It was a decided, even drastic change from the Phantom's accustomed line of action. From the time the Phantom had physically disappeared as Gentleman Laroque, the man had drawn a veil of secrecy and seclusion about himself that had rarely been broken—certainly never to the extent of admitting any one into the secret of his actual retreat before. True, he had many domiciles, many aliases. That was why the Tocsin had first called him the Phantom. But this was the *centre of the web*, the one place that he, Jimmie Dale, had sought and struggled vainly with every resource at his command to find. And now Bunty Myers had been admitted, if not into the secret itself, at least into the precincts of the hidden refuge. Why? Did it evidence weakness? The first cracking of the line of defence? It was certain that the Phantom's ranks had become sadly thinned. Little Sweeney, perhaps the most

versatile and cunning of the Phantom satellites, was dead;
and two out of the four trusted pawns who had had their
rendezvous in the back upstairs room at Wally Kerrigan's
"club," Spud MacGuire and Muller, were dead. The per-
centage was very heavy! There remained only Bunty Myers,
the Kitten, and Mother Margot. The circle was narrowing.
Was that why, where previously Mother Margot had always
been called from the pushcart on Thompson Street to the
telephone in the rear of that malodorous little second-hand
store to act as the mouthpiece of the "Voice," where previously all communications had passed through her, the Phantom had now changed his tactics and admitted his tools to
personal interviews?

A frown, half of perplexity, half of annoyance, gathered
on Jimmie Dale's forehead. This might or might not be the
reason. Very much more likely not! He had forgotten for
the moment that Mother Margot had been away that night.

He brushed his hand across his eyes, as he winced suddenly again with pain. He wondered if Mother Margot were
back yet. That was a curious telephone booth at the back
of the second-hand store where she received her messages!
A side door that opened on the lane—and the booth in a
sort of back storeroom! He had, of course, investigated the
place almost immediately after that night at Mrs. Kinsey's
when Mother Margot had imparted her unwilling information about it, and the result of that investigation had been to
make it plain that the telephone itself was purely a part, just
as Mother Margot's rooms were, of the Phantom's equip-
ment, and that Mezzo himself, who was a doddering, almost
senile old man, was not even a pawn—merely a convenience.
The old Italian, whose hearing was probably just good
enough and no more to distinguish the ringing of the bell,
whose trade was among a clientele far removed from such
luxuries, could have no possible use for a telephone, let alone
one in a booth, and less possible excuse for the expense that
one involved. He was simply paid to keep it there. That
was obvious. Well, it had served still another purpose—
since he, Jimmie Dale, had not infrequently used it himself!

The Phantom was not the only one who called Mother Margot to the phone, or the only one to whom the old hag paid allegiance! He smiled grimly. Perhaps he counted too much on that! Because he, Jimmie Dale, as the Gray Seal, had once caught Mother Margot in the act of double-crossing her own pals, it was no guarantee that, though he might hold her in a sort of allegiance therefrom, she would be above double-crossing him too!

He shook his head. No! He had watched her too closely. He was not prepared to say what she might do if she got the chance, but so far he was satisfied that she had played straight with him—only, so far, the little information she had had to give had not brought him much nearer to his goal.

His mind reverted to Bunty Myers. Bunty Myers had come out of the affair that night at Twisty Munn's when he had shot Kid Gregg without a breath of suspicion attaching to him. Again Jimmie Dale smiled grimly. He remembered that, as he had run down the stairs with the awakened tenement howling about his ears, the thought had flashed through his mind that if Twisty Munn had recognised Bunty Myers the latter would have the police drag-net sweeping the city, yes, and the country, for him, and he would be hard put to it to find cover. But, as it had turned out, whether Twisty Munn had really recognised Bunty Myers or not, Twisty Munn had remained silent on the subject. Yesterday's papers had been full of the affair. Twisty Munn was by nature an ingenious and versatile liar, and he had run true to form. Himself in the very act of receiving the stolen contents of Martin K. Froomes' safe when the shooting occurred, Twisty Munn had, of course, as an incentive for remaining silent the undesirability of implicating himself in a criminal transaction; and again, he might not actually have known who Bunty Myers was, or, if he had, the fear of reprisals if he snitched might also very logically account for his reticence. Twisty Munn, so Twisty Munn swore, knew absolutely nothing about the matter, except that he and Kid Gregg had been sitting in his room talking when the door had burst open and a couple of men he had never seen before had entered. Kid Gregg had jumped to his feet and pulled his gun, and just as he fired one of the others had dropped him. He, Twisty Munn, didn't know what it was all about, s'help him God! but he had a hunch it was a personal row between Kid Gregg and one of the other men over some moll or other.

Quite so! Into Jimmie Dale's dark eyes there came an ironical gleam. There was nothing to disprove it. Twisty Munn's story fitted into the balance of the night as perfectly as though it were the truth! Well, that left Bunty Myers free! That was what counted. It would be easier to find Bunty Myers now than if he had taken to cover from the police. And it was Bunty Myers that he, Jimmie Dale, wanted now!

And then Jimmie Dale shook his head again—in sudden irritation now. Had he forgotten too that since the night Little Sweeney had masqueraded as Isaac Shiftel and paid for it with his life, Bunty Myers had already sought cover, perhaps more as a precautionary measure than because he was actually "wanted" for that affair, but nevertheless had completely forsaken his usual haunts; and had he also forgotten a night not long ago when, as Smarlinghue, he had searched vainly through the length and breadth and in the most hidden places of the underworld for the man? He had wanted Bunty Myers then, hadn't he? And he had not found him.

The strong, square jaws locked with a snap. Yes! That was true! But he wanted the man *more* now, wanted him vitally. He would find him, that was all!

And then, what?

Jimmie Dale's laugh, short, hard, mirthless, rang low through the room. And then, what? The answer to that was simple. The buttons were off the foils. What Bunty Myers knew he would be *made* to tell. Bunty Myers wasn't tired of life, and if he found himself cornered by, say, the Gray Seal, and given the choice of telling where he had had that conversation with the Phantom or of paying the price of silence with his life, there was very little question as to what the man would do, for out of his own experience

Bunty Myers would not credit the Gray Seal with trifling! Nor would there be any trifling. The knowledge Bunty Myers now possessed meant that the Phantom at last could be trapped; it meant that at last *her* life, the Tocsin's, could be made safe; that the nightmare of horror which must even now be turning her soul sick within her could be brought to an end; that sunshine could come, and love and the joy of living could be hers once more, and——

With a low cry, Jimmie Dale leaned suddenly with his elbows on the window sill, staring out into the blackness of the night. It seemed to be beckoning, calling to him.

She was out there somewhere.

Was she? Was he even certain that she was still alive? Something cold, an icy grip, seemed to clutch at his heart. Since the night at Miser Scroff's, true to her stated determination to keep him out of the shadows, as she called them, that enveloped her, that held her life in peril, he had had no word from her.

Jimmie Dale was gnawing at his lips now; his arms fell from the window sill, and his hands clenched at his sides. She had simply kept her word. That was what she had said she would do. Why then this sudden access that verged on panic? He laughed out shortly again. It wasn't sudden. It wasn't a new phase. It hadn't just at this moment germinated in his brain. It was what had been growing there ever since he had lain wounded in bed. It was the seat of that constant disquiet and restlessness that was culminating now in— What?

He was on his feet; and now he began to pace the room. To protect her life she had arrayed herself against the merciless cunning of the Phantom—not a man; a monster. There was no middle course between them. There was but one end. One of the two must fall. And the Phantom was still safe, still secure, still at his hell-born deviltries.

And she?

A bead of moisture oozed out on Jimmie Dale's forehead. He flirted it away with a sweep of his hand. It meant little that her silence was exactly in accordance with what she herself had stated was her proposed line of action. There was something that meant infinitely more. She might propose, but immeasurably true was the trite old saying applied to her that she could not always dispose! He, as Smarlinghue, as the Gray Seal, excluded from working in conjunction with her, had worked nevertheless in the days and weeks that were gone with identically the same end in view as she, working independently, had had—the unearthing of the Phantom. Why had their paths then, in spite of herself, not crossed since that night in Miser Scroff's room, save perhaps on the one occasion when he had *presumed* that the tip to the police in reference to the jewel robbery at Linesthal's had come from her? *He* had been in touch with the Phantom, with the Phantom's criminal efforts since then. And if she were still free, still alive, and making progress in her fight, how was it that she and he had not inevitably been brought into contact with each other?

His hands clenched tighter. And there was more even than that; one outstanding brutal thing, ugly in its promise, that brought him a deadly fear. She *had* made progress while she had been mistress of her actions; she had said so in her notes up to the time when those notes had ceased; her appearance at Miser Scroff's that night had proved that she had penetrated the Phantom's outer defences, and had had a certain foreknowledge of the man's proposed coups. Therefore the presumption was that, had all still been well with her, she would have had knowledge of what had happened three nights ago, and she would have known that he, Jimmie Dale, had been shot.

His brain seemed to whirl; the blood to pound in hammer beats at his temples. Not a sign had come from her, not a word over the telephone, not a message of any kind, direct or indirect. His mind, his soul, seemed to falter now before the ugly deduction that flung itself pitilessly at him. She loved him, as he loved her. He knew that. She loved him with a love so great and unselfish that daily, hourly she had faced alone the peril that menaced her so that he might not also be in danger, so that he might be sheltered from it.

Would she then, if she knew he had been shot, and if she were able even with her last effort to communicate with him, have remained silent, made no attempt to discover how serious was his condition, or whether indeed he were alive or dead?

Alive or dead! The phrase battered at his brain. It applied to her. White-faced he stood at the window again, and stared out into the darkness. It was black! How black it was! And she was out there in the night somewhere—somewhere—alive or dead.

Inactive! His wound as an excuse! He swore savagely now in his emotion. What was he—a weakling! Too long he had stayed here now inactive when she—she was out there somewhere—perhaps dead. Something caught in his throat. His hands raised above his head and clenched until under the tightened skin the knuckles showed like knobs, bloodless, white.

If she were dead! He laughed! It was a merciless sound. He swung from the window and went into the dressing room. He began to dress. How should he dress? Tweeds or dinner clothes? That sounded queer—as though his brain were unhinged. He wasn't going to a party! Foolish word that—party!

He began to get into his dinner clothes. He knew what he was doing now. There had been what Jason would have called a rush of blood to the head for an instant, blurring him a bit, as it were. His side wasn't so bad—a twinge or two—nothing to speak of. There was something else out there in the night—a clue to pick up somewhere. He didn't know how—or where. It might be as Smarlinghue, somewhere in one of the hidden sink-holes of the underworld, that he would pick up the trail of Bunty Myers, or Bunty Myers' pal, the Kitten; or, if Mother Margot were back—— Well, it was as a man in a dinner coat and masked that Mother Margot knew the Gray Seal. He was dressing for Mother Margot. Quite the thing, wasn't it—to dress for the ladies?

Damn it! He must hold himself in! He stepped to the liqueur stand and poured himself out a little brandy, and drank it. He responded instantly to the stimulant. It steadied him. Over his underclothes he strapped on the leather girdle with its kit of blued-steel implements nestling in the little upright pockets, and where nestled, too, the thin metal case that contained the diamond-shaped, gray-paper, adhesive seals, the insignia of the Gray Seal. He put on his shirt, his waistcoat and jacket, and into the side pocket of his jacket he slipped his automatic. He was dressed now.

He stared at himself in the glass. Jason would have to be told. It wasn't fair to the faithful old man to slip out without a word. Jason would be mad with anxiety if he found him gone. Jimmie Dale rang the bell.

The reflection in the mirror returned him a twisted contortion of the lips. The damned thing was trying to ape a smile, wasn't it? It looked like a death's-head, gaunt and pasty-white, with lines like an old man's. Well, what of it? He felt all right, except that the bandage was infernally tight.

A knock sounded at the door.

"Come in," said Jimmie Dale.

Jason's white head appeared in the doorway—and then the door was shut with nervous haste, and the old butler came hurriedly forward across the room.

"Master Jim, sir!" he gasped. "Master Jim, what—what are you doing, sir?"

Jimmie Dale smiled.

"I'm going out, Jason," he said.

The old man cast an anxiously suspicious glance at his master.

"Yes, of course, Master Jim, sir," he said soothingly. "But the exertion of dressing, sir—if you'll just sit down for a little while now, Master Jim, then by and by——"

"Jason," said Jimmie Dale, whimsically, "you couldn't be a fraud even in a minor degree—you're too transparent. I'm quite myself. I'm not in delirium. I'm simply going out."

The old man's face grew a little white.

"You can't mean it, Master Jim," he faltered. "In the state you're in, sir, it's likely to cost you your life to go out."

"It's likely to cost me more than that to stay in," said Jimmie Dale, quietly.

The old man twisted his hands together; he coughed in a sort of helpless way.

"I'm an old man, Master Jim, sir"—the tears were welling into Jason's eyes—"and you'll pardon me, Master Jim, for taking liberties, but when you were a baby I dandled you, Master Jim, on my knee, and—and I know there's something strange and—and danger—that's come into your life—and it isn't my place to ask what it is, but—but for God's sake, Master Jim, sir, don't you go out until you're well enough."

Jimmie Dale stepped toward the old man, and laid both hands on the other's shoulders—gently.

"Jason," he said, steadily, "get me an overcoat, light weight, dark color—and a slouch hat. Tell Benson I'm waiting for him—and to pamper my infirmities we'll take the limousine to-night." He turned Jason around, and pushed the old man quietly toward the door. "Look sharp, please, Jason," he said.

The door closed behind the old butler. For an instant Jimmie Dale stood staring at the door, his face softened, almost a mistiness in the dark, steady eyes; then he turned abruptly to the liqueur stand again.

"I guess perhaps I'll need it," he muttered.

He took out a small silver flask, filled it with brandy, and slipped it into his pocket. He went out then, closing the door behind him. As he descended the stairs he caught the sound of the car on the driveway coming from the garage at the rear of the house. That was Benson—another Jason! He felt suddenly humbled. Benson young, Jason old—at the extremes of life—and each without an instant's hesitation would give their all for him. It was a strange, strange thing, the love of men one for another—the love of these two for him. He had accepted it all too matter-of-factly perhaps in the past, not stopping to appraise it always for its immeasurable worth, or, when he thought of it, perhaps priding himself on it only as a possession that other men did not have, like a suit of clothes perhaps made by an exclusive tailor where the same pattern was not supplied to any one else. He did not know how he had won it.

He took his coat and hat from Jason in the hallway. The old man's lips were twitching.

"God bless you, Jason!" said Jimmie Dale suddenly, and swung through the door.

At the curb Benson, the chauffeur, touched his cap, as he reached out to open the door of the big closed car—then hesitated.

"You'll excuse me, Mr. Dale," he stammered, "but—but I——"

Jimmie Dale smiled.

"It's a wonderful night, isn't it, Benson—for a drive?" he said. "West Broadway, Benson—and, oh, yes, stop anywhere within a block of Thompson Street."

"Yes, sir," said Benson mechanically—and opened the door.

Jimmie Dale stepped into the car. The door closed. He saw Benson, in the act of swinging into his seat, turn and face for an instant the open doorway of the lighted vestibule where Jason stood. Benson's shoulders lifted in a helpless gesture.

"What the hell can I do?" said Benson's shoulders eloquently.

XXII

A TAPPED WIRE

JIMMIE DALE settled back in his seat. The car moved swiftly, smoothly downtown. It wasn't so bad; not so very much worse than being in bed. He was quite all right.

He stared out of the windows. He had no plans—no definite plans. How could he have? Somewhere, somehow, he must pick up the trail of the Phantom's associates. That was all. And Mother Margot offered by far the best and surest way—if she were back. Obviously, therefore, the first move was to find out if Mother Margot had returned, and he would know that in a few minutes now.

And if she were still away?

His lips tightened grimly. The Sanctuary—Smarlinghue—a spectre haunting the Bad Lands through the night! Perhaps hopelessly! He had done that on so many nights before. What other way was there—to find Bunty Myers?

He lighted a cigarette. Occasionally he shifted his position. He told himself that it was only because the bandage was so tight that he was beginning to experience a little discomfort.

The car circled around Washington Square, and made its way into West Broadway. Presently it stopped. Jimmie Dale got out.

"Wait half an hour for me, Benson," he said quietly. "No more. If I'm not here by then take the car back home."

He did not wait for a reply. Half a block ahead was Thompson Street. He started toward it. His coat was tightly buttoned around his throat, his collar turned up, his slouch hat pulled toughly down over his eyes.

He swung around the corner, walking with his hands in his pockets. The narrow street seethed with its usual night life. Half naked children tumbled in the gutters, and played beneath the wheels of the pushcarts that flanked the side-walks on both sides of the road. Banjo torches spluttered and flung out fantastic flares; shawled women, dark, swarthy, elbowed about the carts; men who wore earrings and chat-tered in strange tongues lounged on the sidewalk or jostled their way along in a sort of aimless fashion. The place was a din, a hubbub. The hawkers cried their wares.

Jimmie Dale made his way along with studied carelessness, and suddenly, nodding sharply to himself in satisfaction, he edged out to the curb. Mother Margot was back! True, the old hag herself was nowhere in sight, but this was her push-cart here laden with its miscellany of small articles like the notion counter of a department store. He picked up a cheap, gaudy, colored kerchief and pretended to examine it. At the next cart was the old Italian whom he, Jimmie Dale, as Smarlinghue then, had accosted three days before when, as now, he had been in search of Mother Margot.

"How much?" he demanded, holding up the kerchief.

The Italian shrugged his shoulders.

"Wait-a da minute," he said. "She just gone-a da tele-phone. She come-a right back."

Jimmie Dale put down the kerchief.

"I don't want it bad enough to wait," he said indifferently —and drew back into the throng on the sidewalk. But the next instant he had sidled out of the crowd again into a dark, narrow and dirty little alleyway that made the side of an equally dirty and uninviting second-hand shop, on whose unwashed window painted letters, that had once been white, announced that its proprietor was one Antonio Mezzo.

The telephone! Luck! He felt his pulses quicken. There were only two persons who ever called Mother Margot to this telephone here, himself and—the Phantom. His fingers had crept to a pocket in the leather girdle. They came out with his mask. He slipped it quickly over his face. Mother Margot would have news to-night, then! He was at the side door now. It was slightly ajar; and, yes, he could just catch the old hag's miserable jargon, the shrill, complaining voice, muffled, of course, by the telephone booth itself that stood just within beside the door:

"I can't hear youse. De buzzin's got me feazed."

Jimmie Dale's lips straightened suddenly. It wasn't Mother Margot he wanted to hear. Why trust her? He had never caught her at the phone before! He could make her *talk,* but he had no guarantee that it would be the whole truth. He pushed the door open softly and stepped inside. There was a dim light coming from a blackened, nearly burned-out incandescent that dangled from the ceiling. The back room here, littered with old junk and broken furniture, was cut off from the front by a closed door. Being inside the booth, she had not seen him. She was still reiterating the fact that she could not hear distinctly.

Jimmie Dale crept a step forward, another—then with a swift movement he jerked the door of the booth open, and leaning forward clapped his hand firmly over the mouthpiece of the telephone.

There was a startled cry from the old hag, as she shrank back. The side of the booth creaked with her weight.

"My Gawd!" she whispered wildly. "De—de Gray Seal!"

"Yes!" said Jimmie Dale grimly. "Give me that receiver. Quick! You answer as I tell you."

He put the receiver to his ear.

"What's the matter?" demanded a voice imperatively. "What's that noise?"

"Tell him it's Mezzo moving some furniture about," ordered Jimmie Dale swiftly.

He took his hand from the transmitter.

"It's de old dago shovin' some of his junk around," said Mother Margot into the phone.

Again Jimmie Dale's hand closed over the transmitter.

"All right!" snapped the voice. "Can you hear now?"

"Tell him you can hear now," breathed Jimmie Dale.

"Sure," obeyed Mother Margot. "Sure—I gets youse now."

"Go to the Crescent as I told you, then," said the voice, "and give Curley this message: *The black box. Sadie Foy's at eleven o'clock.* Understand?"

Jimmie Dale nudged Mother Margot significantly as he nodded his head affirmatively, and again removed his hand from the phone.

"Sure!" said Mother Margot.

"Hurry!" said the voice, curtly.

The receiver at the other end of the wire was hung up.

"Let's get out of here," said Jimmie Dale, coolly.

Mother Margot stumbled out of the booth. She was twisting her hands together, casting frightened, hurried glances toward the closed door that led into the second-hand shop in front, glancing furtively, too, at Jimmie Dale from under her hooded shawl.

"My Gawd!" she mumbled thickly. "My Gawd!"

Outside in the lane, the side door closed, Jimmie Dale drew the old woman against the wall of the building, and for a moment stood staring at her speculatively in the darkness.

Suddenly she reached out, and clawed at his sleeve.

"Wot youse goin' to do?" she whispered wildly. "My Gawd! De Gray Seal! Wot youse goin' to do?"

Jimmie Dale ignored her question. He spoke sharply.

"So Curley down at the Crescent Saloon is one of the gang too, is he?" he demanded.

"No; he ain't!" She shook her head vehemently. "Not de way youse means, he ain't."

"I suppose that is why a message is sent to him, then," observed Jimmie Dale caustically.

"He gets lot of 'em," she said quickly; "but he don't know wot any of 'em means, an' he don't know where any of 'em goes to. I watched him once. Some one calls him up on de phone, an' he just says de message over, dat's all."

"Quite so!" said Jimmie Dale softly. "But in that case, did it ever strike you that the Voice, as you call him, would save quite a little time, to say nothing of making you trudge around town, by phoning Curley direct?"

Mother Margot was twisting her hands again.

"Youse don't believe me!" she cried out hoarsely. "Youse t'ink I'm stringin' youse. I ain't! Honest to Gawd, I ain't! I'm handin' youse de straight goods. Dat's why no one gets next to de Voice unless he wants 'em to. De trail's gummed up. See? He don't trust no one. He was gettin' leery of me. Dat's why he sent me away. See? Dere's been a lot of leaks. He sent me away for three days on a fake lay. An' w'en I was away one of his games gets a hole all bust in it again, an' I guess it was youse did it. So he's sure it ain't me dat's spillin' any of de beans. Youse see, don't youse? Say, for God's sake, youse see, don't youse, dat I ain't stringin' youse?"

The old hag's voice was full of nervous anxiety. She kept wringing her hands together. Jimmie Dale nodded. She was undoubtedly telling the truth. He could quite understand now why she had been away—and could understand, perhaps better than she could, the Phantom's dire need of looking to his fences.

"But the phone?" he suggested.

"Well, dat's de answer, ain't it?" she said. "It ain't so much of a trick to trace a telephone call, is it? Not if de dicks want to do it. Dat's why he don't telephone dat sort of stuff nowhere except here, an' not to nobody except me. An'—an' if he was wise to wot happened in dere just now he'd—he'd—my Gawd, youse know wot he'd do! Say, youse ain't goin' to stop me, are youse? Youse're goin' to tell me wot dat message is, ain't youse, an' let me put it acrost?" She was clawing pitifully, frantically at Jimmie Dale's sleeve again. "If youse don't, an' I don't give Curley dat message, dey'll kill me. Mabbe youse got away wid it bein' de dago bumpin' furniture dat made de row in de booth, but if de message don't go, dat don't go neither, an'—an' dey'll slit me troat. Aw, for Gawd's sake! Youse knows dat! Dat's wot dey'll do!"

It was literally true. The failure of Mother Margot to deliver the message was exactly equivalent to her death sentence. Jimmie Dale's lips were a straight line. There was no quibbling on that point. The Phantom's trade was murder. He would strike without an instant's hesitation at the slightest indication that the old hag had played him false. On the other hand if he, Jimmie Dale, allowed Mother Margot to deliver the message he delivered himself without reservation into her hands—either that, or go back home to bed and leave Sadie Foy's alone. But again, if the message were delivered it promised almost to a certainty that at Sadie Foy's he would pick up the trail he had come out to-night to find. The Crescent Saloon and Curley did not interest him. That was only a relaying station. The rendezvous was at Sadie Foy's. Suppose he refused to give Mother Margot the message? Would it stop the projected devilry that was obviously afoot? And on that basis alone ought he to refuse? If he did, it would cost the woman her life. There was no supposition about that. That was fact. He couldn't do that, could he? And yet, since he must then assume the moral responsibility, and if for no other reason than that play a hand at Sadie Foy's, his own life very probably hung on whether Mother Margot would keep faith with him or not.

"Dey'll kill me!" Mother Margot whispered hoarsely. She pulled at his sleeve, clung to it; she was rocking queerly on her feet.

"Yes," said Jimmie Dale calmly, "they'd kill you; and they would equally kill me if, once out of my sight, you added to the message the information that I was in this game again to-night. And so you see it's a case of you being killed to a certainty, or the *chance,* depending on you, of the same thing happening to me." He smiled suddenly, whimsically. "I haven't very much choice, have I? I can't send you to your death. The message? Oh, yes! It's this: The black box. Sadie Foy's at eleven o'clock. That's all."

She drew in her breath suddenly.

"My Gawd, youse're *white!*" she said in a low, catchy way. "I gets youse. Youse're goin' to be at Sadie Foy's, an' youse're takin' de chance of me splittin' on youse. Well, youse needn't worry, an' I'll tell youse why. I ain't forgot de night at Pedler Joe's. Youse made me go dere, I knows;

but youse risked yer life to get me out of it, an' I ain't forgot."

"I've wondered about that," said Jimmie Dale, half to himself; then, briskly: "Do you know anything about this black box or what the message means?"

She shook her head.

"Do you know where Bunty Myers is?"

Again she shook her head.

"I ain't heard anythin' for three days until in dere tonight," she said earnestly. "I only just got back."

"All right," said Jimmie Dale quietly. "You'd better go now. And hurry—in case there's a check on the time when you should be at Curley's."

She hesitated an instant. Then she brushed a hand quickly across her eyes.

"My Gawd, youse're white," she said again, huskily—and turned, and shuffled hurriedly down the alleyway toward the street.

Jimmie Dale watched her until she had disappeared.

"Perhaps!" said Jimmie Dale grimly. "And perhaps I am —a fool!"

XXIII

THE PIECES OF A PUZZLE

FIVE minutes later Jimmie Dale was staring at Benson's back through the plate glass, as the big limousine, continuing its progress in a downtown direction, rolled rapidly along.

He was frowning heavily. He did not like this! He did not like having Benson along like this. Not because Benson could not be trusted to the uttermost, but for Benson's own sake. There wasn't much risk for Benson, of course; in fact there wasn't any, as far as he could see, but he would have felt easier in his mind had he been alone. They were going ostensibly now to the Silver Dragon, a famous resort of slumming parties in Chinatown, and Benson would park outside where other cars were parked, and simply wait. But for all that, there was——

He shrugged his shoulders. What else could he do? His side was behaving very nicely so far, better than he had hoped for, in fact, but that condition was dependent, he knew very well, on saving himself all he could. That was why, for example, he had not gone to the Sanctuary, and, as Smarling-hue then, gone alone to Sadie Foy's. There would have been time—ample time. But he wasn't fit to play the rôle of Smarlinghue to-night.

He dismissed the subject from his mind. He had done what had seemed the wisest and best thing. The rest was in the lap of the gods. He began a little mental calculation as he took out his watch. It was twenty minutes to eleven now. It was roughly about ten minutes ago when Mother Margot had started on her errand. She should be at Curley's by now. That left a leeway of twenty minutes for somebody to telephone Curley and, presumably, make the rendezvous at Sadie Foy's at eleven o'clock.

Jimmie Dale replaced the watch in his pocket—and stared again at the back of Benson's head. The black box! Sadie Foy's! He shook his head. The combination meant nothing to him, of course. But Sadie Foy herself was quite a different matter. In Chinatown Sadie Foy was a celebrity—a very shady and notorious celebrity. She was seldom sober. She was a white woman, old now, who had married a Chinaman. But Charley Foy, her husband, had perished in a Tong feud. That was many years ago. Since then she had lived in a little rat-hole of a place as dissolute as herself, a few blocks from Chatham Square, supported, according to the police, by a pension from the Tong for which her lamented Charlie Foy had given up his life.

A queer smile flickered across Jimmie Dale's lips. As Larry the Bat in the days of old, as Smarlinghue of to-day, he was in this particular very much better informed than the police. There was no question whatever about the pension; but the pension was not based on purely philanthropic motives, or due to a deep-seated sorrow for Charlie Foy's untimely and violent decease. It satisfied the police. Actually, Sadie Foy drove a lively trade in bulk opium, or in anything else of an illicit character that promised her a profit. The bulk opium accounted for the pension; an innate evilness and cunning accounted for her general depravity. It was a choice place for a rendezvous of any questionable sort, or for any purpose!

The minutes passed as the car sped along. Jimmie Dale half closed his eyes. Sadie Foy, or for that matter her iniquities, meant nothing—it was the trail now that so obviously led to Sadie Foy's door. The Phantom was interested in something at Sadie Foy's at eleven o'clock. Would the trail broaden—or break? What did the night hold? A final reckoning with the Phantom? Freedom for *her*—if she still lived? Success, partial or whole? Failure? What?

The car slowed, and stopped. Jimmie Dale stepped to the sidewalk.

"We'll raise the limit a little this time, Benson," he said. "Wait an hour."

Jimmie Dale mounted the steps of the garishly lighted restaurant before which the car had stopped, and passed inside. The place was a riot of noise; the clatter of dishes, laughter, song, the never ceasing hum of numberless voices from numberless tables where the diners sat. He walked leisurely from room to room, making for the rear of the establishment—and here nonchalantly walked out into the cross street behind. The Silver Dragon was blest with two entrances.

And now Jimmie Dale quickened his step. He was in a narrow, twisting, ill-lighted little street in the heart of Chinatown. Shuttered windows threw out stealthy gleams of light from their interstices; scuffling figures sidled by him. He passed a small frame house, mouldy and in decay, weather-streaked, which paint had not touched in years. It was in complete darkness; not a light showed from it anywhere. And then in another minute he had slipped into the adjacent lane, and in still another was creeping cautiously across a filthy back yard—with the rear of the small house that was mouldy and in decay looming up before him. This was Sadie Foy's.

His eyes narrowed now a little grimly. It was black here all around him, but the house itself was not quite so dark at the rear as it had been in front! From a lower window just ahead of him little undulating threads of light seeped out from behind the edges of a drawn shade. It was the air did that, of course—made the shade sway slightly. Therefore the window must be open.

Voices, in what seemed like low, guttural undertones, began to reach him. He stole cautiously forward. There was refuse in the yard, and it was pitch black. It was not easy to assure silence even from step to step. A tin can became an object of dire menace. A minute, two, passed—and then Jimmie Dale, from a stooping position, stood upright. His head was just on a level with the window sill. He could hear now distinctly.

"Well, we're gettin' fed up waitin'!" said a silky voice. "It's eleven o'clock, and we've been patient for about a couple of hours. If youse ain't comin' across nice an' pleasant, mabbe we can help yer memory a little more de other way. Sadie's got everything locked up nice for de night in front, an' nobody'll disturb us. Ain't youse, Sadie?"

Jimmie Dale's dark eyes lighted with a sudden gleam. He could see little, scarcely more than a group of shadows on the shade, but he had recognised the purring voice. The trail was here! It was the Kitten's voice—and with the Kitten at work, hand in glove with him somewhere should be the Phantom and Bunty Myers. If the light breeze would only stir that shade a little more—just half an inch!

A woman cackled hoarsely.

"Sure! I'll take care of dat! Don't youse worry!"

"D'ye hear?" It was the Kitten's voice again. "We've let youse off easy so far, but we're gettin' fed up. I ask youse for de last time before youse gets hurt some more, where's de black box? Yer brother didn't take it up de river wid him; an' de mob of boobs youse played for suckers ain't got it, 'cause dey're mostly on de street now wid de kids pickin' up deir free lunches in de gutters; an' it wasn't left around loose in de crib w'en yer sweet little Banco Santos was pinched; an' youse've been hidin' all de time—so where is it?"

There was no answer. In the silence Jimmie Dale, almost involuntarily, startled, had drawn back a little. The Banco Santos! He did not need to see in there. He knew what the black box was now! The trial was scarcely a week old. The papers had been full of it. Two brothers, two Portuguese, Georges and Manuel Santos, had run a private bank, garnering in the savings of, for the most part, the poorer element among the foreign class, the tenement dwellers. They had played the game craftily, with vicious patience, for nearly two years, piling up the savings of the poor—only the final coup had been disrupted a little by a sudden suspicion that had arisen in the minds of the authorities. And one evening, as the latter had descended on the place, the two brothers had decamped by the back window, one of them carrying under his arm a black, oblong security box. One of the brothers, as likewise the black box, had not been seen or heard of since. The other brother, Georges, had been caught, and only a few days ago had started to serve a fifteen-years' sentence in Sing Sing. The missing funds were estimated at between twenty-five and thirty thousand dollars.

The Kitten purred again:

"Ain't it too bad he's lost his voice as well as his memory! An' we ain't done hardly anythin' but be civil to him since we runs into him back dere in Mickey de Cobbler's dump. Mabbe he's sore 'cause we didn't go right up an' shake hands wid him den! But youse see we was just sittin' around havin' a drink, an' thought mabbe we'd had one too many an' was seein' things w'en de cellar door opens, an' one of dese guys here says he'll bet a million bucks dat it was Manuel Santos, an' by de time we gets our breaths back he's slipped out. We hadn't never travelled together none of us before, but dis looked like we all had tickets for de same place. So we follows him. An' over he sneaks to Sadie's here to buy some coke, an' we trails in, an' sure enough w'en we gets a real good look at him Steenie's right an' it's Manuel Santos. Only he ain't got de black box dat dey talked about in de papers wid him." He laughed a little, low, viciously. "I'm sick of askin' him. Youse ask him, Steenie, same as youse did before—only a little harder."

There was a sudden blurred movement of the figures on the shade—a sudden low, throttled cry of pain and fear.

Jimmie Dale's fingers touched the lower edge of the shade. They were not occupied in there with the window now! And it might even have been but the stirring of the night breeze. The shade swayed gently inward an inch, two—and floated almost imperceptibly back into place again.

Jimmie Dale's face was hard and strained. It was not difficult to pick out Manuel Santos from the group! The man's hands were tied, and he drooped over the table as though in a half swoon; his face was battered ferociously, and blood trickled in two or three little streams from his cheeks. Behind him stood the Kitten. In a corner Sadie Foy cackled applause, and rubbed skinny hands together joyously. There were four other men—dregs, rats, jacks-of-all-trades in the underworld. He knew three of them by name: Steenie Klotz; Red Jack; the Bummer. Nice names! But in the underworld the monikers were apt!

There came the sound of a blow, another, and another—and then a cry again. A voice gasped out weakly:

"Stop! For God's sake, stop! I—I'll tell."

"Blamed if youse ain't a great memory worker, Steenie!" purred the Kitten's voice. "He's goin' to tell. Well, Manuel, where is it?"

"It—it's at the camp." The man's words came painfully.

"Where's dat?" demanded the Kitten.

"It's on the Sound. It—it's just this side of the Martin-Holmes place."

Jimmie Dale's brows contracted suddenly. The Martin-Holmes had nothing to do with this, of course; but he remembered now——

"Youse mean dat summer shack youse an' yer brother had?" inquired the Kitten softly.

"Yes," the man answered.

"Nix on dat!" The Kitten jeered suddenly. "De bulls lived dere for about two weeks pawin' it over. Don't youse try any of dat stuff, my bucko! If it'd been in de house dey'd have found it. I heard dey even pulled de floors up. Say, Steenie, *youse'd* better try again!"

"No, no!" Manuel Santos' voice rose shrilly. "It's true! I'm telling you the truth. The police could never find it, but it's there."

"All right," said the Kitten evenly. "Tell us about it, den."

"It ain't really in the house, it—it's outside the attic window." The words came slowly in a mumbling sort of way. "It looks as though the eaves were all boarded in around the house, but you can move one of them above the window. There—there's only one window. It—it's there."

There was a low, muttered chorus of exultant oaths; and then the Kitten's voice:

"Dat sounds good enough to be true." He was purring again. "I'll get a closed car, an' we'll hike along out dere, an' youse'll come too, Manuel, so's dere won't be no tricks. Youse ain't such a fool after all, Manuel! A little trip to South America where youse'll be out of everybody's road, an' a lot safer yourself dan youse have been for de last six weeks tryin' to hide yerself away, is better'n takin' a last ride in a wooden box where youse can't look at de scenery! Youse're among friends, Manuel, if youse only knew it. Dere's some——"

Jimmie Dale was retreating from the window. A moment more, and he had gained the street; and, hurrying now, returning by the same way he had come, he reached his car in front of the Silver Dragon.

"Benson," he said quietly, "we seem fated to make quite a night of it. Off and on, you've driven me a number of times to Mr. Martin-Holmes' summer residence out on the Sound. I know it's closed now for the season, but do you remember just exactly where it is?"

"Perfectly, sir," said Benson.

"Good!" nodded Jimmie Dale. "Drive there now—that is to within, say, half a mile this side of the place. If I remember correctly, it's quite thickly wooded there. I leave it entirely to you to find a convenient spot in about that neighbourhood to run the car off the road and park it where it will not be seen."

Benson stared, a hesitant, anxious expression creeping into his face.

Jimmie Dale smiled.

"I'm still quite all right, Benson," he said.

"Yes, sir," said Benson mechanically.

"And, by the way"—Jimmie Dale paused in the act of stepping into the car—"I might say that I am in a very great hurry, Benson."

"Yes, sir," said Benson heavily.

For a moment, as he settled back on the cushions and the

car started forward, the smile held on Jimmie Dale's lips. Benson, like Jason, was comparable to a hen with her chick. Benson at this precise instant probably—to mix metaphors—was inwardly wriggling like an eel. He was probably debating with himself whether he should not drive directly home, and there, by brute force if necessary, with the assistance of Jason, put him, Jimmie Dale, back to bed again—even if he got fired for it! Benson, however, in the last analysis wouldn't do anything of the kind—he would play the game.

The smile faded now from Jimmie Dale's lips, and a puzzled, anxious look settled on his face as he dismissed Benson from his mind. He had acted quickly back there at Sadie Foy's because he had realised that there was no time to lose; and though, even then, he had realised too that the pieces of the puzzle seemed somehow strangely mismated, he had also realised that the final act in any case would be played out where he was going now—at the Santos' camp. Further, there was the moral responsibility to save that money, and nothing would have induced him to shift that responsibility to, say, the police, when instinctively he sensed, as he did, that the Phantom had still a card to play, a card that also must be played out at the same place. But what was that card? If it were only the Kitten who was involved, he could pick up the Kitten's trail again at the Santos camp; but it was more than the Kitten that he wanted, more than the Kitten that he still hoped for, and in which hope intuition told him he was justified. He wanted the Phantom—or Bunty Myers.

He had time now to solve the puzzle—if he could. But the pieces on closer examination only seemed the more mismated. They contradicted even the sense of intuition that was so strong upon him. Where was the Phantom's hand in this? The Kitten? Well, then, why that message?—"Sadie Foy's at eleven o'clock." The Kitten had said himself he had been there long *before* eleven. The Kitten was therefore *already* at Sadie Foy's when the message was delivered to Curley at the Crescent Saloon. And then, again, the four men who were with the Kitten, he was absolutely certain, had no intimate connection with the Phantom; they were not the kind the Phantom gathered around him; they were simply apaches, buzzards of the underworld, mentally the lowest type of criminal, whose only knowledge of finesse was embodied in the use of a black-jack, a knife, or a revolver. They did not belong! Suppose then they had been hired for this special occasion? In that case the Kitten was already fully equipped to carry through the night's work. Why, then, the message?

The miles flew by; the minutes passed into quarter hours. They had long since been out on a country road.

What did it mean?

Jimmie Dale, save that at long intervals he subconsciously eased his position, sat motionless, staring introspectively at the window.

What did it mean?

And then suddenly Jimmie Dale sat erect. He had it! It had come like a flash. It dovetailed; it fitted in its minutest part. It postulated only that the Kitten had a means of ready communication with his unhallowed master, the Phantom, which in itself was axiomatic. The Kitten had haphazardly been in the company of the four apaches when one of the four, this Steenie, had recognised the fugitive, Manuel Santos. It was a "find" worth thirty thousand dollars—which the Kitten did not propose the other four should share. It was very simple! The Kitten had taken the leadership, and in the early stages at Sadie Foy's had undoubtedly gone out on some excuse and sent the Phantom word of what was afoot, stating probably that he was sure they could make Manuel Santos talk, and if so he would somehow stall on any move being made until the Phantom had time to act, setting that time at eleven o'clock. Obviously, then, some one would be on hand at that time to receive from the Kitten the information as to where the black box was hidden, if that information had been obtained, and the "some one" would then arrive first at the hiding place, while the Kitten and the four thugs would arrive later only to find a rifled nest! And the Kitten would be secure from any complicity in the eyes of the four thugs—wherein the Kitten was very wise!

Jimmie Dale stooped suddenly forward and picked up the speaking tube. He wasn't racing any more then against the Kitten on whom he had a known start. He was racing against "some one" else, some one who would race like mad so as to keep the Kitten in countenance and not force his stalling to become apparent through lingering on the road when his hungry dupes would be urging speed.

"Faster, Benson!" he said sharply. "All you've got the rest of the way!"

He leaned back in his seat again. It was clear enough now. But who was this "some one?" It wasn't the Phantom himself, for the Phantom had sent the message. Who, then, was the Phantom's delegate? Jimmie Dale's lips drooped curiously until grim little lines formed at the corners of his mouth. It was more likely than any one else to be the man he had started out to find—Bunty Myers. He frowned quickly. Had he made a mistake? Should he have remained at Sadie Foy's? This delegate must have been there somewhere at eleven—when the Kitten was going out again with the excuse of getting a closed car. And then he shook his head impatiently. Perhaps! If he had known what he was so sure of now, he might have acted differently—perhaps not. This, after all, was the surer way, both of finding that delegate, and securing possession of the black box.

The car was eating up the miles now, keeping check almost with the minutes as they passed.

He ran his hand through his hair. Dog eat dog! It was dirty, miserable work all the way through, beginning with Manuel Santos, who was perhaps the most despicable of the lot. His hands clenched suddenly. If nothing else came of it, getting that money back to those to whom it meant their all was worth whatever it might cost him to-night. Thirty thousand dollars! There was something fiendish, damnable, in the vicious premeditation, the vicious patience with which the two Portuguese had worked! He remembered in the

account of the trial it had come out in evidence that the
authorities had not been lax. Always on demand securities
in the shape of bonds had been produced to make the bal-
ances. Of course! And of a sudden those bonds had been
transferred into cash, and—presto!—the squalid little bank
was no more! He smiled grimly. It was probably the steady
demand for so many bills of large denominations during the
two or three days prior to the end that had first aroused
the suspicions of the authorities, and——

The car was slowing down. And now it jolted over rough
ground. A branch slapped smartly against the window pane.
The headlights, streaming out, threw tree trunks into spectral
relief against a background of utter blackness. And then
the headlights went off, and the car stopped.

Jimmie Dale stepped out.

"You're sure of the place, Benson, and that you're hidden
from the road?" he asked crisply.

"Yes, sir," Benson answered. "Quite sure, sir."

"Very well!" said Jimmie Dale. "Keep your lights off,
wait for me, and don't leave the car under any circumstances." He sensed a protest anent himself rising to Benson's lips, and he turned quickly away. "I'll be back in a
few minutes, Benson," he said.

XXIV

THE BLACK BOX

JIMMIE DALE moved forward through the trees. It could not be far, not more than three or four hundred yards, for the Santos house lay between himself and the Martin-Holmes estate. That was why he had told Benson to stop half a mile this side of the latter place. The general direction, he knew, was a diagonal one—toward the Martin-Holmes' residence, and toward the shore, away from the road. He smiled a little queerly to himself as he went along. He remembered that during a week-end visit to Holmes a year or so ago, the latter had expressed his annoyance at what he had called an unsightly shack that two Portuguese had put up on the beach close to his place. He, Jimmie Dale, had not been very much interested then; he was vitally interested in that so-called shack now!

He frowned suddenly. He had been making fair progress, and should have reached his destination by now; but, instead, he was still in the woods and the ground was growing wet and soggy underfoot. He edged off in the direction of the shore—the house was at the water's edge, Holmes had said—and went on for another hundred yards. It grew worse. He could hear now the lapping of the waves. The trees grew fewer, and began to be replaced by a reedy growth —and then of a sudden Jimmie Dale halted. A glimmer of moonlight flickered on water and waving marsh grass. It was impassable—it reached out into the Sound itself.

It was disaster! He felt his face whiten. He must already have been ten minutes on the way—and ten minutes was the utmost limit of margin he had any right to count upon. Ten minutes! It was far worse than that! It would take that much more to retrace his steps and circle around the other way before he could get started again.

He gnawed at his lips now as he turned and began to run. It was almost certain disaster; disaster to the moral responsibility he had assumed, disaster to the hope he had cherished that to-night— He stumbled. He could not be careful of his footing now. Defeat, yes, perhaps—but he would not accept it. He ran doggedly. Again he stumbled, and again. And now he winced with pain. This hurt his side brutally. It wasn't like riding on the cushions of a luxurious limousine, or even of walking when no unusual effort was required.

He went on. His breath came hard. He swept beads of moisture away from his forehead—and then once he reeled. It was hours, wasn't it, since he had started over again? There wasn't much chance—one perhaps in a thousand—not that much! His jaws clamped hard together. He was making a mess of it with that cursed side, and——

Jimmie Dale came suddenly out of the edge of the woods. Well, at least, this was better! Fifty yards away across a clearing a house loomed shadowy out of the darkness. He listened intently. There was no sound. He darted silently across the clearing and gained the house. It was a small place so close to the shore that, as he crept now noiselessly up the steps of a verandah that apparently ran all around the house, he could make out a little wharf and what looked like an old, neglected boat drawn up on the beach. Certainly, there was no mistaking the house for there was no other of this description, he knew, in the neighbourhood.

A pick-lock came from a pocket in the leather girdle, and with it again the black silk mask. A moment more, and Jimmie Dale stood inside the house. And now he listened again, straining his ears for the slightest sound. Nothing! His face was white and haggard. There was only one answer of course—the Phantom's delegate had been and gone. There had been time enough—so much and to spare that even the Kitten was due now.

He took out a flashlight and circled it around him. The place was crude, to a certain extent unfinished; exactly what

Manuel Santos himself had called it—a camp. It seemed to be divided into several rooms by thin, unpainted partitions. Here at his right, steps led upward. Well, he had come this far, and even if the chances now were all against him, he was still going up there, but he had to think of the Kitten now—the possibility of being trapped himself by the Kitten and his thugs. There was time enough now to take the precaution of arming himself with a knowledge of the general plan of the place. He stepped hurriedly through the several rooms that made the depth of the house. He nodded in quick understanding. The "camp" was of uniform design. One took his choice as to which was the rear and which was the front. Here, where he stood now, a door opened on the verandah; and here, too, a rough staircase led to the upper story, or attic, as Manued Santos had called it.

Well, the attic now! That window! He went quickly up the stairs. At the top, his flashlight disclosed a broad landing and a closed door. The door was unlocked, and he stepped forward over the threshold. The flashlight circled the interior. Again he nodded. It was an attic, nothing more or less, without partitions, that reached from one end of the house to the other. There was a single window, halfway down one side—the right-hand side from where he stood now facing the Sound.

He was at the window now. He opened it, and stood up on the sill—and suddenly, poised there, he remained motionless. From the direction of the road he thought he had caught the sound of a motor. It was gone now. Perhaps he had been mistaken. The road was, as nearly as he could calculate it, a good hundred and fifty yards back from the water.

He felt swiftly up above his head outside the window. He did not dare use the flashlight now. Whether he was mistaken about the motor or not, the Kitten was already due, and a light would show a long way through the darkness. And, besides, there was partial moonlight, and he could see a little. His fingers were feeling, searching, prying over the rough boarding. It was very ingenious, this—the eaves boarded in to meet the wall of the house—only he could not find any section of it that seemed at all loose or movable. It would be craftily done, of course; he would hardly expect anything else, but—— It was strange! Very strange! The Kitten had been able to pass on no more detailed information about this than he, Jimmie Dale, had overheard; and if he, Jimmie Dale, could not open it, how could the Kitten's confederate have done so? Just luck? A stumbling on the trick of it? It was rather strange!

Jimmie Dale became motionless again, intent, alert. There could be no question about it now. There was the unmistakable crunch of *several* footsteps approaching the house from the direction of the road. The Kitten was coming!

In a flash Jimmie Dale reached into the leather girdle, and a powerful little blued-steel jimmy was in his hand. It was very strange! So strange that he meant to see inside there, Kitten or no Kitten! The jimmy ripped into a board above his head, and pried one end of it loose. He felt quickly inside. It was naturally hollow here, and he reached in as far as he could, feeling in both directions. Nothing! He tore the board completely away now, and moving a little along the sill, reached in from the other end. *It was here!* He was wrenching out an oblong shaped, black metal box of the style generally used in the safe deposit vaults. It was here! His brain seemed stunned for a moment. He did not understand. He could not understand—except that he had been wrong— wrong in his deduction from that scene at Sadie Foy's, wrong in his theory of the meaning of that message. And yet it had been so logical, so surely the truth! And yet, just as logically now, he was forced to the conclusion that he had been wrong. There had seemed, still seemed, to be no other possible explanation of that message, and yet—and yet he must have been wrong. Nobody—no Phantom's delegate—had been here. And the Kitten himself was coming now—because those were the footsteps of four or five men. Perhaps the— He pried the box itself hurriedly open. No; the contents had not been taken and the box left! The faint light disclosed package after package of banknotes.

The crunch of footsteps came again, still nearer to the house. Jimmie Dale lowered himself from the sill, and, carrying the box, retreated quickly across the attic to the door opposite to that by which he had entered—the door that faced the Sound. He opened it silently, stepped out on the landing—and the next instant crouched quickly back in the angle between the door jamb and the wall, on the side of the jamb away from the stairs. Too late! He had not thought they were so *near*. There was a footstep below. One of them was coming up this way—was even on the stairs now. He could not see, he could only *hear*. His automatic swung forward. Some one was close to him now. His jaws clamped. No, he had not been seen, either. The footstep passed the threshold of the door, entered the attic, and was crossing it now in the direction of the window. And now through the open door Jimmie Dale could make out a figure, little more than a shadowy outline, in the faint ray of moonlight from the window.

And then Jimmie Dale hung there riveted to the spot. It was quick—quick as the winking of an eye. The figure, at the window now, halted abruptly, and swung sharply around to face the opposite doorway. And, coincidently, it seemed, the door opened, and as a flashlight streamed in and fell full upon the figure, and Jimmie Dale saw the man's face, there was a chorus of savage oaths, and almost simultaneously the flash and roar of a revolver shot. And the figure turned and ran toward the doorway near which Jimmie Dale stood.

It was Bunty Myers.

A voice screamed out in rage:

"Blast youse, Kitten, if youse hadn't bumped against my arm I'd have got him, an' got him good!"

Jimmie Dale's face was set, drawn, rigid, a queer tightness about the corner of his lips. He had been right, a thousand times right! It was not he who had been wrong, nor his intuition, nor his logic at fault. It was Bunty Myers who had been wrong—something had gone wrong with the man's plans, something had——

A fusillade of shots poured into the room after the flying

figure. Bunty Myers stumbled, recovered himself, came on again, staggered through the doorway, and stumbled again—this time dropping to the floor.

And then Jimmie Dale was at work. He slammed the door shut, and snatching out his pick-lock, locked it. Bunty Myers! *He* wanted Bunty Myers! This was the man he had set out to find to-night, and— No, it wasn't only that! Thank God, he wasn't quite so raw as that! Those thugs in there, those apaches, would kill the man like a dog, as they had already tried to do, for interfering with their meat. And the more so now that they would find that meat gone! The Kitten couldn't stop them without giving himself away. It wasn't Bunty Myers, it was a man's life now—if the man were not already too far gone.

He held the box under his left arm, as he bent forward to the huddled form on the floor.

"Quick!" he whispered. "Put your arm around my neck. Do you hear? Make an effort! It's your only chance."

The man, with Jimmie Dale's assistance, lurched to his feet. They staggered, half fell down the stairs together. Bunty Myers was mumbling almost incoherently:

"I—I had a breakdown on the way—out—Kitten. Damn fool, Kitten, why couldn't youse hold—back—eh?—only a—a little late—youse——"

A sweat of agony was standing out on Jimmie Dale's forehead. He was half carrying the man. His side was torturing him.

"My God!" whispered Jimmie Dale between drawn lips.

Behind, upstairs, they were smashing at the locked door. They would either have to break it down or come around the other way through the house. It was worth a couple of minutes' start—and there was the boat there now on the shore just a few yards away.

He plunged on, staggering. Bunty Myers had become almost a dead weight. Well, he couldn't leave the man to be *killed*, could he? The man kept muttering now, muttering, muttering:

". . . Up an' down—see?—'ell of a note—up an' down—up an' down——"

Bunty Myers collapsed a limp heap in the bottom of the boat. Jimmie Dale shoved it off, and jumped in. There were no oars, save a broken one. He seized it, and began to paddle. Footsteps pounded on the verandah, racing around the house. A yell went up:

"Dere he is! Dere he is—in de boat!"

There was the crash and flame spurt of shots, the spat of lead on the water. Jimmie Dale threw himself flat in the boat beside Bunty Myers. With the initial push, and the few strokes he had managed, the boat was quite a little distance from the shore, and what breeze there was was carrying it still farther out and also in the direction of the marshy tract through which he had first tried to reach the house. They could not, therefore, follow him along the shore.

A medley of voices from the shore, punctuated by oaths, reached him:

"Get a boat. . . . Dere'll be one up at dat swell ranch even if it is closed for de summer. . . . Sure! Bust de boathouse in. . . . Beat it quick. . . . He's good an' hurt, an' he won't get far. . . . He was winged upstairs in de attic w'en he fell——"

Jimmie Dale wrenched his flask from his pocket. They had only seen *one* man. Of course! His head was swimming crazily. He gulped down some brandy, and then felt for Bunty Myers' lips.

"Drink this!" he said hoarsely.

The liquor gurgled queerly. He felt it run down the man's chin—but Bunty Myers must have swallowed some of it, for he began to mutter again, obviously in delirium now.

"Up an' down, I tell youse!" mumbled Bunty Myers. "It's honest to Gawd's truth. She don't know it, 'cause it's in de next house. It goes up an' down, I tell youse. I saw it. Up an'—" His voice trailed off.

What did the man mean? Jimmie Dale swept his hand across his eyes. It encountered his mask. He pulled it off and put it in his pocket. They were both delirious, weren't they—he and Bunty Myers? This was the man he had come to find, and from whose lips he had sworn he would tear the Phantom's secret, and all the man did was to croak, "Up and down, up and down!" Why didn't he say, "See-saw, Marjorie Daw!"

He gulped down another mouthful of brandy. Yes, that was better now. He raised his head. The shore was indistinct; not so much through distance, but because what little moonlight there had been was gone now—under a cloud. They would have a boat after him pretty soon. He must paddle now—risk a shot—he wouldn't be very distinct, either.

He dipped in the broken oar. It brought a moan of agony from his lips. The shots he had invited from the shore came —and missed. He *must* paddle—if it tore his side to pieces.

Only *one* man in the boat. That's what they thought. Well, then, why not? He could easily save himself. Drop overboard and swim ashore somewhere in the marshy tract. He had strength enough for that. They'd find the boat—and find a man in it! But there was some reason why he couldn't do that. He shook his head fiercely as though to clear his brain. Yes, of course! He couldn't leave that huddled figure there at his feet to be killed, could he? So it would have to be a fight, unless he could evade them in the darkness. And—and there wasn't much chance of that. He listened. That sounded like a boat coming from somewhere far behind now. But there weren't any more shots from the shore. Naturally! He must be opposite the marsh now, and they couldn't follow him any more on the land.

He couldn't leave the man to be killed—and that's what they'd do, kill the man. The Kitten couldn't prevent it without the others understanding the whole game and turning on the Kitten too. The Kitten had done all he could when he had bumped against the arm of the man who had fired that first shot. Funny, that Bunty Myers should be here! No, it was clear, quite clear! Bunty Myers had started out all right for the box, but a breakdown had made him late, so late that he——

A shout came from the shore behind. It was answered

from the water. There was no further question but that they had secured a boat, though it was still a good way off. His broken oar suddenly touched bottom as he made a stroke. It wasn't the shore—it was just shallow water here fronting the marshland. Well, it didn't matter! He couldn't paddle much more, and not fast enough anyway to escape them, nor run fast enough with a wounded man even if he were ashore to get away from them. He laughed a little harshly. It was a case of fight for it, then. Perhaps Bunty Myers might be roused, propped up against a seat to help. It would be ironical if Bunty Myers hit the Kitten!

He stopped paddling, and leaned forward with his flask once more.

"Here! Quick! Take some more of this!" he said.

There was no answer. The head he lifted slid from his grasp, and thudded with a dull, ugly sound against the side of the boat. And for an instant Jimmie Dale stared at the limp, huddled form. And then, with a low, quick cry, he reached for the other's wrist, searching for the pulse—and then for the man's heart beat. There was none. He drew his breath in sharply. The man was dead.

The splash of oars mingled with the growl and snarl of voices came distinctly now across the water. *Bunty Myers was dead.* It was queer! Strange! It seemed to carry with it some significance beyond the mere fact of death. What was it? He had started out to find Bunty Myers for something or other. His head was swimming miserably again. It had nothing to do with that black box there on the floor of the boat. Nothing to do with——

He spurred himself to action. One man in the boat. There need be only *one* man in the boat now! He looked behind him, straining his eyes through the darkness. He could not see the other boat. Therefore they could not see him. He picked up the black box, and slipped over the side. The water could not be very deep since his oar had touched the bottom—no—it was less than waist high. He began to wade as quickly as he could, and still avoid making any splash, toward the shore.

The sounds from the oncoming boat grew louder, the voices more distinct. And then Jimmie Dale, reeling a little, stepped from the water's edge, and began to make his way silently through the woods. He knew the way. There was no danger of losing it. He was on the same side of the marshy tract that Benson was. He had only to keep straight ahead toward the road. And it wasn't far.

Curious, how heavy the black box was! He smiled grimly. Back there they would think Bunty Myers must have let it drop overboard. What else could they think? But to-morrow the police would get it—with the compliments of the Gray Seal. And the Phantom—no, Bunty Myers! His head was swirling again, but his brain seemed to be fighting desperately to tell him that what Bunty Myers had said about "up and down" and a "next house" somewhere was something he should understand, because he was to make Bunty Myers tell him something if Bunty Myers died for it, and he knew very well that Bunty Myers had died.

He gnawed at his lips. His head was very bad—very bad. He couldn't think any more. Not now! Not to-night! But he had no need to think any more now, had he? There was Benson and the car looming up just ahead of him. The rest was for to-morrow, and the to-morrows.

The to-morrows. . . .

XXV

A DOOR opened and closed softly. A shadow moved in the darkness. Came then the crackle of a match, and a gas jet, air-choked, wheezing in protest, emitted a thin blue flame, grew yellow, and cast a meagre glow over its immediate surroundings. Unkempt, disreputable in his ragged, threadbare attire as Smarlinghue, Jimmie Dale stood for an instant staring around him at the squalid appointments of the place, and then moving abruptly to the far end of the room, flung himself down upon the already crumpled coverings of the dilapidated cot bed against the wall.

This was the Sanctuary. He half closed his eyes, staring at the asthmatic, stuttering gas jet. Well, it would be in every verity a sanctuary for another hour or so; a retreat where he could strive quietly to bring mental order out of chaos, and, yes, physically rest for a little while until it was time to carry out the plan that he proposed to put into execution before another morning came.

Since last night, all through the day, those mumbled words of Bunty Myers, the dying gangster, had been ringing in his ears. They had become an obsession. He could not rid his mind of them—or of the insistently growing intuition that they were the key to the Phantom's lair if he could only make head or tail of them. "Up an' down, I tell youse. . . . She don't know it, 'cause it's in de next house. . . . It goes up an' down, I tell youse. . . ."

Who was "she"? He could not actually deduce it logically, but he was nevertheless sure that "she" was Mother Margot. The voices he had heard in her room but could not locate, the certainty that the clue, the phantom clue as he came to call it, was to be found in Mother Margot's rooms, was of course the basis for this interpretation; but it was the "next house" that bothered him. What did that mean? If he were right, and it was Mother Margot who did not know " 'cause it's in de next house," where was this "next house"? There was nothing there but another tenement across the narrow areaway.

He frowned suddenly, impatiently. His mind was simply beginning to go over again, vainly, ineffectually, what it had already gone over a thousand times, it seemed, since last night. He had already made a decision—hours ago. He would know to-night whether he was right or not; he would know before he slept whether Bunty Myers' dying words linked up the Phantom's secret with Mother Margot's rooms or not. To-night, finally, the phantom clue that *was* in any case connected with the old hag's rooms would be a mystery no longer if he literally had to wreck the place to unearth it.

Jimmie Dale nodded grimly to himself. *To-night!* In a little while—it was too early yet. Just ten o'clock.

His lips tightened. Yes; wreck it! His was a single purpose now—that to-night he would strike with all his might; strike without counting the personal cost; and, above all, strike while for once he possessed the certainty that it would not be too late in the sense that even success in the unearthing of the Phantom and in a final reckoning with the man might only hold a bitter emptiness because she, the Tocsin, the woman he loved, would already have been beyond all aid.

There would be no thought of that. He was lighter of heart on that score than he had been for many days. She was alive; yes, and well, and safe. He knew that to-night. The torment, the fear for her safety that, finding no trace of her, he had known yesterday, and for so many yesterdays before, was gone now. She was alive; and, so far, she was safe. His lips moved silently. Thank God for that! And now he asked only that, whatever the outcome to himself in what he was about to do, she might after to-night be safe for always.

He shook his head a little grimly. Suppose, instead of success, he failed? Too often the Phantom had slipped from his grasp; and he was only too well aware that to-night he was almost literally going up against a stacked hand held by the other. Mother Margot had warned him that her rooms were a trap for the Gray Seal; the Tocsin had warned him. He had' never doubted this simply because more than once he had ventured into those rooms and emerged unscathed. And, though it might well be, as he had argued with himself on his last visit there, that it was now so long ago since the trap had been baited that the Phantom no longer built any hopes upon it as a means of snaring his prey, that argument, however well founded, did not apply to-night. He could not very well expect to attack the trap itself and proceed to demolish it without *inviting* the attention of the trapper, which was, indeed, his prime intention.

A fool? Perhaps! But there was no other way of getting to grips with the Phantom. And to-night she was alive and safe; and there might be no to-morrow night. And, besides, if the worst happened, he would not go out *alone*—the Phantom would go with him. He was somehow sure of that; it was like a deep-seated consciousness, a strange reassuring certainty. And if that were so, he had no quarrel with the price, whatever it might be!

His fingers, fumbling in the pocket of his ragged jacket, found and drew out an envelope. He stared at it for a long time. Hers! The Tocsin's! The first word he had had from her for so many days! His eyes softened. Alive! And he had known so great a fear—a fear that had grown day after day into an almost hopeless agony of dread. She who loved him, and had made no effort to communicate with him after he had been wounded that other night—no effort when he knew that under ordinary conditions she would have moved heaven and earth to do so. That was why, last night, in spite of Jason, in spite of his wound, he had tried to pick up the Phantom's trail again through Bunty Myers—and in a measure had succeeded. He had found Bunty Myers, but Bunty Myers was dead now.

A strange, grim light crept into Jimmie Dale's half-closed eyes. The circle had indeed narrowed. Of the Phantom's satellites, of all those who once had gathered in that back, upstairs room of Wally Kerrigan's "club," there were left now only two—the Kitten and Mother Margot. Those two —and somewhere in his hidden lair the Phantom. Well, to-night then——

He nodded quickly to himself. He was only waiting until it was a little later. He turned impatiently on the cot. Time seemed to drag interminably. The stage was already set. He had warned Mother Margot to keep away from her rooms to-night; to find an alibi for herself. It was a little quixotic, perhaps, a little of added danger to himself; but again, as it had been last night, her life, if things went wrong, might very well pay part of the forfeit, and even Mother Margot was entitled to her life. What else could he have done? It was true that, at best, he could consider her but an unwilling sort of ally; but nevertheless, even though it might have been but through fear, she had, he was sure, always played straight with him. And so to-night he could have done no less than to have given her her chance again.

Jimmie Dale rose abruptly from the cot, and, with the envelope in his hand, stepped back across the room again to a position under the gas jet. He had found the note here in the usual place behind the movable section of the baseboard when, late that afternoon, after having previously called Mother Margot from her pushcart on Thompson Street to that rather singularly-placed telephone in the rear of Antonio Mezzo's shop and had given her her warning, he had come to the Sanctuary for the purpose of assuming the rôle of Smarlinghue, and of spending at least a portion of the waiting hours in the underworld's inner circles which were always pregnant with the possibility of affording an additional thread or clue that might lend strength to his intended stroke against the Phantom. He read the note again. It was dated that afternoon:

Dear Philanthropic Crook:—What have you been thinking? With you wounded, and believing I would be in a position to know of it, and no word from me, it could only have been one of two things. Either I was heartless, or—or what you had feared so greatly had happened. It could not be the former, and so I know that in your love you must have been, as I would have been, mad with anxiety.

I said I would not write to you or communicate with you until the shadows had all gone out of our lives again, but this afternoon I would indeed be heartless if I did not send you this word. I am well; and I am safe. Through circumstances that I shall not enter into, I did not know that you were wounded until last night, and then, almost coincidently, I also knew that from last night's activities your wound could not have been serious, and so *my* anxiety was relieved.

Just one word more. Once before, long, long ago, so long ago that it seems now it were in some other age, I wrote you that it was near the end, that I had all but won, that victory was in sight, and—and, Jimmie, only disaster came. And so now I hesitate to say anything but just this: Things are going very well, and it may be, Jimmie—oh, I can not help but say it—only *hours* before the shadows will have gone forever.

MARIE.

Jimmie Dale replaced the note in his pocket. Somehow, he could not bring himself to destroy it, as he had always done before. It had been so long since he had heard from her; it was physical, tangible evidence that she was *alive*. He swept his hand across his eyes. Those fears of last night—that had driven him, wounded, from his bed! It was as though she had almost read his mind, read the argument he had followed and from which he had deduced the worst. It was strange, though, that she had not known—if things were going so very well! Circumstances! What circumstances?

He began to pace up and down the squalid room; and then, as abruptly as he had left it, he went and flung himself down on the cot again. He was restless. It was not his wound. His wound was all right, and was none the worse for last night's experiences. His side was sore and stiff, of course, and in that sense caused him a certain discomfort, but otherwise he was quite normal.

It was not his wound that caused his restlessness; it was this dragging of time, this waiting for the moment to arrive when he could supplant inaction with activity. Perhaps he would have done better to have remained longer in those various hidden places of the inner circles of the underworld that he had visited after he had received the Tocsin's note? He shrugged his shoulders. No; he was better here. He had learned all that he could have hoped to learn—yes, and more! No; that was not quite true. He had, rather, only substantiated beyond question what he had already decided in his own mind could be the only logical conclusion to the affair of last night when the Kitten and Bunty Myers, playing Steenie Klotz and his companion apaches for dupes, had attempted to secure the stolen funds of the defunct Banco Santos.

His jaws closed with a snap. Whisperings! How many times before had he listened to the voice of the underworld breathing its secrets through the underground exchanges where none save those of the aristocracy might find entrance, and where the peers of that abandoned realm of Crimeland kept their fingers on the pulse of a seething, disturbed and moiling citizenry! And to-night the underworld was in a sort of tense ferment, watching in unholy anticipation a game of life and death that was being played out behind its guarded doors that were so effectually closed to the outer world.

Jimmie Dale smiled suddenly, grimly now. He had found the underworld viciously agog, intent with gluttonous eagerness upon a drama whose dénoûement promised to be bloodthirsty and murderous enough to satisfy even its unbridled lusts! Steenie Klotz, Red Jack and their companions had been played for dupes by Bunty Myers and the Kitten, but the dupes were not altogether fools, nor their intellects fallen to so low an estate that they had failed to absorb the fact that one plus one made two! The Kitten, and very certainly indeed Bunty Myers, had not expected that the night would end with the dupes finding Bunty Myers dead at their hands in that boat on the shore of the Sound! And of the two now Bunty Myers was perhaps in the better case! The Kitten, it transpired, had had sense enough not to stand on the order of his going, and had incontinently fled for his life. He had not been heard of since last night.

Again Jimmie Dale smiled grimly. It was the logical conclusion—and it was very simple. Bunty Myers and the Kitten for years had been well known characters in the underworld; and for years they had been known to work *together* in Gentleman Laroque's gang. And one and one made two, that was all!

Whisperings! Whisperings, as ghouls might whisper in hideous enthusiasm at the promise of some abominable feast to come, whisperings everywhere through the underground exchanges of Gangland! Of the passing of Bunty Myers the police as yet were apparently in ignorance; but Steenie Klotz and his outraged apaches had not hesitated in "safe" quarters to spread the story and make known the sentence they had passed upon their betrayer. And the underworld in its blood lust waited. It was the law. The Kitten was being hunted mercilessly to his death. But so far they had not found the Kitten.

Jimmie Dale nodded at the gas jet. That was what he had learned in the underworld's inner circles; and then he had returned here to the Sanctuary, for it was not as Smarlinghue but as the Gray Seal that he meant to play out the night. And now time dragged. He could not even begin to strip off these rags and discard the character of the drug-broken, dissolute artist until the moment arrived when he was ready to leave. It was too dangerous, for in the meantime some one, any one, a lodger even in the same tenement here, might come, and——

He sat up suddenly erect on the cot. Some one *was* coming. He listened. A footstep shuffled along in the hall outside and reached the door; and then some one knocked guardedly upon the panel.

It was Smarlinghue, not Jimmie Dale, who spoke.

"Who's there?" he demanded ungraciously.

"It's me," a voice croaked hurriedly. "Let me in, Smarly. It's Mother Margot."

Mother Margot! A queer smile flickered across Jimmie Dale's lips, as he rose from the cot and started across the room toward the door. Mother Margot who *obeyed* him as the Gray Seal, when she couldn't help it perhaps; Mother Margot who accepted Smarlinghue as one of her own ilk, and, on one occasion at least, as a source of assistance and an ally in her turbulent life! What did Mother Margot want with Smarlinghue to-night? He opened the door, and, as the old hag, her shawl drawn closely around her head, entered, he closed it again behind her.

"Hello, Mother!" said Jimmie Dale facetiously. "Ain't business good down on Thompson Street to-night?"

She glanced around her furtively.

"Dere ain't no one here, is dere?" she asked anxiously.

Jimmie Dale shook his head.

"Spill it!" he invited. "What's the matter?"

Again she glanced around her, and it was almost a minute before she spoke. She twisted her hands nervously together.

"Youse helped me once before, Smarly," she whispered finally. "I—I ain't got no one else to ask, an'—an' to-night I'm in bad. Youse—youse'll help me again, won't youse, Smarly?"

Jimmie Dale pushed one of the two rickety chairs the Sanctuary possessed toward her.

"How do I know?" he countered cautiously. "I ain't making promises on the blind. Help yourself to the chair, and I'll listen."

Mother Margot shook her head quickly.

"I ain't got no time to sit down. An' I ain't got no chance for anythin' only mabbe to get croaked to-night if youse won't help me. I ran all de way over here, an'—an' I was scared youse wouldn't be here." She was wringing her hands together again in evident terror and nervousness. "Oh, my

Gawd, if youse hadn't been here, Smarly, I——" Her voice broke and ended in a choked sob.

Jimmie Dale's eyes, from the crouching, dishevelled, shawled and spectacled old creature, sought the shadows cast by the flickering gas jet that played along the edge of the threadbare strip of carpet at his feet. He did not question the genuineness of her distress. He had very good reason to believe in it most thoroughly. He was even vitally, personally, intimately concerned in it; for, back of it, where Mother Margot was involved, must be the Phantom's hand. He smiled queerly to himself. What it was that had brought her here he, as Jimmie Dale, *must* know; but that knowledge could only be obtained through Smarlinghue, and Smarlinghue was—well, Smarlinghue was Smarlinghue.

"Well, don't lose your nerve," said Smarlinghue a little sharply, "or maybe you'll get me scared too, and the deal'll be off before it's started. The time before you got me to go hunting for English Steve, and I found him—murdered. What is it this time?"

"I—I've got to try an' get a message to some one," she said anxiously.

"That's what you said when it was English Steve," observed Smarlinghue judicially. "Well, shoot! Who is it to-night?"

Again she did not answer immediately; again she glanced furtively around her. And then she spoke, her voice scarcely audible:

"De Gray Seal."

"The Gray Seal!" Involuntarily Jimmie Dale gasped. He stared at her. He could quite understand that she might seek the Gray Seal; but this was irony in its sublimest form, wasn't it? And then suddenly he remembered. The night he had saved himself here by playing his dual rôle! The new heights to which Smarlinghue had risen in the underworld through that supposed encounter! It had almost secured him initiation into the confidences of Bunty Myers, and the rest of the Phantom's followers, of which Mother Margot here was one. That was it! Because he had *once* been known to have been in actual, physical touch with the Gray Seal, and would therefore perhaps be able to recognise him again! And she had come to the Gray Seal himself! It was exquisite!

He felt her eyes boring into him from behind her heavy-lensed spectacles. He smiled with exaggerated derision. But mentally now he knew no mirth. That was only one side of it, the strange irony of it. There must be something of no ordinary importance that could have prompted her to act like this. What was it? She who, again and again, had been compelled to act under the Gray Seal's orders, under *his* orders; who, only that afternoon, had received her instructions, or, perhaps better, warning from him over the telephone!

"It's too easy!" scoffed Smarlinghue, and grinned broadly. "All anybody's got to do that wants the Gray Seal is to go out on the corner and whistle for him."

"My Gawd!" The exclamation came piteously. She wrung her hands the harder together.

"Well," said Jimmie Dale, still facetiously, "what's the idea, then? Do you think just because he rough-housed me here one night that he left his calling card, and wrote his address on it before he went away? Or maybe you think he took his mask off, and says: 'Smarly, drop around any afternoon for a cup of tea; I'll always be at home—to you!' Well, he didn't! There ain't a bull or a lag that ain't been hunting him for years—and they're still hunting! How'd you expect me to find him?"

She seemed hardly to be paying any attention. Her fingers were working nervously with her shawl, now loosening it, now tightening it around her throat; and she still kept on glancing in all directions furtively around her.

"Smarly, for Gawd's sake, listen!" she burst out wildly. "I ain't askin' youse to find him. I'm askin' youse to help me. I got to have some one I can trust. Mabbe youse won't have to do nothin' at all. Youse won't see him; it'll only be on de telephone. I—I've been workin' wid him for weeks now."

It was exquisite! There was humour here for Jimmie Dale —but Smarlinghue's jaw dropped helplessly.

"The Gray Seal—and *you!*" He gulped, swallowing hard. She nodded her head in a sort of helpless way.

"Yes," she said. "My Gawd, I'm handin' it to youse straight, an'—an' I'm in bad to-night. Youse helped me once, an' dere ain't no one else I dares go to. An' youse *will* help me, won't youse, Smarly, if I swear to youse dat dere ain't no risk or nothin' like dat for youse, an' dat dere ain't no one goin' to know youse was in it at all?"

Jimmie Dale, as Smarlinghue, examined meditatively the ragged, frayed sleeve of his coat.

"All right," said Jimmie Dale cautiously. "If I'm as safe as that, I won't see you stuck. But you've got to show me first. What do you want me to do?"

She reached out and caught his hand impulsively, and wrung it hard.

"Gawd bless youse, Smarly!" There was a world of relief in her voice, husky and broken though it was. "I knew youse would, Smarly; I knew youse would. Listen! Youse knows where my pushcart is on Thompson Street. Well, just near it is Mezzo's second-hand shop, an' dere's a side door to dat—up de lane. Dat door ain't locked, an' old Mezzo's away to-night, an' de shop is shut up. Dere's a telephone in dere in de back storeroom. It's kept dere on de quiet—see? All youse've got to do, Smarly, is go in dere an' wait, an' answer de telephone if it rings. Dere ain't nobody goin' to see youse, an' dere ain't nobody goin' to know youse're dere. If it rings it'll be de Gray Seal, an' youse'll give him a message from me."

Jimmie Dale, as Smarlinghue, whistled a little dubiously under his breath.

"And they said he always worked alone!" he observed plaintively. "Say, you'd get bumped off for this if any of the fleets knew about it! You're pretty thick, ain't you? He puts in a telephone for you, and——"

"No, he didn't!" She shook her head vigorously. "He had nothin' to do wid it. It's—it's another crowd. He got wise to it, dat's all, an' one night he caught me cold in—oh, my Gawd, Smarly, never mind about dat! I—I'm in wrong wid de whole works. I—I got to get a message to him to-night if I can."

"Well, why don't you go and find him then, and can the telephone stuff?" inquired Jimmie Dale, in his rôle of Smarlinghue.

" 'Cause I don't know where he is, an' no more about him dan youse does," she said almost hysterically. "Don't youse understand, Smarly? He calls me to de phone when he wants me, an' de times he's shown himself was when he was wearin' a mask like he had de night he bust in on youse here."

"Well, then," prodded Jimmie Dale, "why don't you stick around and listen for the telephone yourself to-night?"

Mother Margot was wringing her hands again.

"D'youse t'ink I'd have come here an' put youse wise to wot I have, if I could've done dat?" she cried wildly. "Dat's wot's de matter. It—it's de other crowd dat's pullin' somethin' to-night, an'—an' I got to go an' do somethin' dey's told me to do. I got to go. I don't dare not to go. Dey— dey'd cut me t'roat if I didn't—an'—an' it's somethin' de Gray Seal's got to know about, or else he—oh, my Gawd, Smarly, can't youse understand?—he'd put me in wrong, an' I'd get finished anyway. He's pullin' somethin' himself to-night, but it's no good now, 'cause somethin' else is goin' to happen, an' he'd know afterwards dat I knew, an' if I didn't wise him up dat's my finish too."

Smarlinghue circled his lips with the tip of his tongue, and scowled unhappily.

"Say," he said heavily, "you're in nice, ain't you? How do you know it won't be the other crowd you're talking about, the bunch that you said put the phone in there, that rings up—and then I'd get stung too?"

" 'Cause dey knows I ain't goin' to be dere. Ain't I tellin' youse dat?" Mother Margot answered miserably. "If de phone rings, it'll be de Gray Seal. Dere's no one else'd ask for Mother Margot."

"And suppose he don't ring up at all?" inquired Smarling-hue.

"I dunno!" Mother Margot's face seemed to whiten a little. "My Gawd, Smarly, I dunno—dat's wot's got me so scared. I ain't even sayin' he will; I—I'm only hopin'. It's de only chance I got. I know mabbe where I could find him a couple of hours from now, but it'll be too late den. I—I can't do nothin' more, Smarly, can I? I can't do nothin' more. If he don't telephone, de only chance I got is to try an' make him believe I did me best—dat's all! An' if he don't believe me, I—I guess I goes out for keeps."

Jimmie Dale for a moment appeared to consider the matter.

"I ain't quite sure I get you," he said slowly at last, "except that it looks to me like, between the two of them, it don't make much difference whether you're coming or going. And this telephone stunt looks like a long shot to me. But I don't see where I get hurt any, and if it's going to ease your mind I'll stand in. So what's the message I'm to give if he telephones?"

Mother Margot's face brightened.

"T'ank God for youse, Smarly!" she faltered. "Youse're as white as dey makes 'em. Youse just say dat de message is from me, an' dat de Voice is goin' to pull de big bump to-night, an' to watch French Jeff down at de White Rat. Y'understand, Smarly?"

Jimmie Dale shook his head.

"No; I don't," he said. "But if he does, it's all right, I suppose. I'm satisfied. I'm not for mixing in and getting my hair singed. But if he asks me what the bump is, and what time it's going to bust loose, what do I say?"

"Nothin'," said Mother Margot. "Dere ain't nothin' more to tell him, 'cause dat's all I knows myself; but I knows it's de big showdown all right, an' de dope is straight. He won't need nothin' more, I guess, if he wants to butt in."

Jimmie Dale nodded indifferently. It was precisely what he wanted to know—the exact extent of the old hag's information.

Mother Margot shuffled her feet nervously.

"I got to go, Smarly," she said anxiously. "De Dago's runnin' me pushcart for me for de rest of de night, but he don't know nothin' about dis, so don't youse give him de high sign. Youse understand about de side door in de lane?"

"Sure!" said Smarlinghue. "And while we're standing here talking maybe he's telephoned already and pulled a bone."

Mother Margot shook her head.

"Dat don't matter," she said. "He knows Mezzo don't always hear, an' sometimes it's hard to get an answer. If he was tryin' to get me, he'll try again until he does." She hesitated, drew her shawl tightly about her head again, took a step toward the door, and once more hesitated. "Gawd bless youse, Smarly!" she said brokenly. "Mabbe youse t'inks youse does, but youse don't know wot youse're doin' for me to-night. Mabbe I'll pull out of dis alive, an' mabbe I won't, but don't youse ever forget, Smarly, if youse never sees me again, dat dere ain't no one in dis world means anythin' to Mother Margot like youse does, Smarly. An'—an'——" Her voice broke.

She was crying. Jimmie Dale started forward impulsively as he saw the old shoulders shake, and a tear, followed by another, trickle unchecked down her cheek. But she turned her head quickly away, and scuffled hurriedly toward the door before he had reached her.

But at the door she turned again.

"Gawd bless youse, Smarly!" she called again—and closed the door behind her.

XXVI

MOTHER MARGOT'S footsteps, shuffling, receded along the hall, and died away with the opening and closing of the street door.

Jimmie Dale stood staring across the empty room. He had not fully realised before how secure was the hold that he, as the Gray Seal, had upon the old hag! She was afraid of the Phantom, or the Voice, as she called the man; but she was equally afraid of the Gray Seal, it now appeared—and between the two, unable to steer any middle course to-night, she was in mortal terror.

He frowned. He might have eased her mind a little in some way, perhaps. No! He shook his head decisively. Her coming, the story she had told, changed materially, and of necessity, his own plans for to-night—at least for the next few hours. Mother Margot's rooms had interested him only because of the probability that they were the outer portal to the Phantom's sanctum; but if the Phantom's movements to-night centred around French Jeff and "The White Rat," it was French Jeff and The White Rat that automatically and at once became the centre of attraction for him as well. And particularly so since, deprived of the Kitten's assistance, practically the one remaining satellite, any play that the Phantom made must, leaving Mother Margot out, be made in *person*. It was the Phantom that he sought!

Jimmie Dale stepped swiftly across the room and locked the door, then kneeling on the floor near by lifted aside the movable section of the baseboard. He could no more have afforded to risk the character of Smarlinghue by some well-meaning but ill-advised word in an effort to calm her fears,

than he could afford, after what she had said, to go to The
White Rat *as* Smarlinghue. She was as likely to be there as
not. If she saw Smarlinghue there it would be— Well,
she would never again after that have need to fear the Gray
Seal! A hint that Smarlinghue was not what he seemed
would be the end, swift and inevitable, of the Gray Seal and
Jimmie Dale!

He nodded sharply to himself as he stripped off his ragged
attire, and, quickly now, removing the little pieces of wax
from nostrils and from beneath the lips, that distorted the
contour of his face, and removing, too, the stain of make-up,
began to dress again as Jimmie Dale in the carefully folded
suit which he took from the hiding place behind the baseboard. Again he nodded to himself. Tweeds to-night. It
was fortunate! He had naturally been wearing tweeds that
afternoon when he had left his house. The White Rat was
not usually frequented by gentlemen in evening dress!

A minute, two, three passed. The gas jet, spitting like an
angry cat, became suddenly silent. The room was in darkness, save for a queer, nebulous shaft of night light that came
in through the top-light high up over the French doors that
opened on the small, ill-kept courtyard without. And now
a shadow moved and bulked itself against the French doors,
and one of the French doors opened without sound and closed
again, and the shadow crept along the wall of the building,
and strangely, like an apparition, disappeared through the
fence that bordered the lane.

A moment more, and Jimmie Dale, as though Smarlinghue
had never existed, was walking quietly along the street. His
mind was working now with cool, judicial precision, sifting,
weighing, appraising the factors of the problem before him.
Mother Margot would not be near Thompson Street again
to-night. If the Gray Seal's hand appeared to-night, it would
be no more than she expected. Whether it was as the Gray
Seal or as Smarlinghue that first he next saw Mother Margot,
the statement that the Gray Seal had phoned and received his
information was wholly in accord with the old hag's own
suggestion. He, Jimmie Dale, was free to go at once to The

White Rat. He was not even abusing the trust that she had reposed in Smarlinghue! There was something ironical in that!

Her distress had been genuine enough, and her story was beyond doubt or question. Who should know better than himself? She had said that later on she might have known where to find the Gray Seal, but that it would be too late then. She had meant, of course, her own rooms that he had, that afternoon, warned her to keep away from. That statement alone stamped her story with the ring of truth. But why bring distrust of Mother Margot even into question! She had never yet played him false; and to-night it was glaringly obvious that, voluntarily, in the only way she could, though that way depended purely on chance, she had done her utmost to keep her pact with him.

He shrugged his shoulders. Mother Margot, as a factor in the problem to-night, could from now on be eliminated. French Jeff and The White Rat, then! What was the game that the Phantom was playing, the key to which, which was all the information that Mother Margot had possessed, was French Jeff and The White Rat?

Jimmie Dale was walking more quickly now, threading his way through the more unfrequented streets, as he worked deeper into the lower East Side. French Jeff and The White Rat were equally notorious; the one as a sort of plenipotentiary of crookdom from the other side of the water, and the other as the favourite hostelry of foreign visitors whose credentials were properly viséd. This was the understanding that the New York underworld had of French Jeff and The White Rat; ostensibly, however, to the police, and to the public at large, the man was but the quiet, law-abiding proprietor of a small establishment that, while it could not be dignified by the name of hotel, yet, nevertheless, embodied in itself a bar, a restaurant, and a few rooms for guests— which latter, to the public, were always "engaged."

Quite so! In the enormously fat little Frenchman and his White Rat lay potentialities for evil that were limitless. Suave, cunning in his international affiliations, the man was

credited with playing big games for big stakes. That he
was successful was evidenced by the fact that for years now
he had carried on business without coming under the ban of
the police.

Jimmie Dale frowned. He, like the rest of the underworld,
for his eyes were Smarlinghue's now, could only view the
man in the large; there were no details to the picture. And
this was so, naturally enough, because French Jeff confined
himself strictly to his own foreign connections, and stood
wholly aloof from local entanglements no matter how allur-
ing the promise of their reward might be. What then was
the Phantom's interest in this man to-night? Had French
Jeff at last broken his rule and gone in on some deal, working
hand in glove with the Phantom; or was the Phantom preparing, as he so often did, to pick the ripened plums from
another's tree? Or was it——

Jimmie Dale had halted before an uninviting three-story
frame building on the corner of an equally uninviting street.
A sign, somewhat battered and aping the Continental style,
swung in the breeze over the front door. It bore the design
of an animal, its species none too easily recognisable, done in
white on a green background; the lettering, however, below
this inartistic effort was informative: THE WHITE RAT.

Within, as could be seen from the street, the ground floor
was a sort of combination restaurant and bar. A few customers occupied tables; a few more were at the bar. Jimmie
Dale's slouch hat was pulled rakishly down over his eyes,
his cravat flashily tucked into the bosom of his shirt, as he
stepped now inside, and, walking up to the bar, ordered a
drink. He glanced around him nonchalantly. He had never
been in the place before, but in common with everybody else
in the underworld he knew the fat proprietor by sight.
French Jeff was not in evidence.

"Ain't the boss around?" inquired Jimmie Dale casually
out of the corner of his mouth, as the barkeeper slid a glass
toward him across the bar.

"Sure! He's upstairs on de office," replied the man, evidently, too, a Frenchman, in broken English. "You want to see him?"

Jimmie Dale shook his head.

"Nope!" he said indifferently. "Not hard enough to bring him down. I'd have said hello to him if he'd been handy, that's all."

Jimmie Dale set his now empty glass back on the bar, and with a wave of his hand to the barkeeper, went out again to the street. French Jeff was "upstairs on de office." He went on around the corner. The White Rat, if it were efficient along the lines upon which it was supposed to run, would certainly possess a side entrance for the benefit of those who, with the necessary credentials, were privileged to occupy rooms there. Yes, here it was.

Jimmie Dale opened the door quietly and stepped inside. Even if seen, it meant only that he must then find some other means of getting into proximity with French Jeff. The glib excuse that he thought this was but another entrance to the restaurant, as indeed it might well be also, would be quite sufficient to guarantee an orderly retreat on his part. And then he flung a mental gibe at himself. He was borrowing trouble, whereas, as a matter of fact, he appeared to be playing in wholesale luck.

He found himself standing in a dimly lighted hall, rather seedily furnished, and quite deserted. The only sounds were those that sifted through from the restaurant in the front of the establishment, the clatter of dishes, the muffled voices of those at the tables and at the bar. No; he was wrong! From above him, up the stairs that were directly in front of him, his ear caught now a curious, irregular rasping sound. He could not at once definite it as he began quickly and silently to mount the stairs, but half-way up the sound took on a concrete meaning, and a smile broadened his lips. The sound had resolved itself into nothing more than a series of well defined snores!

And now at the top of the landing, he placed the direction of the sound. Doors here opened off on each side of the hall, and at the far end the light streamed out through one that was open, and disclosed, facing it, the door on the opposite side of the hall to be ajar. It was from the lighted room that the snores emanated.

Jimmie Dale moved softly along the hall, keeping close against the wall on the opposite side from the lighted door, and finally paused. From where he stood now, he could just see at an angle into the lighted room. For an instant he stood listening, then he slipped through the already partially opened door beside him that faced the lighted doorway. He was playing in luck, in unbounded luck! Here was a vacant room, and across the hall, the door wide open, French Jeff and his "office" were in plain view. Perhaps it was almost too much luck! This room here might be occupied after all, the "guest" out only temporarily, and likely to return at any minute.

He glanced critically around him. There was light enough from across the hall to see. No; it was quite all right. There was no sign of occupancy, no clothing, no belongings of any kind in evidence. And if by any chance a new arrival should be allotted the room, it would certainly not be until French Jeff in there had been advised and had passed upon the applicant's desirability, and there would be time enough then to consider a means of retreat.

Jimmie Dale, leaving the door no more ajar than would enable him to see readily into the opposite room, drew up a chair and coolly seated himself for his vigil. The fat little French crook was sprawled back in his desk chair, his hands folded over an ample and undulating paunch, his feet up and resting on a black handbag that in turn occupied the seat of a second chair. The man was fast asleep.

What was it? What was the game? Had that black handbag, guarded by the other's feet, anything to do with it? "Watch French Jeff at The White Rat." That was all Mother Margot had known.

The minutes passed, became quarter hours, a half hour—more. Occasionally French Jeff stirred uneasily, awakened, settled himself drowsily, and went to sleep again; occasionally Jimmie Dale silently changed his own position.

What time was it? It had been well after ten o'clock when Mother Margot had come to the Sanctuary; it must be long after eleven now. He began to know not so much a sense of impatience as one of disquiet. It was still early yet, of course, and the hours, most likely of all the twenty-four for criminal activities, were still to come, but somehow the pig-like serenity of the fat Frenchman disturbed him.

Still the minutes dragged by. Another quarter of an hour passed. And then Jimmie Dale suddenly straightened up alertly. There was a footstep now on the stairs; and now it came along the hall. Jimmie Dale retreated a little from the door, his automatic in his hand.

It was one of the waiters from downstairs. The man passed into the other room.

"It's time to go, monsieur," he heard the waiter say in French.

French Jeff, with a grunt, roused himself.

"All right, Emile," he said shortly.

The waiter left the room and went downstairs again.

French Jeff spent a moment at his desk, then closed it down, picked up the black handbag from the chair, extinguished the light, and left the room.

Jimmie Dale stole out into the darkened corridor. French Jeff descended the stairs, and went out through the side door. Another minute and Jimmie Dale, too, had gained the street, and crossing to the opposite side took up the fat proprietor's trail.

It led to the nearest subway station, and an uptown train. French Jeff got off at the Grand Central Station, and Jimmie Dale followed. At a ticket window, French Jeff bought a ticket and berth on the midnight train for Boston. Jimmie Dale, for the first time in evidence, and now at the other's elbow, made exactly the same purchase—but on Jimmie Dale's lips now there was a smile of almost self-pity.

"If I'm going where I think I am," confided Jimmie Dale softly to himself, as he followed the other through the gates and to the Pullman, "it'll be a rather expensive ride for the mileage—but the gatemen are inviolable and the porter might not have stood for a bribe."

The berths in the car were all made up. The fat little Frenchman swished down the aisle, waddling after the porter. Jimmie Dale, finding his berth to be opposite that of French Jeff, sat down on the edge of it, and drew the curtains together in front of him. A few minutes passed. The train pulled out. A wry smile began to settle on Jimmie Dale's lips—and at 125th Street it had hardened into lines of grim, unmirthful chagrin.

French Jeff had undressed and gone to bed, and the car was already reverberating to the fat man's snores.

Jimmie Dale got off the train.

— XXVII —

THE LAIR

TIGHT-LIPPED, Jimmie Dale stared out at the black, flying walls as the subway train roared its way back to lower New York. He had been properly done! There could be no question about that. But by whom? And why? What did it mean? Intuition, even back there in The White Rat, had warned him that something was wrong, but he would in no way have been justified in being swayed wholly by intuition. He could not in justice blame himself for that. What was it? What was the meaning of it? Something *had* happened somewhere—but not at The White Rat. And he had been very neatly side-tracked. All that was obvious.

Was it Mother Margot? He shook his head. She had never yet double-crossed him, and he did not believe that she would dare to do so. Even her visit to the Sanctuary to-night, and her very evident wholesome respect for the Gray Seal, not to say fear, was almost proof in itself, it would seem, that she had not deliberately tried to mislead him.

What, then? There seemed to be only one logical explanation left. The Phantom. It would not have been altogether a new move on the Phantom's part, for, while not wholly analogous, the man had in a way tried the same game before. The Phantom knew only too well, and to his cost, that there had been a leak somewhere in his entourage, a leak that had brought the Gray Seal very inopportunely on his heels more than once. But to-night that entourage, in view of the fact that the rest were dead and that the Kitten was being hunted mercilessly by his own fellow crooks of the underworld, was reduced now to Mother Margot alone. Therefore, if the

leak still existed, it must exist in the person of Mother
Margot, and therefore, as a precautionary measure if nothing
more, should the Phantom be up to some play to-night in
which he particularly wanted to guard against any interference, he would logically turn the possibility that the leak
still existed to his own advantage, and at the same time,
perhaps, test out, and even trap, Mother Margot.

"Yes," said Jimmie Dale grimly to himself. "I guess
that's it."

He nodded sharply. He had been side-tracked from his
original plan to-night, but the night was not yet ended, and
if he had the Phantom to thank for the bubble he had been
chasing, the Phantom might yet have reason to remember
to-night from another cause very different indeed! The
phantom clue at Mother Margot's rooms was again his goal.
The delay had mattered little. What he had meant to do as
he had lain there on the cot in the Sanctuary, he meant to
do now.

Jimmie Dale looked at his watch, as he left the subway at
Astor Place and headed into the Bowery. It was ten minutes
to one. He walked quickly now. It was not far to those
two tenements with the narrow areaway between, in one of
which Mother Margot had lived since Gentleman Laroque,
alias Isaac Shiftel, alias the Phantom, had so mysteriously
made his escape from the room which the old hag now occupied; just a little lower down, a little off the Bowery, in
one of the East Side's most unenviable neighbourhoods.

Five minutes brought him to his destination. It was quiet
here, save for the distant sounds of night life from the Bowery, dark, deserted. A light showed sparsely here and there
from a window—that was all. He passed the areaway between the two tenements, smiled grimly at the recollection
of the officer who had stood guard therein beneath the window on the night the Phantom had escaped and he, Jimmie
Dale, had been so nearly trapped, and slipped unobtrusively
into the dark hallway of the further tenement.

A moment more and, masked, he stood listening, at the
door of Mother Margot's rooms. There was no sound from

within. Why should there be? Even if Mother Margot,
according to her own story, had not been ordered somewhere
else by the Phantom, she would not be here since he, Jimmie
Dale, had warned her to keep away. There was no sound,
but—the slim, sensitive fingers were working tentatively at
the doorknob—this was a little strange. The door was unlocked !

It swung open now silently, an inch at a time, under his
hand. He stepped inside and, as silently, closed the door
behind him. It was black in here. He could not see a yard
in front of him. But he was familiar, a little more than
familiar, with his surroundings ! He stole forward to the
doorway connecting with the inner room, moving without
sound, as Larry the Bat in the days of old in the old Sanctuary had moved, and paused on the threshold. It was from
here those voices that other night had come; here was the
mise en scène of the phantom clue.

Again he listened. There was still no sound. Jimmie
Dale's automatic was already in his hand, and now from his
pocket he took out a flashlight. Still he waited another instant, listening; and then, the round, white ray stabbing
through the blackness, Jimmie Dale, his face set hard and
grim, his lips a straight line, stood staring at the wall opposite him.

The phantom clue was a phantom clue no longer. It lay
there clothed in tangible, yes, even mocking, form, so blatantly did it flaunt now the disclosal of its own existence !
The flashlight was boring into a great oblong-shaped opening
through the wall.

Still Jimmie Dale stood motionless. Through his mind in
swift, lightning flashes swept the oft-repeated admonition of
both the Tocsin and Mother Margot. A trap. He had been
told the place was a trap for him. Was the door of the trap
open now—a little *too* invitingly open—the door he had never
been able to find before, patiently and thoroughly though he
had searched? Had this anything to do with what had gone
before to-night, with the fool's errand upon which he had

run to French Jeff and The White Rat? How could it have? And yet——

His eyes swept the opening, and the wall adjacent to it, above and on both sides. He understood now, of course. And it brought no sense of self-reproof that, though knowing it had existed somewhere here, he had not, in the times he had searched before, been able to find it. It was clever, ingenious, a replica almost of the old Crime Club with its false, movable walls, though here not nearly so elaborate— but perhaps even built by the same men, at that, as one of their outposts, since Clarke, alias Wizard Marre, who had been the Phantom's confederate in the murder of Jason Lane, had been a member of that original organisation. A dado of cheap, painted burlap at the height of some five feet ran around the room; this was surmounted by a wide moulding, and the whole divided into oblong panels by vertical, though narrower, strips of moulding again. It was one of these oblong sections that now had disappeared into the floor, disclosing an inner wall, that was obviously the real wall of the room, set back perhaps slightly more than two feet from the false wall with the dado. This made a little passageway within, so that while he, Jimmie Dale, might have tapped the entire length of the wall in an effort to discover the opening by the sense of sound, in no place would it have sounded *more* hollow than in any other; and, again, the mouldings covered the joints, and the section slid up and down behind them, so that unless they had been ripped off bodily it would have been impossible to——

His face grew harder. That was what he had meant to do to-night, *wreck* the room if necessary, throw the caution that before had actuated him to the winds; but to-night all lay there *open* before him, starkly, vauntingly open. It was obvious enough now. The section slid up and down through the floor and— *Up and down!* That was what Bunty Myers had said. But Bunty Myers had said too that *she* didn't know because it was in the next house. That passage there! Invitingly open now! It could only lead to one place then—the next house—and there was only one next house on this side. The other tenement! A trap! Well, he had come for this, hadn't he?—to find the trap, no matter what the consequences, no matter what the cost, if it would but bring him into touch with the Phantom.

He stepped forward now silently across the room, and, with his flashlight switched off, knelt down at the opening. The passage in there was very narrow, certainly quite long, and certainly inky black. One could therefore fairly expect that somewhere in the passage between here and the other tenement there would be a light; and if so, and if it were lighted now, it would disclose for the benefit of the "quarry" any "trapper" who might be lurking there. Also if there were a light it would naturally be readily accessible from the entrance here.

Half crouched, he leaned forward into the opening, and felt inside, up and down along the edges of the wall. His fingers encountered a switch button. He pressed it now— but instead of a light showing anywhere, the movable section of the wall under him began to rise. He jabbed at the switch quickly again, even as he flung himself clear of the opening, and then found that the section had receded once more to its original position below the level of the baseboard.

Jimmie Dale drew in his breath sharply. So that was it! The thing was electrically controlled. That was plain enough, and from the *inside* there was no concealment of how it was set in motion; but how was it operated from within the room? He might not have been able in his several previous searches to have located the position of the opening, but he was quite certain that had there been a concealed switch, say, anywhere along the wall under the dado, or at the edges of the mouldings, he would have found it, for his fingers had felt over every inch of that space.

He shrugged his shoulders. Well, it didn't matter now, did it, since some one else had supplied the "open sesame!" And since there was no other light——

His body well back from the opening, he reached his hand inside, and, pointing his flashlight parallel with the passage in the direction of the other tenement, flung a beam of light along it. It brought no response; no answering shot, for example, that he had half expected. He risked more now. Flat on the floor, with head and shoulders this time inside the opening, the flashlight's ray shot out again. But this time he could see. What was at the other end he could not tell, but immediately in front of him the way was clear. A series of steps led downward, then seemed to reach a level, until, in perspective, from where he lay, the roof and the base of the passage merged together.

The passage, then, beyond surmise, led down under the narrow alleyway to the "next house"—the tenement which was the counterpart of this one here. He rose to his feet, and cautiously, without sound, moved forward, descending the steps. The passage was extremely narrow, his shoulders kept brushing the walls on either side.

At every few steps he stopped to listen. His flashlight was out now. When he moved it was the sense of touch alone that guided him. He reached a level. This would be the section of the tunnel directly under the areaway, of course. And now, as the series of steps began again, this time leading upward, a faint glow of light showed through the darkness, and for the first time his ear caught a sound—it was like a low, strange moaning.

Jimmie Dale went down on his hands and knees now as he crawled upward. He would be less a target in that position, for it was obvious that the other end of the secret passage was open, and that the room or the space into which it opened was lighted—*and occupied*. Also, it was no longer a mystery where the voices had come from that had been heard in Mother Margot's rooms!

Noiselessly he reached the top step. Here the arrangement was the exact duplicate of the other end of the passage. A wall section was open, a lighted room beyond. The moaning, naturally more distinct now, continued unabated.

Cautiously Jimmie Dale edged forward until he could see into the room—and then, in an instant, he was on his feet and through the opening, and running toward a man's form that was stretched out on the floor.

The Kitten!

The man's face was gray with the pallor of approaching death, and there was a great crimson blotch over the left side of his shirt where the vest had been torn open, but he roused himself now with almost superhuman energy, staring in most strange eagerness and excitement at Jimmie Dale.

"Who are youse?" he cried out. "Who in 'ell are youse wid dat mask on?"

"It doesn't matter," said Jimmie Dale gently. The man was dying; it needed no professional eye to discern that fact. The Kitten! Well, even the Kitten was a fellow-human. "It doesn't matter," he said again; "let me try and make you more comfortable, and——"

"It does matter!" There was fierce insistence, so fierce that it was almost bizarre, in the man's gasping words. "It matters more'n anythin' else whether a guy dat wears a mask is a friend of Laroque's or ain't. Youse can't do anythin' for me. I—I ain't got but a few minutes left. If youse're a friend of Laroque's beat it out of here an' leave me alone; if youse ain't, I got somethin' to tell youse. Quick! Who are youse?"

Gentleman Laroque, alias the Phantom! The Kitten the last remaining satellite! What did this mean? The man's mind was wandering, perhaps—and yet he seemed coherent enough.

"I think you'd know me best," said Jimmie Dale simply, "as the Gray Seal."

The Kitten struggled to his elbow.

"De Gray Seal! Prove it! Prove it for de love of Gawd!" he cried out wildly. "Mabbe dey've got him, but if dey ain't, youse will—if youse *are* de Gray Seal. Prove it!"

There was something of vital, paramount moment here. The man seemed possessed of a hatred and fury that had given him, in his dying condition, an unnatural strength. From the leather girdle Jimmie Dale took out the thin, metallic case that was the receptacle of those diamond-shaped, gray-paper seals that had given him his name, and, lifting one out, held it up before the Kitten's eyes.

The man laughed. It seemed to carry a shudder in its depths. It echoed around the room in a strangled, horrible way.

"Dat's enough!" screamed the Kitten. "Youse're de guy dat's been after him for weeks. Youse're de guy he's afraid of. Mabbe dey've got him, but I ain't takin' no chances, for if dey ain't, youse will. Damn him! It was Laroque dat give me dis—in dere—in de passage. It was Laroque dat plugged me cold, an—" He caught at his throat, choking, struggling for breath.

"Laroque!" exclaimed Jimmie Dale tensely. "Do you know what you are saying—that it was Gentleman Laroque who shot you?"

The Kitten clutched at Jimmie Dale's arm, dragging himself up again.

"Yes, I know wot I'm sayin'." He was whispering hoarsely now. "Listen! Mabbe youse heard I was up against it wid a gang dat was after me, mabbe youse didn't—it doesn't matter. I hid since yesterday. To-night dey nosed me out, an'—an' I had to beat it for me life. I didn't have much start. I pinched a car, but dey got another—see? I didn't have nowheres to go but here, den—I thought Laroque'd hide me—it was de only chance I had."

He fought for his breath, paused, and struggled on again, his words coming more thickly and with greater effort.

"I left de car around de corner, an' came in here. Laroque an' Mother Margot was here. I—I was tellin' 'em about it. I thought I'd given de gang de slip. But I hadn't. Dey came smashin' at de door. Laroque didn't say nothin', only he looked wicked when he jumped for de electric wall bracket an' gave dat brass fittin' against de wall a twist. Dat opened de door in de wall—see? 'Come on!' he says den to Mother Margot an' me. 'De two of youse! Quick!'

"De gang was bustin' in de door of de room by now, an' dey saw us. We followed Laroque through de wall, an' he pushes de switch inside an' de wall closes up. It—it was black in dere. My Gawd, it was black! An' Laroque kind of laughs. 'Dat was a close squeak, an' mabbe we ain't safe

yet,' he says. 'Mother, youse an' me'll go down to Blind
Peter's, since de Kitten's been thoughtful enough to bring
us a car; an' youse, Kitten, youse'll go where youse deserves
to go for takin' any chance on givin' me away.' Just like
dat he said it, an' he was laughin'. My Gawd, he was
laughin' all de time. 'Youse overrated de value of yer life,
Kitten,' he says, an'—an' shot me—cold."

The man with a nervous grip that locked like a vise around
Jimmie Dale's arm and shoulder, had heaved himself up into
a sitting posture. His lips and face were working.

"D'ye understand?" he choked.

"Yes," said Jimmie Dale through tight lips.

"Quick!" gasped the Kitten. "Listen! I—I ain't got
much more time. He thought he'd finished me. I—I guess
I lost consciousness. Den I heard de gang in here poundin'
at de wall. Dey couldn't do me no more harm. I knew
Laroque had put me out for keeps, an'—an' he was goin' to
pay for it—see?—pay for it—pay for it. I crawled to de
switch an' opened de wall. Dey made a rush for me, but I
gets a chance to speak. Dey thought I'd got away wid some
money last night—a—a black box—Banco Santos—but I
hadn't—I don't know no more'n youse where it is—see?"

The Kitten's voice was growing weaker; his grip was
loosening, the strength ebbing from his fingers.

"I told 'em it was Laroque an' de woman put up de whole
plant, an'—an' dat dey had de money, an' dat I'd only done
wot Laroque told me—an' de proof Laroque an' Margot was
in de game was dis hole in de wall an' de passage—an' dat
dey was runnin' for Blind Peter's." He caught at his throat.
"De gang went through de hole dere after Laroque—ten
minutes ago—Blind Peter's—understand? Double chance—
de Gray Seal'll get 'em if Steenie don't—de Gray——"

Jimmie Dale stood up. The Kitten was dead. For an instant he looked around him. He seemed most curiously to
be possessed of two entities—one that rejoiced fiercely over
what now seemed a certainty that the Phantom, either at the
hands of the apaches that the Kitten in his dying vengeance

had set upon the other, or, failing that, through himself, Jimmie Dale, would be finally and irrevocably trapped to-night; the other that looked out as through a strange veil of unreality upon his immediate surroundings. This was the Phantom's lair at the end of the phantom trail.

XXVIII

JIMMIE DALE stepped swiftly across the room, and with a small steel jimmy which he took from his leather girdle, ripped aside, from where it fitted close against the wall, the round brass plaque or fitting, technically called the canopy, of the electric-light fixture. There was no time to lose, but he could spare an instant for this! Yes, it was as the Kitten had said. It concealed an electrical connection quite apart from the electric light itself; and by giving the canopy a half turn the contact could be made.

He nodded, as he turned now in a flash toward the window. He was satisfied. That was how the movable section of the wall was manipulated from within. And the window here, unless his calculations were hopelessly at fault, faced, exactly across the areaway, the window in Mother Margot's room. He raised the shade—and suddenly, with a low, suppressed cry, wrenched it down again, and leaped for the opening in the wall. In an instant he was inside, and, pressing the switch, the movable section had closed behind him.

The police! The window *did* face Mother Margot's, and, as there had been on the first night that he had come here, so too to-night an officer was lurking outside there now in the alleyway. The light streaming out from the window with the lifting shade had disclosed a man in uniform crouched against the wall. And also, even as he had wrenched back the shade, his ear had caught the muffled tread of several men in the hall outside the room. And that, too, was as it had been on the first occasion!

He ran now, his flashlight streaming ahead of him, through the tunnel, gained Mother Margot's room, and, indifferent now as to whether the movable section here was left closed or not, since it could in no way affect his own movements, and since the tunnel was now an open secret through its discovery by the apaches, he made no attempt to close it behind him; and, as he had done before when wary of the police here, he slipped out at the rear of the tenement, sped silently across the backyard in the darkness, and disappeared in the lane behind. And thereafter, keeping always when he could to the lanes and alleyways, grudging the sedate though crisp walk when forced out into the open, he went on at top speed.

But swiftly as he went, his mind ran the swifter. The police—not at Mother Margot's, but at that *other* tenement! His own escape had been a sinecure, thanks to the Phantom's secret passage. It would take the police some time to find that movable section in the room where the Kitten lay! But he did not understand. Why were the police there at all? They had not followed on the heels of the Kitten and the apaches, for in that case they would have been there much *sooner*. It was not the sound of the shot that the Phantom had fired, for that had been deadened inside the walls of the passage; nor did it seem possible that any other disturbance made there had been reported to them, say, by the inmates of the tenement, for in that case there would have been commotion amongst the tenants themselves, who would have been swarming about like bees. It was strange! The whole night was strange! He did not understand.

He ran on. The point was not vital. It was vital only that he should reach Blind Peter's without delay. Thank God, it wasn't far! But they had had ten minutes' start, and it was almost certain that neither the Phanton nor the apaches had gone on foot. Blind Peter's! He was not so sure after all that men like Steenie Klotz and Red Jack would be able to trap the Phantom there. It was the *safest* place in the underworld if one knew its secrets, and on that score the Phantom had made no mistake. But Steenie Klotz and his followers were of the lesser breed, the hangers-on, the purely thug element, not of the élite, not of the initiated, and Blind Peter's might well be to them but a name, a place whose mysteries were reserved for the upper strata of the criminal realm from which they themselves were far removed. It might well be—but against this was the fact that the underworld, its aristocracy and its proletariate alike, were behind Steenie Klotz and his companions in their determination to wreak vengeance upon the Kitten, and with the explanation made of why it was Gentleman Laroque now instead of the Kitten who was the object of this vengeance, the Phantom might find far else but sanctuary at Blind Peter's.

He did not know. He knew only that if he were in time the Phantom would not only find no safety there, but, forced to attempt flight again, would find no escape. And he would be in time! He *must* be!

It was the end! The end! The end! The words pounded over and over again at his brain, as he ran on. In either case, it was the end to-night. What Steenie Klotz and his pack might not know of Blind Peter's, he, Jimmie Dale, knew as perhaps few outside Blind Peter himself knew. It was the years of Larry the Bat, the years of Smarlinghue, the knowledge he had thus garnered, the height to which those alter ego characters of his had risen in the inner circles of Crimeland, that were bearing fruit now.

Yes, he knew Blind Peter's! Blind Peter was a very old and wizened little man of dark-skinned, doubtful origin, who wore spectacles with lenses that were coloured and that were of the thickness of heavy plate-glass, and who groped out with hands and stick when he walked—and who was not blind. He ran, supposedly, a small general store in one of a block of four houses in a neighbourhood that, to speak mildly, was unsavory at best. The other three houses were, supposedly again, lodging houses, and in a sense they were lodging houses, just as in a sense they were anything else one wished to call them. But Blind Peter owned them, and they had made Blind Peter rich—or, rather, a maze-like cavern of vice beneath their cellars had. Here, where sound never reached to the outer air, where the cellars above, rubbish-filled, were a benign and protecting mantle, toll from the lusts of the gaming table, toll from the overlords of crime who rented council chambers there, toll from the fear-stricken who had fled from daylight and the law, toll from every human weakness, was paid to Blind Peter. And, discreet beyond any of his ilk in the selection of his clientele, Blind Peter's place was safe. There was but one entrance and one exit—through the back of Blind Peter's store, where none might enter or depart except under the closest scrutiny.

Jimmie Dale had halted. A queer smile twisted his lips. Was there? Well, in the old days there had been another entrance, guessed at by many, but known only to a few, of which he, as Larry the Bat then, had been one—and it was here. He was crouched in the darkness before a low basement door, that of the house in the block farthest away from Blind Peter's store. Behind him was a small backyard, and behind that again the lane. The door was locked of course. But his pick-lock was at work now; and now the door opened slowly, gradually, wary of a protesting creak.

Jimmie Dale closed the door behind him without locking it, and descending a short flight of steps, stood still to listen. He was in the cellar now. He could hear nothing either from above or *below*. There would be no guard here. This entrance was for emergency only, a reserve margin of safety that Blind Peter held up his sleeve for himself and his intimates; it probably had not been used in months, and naturally any one using it at all was, in the very fact that the secret was in his possession, beyond the necessity of challenge. Besides, a guard of any kind would but scream out aloud to Blind Peter's entire clientele the fact that this entrance, or exit, existed. Nor would one entering by this means, if he took but ordinary precautions, blazon the existence of the entrance to those already below. Blind Peter was far, very far, from being a fool! Here in this cellar the entrance was craftily hidden; but below it was still more so.

Jimmie Dale's flashlight winked through the blackness. He moved quickly forward to the far corner of the cellar. Rubbish, an untidy heap of kindling wood, the flotsam and jetsam of broken and discarded household effects littered the place. He worked rapidly now, brushing aside a thin, scattered layer of the kindling wood at the edge of the pile—and lifted up a small trap door.

It was black below, intensely black. The flashlight sent its ray streaming down a steep flight of steps—and went out. Jimmie Dale nodded sharply to himself. It was as it had always been. These steps led to the rear wooden wall—of a coal bin. But the coal bin would not be inconveniently full, and the front of it was quite open, and in the back of it a board or two could at a touch be moved aside.

He began to descend the steps cautiously. Across the narrow little chamber that contained the coal bin was a door leading into Blind Peter's unholy nest. And since that door must exist in order to make this exclusive entrance of any practical avail, a door the existence of which must almost of necessity be a matter of common knowledge to all who frequented Blind Peter's, that door itself must excite no suspicion. Therefore when it was opened it exhibited to all but the initiated in Blind Peter's nothing more than an apparently essential adjunct to the establishment—a storeroom that contained boxes of supplies, many of them, and a coal bin!

Almost down the steps now, Jimmie Dale paused suddenly —and as suddenly took the remaining ones at a leap. Dull, muffled, the report of a revolver shot had reached his ears. It was echoed by another—still another. The flashlight was in play again. Those boards! Yes, here they were! He moved them aside—and stepped through into the coal bin, so innocently almost empty.

The coal rattled a little under his feet, but the sound was drowned out now by shouts that added their quota of muffled uproar to the quickened reports of the revolver shots—and the sounds were coming nearer, nearer to that door there that opened into this supposed storeroom. The Phantom and the apaches! It could be nothing else! Steenie Klotz had gained admittance—the law of the underworld was at work. Blind Peter had evidently not dared oppose it. Did the Phantom know of the existence of this exit? A trapped rat, was he fighting for escape this way?

Jimmie Dale's lips were a thin line. Well, the Phantom would *not* escape this way! Whatever the penalty that he, Jimmie Dale, might pay, the Phantom's career ended to-night. That was what he was here for. No matter what happened to himself, the price would be a small and pitiful thing to pay. To-morrow, no, to-night, the Tocsin, the woman he loved, she who in her great unselfish courage, aye and her love, had chosen to risk death alone, to fight out her fight alone that he too might not be sacrificed, would be free, free from peril, free to live in God's sunshine as——

He was at the door now. The sounds from the other side had risen into almost riot noise. The panel here—it used to move a little so that one intending entrance might first satisfy himself that he was not observed. Yes, it still moved—the space of a few inches.

He could see through—into a small room, garishly appointed, its roof supported by ornamental rafters from which hung several lanterns of curious, antique design, its walls draped with oriental hangings, the whole furnished in a sort of barbaric luxury. It was Blind Peter's private retreat —and naturally again offered a further bulwark and protection against the detection of the hidden entrance.

The door opening out on the other side of this room and directly opposite the ‚one behind which Jimmie Dale stood was closed, but now suddenly it burst open. Shots, yells, curses, rose crescendo in a hideous uproar. A figure reeled in, stumbled, fell upon its knees, and began to drag itself away from the threshold. The old hag! Mother Margot! But Jimmie Dale's eyes rested for but an instant on her. There was another figure, the figure of a man, on the threshold itself now, a man at bay, fighting, pumping his shots from his automatic, cursing as he fought—Gentleman Laroque, alias Isaac Shiftel, alias Limpy Mack, alias the Phantom!

Outside, beyond that door, Jimmie Dale could not see. He could only hear—above the shots—the oaths and yells from, it seemed, a multitude of throats, like the screech of beasts, like animals giving tongue to a blood lust that was upon them.

It was very plain! They had dug the Phantom out of wherever he had been in hiding in Blind Peter's here, and had driven him in a running fight to the end of the chain of underground rooms and passages. It was the end! The Phantom could go no further—*save through the door behind which he, Jimmie Dale, stood.* And through that door the Phantom, for the Tocsin's sake, would never pass while he, Jimmie Dale, lived!

The end! Yes—but it was ending there on the threshold now. The Phantom half spun around, and screamed as a bullet struck him, made a desperate effort to slam shut the door and, instead, crumpled to the floor.

A strange, queer look was on Jimmie Dale's face. His jaws were clamped, his features set like iron. The end! Well, he could go now. Go the way he had come—unseen. It was over! The Tocsin was free. And *he* too was free, free of hurt or harm, free to the years that stretched ahead where only love and happiness should hold sway, and the—

"Kill 'em! . . . Bump 'em both off! . . . The cursed snitches. . . ."

Shots seemed to be still pouring a leaden hail into the prostrate form of the Phantom on the threshold, as he lay there, sprawled out, a dead thing now. Then a rush! Faces appeared at the doorway—Steenie's! The man levelled his revolver at the old hag on the floor as she crawled for protection toward the end of a sort of divan at the side of the room.

The mind works swiftly, swift beyond all measure of time. She was only an old hag, an abandoned thing steeped in her crimes, the last of the Phantom's satellites—all the rest had gone—it was justice that she should go too. What had he to do with it? The road to life and happiness lay the other way. Suppose she was a woman, suppose it *was* murder that would be done in the next second, what had he to do with it! What had——

Through the opening in the panel Jimmie Dale fired. The

revolver in Steenie Klotz's outstretched hand clattered to
the floor, and the man with a yell of mingled pain, fury and
surprise leaped back from the open doorway—and with him,
from this new attack, the others took hasty cover, leaving
the doorway clear again.

"Quick! This way, Mother Margot!" Jimmie Dale
called out sharply. "Don't stand up! Crawl!"

He fired steadily, coolly, sweeping the opposite doorway
with his bullets—working with pick-lock in his other hand at
the door behind which he stood. The old hag came crawl-
ing, weakly it seemed, across the floor, nearer and nearer to
him. The shots were pouring into the room again—but they
were coming at an angle. He laughed a little—without
mirth. Steenie Klotz and his men were crouched on both
sides of the door casing out there beyond, of course, and
they could not fire in a direct line now without exposing
themselves. But how much could they see? The danger
would come when he opened the door for Mother Margot,
and when he could not for the moment command the other
doorway.

It would be a race for it then—nothing else.

"You fool!" an inner voice snarled at him. "Don't you
know the Phantom is dead! You fool, to have risked this
now! You poor, feeble, quixotic fool!"

The old hag was close to the door now. He called to her
again.

"When I open the door, jump for it!" he said grimly.
"Are you ready?"

He caught a faint, affirmative reply. He fired at the opposite doorway again, then closed the panel; and then with a
sudden wrench pulled the door before him halfway open;
and, as Mother Margot scurried through, he flung it shut
again, locked it, and reaching out in the darkness for the
old hag, jerked her forward, making for the rear of the coal
bin. She staggered weakly, making a strange, half crooning
noise. If he could win behind the bin to the stairs, there
would be comparative safety, time enough at least to get
to the lane above. Blind Peter, if he, Jimmie Dale, knew

the man at all, having profound respect for his own skin, would not be taking a *personal* part in the fight, and those apaches back there would certainly never find the opening until they had gone for Blind Peter and had either persuaded or forced him to disclose it.

An age of time seemed to have passed, though he had reached the rear of the bin now. And now the boards swung back—but they were smashing at the door behind, battering at it, raining blows upon it. Just an instant more— if the door would hold for but an instant more, so that when the light poured in they would not *see!*

She was slow—God, how slow she was! He pushed her roughly through the opening, and sprang quickly after her. And as he swung the boards back into place, he heard the door crash open. But he was safe now—safe for a moment anyhow.

"Quick! The stairs! Right ahead of you!" he whispered.

But there was no answer. He stretched out his hand, groping down and around him. Mother Margot lay an inert heap at his feet. His jaws shut with a snap. Where was his margin of safety now? She was either hurt or wounded, or had fainted, and——

"You fool!" snarled that inner voice again, as he picked the old hag up in his arms, and began to climb the stairs.

XXIX

THE PORT OF DAWN

MUFFLED voices reached Jimmie Dale's ears from below. He staggered on upward, making what speed he could. It was not easy with this burden in his arms. In the darkness he gained the cellar; and from the cellar emerged on the small backyard, and thence on the lane.

Here, he drew a great, gasping breath of relief. He was safe so far, but he had still to get away from the immediate vicinity of that cellar entranceway. Blind Peter, at any moment, might solve the problem for Steenie Klotz and his pack!

He went on again, running heavily, lurching under his load. Thank God for the darkness! He looked, as he ran, for some place of shelter or hiding. He could not go out into the open street with Mother Margot unconscious in his arms—certainly not anywhere in *this* neighbourhood; nor could he run on indefinitely like this, whether by lane or street.

Fifty yards, a hundred he covered. There were no sounds of pursuit, and now he had no further anxiety on that score, for he was already too far away for them to pick up the trail if he could only find temporary cover somewhere until Mother Margot's condition, which must necessarily govern his future movements, could be——

She was stirring in his arms now uneasily, commencing to mutter incoherent words. He kept straining his eyes to right and left as he ran—and suddenly swerved close up against the left-hand side of the fence. This would do admirably. He could ask for nothing better. There was a

shed here, or an outhouse of some kind.   He laid Mother
Margot down, worked swiftly for a moment with the door
lock, then picking her up again carried her inside and laid her
upon the floor.

But now, her senses evidently almost fully back, she raised
herself quickly to her elbow, and tried to struggle to her
feet.

"It's all right!" said Jimmie Dale reassuringly.   "We're
safe now.   Are you badly hurt?   Let me see."

He bent down and played his flashlight upon her—and like
a man dazed and stunned then stood swaying on his feet.
The flashlight trembled in his hand, throwing wavering beams
across the floor.   And then he was on his knees, and with a
great cry he had gathered her into his arms, and was calling
out hoarsely, calling her name over and over, a man unhinged,
almost, with the mad uplift that had surged upon him.

"Marie—it's you!   The Tocsin!   Marie!   Marie!"

The hooded shawl had fallen from her, the gray, tangled
wig was awry.   The Tocsin!   Marie!   And he had not
known—he had known only that in some character here in
the underworld she had been bravely striving to fight out her
battle alone—just as she once had as Silver Mag.   Silver
Mag!   Mother Margot!   And he had thought that Smarlinghue was unknown to Mother Margot!

She was crying softly.

"Jimmie," she whispered, "dear Jimmie, I—I was afraid
that I was saying good-by to you for—for always in the
Sanctuary to-night."

He held her closely.   His face was buried in her hair.   His
shoulders heaved—as though a strong man sobbed.   It was
a long while before he answered her.

"I know.   I know now," he said at last.   "I didn't understand then.   How could I?   I had investigated Mother Margot and she had been in existence long before you left me
that night in the boat on the East River.   If it hadn't been
for that I might——"

She stroked his face with her hand, very gently, very
tenderly.

"Yes," she said; "but I was always Mother Margot—after Silver Mag. I was Mother Margot when they forced me into hiding the time before this. Don't you remember in the boat, Jimmie, that I would not tell you even then, even when Clarke was dead and you thought everything was all right again, how or where I had lived all through that time?"

"Yes, I remember," said Jimmie Dale; and then, with a quick, anxious cry: "And I remember now that you've been hurt, wounded, I am afraid, and need——"

"No," she said, and shook her head. "It is true that I was hit with something, a heavy stool that one of those gangsters threw when the fight first started at the upper end of Blind Peter's cellars, and it made me a little dizzy and giddy perhaps. But I am not hurt. I am afraid I only fainted, Jimmie, just—just like a woman." She laughed a little, bravely, tremulously, as she looked around her. "I know you said we were safe now, and I know that the Phantom is dead, but I'm all right again, and I'm able to go on. We can't be very far away from——"

"We're safer here just now, quite safe," Jimmie Dale answered. "If we went out we might only invite a chase and have to run for it, and you haven't got your strength back yet. And"—he too laughed a little tremulously now—"besides I want you—like this, Marie—like this for a little while."

Her head was on his shoulder now. He brushed back the hair from her forehead, and kissed her, and laid his face against hers.

"Like this." Her voice broke a little. "God is very good, Jimmie. I—I did not dare to hope that it would be like this when I sent you to The White Rat to-night."

"That was a plant!" said Jimmie Dale a little ruefully. "Why did you send me there?"

She drew slightly away from him so that she could lift her hands and clasp and hold his face between them.

"What else could I do, Jimmie?" she said with a catch in her voice. "You—you were so persistent. I had to get rid of you. I knew you were going to those rooms to-night—

you had told me so. Well, the Phantom, or the Voice, had ordered me to be in the hallway of the *other* tenement at half past twelve. I knew then that there must be some connection between the two tenements, which would account for the voices that I had heard when I had been alone in the rooms where I was supposed to live. But I didn't know how, or where. It was certain, though, that if the Phantom brought me that far to-night, he would bring me all the way—you see, he was at the end of his rope nearly; there were only the Kitten and myself left. Well, I meant to end it to-night with the help of the police, and——"

"The police!" Jimmie Dale smiled strangely. "It was you, then, who were accountable for the police!"

"Yes," she said. "But I had first to get you out of the road, or you would almost certainly have been trapped in those rooms either by the Phantom or the police. I hadn't the least idea of what French Jeff might be doing to-night, but his reputation made him a likely subject for *anything,* and I felt sure that once set on his trail with the idea that the Phantom was mixed up in it too, you would watch him until something happened—which, since I expected nothing to happen, would mean all night. I don't see why you didn't."

"He went to bed on the midnight train to Boston," said Jimmie Dale grimly.

She laughed a little now, still holding his face captive with her hands; and then abruptly her voice was grave and serious again.

"Just before going to the other tenement at half past twelve," she said, "I notified the police to be there at one o'clock—if they wanted Isaac Shiftel; and that if they came before they would only ruin their one chance of getting their man. I needed that half hour to find out all I could, to get to the bottom of the Phantom's secret, or to make sure at least of where he lived in that other tenement, so that there could be no possible means of escape for him; and I wanted that much time in case he was late in keeping his appointment, and so that I would be sure to be with him and make sure that he did *not* escape. I—I am not sure that I expected to—to live through it myself. If he had any suspicion aroused it—" Her voice broke suddenly. "But—but he hadn't, Jimmie, and—and you must know what happened afterward since you, too, went to Blind Peter's."

"Yes," said Jimmie Dale simply. "I know. And I know a great deal more now. I know now that the night I caught you, as I thought, double-crossing Limpy Mack, you were trying to save what you could of old Mrs. Kinsey's money. And I understand now that the reason you did not know when I was wounded was because it happened at the time when you, as Mother Margot, were away. And that night in the tunnel at Morley's place, when you wouldn't let me show any light or come near you, you were Mother Margot, weren't you?"

"Yes, Jimmie," she whispered.

For a moment he was silent, and then suddenly he cried out, and in his voice was the yearning of the days and weeks when it had seemed this moment could never be:

"Marie! . . . Marie! . . . Marie! . . ."

He was holding her close to him again, his arms around her, her face against his own. And neither spoke now. Here in the shed it was very dark and very silent; but radiant in their souls was the glad sunrise of a new life, and in their hearts was song, like the song of springtime, a song of great joy, and of peace.

For they had come at last to the Port of Dawn.

THE END